THE HOUSE IN THE HILLS

THE HOUSE IN THE HILLS

BY

OLIVIA FITZROY

ILLUSTRATED BY PHYLLIDA LUMSDEN

Published by Fidra Books, 2009

First Published 1946 by Collins Publishers

British Library Cataloguing in Publication Data
A catalogue record for this book is available from the British Library

Printed in Great Britain by
the MPG Books Group, Bodmin and King's Lynn

ISBN-13 978 1906 12318 5

Published by Fidra Books Ltd
219 Bruntsfield Place
Edinburgh
EH10 4DH

www.fidrabooks.com

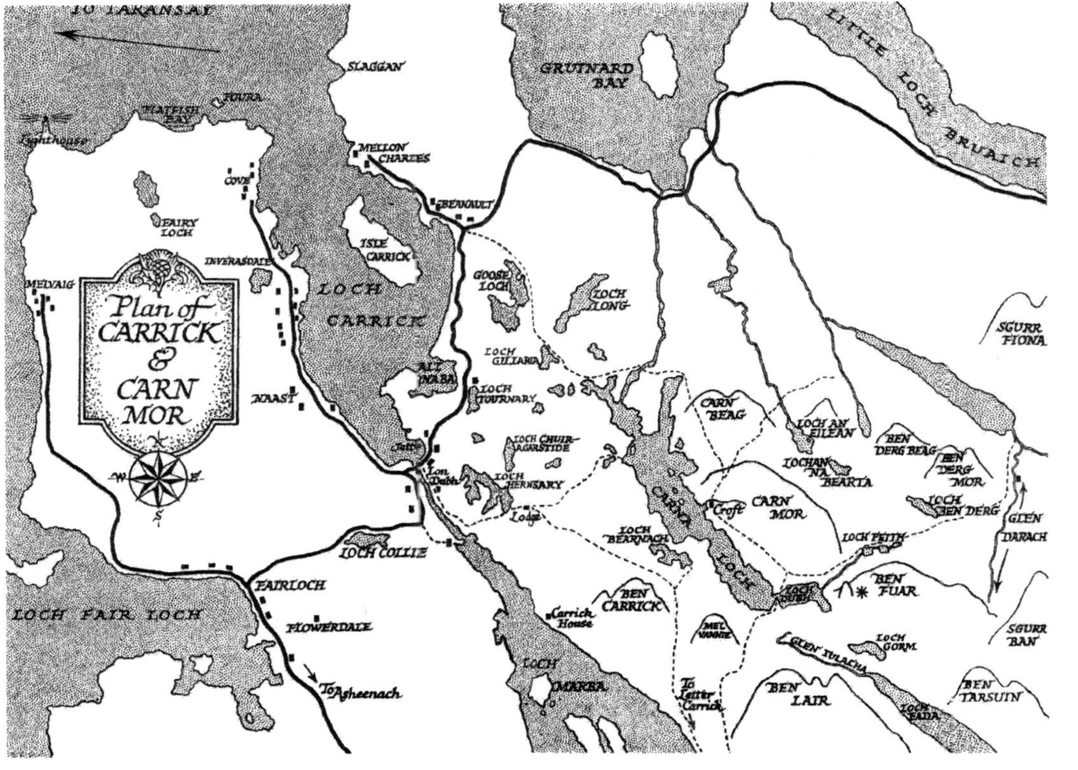
Plan of CARRICK & CARN MOR
TO TARANSAY
SLAGGAN
GRUINARD BAY
LITTLE LOCH BRUAICH
FOURA
FLATFISH BAY
Lighthouse
MELLON CHARLES
COVE
BEANAULT
FAIRY LOCH
ISLE CARRICK
INVERASDALE
MELVAIG
LOCH CARRICK
GOOSE LOCH
LOCH LONG
SGURR FIONA
LOCH GILLAIRD
ALT NABA
LOCH TOURNARY
NAAST
CARN BEAG
LOCH AN EILEAN
BEN DERG BEAG
BEN DERG MOR
LOCH CHUIR-AGARSTIDE
LOCHAN NA BEARTA
LOCH HERNSARY
Lon Dubh
CARN MOR
Croft
LOCH BEN DERG
GLEN DARACH
Lodge
LOCH BEARNACH
CARNA LOCH
LOCH PEITH
LOCH COLLIE
FAIRLOCH
BEN CARRICK
LOCH DUBH
BEN FUAR
LOCH FAIR LOCH
Carrick House
MEL VANNIE
FLOWERDALE
LOCH GORM
SGURR BAN
GLEN TULACHA
LOCH MARBA
To Asheenach
To Letter Carrick
BEN LAIR
BEN TARSUIN
LOCH EADA
N
S
E
W

Olivia FitzRoy – her childhood

By her sister, Barbara Ormrod

Before the Second World War, my mother and father lived at 112 Sloane Street in London, in a house that they bought in 1930. My father was in the Navy, almost continuously at sea and except for an occasional two weeks' leave we saw very little of him. In those days no provision was made for Naval families so if my mother wanted to see him we were sent to stay either with my grandmother, Lady Manners, who lived in Sussex near Midhurst or with my great-aunt at Rockingham Castle in Northamptonshire.

My father Captain R O FitzRoy, RN was the eldest son of Captain The Right Hon E A FitzRoy who was the Speaker of the House of Commons from 1928 to 1943 where he and my grandmother lived in Speaker's House. When my grandfather died just before the end of the War, he was posthumously created Viscount Daventry (his constituency). My grandmother cleverly had herself made a Viscountess in her own right and so my father didn't become 2nd Viscount Daventry until she died. As my father had five daughters and no sons, the title passed to his brother who had two sons. My mother was Grace Zoë Guinness and she married my father in September 1916.

I was one of five sisters. The eldest three were

Mary (born in 1919), Olivia (1921), Katherine (1924), myself (Barbara, 1928) and Amelia (1930). The older sisters were mainly looked after by a governess whilst Amelia and I had a nanny and a nursery maid.

Every summer our aunt, Nancy FitzRoy, used to rent a cottage in Scotland, seldom the same one, and invite her nieces and nephews to stay. Up until the War, Amelia and I were considered too young and went to the seaside with Nanny, whilst Mary, Olivia and Katherine went to Scotland. The cottages were small and fairly primitive and all housework and cooking were done by the guests and my aunt. At the time this was very exciting as we never did anything like that at home! The cottages were also near the sea and the days were spent fishing in the sea, rivers, burns and lochs with much exploring and picnicking.

1939 was the first year that Amelia and I went and, when in early September most people went south and war was inevitable, my father sent a message "Don't move, stay where you are, you will be safer." He was sure that Hitler would invade. Mary and Kathy had already gone, so Olivia aged 18, and Amelia and I aged 9 and 10 stayed behind. It was very challenging for Olivia, a Debutante who had just finished her first Season, now without telephone, electricity, or even a wireless! How she managed from the very minimal village shop I can't think. In September she walked up to the 'Big House' to hear the news, leaving Amelia and I in bed. She heard war declared and brought the news back to us. At our age war was exciting so we were thrilled and sure that we would find enemy submarines hiding in the loch. Fairly soon my mother and sister Mary came back to Inverewe. Kathy had insisted on going to boarding school.

My father was Captain of the 1st Minesweeping Flotilla and his was the first ship to come into Loch Ewe. He was spotted by Amelia and I when we were on our way to take up the lobster pots and set the long line. Eventually, the whole Northern Fleet came in – Repulse, Renown, Prince of Wales, Ark Royal and so on and we had a ready market for our lobsters and fish! We lived in The Lodge, the gate lodge to the big Inverewe House, now all incorporated into the National Trust garden. It was a little black and white bungalow that will be familiar to visitors to Inverewe gardens and not at all like the Lodge in Olivia's books about the Stewart family! We had no staff so did everything ourselves.

Living in such remote area during the war shopping opportunities were limited and we soon ran out of reading matter so Olivia wrote *Orders to Poach* to entertain Amelia and I. Our tastes in books were, I suspect, typical of our time – *Swallows and Amazons*, Violet Needham, Sapper, Leslie Charteris, Baroness Orczy, Dennis Wheatley, R L Stevenson, Charles Kingsley, J M Barrie, Georgette Heyer and many others. Books were always favourite presents.

Orders to Poach was published by Collins. I think that they were the first publishers to see the book as Billy Collins lived near Rockingham and was a friend of the family. Olivia later moved to Jonathan Cape.

After one and a half years at Inverewe we moved to Strontian near Fort William to a house owned by our father's brother – large, freezing cold, again no electricity, miles down an unmade road in a bus. We spent a year there and Olivia kept us alive by stalking hinds in the winter. She wrote her second book, *Steer by the Stars* whilst living there.

My mother hated it. She was very talented - a very good artist, she also wrote well, was musical and extremely amusing, original and wise. Although totally impractical, she was a wonderful mother, grandmother and surrogate grandmother to many. She never got up until lunchtime and never went to bed before 3am! My maternal grandmother came up to visit us and spent her time picking sphagnum moss from the bogs and drying it to send south for wound dressings!

My father left the Navy when the war ended. He was a Captain and commanded the battleship Rodney. They bought an old rectory in Rutland – still without electricity! He became a Governor of Uppingham School, a county councillor and a head of the Red Cross.

Our rather nomadic life meant that we did not have many friends beyond ourselves. I think it was not a person who had the most influence on our lives, but the places where we lived – Rockingham was the most wonderful place to be brought up: steeped in history with huge gardens and a ruined keep. Sussex, quite different, had the South Downs to roam over and all these places came into Olivia's books and poems.

We were all musical, artistic and literate, Olivia being the best at writing. Mary went to school at

Owlestone Croft, Cambridge when she was about 15. Prior to that she was taught, like all of us, by various governesses and local tutors. Olivia had too many animals – ducks, pigeons, rabbits, dogs and ponies – to go away to school. She was very intelligent and masters from Uppingham School came to Rockingham Castle to coach her in Mathematics, History, Literature and English. Katherine was determined to be conventional and went to boarding school during the War where she was very good at games and music. Amelia and I had various local teachers – we also went to the village school in Strontian, the next place in Scotland that we lived after Inverewe. Here we learned the Lord's Prayer in Gaelic! We also went to various small schools in Sussex, which usually entailed bicycling miles.

My mother was not in favour of formal education which explains our idiosyncratic schooling. However, I think that if Olivia had had to conform to school rules, her writing might have lost its originality.

Barbara Ormrod, 2006.

THE HOUSE IN THE HILLS

FOR MY

MOTHER AND FATHER

CONTENTS

Illustrations

CHAPTER I

WINTER EVENING, CARRICK

Tuesday, 12th December

FIONA, coming down the shoulder of Ben Carrick above the Lodge, blew on her cold fingers and shifted the rifle to the other arm. Behind her the hill looked cold and black against the winter sky, already darkening as a watery sun set over the headlands. The bogs and mud were frozen hard and the edges of her heavy boots left no impression on them. A thin sheet of cat-ice crackled as she crossed the remains of what had been a puddle; in the hollows under the shade of tall rocks where the sun had not penetrated, the frost was still white; by the feel of the air and the stillness there would be another one to-night. However, if the weather continued in this way, frosty and sunny, there was nothing much to complain about. But it was cold.

Ahead, a mile or so farther on and below the wood in front, lay the Lodge. Fiona could see the blue peat-smoke rising from its chimneys and hoped very much that the bath water was hot and that Maggie had lit all the fires. Her elder brother Ninian was there, fuming at being tied to the house in the last stages of convalescence from 'flu.

Fiona, puffing clouds of vapour into the air in front of her, considered that to-day, although pleasant, had been singularly unfruitful. She had been out after a hind to replenish the larder, and although she had seen several, had been unable to get near any. Either the wind had changed at the last moment, or a sheep had run, bleating like a lost soul, from under a rock, or else a stone, frozen hard into the hillside, had responded to the sun's faint warmth and had, with Fiona's added weight, gone bounding and crashing over the hard ground, frightening everything within miles. Lastly there had been a long cold wait when her bare fingers had nearly frozen to the rifle and she had lost all feeling in them. Then when the time came to fire she found she could not press the trigger, and the sudden jerk had sent the bullet wide and the hinds loping off down the hill and out of sight. Ninian would be scathing about all this, and say she wasn't fit to go out alone and why didn't she take Davy the old gillie, who lived in a croft by the river. Fiona smiled to herself: Ninian had not changed at all.

Fiona, at nineteen, was tall and slim and dark. Her hair was kept back from her face by a green ribbon, she was dressed in an ancient tweed coat and breeches, the colour of dried grass and greeny moss, her stockings were referred to by Ninian as sky-blue, which was an exaggeration, and ended in enormously thick black boots dubbined and nailed. Under the coat was a brown Shetland jersey. Notwithstanding all these clothes Fiona's feet were frozen. At one time she had stepped into a burn that had come above the top of her boot, and she was convinced that she must have frostbite. She jumped from rock to rock, her body tingling, and the rifle banging on her shoulder. In the mud in front of her were the slots of deer, frozen hard: she kicked at them but made no impression beyond vaguely stubbing her toe. Small cold birds sprang up from the heather and fluttered for a moment or two, whistling sadly. Fiona felt sorry for them but hurried on. It would be dark soon, although only four, and she had no desire to be left out on the hill with the night coming on.

What to do to-morrow? Hugh Murray was arriving in the afternoon; Ninian would be recovered enough to come in to Asheenach with her to fetch him. And in a day or two Sandy Stewart, her cousin, and her twin brother and sister would be back from school and arriving either in the bus or fetched by herself or Ninian. And then she supposed

FIONA

another long holiday of days spent on the hills or in *Black Swan*, their boat. It all rather depended on the weather but it was sure to be fun: Ninian and Hugh would think of things to do, and they might even meet Fergus somewhere in the hills. One never knew with Fergus; he came and went of his own accord, leaving no word of where or when or whether he would ever come back. And when he did reappear it was to pick up the threads of old conversations and ideas as if he had only left them yesterday.

The sun dropped swiftly behind the headlands. The islands were cold and grey in the sea, like the hill behind her. Fiona ran the last half-mile, her boots clattering on the stony track.

The lighted windows of the Lodge showed that it was much darker outside already than she had imagined. It looked warm and inviting. At the sound of her footsteps Ninian came to the door and she saw his tall figure standing in the porch watching her.

Ninian knew that if Fiona had had any luck she would have called out to him, and would already be pouring out the story from half-way along the track.

"You useless woman," he called to her, "thundering over the hills like an army. Did you get anywhere near any?"

"Beast." Fiona pushed past him into the hall. "Yes, I did. But it was as cold as the North Pole on the hill."

"Well, Hugh and the others will just have to starve." Ninian followed her into the gun-room.

"In a day or two you'll be able to go out yourself and bring them back by the thousand," retorted Fiona.

"S'matter of fact," said Ninian, "Davy brought up some rabbits."

Fiona took off her coat and boots and padded on wet, peat-stained feet to the foot of the stairs. She was very like her elder brother, in all but character, and would fly into a rage over things that only made him smile.

"I'm going to have a bath," she announced. "If Maggie hasn't made the water hot I'll wring her neck."

She vanished round a bend in the stairs, and Ninian followed her more slowly into what used to be the old nursery.

Here a huge peat and pine log fire was burning, filling the room with shadows that danced and bobbed on the walls. It hissed and crackled and the room was full of the soft smell of peat. Maggie had not yet brought the lamps, so he sat in the dusk and watched the faint thread of the road and wished that his cheeks and nose were glowing like

Fiona's, and that he had spent the day on Ben Carrick instead of cooped up in the house.

Half an hour later Fiona appeared, smelling faintly of soap and talcum powder, and dressed in a long blue housecoat. She joined Ninian on the window-seat and announced that she had dropped her book into the bath.

"Well, if you must read in the bath," said Ninian. "By the way, what was it?"

"Well," Fiona paused, "well, actually it was *The Thirty-Nine Steps*."

"You are the absolute end," said Ninian. "Why don't you read your own books if you must read in the bath?"

"Well, you read in the bath too," pointed out Fiona.

"Yes, but I don't drop them in," said Ninian.

"Oh, dear, I'm very sorry, but I think it'll be all right." She produced it from where it had been hidden behind her back. The edges of each page had become large and curly. Ninian looked at it with horror as she wiped it with a dishevelled handkerchief and stood it up by the fire.

"Absolutely ruined," Ninian growled.

Fiona knelt in front of the fire, throwing small pieces of peat and twigs on to it so that it blazed and crackled and made her face glow orange.

"What time's Hugh arriving to-morrow?" asked Ninian, from the depths of an arm-chair.

"The 2.40," said Fiona. "Can you come and meet him too?"

"Gracious, yes. You seem to think I'm a sort of invalid," said Ninian.

They were both silent for a moment until Fiona said, "Listen!"

There was the sound of a far-away roaring in the trees down by the burn.

"Wind," said Ninian. "Probably means the frost will stop."

"It would be too much if it rained." Fiona sat back on

her heels and the fire flickered over her back. There was another roaring, in the chimney this time, and suddenly the burn sounded nearer and then grew faint again.

Ninian went over to the window and looked out. Clouds covered the stars and it was very dark. He could see the tops of the birch trees dipping and swaying.

"I'm sure it'll rain," he said.

"How typical," said Fiona. "Now I suppose it'll pour and pour and we shan't be able to stir out of doors."

The window rattled at a sudden gust and downstairs a door slammed.

"It was such a heavenly day on the hill, too," said Fiona. "I had hoped it might snow, but there's not much chance now. Where's the toboggan, Ninian?"

"Somewhere about, in the byre, I think. Tin trays were the fashion last time, I seem to remember."

"Well, we've all grown rather since then," Fiona pointed out. "Do you remember Jamie in the big meat dish?"

This led to long reminiscences, until Maggie appeared and asked them if they would not rather have dinner in the nursery as it was so cold.

"Oh, yes, please," said Fiona, "like we used to, on a table in front of the fire."

Ninian, who felt this was only another instance of his being coddled, said nothing, but there was something rather nice and cosy about the thought of dinner in front of the fire. He threw some more peat on and then remembered the chestnuts he had brought up from London. He reached a long arm up to the mantelpiece and pulled down a brown paper bag which split and showered its contents over Fiona.

"Typical," she said, scooping them up in handfuls. "Doesn't one have to prick them or something?"

There was a toasting-fork in the grate and with the aid of that and Ninian's penknife they pricked them and set them to roast among the peat. Then they sat on cushions before the fire and had dinner off a tray on a low stool.

"Like we used to when we were small," said Ninian, rescuing one of the chestnuts from the flames. He looked at Fiona, who, with her hair tied back and her nose pink and shining from a hot bath and roasting the chestnuts, looked about twelve.

"You don't look any different either," she said, reading his thoughts, "now you've shaved off that ridiculous moustache."

The sound of a car made them both look up.

"Who on earth?" said Fiona.

"At this time of night," said Ninian.

They leapt up and ran to the window. The car had come through the last gate and was just rounding the bend before the bridge. Powerful headlights shone on the bare branches of the birch trees and over the tumbling water of the burn.

"He must be lost," said Ninian, "unless something frightful has happened."

"It's not Murdoch's car," said Fiona (Murdoch being the policeman).

They watched while it crossed the burn and climbed the hill just below the Lodge. Then the horn began to blow. Four short blasts.

"H!" murmured Ninian.

Two short, one long.

"U!"

"Hugh!" shrieked Fiona, and dashed out of the room just as the car stopped. Ninian followed her and they flew downstairs and opened the door. A rush of cold damp windy night came pouring in and Fiona shivered. The car door slammed.

"Anyone at home?" called Hugh.

"Hugh!" they both shouted.

"What are you doing here?" cried Fiona.

"I got off a day early, so here I am." Hugh came

towards them, enormous in a greatcoat buttoned up to his nose. He thrust a parcel into Fiona's arms and murmured something about ham.

"Delicious." Fiona sniffed. "Ninian, come back; you'll catch pneumonia."

"Oh, rubbish!" Ninian was at the car, delving into it and producing suitcases and rugs. "I've finished with coddling. And it's not very cold."

"Personally I think it's freezing." Hugh followed Fiona into the hall. "And talking of freezing, what about the car?"

"There's room in the byre; I'll show you." Fiona started towards the door.

"No, I refuse. You look much too glamorous in that blue thing to come messing about in any byre," said Hugh firmly. "Anyway, as if I didn't know the way blindfold."

He vanished into the night, shutting the cold out. Fiona flew into the kitchen with the ham to tell Maggie to bring some more dinner and for Morag to light a fire and make the bed in Mr. Murray's room. Then she went upstairs to put some powder on her nose. Hugh might have said she looked glamorous but Ninian had just told her she looked about twelve.

When Hugh and Ninian came stamping and shivering into the nursery she was standing by the fire with a decanter of sherry and three glasses beside her.

"Transformation," grinned Ninian, and Fiona put out her tongue.

They drank each other's health in the sherry, found some cushions for Hugh and sat once more round the fire.

"It's going to be a deadly dull winter," said Fiona, between mouthfuls. "There's simply nothing to do, apart from occasional hind-shooting. It'll be icy cold on the sea, and if it's raining it'll be simply hell."

"What rubbish you do talk." Hugh seized the drumstick of a chicken in his fingers and tore mouthfuls off it. "Have you ever known a dull time up here yet? There's always plenty to do. What shall we do to-morrow?"

"It sounds to me," Ninian nodded at the window, "as if it's going to rain."

The door rattled and the trees down by the burn made a long sighing noise. Fiona, licking her fingers, picked up a blackened chestnut and started to peel it.

CHAPTER II

REDISCOVERY

Wednesday, 13th December

SLEEPILY Hugh opened an eyelid and looked out over the heap of blankets above him. Nice though Carrick was, it certainly was cold. He shut his eyes and decided to try and sleep again as the room was not yet light. It must be very early. Half-consciously he heard banging and brushing downstairs, which meant that at least some of the household were up. He guessed it was neither Ninian nor Fiona. Then a new noise penetrated his muffled ears. The steady pattering of rain on the windows. Hell! Ninian had been right. More determined than ever not to become any more awake, Hugh pulled the bedclothes right over his head, but at that moment Morag knocked on the door and came in with a cup of tea.

"Mind you don't let it get cold," she said, shutting the window and putting a can of hot water on the washstand.

"What's it like outside?" asked Hugh.

"Och, it's verra cold." Morag paused at the door. "Breakfast will be in half an hour."

Slowly Hugh propped himself on an elbow and sipped the tea. Then he lay back and stared at the uneven ceiling of the room. It was part of a long, low garret under the tiles, with a roof so sloping that you could only stand up with comfort in the middle. Though the furniture was old and battered the room had a homely atmosphere with its brightly flowered carpet, deep fireplace and the old screen from the nursery. There was another bed in it, ready for Sandy Stewart, and the traces of his former occupation of it lay about in the shape of fishing-rods, two cormorants' eggs and part of the skull and horns of a stag that he had shot the year before. On the walls were several pictures, "Bubbles" being one and the others religious, doggy, or gondolas in Venice. The chintz curtains and bedcovers were also bright and flowery and clashed with the carpet. A varied assortment of books on the chest of drawers showed that the room was often occupied by different people. Turning on his side to drink some more tea Hugh saw, scrawled on the wall by the bed, in pencil, "I hate her, I hate her." The letters were uneven and he wondered which small angry Stewart had been sent to bed in disgrace.

Footsteps were coming upstairs. In another moment the door was softly opened and Ninian's tousled head appeared round it.

"Yes, he is awake," he said, and came in, followed by Fiona, who was carrying two cups of tea.

They ensconced themselves on the end of his bed and pulled up the eiderdown.

"Yes, do sit down," said Hugh, removing his feet from under them. "I just love having people sitting on my feet."

"Sorry. I say, isn't it absolutely the most repulsive day you've ever seen?" said Fiona. "So typical to be simply teeming with rain."

"I think it'll stop," said Ninian cheerfully.

"Well I hope it does, or Maggie won't allow you out." Fiona blew on her tea to cool it.

"Rain before seven, fine before eleven," murmured Hugh.

"Yes, but it never is," said Fiona.

They sat and talked and shivered until a low booming sound announced the fact that breakfast was ready. Wrapping their dressing-gowns round them, they ran downstairs to warm themselves up with porridge and bacon and eggs.

At about half-past two the rain did stop and a weak and watery sun shone out from behind the clouds.

"Oh, let's go out," said Fiona.

"You must wrap up well, Master Ninian," said Maggie, who happened to be in the room with a basket of peat.

"Of course I will." Ninian heaved himself out of the huge arm-chair where he had been sprawling since lunch. They had spent a pleasant day talking and gossiping about old times and people that they all knew, but he was longing to go out and get a breath of air, however cold. Although he had been back several days, he had hardly been out at all and was growing impatient to see Carrick.

"Where shall we go?" he asked, when they were gathered in the hall. They were dressed more or less alike in tweeds and thick shoes but Ninian had given in to Maggie to the extent of wearing a scarf.

"If ye're goin' anywhere near the village, Miss Fiona, we're needin' another loaf of bread and some matches," Maggie called from the kitchen.

"Let's go down and see the *Black Swan*," suggested Fiona. "Then we could get the bread on the way back."

"Good idea." Ninian chose his hazel stick out of the rack in the hall and they opened the door and went out.

The cold wintry air came rushing up the glen. It came from the sea, over the village, up the hill and across Hernsary Loch. The track was wet and muddy and in some places washed clean of all but rock. The burn was racing under the bridge, sticks and grass whirling down with it and catching on stones every now and then and building miniature dams.

"We shall have to clear it soon," said Ninian, as they stopped on the bridge to look over. "There's a huge collection of leaves down there."

"Let's do it to-morrow," suggested Fiona. "It'll be dark by the time we get back this evening."

"There's something lovely and messy about undamming a burn," said Hugh. "Which reminds me, when do Jamie and Jean get here?"

"The day after to-morrow, with Sandy," said Ninian.

"There'll be no peace then, I suppose, with them charging about the house."

"Yes," agreed Fiona. "They're always much larger and noisier in the winter somehow. I don't know whether it's their boots or the long evenings or what."

They passed the first gate and went on down the winding track. High tufts of grass grew along the middle of it and shining puddles betrayed its dilapidated state. Ninian sighed. Money was as scarce as ever, and there were so many things he longed to do for Carrick and could not. The track could last in its present state for a long time.

Presently, on the left, the ground curved down to a deep gully with a burn running down the centre. Orange-brown bracken stood in dank masses round it and the wet rocks gleamed faintly in the sun. Beyond the gully the ground rose gradually in small hills to the foot of Ben Carrick. Over to the left the long line of Carn Mor was straight under the grey sky. Fiona picked out some deer feeding half-way up the nearest hill.

"We might go hind-shooting to-morrow," she said. "After my performance yesterday we'll see what Hugh can do."

Although they had known Hugh for two years and had been with him on the hill many times, the Stewarts were always inclined to regard his ability there with suspicion and as though it was luck more than anything else when he got a stag. This amused Hugh enormously, and always had.

"Hardly likely I should succeed where you failed," he said.

"No, hardly likely," said Fiona, unmoved.

Ninian knocked a stone with his stick and sent it spinning into the gully. It landed in a clump of wet heather and a rabbit bounced out. Fiona and he were instantly reminded of how, when they were smaller and had been used as beaters, they had constantly come across rabbits sitting as though hypnotised in clumps of wet heather and had been able to pick them up or, alternatively, knock them on the head.

"Bloodthirsty little beasts," said Hugh.

"Well, didn't you?" asked Fiona, and Hugh had to admit that he did.

They passed the second gate at the bottom of a hill at the beginning of the flat ground above the village. Here the burn that had come down the gully went roaring under a small bridge and they pulled several long sticks out that were considerably delaying its progress.

"Just listen to the river," said Fiona. "It must be nearly washing Davy's cottage away."

"Where's the *Cow*?" asked Hugh, remembering the large unwieldy boat they had sailed on Loch Marba the summer before last.

"Oh, she's up on the bank below Davy's cottage," said Ninian. "At least, she was before this spate started."

They hurried on and were soon in the fringe of the birch wood which bordered the River Carrick. The trees held bare black branches into the wintry sky and raindrops fell from them into the wet grass. The moss-covered rocks looked like huge green sponges, and Hugh could hardly imagine how, in the summer, they had shaded here from the sun, and found it cool and pleasant and one of the loveliest places at Carrick.

The third gate swung and squeaked behind them. Down on their left they could see glimpses of the river between the trees and presently Davy's croft, with a curl of smoke from the chimney. They waved to him but hurried on, it was too cold to stand talking. Fat white sheep, washed extra clean by the rain, scuttered away from them up the hillside.

"They have the most blissful lambs," Fiona said. "Not a bit like English ones, but all white and fluffy like their mammas."

"I've never been up here in the spring," said Hugh. "It must be nice."

Soon they were walking beside the river, which grew wide and shallow as it reached the village. The sound of clanging and rasping announced that a horse was being shod at the smithy at the end of the track, and they stopped for a minute or two to talk to Rody the smith. The horse was a young black farm horse, still nervous at being shod. It rolled a wild eye in the Stewarts' direction, but they made soothing noises and it calmed down.

"Come on," said Ninian at last, and they left the track and turned right down the road.

"We'll leave the bread," said Fiona, "and get it on the way back."

The afternoon was growing cold as the sun dipped. The wind came whistling and moaning over the telegraph wires along the flat piece of road by Londubh. The Stewarts, after having seen the film, called this place "Wuthering Heights," and Jean found it quite creepy at night and hated crossing it alone. The tide was in and small waves chopped and splashed on the rocks by the road. Against the dark chump of pines on the headland, the *Black Swan* was almost invisible.

"Gosh, it's a beastly kind of day," said Fiona, brushing the hair out of her eyes. "And we had been so hoping that it was going to be fine for the next week or so."

"Perhaps it will," but Ninian did not sound convincing as he looked at the sky.

They left the road and turned off into the pine plantation. It was sheltered in here amongst great bushes of rhododendrons and bamboo.

"Although how tropical plants grow in this kind of

weather I can't think," said Fiona, who was finding it quite difficult to talk as her chin was so numb.

The path climbed and dipped between the pine trees

THE "BLACK SWAN" WAS ALMOST INVISIBLE.

and eventually sloped down to the small quay. Beyond it on the grey water was the *Black Swan*, looking forlorn and deserted.

"Shall we go out to her?" suggested Fiona, rather longingly.

"It means launching one of the dinghies which is rather too much of an effort," said Ninian. "They're all up on the rocks."

"Oh, bother. Is it really an awful job to get one down?"

"Well, it is, rather; they're all the heavy ones." Ninian looked at the dinghies lying on their sides by the boathouse and several yards from the water, even though it was high tide.

"Oh, well." Fiona turned away. "I say, let's go up to the Point."

They followed her up the hill and left along it. Their shoes brushed through drifts of pine-needles and crackled on the fir-cones. The hill grew steeper and steeper and eventually they came out on the flat heathery top among scattered pines. There was a seat beneath them, and in the summer it was pleasant to sit here or lie amongst the heather on the edge of the cliff and look down into the still green water and watch cormorants and shag swimming below the surface. But now, beyond a brief glance at the grey water of Loch Carrick and the waves breaking on the next headland, it was impossible to stay long, and they turned and ran back through the top of the wood. Half-way was a bank of deep moss under some pine trees, and amongst the roots the Stewarts had made fairy houses when they were small. Fiona stopped to see if there were the remains of any, but they had been grown over and the only signs were a flight of steps up the moss made with small smooth stones. Down on their left was the bay of Camas Glas, where they sometimes kept a lobster cawl, but it was empty now.

"I say," said Fiona, as they hurried on, "we ought to go right down to the rocks; there might be some northern divers."

"It's too cold," said Ninian, "and too late."

"You are a bore." But Fiona followed him, only protesting slightly, past the ponds on which different waterlilies grew in the summer but which now looked dark and deserted, past the twisted tree that was hung with tropiolum like a banner, and on through a gate to the moor behind the wood. Rabbits, startled by their sudden appearance, bolted back through the deer-fence, white scuts bobbing. A graceful roe-deer, a rare visitor, bounded away up the hill and a brace of grouse flew screeching in front of them.

"Pity we haven't got a gun," said Hugh.

"You wouldn't have us poaching?" said Fiona, shocked.

They came out on the road at the top of the hill between Carrick and Tournary.

"I'd love to walk back through the wood over the hill by Hernsary," said Fiona, looking longingly at the pine trees and distant moors on the left of the road.

"You should have thought of that sooner," Ninian

reminded her. "We've got the bread to get now."

"Bother the bread."

"There was something else, too," said Hugh.

"Yes, but what?"

"Haven't a clue," said Fiona, obviously in a temper over the bread and not even trying to think.

"Salt, stamps, butter, chocolate?" suggested Hugh.

"No, none of them mean anything." Ninian frowned. "Perhaps we'll have a brain-wave in the shop."

Fiona stalked on along the road, hands in her pockets and whistling softly. To Hugh her face looked ominous, and he thought he had better not speak or he might get his head bitten off. Ninian did not seem to notice and started to talk about hind-shooting.

"Haven't been out yet this year," he said. "Actually Carrick is still let but the tenants dare not venture so far north in the winter so the shooting is more or less ours. But we do it for meat more than anything, unless there's a hind that's in really shocking condition."

"Carrick House must be a bit bleak in the winter," said Hugh, with visions of most Scottish shooting-lodges, designed only to be lived in from July till October.

"Well, it is our home," said Ninian. "I mean, we are meant to be living there always so it's moderately civilised. But there are several details like extra bathrooms that I'd like to see put in." And he sighed, wondering how long it would be before the Stewarts would be back in their own house instead of living in the gillie's lodge. Still, it was something to be living at Carrick. Lots of people had had to sell, or at anyrate let, and live somewhere quite different themselves.

It was growing dusk by the time they got to the village shop. Inside was a wonderful warm smell of bacon and oranges and oilskins and tarred rope. An oil-stove burnt in the middle of the floor throwing a mottled pattern on to the ceiling. Behind the counter stood Mr. Swift, reigning supreme in a fantastic conglomeration and muddle. Somehow he knew where everything was, and slowly and surely produced butter from among the biscuits, eggs out of sea-boots, and bacon and string mixed together.

"A loaf of bread, please," said Fiona, warming her hands at the stove. The heat made her sniff and she discovered she had no handkerchief. Luckily Ninian had.

"Will you be wanting anything else?" Mr. Swift put the paper-wrapped loaf on the counter.

"I thought Maggie did the baking?" whispered Hugh. "Perhaps it's for all the sandwiches she'll be cutting," said Fiona. "Or maybe she's just lazy."

Ninian, meanwhile, was choosing some chocolate to chew on the way home.

"What was the other thing?" asked Hugh.

He and Fiona scanned the shop.

"Matches!" they said together.

"How many?" asked Ninian.

"She didn't say."

"And a packet of matches, please."

Outside it was almost dark. They hurried up along the track, through the gloom of the bare birch-wood, past the river and Davy's croft, with a cheerful glow from a window, over the bridge and through the gates and past the roaring gully. A faint star came out and shone on them from above Ben Carrick. They sang songs and their feet sounded louder than usual on the track. In front of them white puffs of breath fogged the air.

"There's the Lodge!" cried Fiona as they rounded the last corner. "Let's run." And they clattered down the hill, over the bridge and up the other side.

Ninian, looking back as they reached the door, saw several more stars over the sea. No clouds, a fine day to-morrow. He followed Hugh inside.

CHAPTER III

MIST ON BEN CARRICK

Thursday, 14th December

"As A MATTER of fact," said Fiona, tugging at the sheet on the opposite side of Hugh's bed, "if you don't hurry up it'll be too late to be worth going at all. It'll probably be dark by the time we see the hinds, just supposing we do, and then we'll go and get lost. I thought you had to make beds at school or in the Army, or something."

"Sometimes," said Hugh, carefully tucking in a corner. "But not often."

"There's Davy." Fiona thumped the pillow and went over to the window. Down on the track she could see the old gillie talking to Ninian. They were both wearing the Stewart tweed, which was, after years of experiment, the most perfect blend with the rocks and grass round Carrick.

Ninian came crunching back up to the house, his large-nailed shoes rasping on the stones. He turned again at the door and looked up at the sky, blue and flecked with racing clouds. The wind came tearing round the corner of the house, dead leaves flying before it, and the branches of the birches dipped and tossed their lace-like black twigs as the wind shook them.

He went into the gun-room to find Fiona struggling with her heavy shoes.

"Davy says there were a lot of hinds in the Corrie this morning," he said, taking down his rifle and slipping it into the canvas case. A couple of clips of ammunition went into one pocket and a thin flask into the other.

"Hugh nearly ready?" he asked.

"He's messing about with his bed," said Fiona. "I've never met anyone who took so long to make a bed. Quite fantastic." From long experience she only took two minutes with her own, unless it was the day for a clean sheet.

"It's a little warmer," said Ninian, slinging his glass in its worn leather case over his shoulder.

"Looks simply icy to me," said Fiona, watching the swirling leaves and bent birch branches. "We shall freeze on Ben Carrick."

Hugh appeared in the doorway with his stick.

"I'm actually ready," he announced. "Looks a nice day, Ninian, where's the wind from?"

"West, it would be," said Ninian, following him into the hall. "That means that we shall have to go all the way to the top by Carrick House and come down on them. Simply miles round."

"But rather nice," said Fiona. "Fun seeing the house and Loch Marba. Shall we go right to the top?"

"No need." Ninian opened the door and stood for a moment stuffing his sandwiches into his pocket. "We can come down over the shoulder."

They walked up along the track towards Carna and then branched off into the wood behind the house. Presently they were out and on to the moor, climbing slightly to gain the first ridge. There they found shelter behind a rock and sat down to spy.

Hugh was the first to see them — a large party of hinds right at the top of the Corrie feeding downhill. There must have been twelve or more there, but it was too far to see for certain, as they were among a screen of rocks. Ninian carefully spied out the ground that they would have to cross before climbing up the lower part of the shoulder. From then on they would work up the back of the hill.

"Tiresome lot of sheep right bang below the Corrie," he said, sliding in his glass. "We shall have to keep well down below this ridge, and it'll mean a long walk round."

"Can't be helped. Let's get going," said Fiona, sliding

back behind the rock. "I'm getting simply frozen."

"Who's going to shoot?" asked Ninian, as they walked on along the sheep-track. He led the way steadily. None of Fiona's mad dashes uphill, regardless of aching legs and pounding heart, Hugh was glad to see.

"Oh, either you or Hugh," said Fiona. "I was out the other day."

"Unsuccessfully," Hugh reminded her.

"Yes, but still I had a chance," she said.

"Well, then, definitely Ninian," said Hugh. "He hasn't been out yet. I know I haven't either, but he obviously comes first."

"Rubbish, I'm not particularly keen."

"Don't tell lies."

"No, but really."

"Oh, go on Ninian," said Fiona. "Hugh's being very nice, and you know you're simply dying to, and at any minute he may accept your offer."

A LARGE PARTY OF HINDS.

"Are you sure, really, Hugh?" asked Ninian.

"Yes, really."

"Well, thanks very much. Of course we may not get a shot, but on the other hand we may get two."

They followed him along the track in single file, Fiona, who was last, with her hands deep in her pockets and feeling cold as the wind blew her along. Her feet squelched in the mud and wet tufts of heather brushed against her stockings. Ninian, in front, was keeping a good look-out as at any moment they would climb up over the ridge and be within sight of the sheep. The ground rose slowly in front of them and then sloped up to the left and the foot of the Corrie, and down, right, to where the burn flowed down a gully which ran alongside the track to the village. Slowly Ninian crawled to the top, Hugh and Fiona behind him. The heather was wet and cold to their hands and the damp peaty ground soon soaked through to their knees. All was well, however, for the sheep, three or four hundred yards higher up and down by the burn, were almost out of sight. Ninian crawled on past some rocks, dragging the rifle and stick in one hand. They would knock against rocks and one small stone clattered down, and this just as they were getting to the burn. Slowly Ninian raised his head, but all the sheep were comfortably grazing. Luckily the burn was rocky just here, although in spate, and, following Ninian, they crawled over and through it, although more through than anything.

"Do let's get a little more wet," hissed Fiona into her brother's ear when they got to the other side. "Can't you find another burn? My right shoulder's quite dry."

"Well, how would you have got across?" whispered back Ninian.

"Further down, idiot." Fiona wrung the water out of the corner of her coat.

"Come on, you two, and stop bickering," said Hugh, "I'm slowly freezing to death and even the sheep will get suspicious soon."

Keeping to a long hollow that had once been a burn they went on across the moor and climbed slowly over the bottom of the shoulder of Ben Carrick. The menace of the sheep left behind, they could proceed with less care and in almost an upright position.

At the top of the rise Ninian stopped again to spy. Both sheep and hinds were out of sight and there was nothing ahead but the bare brown and grey hillside, and, down to the right, the tops of the trees about Carrick House. There was no sound but that of wind in the grass and the distant bleat of a sheep and at times the roar of the burn as it tumbled down the gully.

They went on. It grew colder and yet less windy. Fiona thought at first that they must be sheltered behind the hill, but Ninian turned a minute or two later.

"The wind's dropping," he said. "I hope it doesn't change or we shall be in the soup."

"Perhaps we're just sheltered," suggested Hugh; but Ninian shook his head.

"We'll see at the top anyway," he said.

Presently, below them on the right, was Loch Marba, whipped into cold grey horses and studded with sombre islands. They could see the chimneys of Carrick House amongst dark pines and evergreens. The two Stewarts looked at it and longed to plunge down the hill and through the woods. Then there would be the long, emerald-green lawn and the rhododendrons and azaleas and the old white house looking out from wide windows across Loch Marba. Jamie and Jean, when they returned, were sure to spend a day crawling round the house, getting as near as they could without being seen by the tenants or housekeeper. In this way they revived and discovered old paths and hides and eyries which they were determined not to forget. Fiona often felt like accompanying them, and sometimes did, but as she and Ninian were occasionally asked to tea there, they felt it perhaps a little awkward if they were discovered the next day crawling under the bushes round the lawn. But to-day there was no question of such a thing, and after a long look they turned and walked on along a narrow sheep-track, level with Loch Marba but five or six hundred feet higher up.

There was no wind round here and Fiona suggested it would be a good place for lunch.

"Much too early," said Ninian, hurrying on. "Besides we want to see whether the wind's changed and whether the hinds are still there."

Ahead of them the hills ranged along the banks of Loch Marba, a line of giants falling steeply to the water, their crowns lost in mist. Ninian looked up anxiously. From here it was impossible to see, but the other hills were slowly being covered with mist and there was no reason why Ben Carrick should not be also. The hinds were high up too, and it would be more than maddening if it came down before they had got a glimpse of them.

Ninian hurried on. Presently he stopped, and leaning against a rock, spied out the hill above. Fiona nudged him. Away to the right, as far up as they could see under the summit, five or six hinds were feeding. Ninian looked at them for a long moment, then he slid back behind the shelter of the rock.

"Now what?" he said.

"Or d'you mean which?" said Fiona

"Those hinds are nearer the summit than the others." Ninian thrust his hands into his pockets. "The whole lot will be in cloud quite soon, but I think we can reach the top of the Corrie in time."

"They're certainly nearer than the others," put in Fiona.

"Yes, but we know where these are; the first lot may have moved," said Ninian.

"Well, which is it to be?" asked Hugh, resting his rifle, that he was carrying over the rocks.

The Stewarts looked at one another.

"Yes, I think the first lot too," said Ninian. "It's a long climb round to the others and if the wind's still in the west it means approaching them from below. And fairly soon too, or they'll be getting wind of us."

"What will happen when they do? They're sure to as we get up to the Corrie," said Hugh

"They may not," said Fiona, following Ninian up the hillside. "They're a good bit higher up than the head of the Corrie."

They had left the sheep-track now and were more or less literally crawling up the hill. The Stewarts remembered several occasions when stags that had been shot on this hill had rolled and bumped down to the shore of Loch Marba. They hauled themselves up by rocks while the cold air bit into their bare fingers and numbed their feet. Their shoes were well dubbined and unless water went over the top they kept dry. Fiona's were so large that she wore three pairs of socks, and that at least kept her feet warm.

The sky, which had been so blue and promising earlier in the morning, was becoming grey. Ninian looked up anxiously but the mist was still holding off the head of the Corrie, although by now they could see the first fingers swirling down past the summit towards the small lot of hinds. Ninian's long legs sped on up the hill. It was a race against the mist and he didn't want to be caught in it up at the head of the Corrie. The ground was so uneven there that it was almost impossible to tell whether you were going up or down. And before long you were among the treacherous rocks on the precipice above Bearnach.

It was getting colder. The wind, blowing up the Corrie, came up and over the top. Ninian stopped and loaded the rifle. The bolt shot back and the clip slid in, and then the blot snicked into place, sounding deafeningly loud in the stillness. The wind blew in gusts, died, and blew again less strongly. The mist crept and swirled down the hill above them.

"Carefully now," whispered Ninian. "We don't know how near they are."

The ground was levelling out here at the saddle between the two peaks. Clumps of wet bracken stood dankly about between grey lichened rocks, rudely thrown into place by the hand of a giant. Pools of black water lay on the peat, dully reflecting the grey sky. Fiona and Hugh, numbly following Ninian, crawling in the mud, felt miserable. Ninian leading, had all the excitement of the stalk, and he was also carrying the rifle and would be the one to shoot if the chance came. The rocks stood black and grim on the skyline of the saddle. Ninian reached one and cautiously peered round it. The others slithered and squelched up behind him. Fiona rubbed the hair from her eyes with peaty fingers and left a smear. Hugh thought he was lying on a stone, grovelled to remove it, and found it was his sandwiches that had slid round underneath him and were not profiting by it.

Below him, on the sloping sides of the Corrie, Ninian could see the hinds. They were about four hundred yards away and slightly on the left bank, lying sheltered among the rocks. They were well out of shot, but should be easy enough to get to after a detour round to the left.

Ninian slid back.

"They're still there," he said. "The thing is that I shall have to go round a bit, and I suggest that you two stay here while I do the stalk. It should be more amusing to watch than to do, really, apart from the cold."

"All right," said Fiona. "We'll stay here, only don't be too long."

"I'll do my best. Keep my stick," and Ninian slid back down hill and crawled off below the ridge.

Hugh and Fiona lay behind the rock watching the hinds, and presently saw Ninian appear on the far side of the Corrie.

As they watched him the mist came swirling over them. They looked at each other.

"How silent it is," said Fiona after a moment or two. She hardly dared speak as the mist seemed to have blanketed all sound, and they might as well have been lying in the middle of a huge cloud, miles from the earth.

"What shall we do?" whispered Hugh.

"Just stay here for a bit." Fiona edged nearer to the rock. It was cold and damp, and around them dim shapes of boulders loomed and then disappeared. Sharply a sheep bleated over on their left somewhere and then was silent. Fiona felt the mist, which had beaded in tiny drops of moisture on her eyelashes, lie cold and wet on her cheeks when she blinked. Hugh looked as though he was going grey, and the rough hair of his tweed coat shimmered with tiny diamonds.

"But how can he possibly see?" he asked.

"Well, he'll remember the ground ahead and I suppose hope for the best," said Fiona, "unless he waits for it to lift."

"Heavens, I hope not." Hugh hunched himself in his coat like a cold bird. "We shall be frozen by then. Do you know the way back?"

"Oh, vaguely. We can't just leave Ninian, though, we'd better wait until he calls."

"Supposing he's waiting until we do?"

"Oh, Hugh, don't be difficult! I know, let's have lunch."

The packets of sandwiches were slightly the worse for their journey up the hill. But all the same, thick slices of ham between fresh bread, a hunk of fruit-cake and a ginger-nut, were very pleasant and cheering. Hugh had a flask of whisky too in his hip pocket, and insisted on them both having a nip or two, although they had not yet got a hind.

They sat hunched and waiting behind their rock,

straining their ears for the sound of a shot, watching the folds of white mist blow and eddy round them and lay cold fingers on their cheeks.

"Seen anything of Fergus?" Hugh asked presently.

"Not a thing," said Fiona, watching a rock that was just visible and waiting to see if it grew more distinct or less.

"Heard anything?" asked Hugh.

"No, nothing — nothing since he left us in Flatfish Bay last summer."

"I wonder if he's still there?"

"We haven't been to see. Pretty cold in those caves, I should think."

"He was a strange person," said Hugh thoughtfully. "Sort of person who might suddenly pop up out of this fog beside us."

"Yes." Fiona looked over her shoulder, half hoping that what Hugh said might come true and also that it would be rather ghostly if it did. But no such thing happened. They remained isolated behind their rock, the only two people in the world, waiting for half an hour, an hour.

"I simply must have a cigarette," said Hugh. "Would it absolutely wreck everything if I did?"

"Might, shouldn't think so." Fiona was so cold she could hardly speak: her chin felt numb and stiff.

They lit one each and it seemed almost to warm them. They felt as though they had spent the whole day on the hillside and were gradually losing all sense of time and feeling except in a small patch where their shoulders leant against each other.

"I suppose this is what's called dying of exposure," said Hugh, trying to pretend that he could see a rock in the surrounding white blanket.

Fiona nodded. As she did so there was a sudden shot. In the stillness it sounded just behind them and they jumped. Then there was the rush and patter of feet, and the whole herd came tearing past them and away into the mist, their small feet clicking on the stones and the rank smell of deer left behind them in still air.

Fiona, who had clutched at Hugh in the first moment of fright as the deer came literally bounding over their legs, let go and sat up.

"Wonder if he got it?" she said.

"Wonder where he is?" said Hugh, crawling round the rock and peering down the hill.

A faint shout came drifting up on the mist.

"There! Listen!" cried Fiona.

"What? I didn't hear a thing," said Hugh.

"Sh! Shut up!" They strained their ears.

"Hoy! Fiona! Fiona!" The shout was very faint but it came from the direction in which they had first seen the deer.

They yelled an answer and started off down the hill.

"Go carefully," warned Fiona. "You've no idea how easy it is to go in the wrong direction. We shall probably find ourselves skidding down the rocks above Bearnach."

Slowly they went on, shouting and being shouted at, guiding themselves by Ninian's voice, slightly muffled by the fog but gradually growing louder.

After a hundred yards or so, when they had heard nothing, they stopped and called.

There was no answer.

"Hell!" said Fiona. "It would be the limit if we got lost."

They waited a moment or two but there was no sound. "We'll have to go back. Can you remember the way?" asked Hugh.

"I don't know. Anyway let's try."

With their eyes on the ground they went back, thankful that they had left some footprints in the damp ground.

Hugh was the first to hear Ninian again and they yelled back encouragingly, only to find they had lost touch again in a few moments.

"This is too idiotic," said Fiona as they retraced their footsteps once more, "Ninian will be livid."

"I feel extraordinary stupid," said Hugh. "I mean, he can have only been about four hundred yards away and we must have walked at least twice that already."

"Let's never not have a compass again," said Fiona, stumbling over a rock and dropping both her own and Ninian's stick. "Ouch!"

Again they heard a shout, this time nearer than ever, and in a few minutes were almost on top of Ninian, sitting perched on a rock with his chin in his hands. He looked at them.

"What in the world have you been doing?" he asked at last. "Been back to Carrick or something?"

"Well, as a matter of fact," said Hugh, leaning against the rock and lighting his pipe, "it's easier said than done trying to find one's way in this mist. We didn't exactly hang about, it's much too cold. And now where is the result of all this waiting and searching?"

Ninian gestured over his shoulder and Hugh and Fiona saw a hind lying in the grass.

"Well done," said Fiona generously. "And now let's hurry."

"And while we're going, you can tell us how you did it," added Hugh.

They tied on the rope, shouldered their sticks and set off down the Corrie.

"If we keep going down hill it should be all right for the moment," said Ninian, but all the same they went slowly.

As they went he told them how, when he was about two hundred yards from the hinds, the mist had come down. He had had a rough idea of the rocks and cover in front of him and had crept on expecting, after the first moment or so, to come face to face with a hind. Then something had gone wrong and he had found himself far down the Corrie by a rock he knew well. That meant going back and searching again — all very difficult in the mist. Then suddenly he had heard a hind bark only a little way ahead of him. After a short stalk the back of a beast loomed up in front, then it had only entailed getting into place, as luckily it had happened to be the hind he had originally had his eye on.

They did not return till dark. It took them two hours to get out of the Corrie and there they left the mist behind them. It was much colder here down on the flats and Fiona, carrying the rifle, felt her fingers freezing to the barrel. Suddenly, in spite of the cold and hungryness, she felt very happy, and, catching Hugh's eye, saw he was smiling too.

CHAPTER IV

THE HOUSE IN THE HILLS

Friday, 15th December

AT ELEVEN O'CLOCK next morning Ninian left to meet the twins and Sandy from the London train. It was a lovely day, cloudy and sunny, the tops of the high hills along Loch Marba and all the Corriedon mountains covered in snow. Coming down the hill above Fairloch the sun was sparkling on the sea and across to Skye where the Coolins, too, were white-capped.

He had left Hugh and Fiona happily and messily undamming the burn. They were getting wet and cold, but somehow that did not seem to matter when the sun shone between the clouds and in the crisp fresh air.

The train, as usual, was late and Ninian, meeting an old friend, one of the shepherds from Flowerdale, sat with him beside a large coal fire and had a pint of cool draught beer. The shepherd's small black collie, Moll, lay with her nose between her paws and her bright brown eyes fixed unwaveringly upon her master's face. Sometimes, when he glanced at her, she moved her bushy tail. He never spoke to her nor petted her, but the small dog's devotion to him was greater than that given by any lap-dog.

Ninian and the shepherd talked of sheep and hills and deer, warming their hands before the blaze, puffing their pipes and taking long draughts from the deep creamy ale. The shepherd was a fine old man, small, thin, grey-haired, his face as brown and lined and firm as the crooked handle of his hazel stick.

The train swept into the station and stood there puffing and hissing, while its passengers disembarked. Ninian, finishing his beer in the hotel, could hear the clear voices of the twins ringing above the slow, soft speech of the Highlanders.

He said good-day to David and went out on to the platform, to be nearly swept off his feet by a rush from the twins while Sandy stood by grinning, and larger than ever.

"Aren't you ever going to stop growing?" Ninian asked him, smiling. At seventeen Sandy was almost as tall as he was.

They left their tickets with the collector and went out to the Ford, staggering under suitcases and guns. Sandy, a rug and an oilskin over his arm, brought up the rear.

"Did you have a good journey?" asked Ninian, settling Jean beside him and the boys in the back.

"Oh, lovely. Rather cold, but great fun," said Sandy.

"We were all in a third sleeper together," added Jean. "A dreadfully prim girl was in there too, to start with, but she looked so horrified that I think she got out at Crewe, although her luggage was labelled Inverness."

"I hope you behaved well." Ninian felt sorry for the unknown and probably astonished girl confronted by the three Stewarts.

"We behaved beautifully," Jamie answered him. Jamie, the best-mannered of the family, could usually be counted on not to disgrace them all. He, too, had shot up, leaving Jean far behind.

"Well, fairly beautifully," said Jean. "Except at the hotel at Glasgow."

Ninian drew in to a passing-place and let a lorry go by.

"What happened then?" he asked suspiciously.

"Well, you know how one always has porridge and then bacon and eggs or finnan haddock?" said Jean. "Sandy was frightfully greedy, and would have everything as well as millions of scones and baps and toast.

"It was the first proper breakfast I'd had for ages," objected Sandy.

"It rather horrified every one else," said Jean. "But the

worst part was that when he had finished the eggs and the fish he saw some sausages and asked for them too."

Sandy giggled at the memory of the waiter's scandalised face.

"I feel lovely and full now," he said.

As usual at the top of the hill above Kinlochcarrick, Ninian switched off the engine and they flew silently down the long hill, as different a form of travel as sailing is from a motor-boat.

"Don't all the hills look blissful and snowy?" said Jean. "It was such fun waking up this morning and finding oneself in Scotland."

"What are we going to do these holidays?" interrupted Sandy.

"Nothing special. Shoot, set the lobster-pots perhaps, toboggan if it snows." Ninian did not mind what it was as long as he was at Carrick.

"It's sure to be something special," said Sandy. "Poaching one summer, Fergus last summer. By the way, has any one seen Fergus?"

"I did," said Jean, her flax-fair hair blowing over her eyes. She brushed it out. "At the end of last holidays in Inverness. He was stalking along, looking just the same but much more respectable. In fact, quite tidy."

"Did you talk to him?" Sandy was all agog to hear news of Fergus, who intrigued him as much as he did the others.

"No, he turned down a street and when I looked he wasn't there," said Jean sadly, remembering the long hunt she had had and with no success. Fergus had disappeared as completely as if she had never seen him. The others had been sceptical, but Jean was as convinced that it was Fergus Macloud she had seen as she had been last summer in Flatfish Bay, when she had been the only one to see his boat.

"Perhaps it wasn't him," suggested Sandy. "You might have made a mistake."

"No," said Jean firmly. "No one else has a scowl quite like that."

Lunch was ready at Carrick when they returned, and Hugh and Fiona were there, muddy and cold but triumphant at the now loud roaring of the burn.

There was a great scuffling and laughing in the kitchen with Maggie and Morag until Fiona came in to tell them to get ready for lunch.

"Jean, your face is quite black," she announced, coming closer to inspect more nearly. "And you haven't brushed your hair for weeks."

Her eye fell upon Jamie.

"James, your neck," she shrieked, seizing him and hauling him towards the door. "It's quite revolting."

"Well, no one can wash much in a train." James was resigned to his sister's ministrations, and by the time lunch was on the table they were washed, brushed and shining.

Outside the wind, cold but light, sighed gently in the birch trees and rustled the dead leaves beneath them. The sun was almost warm and tipped the point of each ripple on Hernsary with gold. Fiona, noticing it from the window which she was facing, said suddenly, "Let's go up to Carna and row across this afternoon."

"Oh, yes, let's." Jean loved the Carna Loch. "We could go right down to Loch Dubh."

"Not enough time." Ninian speared the kidney he had carefully scooped out of the rabbit stew and ate it in a gulp. Fiona, who had searched for it in vain, said, "Beast. I know, let's go across to the old cottage."

"Which old cottage?" asked Hugh and Jamie together. "D'you mean the one the Mackenzies used to live in, right under Carn Mor?" said Ninian.

"Yes, do let's. I've never been there." Fiona was now fired with enthusiasm for her idea. "Mackenzie always used to say it was a lovely place and completely deserted. No roads to it at all."

"How did they get there then?" asked Sandy practically. "By boat, like we will, or by pony-path from Beanault and Carrick House."

"And I think there's another path from Lettercarrick," added Ninian, who had seen the estate map.

"Who lives there now?" asked Jean, who did not remember ever seeing any one or any sign of human habitation on the shores of the Carna Loch.

"No one." Ninian helped himself to blackberry tart. "It's been empty for years, at least five or six. I can remember going there once on the way back from a long stalk on Carn Mor, years and years ago."

"When you were young," put in Hugh.

"Yes, almost." Ninian smiled. "The Mackenzies lived there then, and it was a lovely place, but I dare say it'll be rather a ruin now."

"Come on!" Fiona was impatient to be off. There was a moment's wild and desperate searching for coats and shoes. Then they were gone.

They decided to go in the Ford, as it grew dark so soon. The short Highland afternoons were lovely but gone almost before they were realised. Determined to make the most of it, the Stewarts packed themselves into the car and roared away up the track for a mile or so until they came out on to the flat ground by the Carna Loch. At the end of the track was the bothy, in which were kept oars, old rods, a pile of dried bracken, ropes and other things. From there was a short path down to the loch itself and the wooden jetty where the heavy grey boats lay.

These had been hauled up and turned upside down for the winter, but the united efforts of the six of them righted one and pushed her down to the water. Jean found the cork and pushed it in; James was carrying the rowlocks, Sandy the two long oars.

"Whereabouts is this house?" asked Hugh, staring across the loch and unable to see the trace of anything remotely habitable.

Fiona pointed. There were several islands on the loch, some away down towards Loch Dubh, the Black Loch, dark and secret and stiff, between Ben Carrick and Carn Mor.

"It's down there," she said. "Behind the islands, in a green patch at the foot of Carn Mor."

"Not a house, a croft really," added Ninian, who did not want Hugh to have any false hopes about the place they were going to visit.

"Well, come on. I'm getting cold." Sandy sprang into the boat which rocked violently and seized an oar. Ninian took the other and in a moment they were on their way.

It was cold in the stern. Great clouds were banked over the sun. Fiona, Jean and Hugh sat huddled together, while James in the bows had completely disappeared. Their voices and the creak and splash of the oars went echoing across the still, cold loch and up to the snowy hills. Hugh tried to imagine what it would be like living always as remote and distant from the world as the crofters at Carna must have been. He could not imagine it, especially the winter, when the short days and long nights would make life unbearably long, when there would be hardly time to trim and fill the oil-lamps between dawn and dusk, when the pony-tracks to civilisation would be snowed up for half the winter and they would have to be entirely self-contained. No wireless, no telephone, no gramophone, cinema or piano would help to shorten the long evenings. No books, music or dancing. The women must have sat spinning or knitting or mending, while the men tended the beasts by candlelight and repaired broken implements.

They passed the wooden islands where, so long ago it seemed, Ninian, Fiona and Hugh had rowed one night for wood for their fire. Instead of green, the trees were black, stripped of their leaves, save for a few dark pines that reared their shaggy heads above the birch and rowan and hazel.

James, who had reappeared when they passed the islands, was now hanging over the bows with his eyes fixed on the lower slopes of Carn Mor. They were all silent now, peering ahead, except Sandy who gave frequent glances over his shoulder, and Ninian who spoke breathlessly between strokes.

"It'll be a patch of green amongst the rocks and bracken," he said. "You probably won't see the house because it'll be grey, but the fields should still be greenish. And there may be a tree or two."

"I see it!" cried Jamie. "There, look! Past that little point."

They craned forward.

"I see it too." Fiona half-stood up. "Look, Ninian, that point is a little stone jetty."

Ninian rested his oar and turned round. Behind him, in a small curved bay, stood the croft. At one arm of the bay a jetty had been built of rocks and a path led from it to

"I SEE IT!" CRIED JAMIE.

the house. This stood, small and grey and solid, in a patch of bright-green grass which stretched for two hundred yards or so up the hillside, bound by a tumbled stone wall.

He turned, and they rowed on, Jamie hopping with excitement and almost out of the boat before she touched the rocks. They made fast to a rusted iron ring and walked on up the path.

"It's rather heaven." Fiona spoke softly, hardly liking to break the utter stillness of the place. The loch water broke gently on the sandy beach, the wind whistled softly in the grass, a raven, far away on Carn Mor, croaked harshly, and then again, and distantly a sheep bleated. But otherwise there was silence so immense and far-reaching that Hugh had that sensation he had had once before at dawn by Bearnach of being the only living thing in these vast hills.

Their feet clattered on the stones as they walked up to the croft. Either side of the path the ground had been cleared of bracken and brambles, and to the left there was smooth and close-cropped grass, while to the right were stones ending in the loch shore. A burn came roaring and splashing down from the shoulder of Carn Mor, through the fields and over the path. They crossed dry-foot on stepping-stones and went on until they came to the wall. At one time this had run right and left of the cottage and then back up the hill enclosing roughly four acres of ground, divided into three fields. Close-bitten grass and rocks lay in front of the house up to each corner where the stone wall swept back to join the fields. An iron gate on either side led to flower and vegetable plots, and these now stood propped open, leaning on one hinge, while the wall had fallen down on many places allowing sheep and deer and rabbits to feed unmolested in the small fields and in the garden. Two apple trees by the house were bent and broken and saplings of hazel and rowan were growing on the wall and in the garden. Up to the right a small wood of stunted trees sprawled on the hillside. Nettles and bracken grew and flourished in the garden and on the path and the tall withered stems of ragwort showed that they also grew in this deserted place.

They went up to the house. Once, no doubt, it had been a comfortable croft, prosperous and whitewashed with its hens and ducks round it. Now the walls were grey, the tiled roof had fallen right in in one place and a small rowan tree grew out of a chimney.

"There's something rather sad about a deserted house." Fiona turned at the door and looked back over the loch. They had climbed slightly uphill since leaving the boat and now the bay and whole expanse of water was spread before them. Right, the wooded islands and the calm blue surface of Carna stretching to the flat ground around and above Beanault, left the narrowing loch lost in the hollow between the hills. From here Ben Carrick looked especially beautiful, clear-cut and white against the blue winter sky, and around it all the tumbled ground above the Lodge.

"What a wonderful place to live," said Hugh at last. Fiona caught his eye, her own full of a new and delightful plan.

"Come on," said Jean, impatient, "let's look inside."

She turned the handle of the door and it opened quite easily. Inside was the chaos and litter and disuse a house falls into after a few years' emptiness. And this had been empty for over six. A narrow hall faced them, crossed from left to right by a rickety staircase to the loft. Left had been the kitchen. A rusty iron range was still in place and an old and battered dresser; also a kitchen table and two broken chairs. Fiona inspected the cupboards, but all they held were broken cups and a rusty kettle. Right was the bedroom with the remains of a bird's nest half-way down the chimney and the sagging springs of a vast double bed and a chest of drawers. Paper and straw lay on the ground and a ragged curtain by the window. Sandy pushed open a door in the far corner which led into another room, a sort of annexe added after the house was built, but evidently intended for a bedroom as another bed and a chest of drawers showed. The ceiling of this room had never been boarded in so that the bare laths and tiles showed, with plenty of daylight in between.

They left the annexe and went back into the hall. Here Ninian had noticed another door and this led into an even smaller room behind the stairs. Its tiny window looked out on to a grassy yard flanked on the left by the cow-byre and stretching up through the fields to the hill.

"Bit small and poky," announced Sandy, leading them back into the kitchen. They perched on the table and gazed once more round the room. Hugh's eye, resting on what seemed to be another cupboard, lit up. He crossed over to it and pushed. It slid sideways, unwillingly, and revealed a box-bed and another beyond it.

"Oh, what fun!" cried Fiona, leaping up to inspect it.

"Like a bunk in a ship," added James approvingly.

Jean privately thought it would probably be rather smelly, but she said nothing.

"Beautifully warm in the winter," said Hugh.

"We've forgotten the attic," said James.

They crowded up the stairs behind him, going carefully because one step was broken. The attic was a long, low room, so much under the eaves that it was impossible to stand upright except in the middle. It was lit at either end by a tiny cobwebby window and several sacks lay on the ground, one half-full of sprouting potatoes. It was quite light as the tiles had blown off in one place and Ninian stood there with his head sticking through. The darkening sky made him look at his watch.

"We must be going," he said. "It's half-past three."

"Bother, we haven't nearly explored." The twins and Sandy thundered down the stairs and into the kitchen. Here a door led through the scullery and into the yard. The cow-byre on the left was in a worse state than the house as one wall was half-down as well as part of the roof. At the back of the byre was the ruin of what had once been a henhouse, as rotten planks and tangled wire showed, and beyond that several small sheds, all in a similar state of disrepair. This part of the garden was still fenced in and long tangled grass and dead overgrown plants filled it with a depressing confusion. They looked at it and then walked slowly round to the front of the house, crunching tins and glass under foot.

"We must just have a last look at the box-beds," said James, who had never seen any before.

Back in the kitchen, already full of the shadows of dusk, they stood grouped round the old table. It felt dank and cold and smelt of disuse. Ninian lit his pipe and the match flared up in the dim room. Fiona was over by the stove, fiddling with the flues and the oven door and trying to peer up the chimney.

At last she spoke. Somehow they had all been waiting for her; something unsaid seemed to lie heavily on the air, something waiting to be spoken. She turned and looked at them, her eyes bright, her hair dishevelled, her face alight with the eager look they knew so well.

"I say," she said, "do let's come and live here."

They looked at her, Sandy and the twins thrilled as always with Fiona's ideas, Ninian and Hugh more dubious and aware of all the difficulties.

"Don't look like that," she said, seeing their faces. "Just think what fun it would be."

"It's almost a ruin," objected Ninian, eyeing the dilapidated darkening room. "There's no furniture; it'd be icy cold."

"No, it wouldn't," said Fiona quickly. "We could quite easily make it habitable, and with a few fires and some scrubbing it'll look quite different. Oh, do let's, Ninian. We've got nothing special to do, and if it's absolute misery we can stop."

"We can bring lamps and peat and stuff up from the Lodge," added Jean.

Ninian and Hugh looked at each other.

"It sounds rather mad to me," said Ninian. "Fancy leaving a comfortable house like the Lodge for the misery of this bothy."

"We needn't stay long," said Jamie.

"We won't come here until it's habitable," said Fiona. "It'll take some time getting things up here, then there's all the garden to do. We must do it."

"Let's try it anyway." Hugh watched Fiona's eager face light into a smile as she turned to him.

Ninian, privately thinking it would be rather fun but not wanting to involve himself in any rash statements, said, "Well, all right. We'll come up to-morrow early and have a proper look round and see what's to be done. We can't embark on anything very difficult."

"That's settled then." Fiona went to the door and started off down the path. The sky in the west was palest gold where the sun was setting. None of the flamboyant summer sunsets but delicate wintery shades. East, the hills rose black and stern round the end of the Carna Loch and back to where they were standing. The croft was right amongst them, part of them, the calm and quietness proclaimed it so.

The twins were talking excitedly about discovering the path down to Beanault, all the way along the Carna Loch and then past Gillaria.

"Also the one to Lettercarrick," said Sandy. "And there must be one to Carrick House too."

"That'll be the Bearnach one," said Ninian.

They reached the boat and pushed her off. As they rowed down the loch Fiona looked back. In her mind she could see the lit windows and a curl of peat smoke and the voices laughing and talking for which the house in the hills had been waiting for many years.

CHAPTER V

MESSING ABOUT

Saturday, 16th December

THE SAME SUN, cloud and wintery blue sky looked down next morning on the Stewarts. They were up earlier than usual, breakfast by half-past eight, ready to start by half-past nine.

Maggie had been kept busy cutting mountains of sandwiches and slices of cake for lunch. They had filled two knapsacks with these and a Thermos of coffee.

"Just in case it's simply freezing," said Fiona.

The Ford was brought out of the byre and piled high with sacks of peat and coal, scrubbing-brushes, soap, dish-clothes, brooms and buckets, and an enormous kettle for boiling water. Ninian brought a saw and nails and a hammer, Hugh grabbed yesterday's *Times* for lighting the fire, and Jamie brought a billhook for dealing with the worst of the brambles.

It was a tight fit in the car and the back was an indescribable chaos of twins, sacks and brooms. Hugh stood on the step and bitterly regretted it when his hands became numb.

"We can't spend all day in the house," Sandy said. "It's much too fine. We simply must explore the burn."

"And the wood." Jeannie's voice came from under a couple of buckets.

"Probably the stove won't light," said Jamie. "I do draw the line at scrubbing with cold water."

"Somehow I don't think there'll be very much work done to-day." Ninian guided the car carefully over a rut. "We must have a look round at everything and see if we really like the place. No use staying there if it's deadly uncomfortable or not enough room or damp or something."

"It's going to be heaven." Fiona sounded muffled but convinced. "But there's no need to rush madly, we've got weeks ahead of us."

They arrived and staggered down to the dinghy with their load. Sandy went to the hut to get an extra pair of oars and rowlocks. He had suggested four rowing.

"Otherwise the wretched two will expire," he said.

So the boat fairly shot across the water when at last they pushed her off. Sandy, Fiona, Hugh and Ninian each had an oar, Jean was in the bows and James in the stern. He peered over into the dark water half-hoping to see a monster trout that were the Carna Loch's speciality. Perhaps, he thought, they hibernate or migrate in the winter. Jean, in the bows, was thinking much the same thing, only instead of hoping to see one she was wondering if one might possibly rise to a fly. There was just the right amount of ripple; surely a cunningly placed fly might lure one out? But she knew that it would not.

The croft looked more entrancing than ever this morning. The pale sun, shining from over Ben Carrick, lit the small emerald fields and the rusty brown wood. High above towered the long smooth head of Carn Mor, steep, grey with strewn rocks, patched brown and green with heather, bracken and grass. Small, foam-edged waves broke on the coarse golden sand of the bay and a splash of dark brown to the left of the wall betrayed a disused peat-bog. Ninian's eye fell on it and he wondered if they would be able to cut peat and then remembered that it took a long time to dry.

"Might lay in a stock," he thought, and then laughed at himself for taking so much for granted that they would stay here.

They carried their stores up in two loads and dumped them in the kitchen. Fiona pushed open all the windows,

THE CROFT.

much to the horror of several well dug-in spiders, and great draughts of clean cold mountain air came sweeping into the house. The windows, as in most of these cottages, were small, but it made so much difference when they were open that Fiona decided one of the first jobs must be the cleaning of them. She looked round for a twin or Sandy but every one had vanished, and laughter and voices from behind the house indicated that the byre was being explored.

Fiona followed them out. It was stuffy and smelly in the cottage and the day outside was so lovely that it seemed a pity to waste it indoors. The wind was in the west, blowing off the sea, over the low ground and across the loch and Carn Mor. Standing in this small smooth patch at the foot of the hill it looked larger than ever. Almost one had to lean backwards to see the top. It was a long curved hill, full of deer and buzzards and ravens, huge grey boulders strewn along its sides. The summit was almost entirely rock, patched, Fiona guessed, with small blue pools and bright lichen, too bare and windswept for anything but the hardiest tuft of grass and the most stunted of bushes to grow. She herself had never stalked Carn Mor, so the hill was unexplored and full of promise. A long deep gully ran down past the top of the wood, probably the bed of another burn. She could hardly wait to see. Exploring burns was one of her favourite things.

Loud voices from the byre drew her attention and she went over to investigate.

"If we had a pony," Sandy was saying, "we could keep him here; there's a lovely little place next to the cow."

She ducked her head under the low lintel and went in. The byre was divided into four stalls, the left two still in good repair, the others decayed and weather-beaten where the roof and walls had fallen in. A pile of bracken lay in one corner with a battered bucket and stool. The rafters were so low that only the smallest cow could get in with comfort.

Hugh came over to her. "We're going to have a cow," he said. "At least two cows, hens, and probably a pig. Later we'll bring the sheep. Oh, and a pony, of course."

"What is this?" Fiona raised her eyebrows.

"The twins and Sandy are organising a farm," Hugh grinned. "You'll have your work cut out."

"No, but honestly, Fiona," Jamie's face was anxious, "don't you think it'd be fun to have a cow? There are three fields for it and this lovely little byre. We just can't waste it."

"The walls are all broken," Fiona objected, although even she was drawn to the thought of their own cow and plenty of milk and butter. Butter! That meant a churn, and hours of work. A cow meant people coming back in the middle of some lovely adventure and getting up at the unearthly hour of six.

"Too much bother," she said firmly.

"Anyhow, we haven't got a cow, they're Maggie's." Ninian clinched the matter.

James joined Sandy in a corner of the byre. If Fiona

had not been so busy with an old hurricane lantern she had found and was trying to hang from a beam, she would have seen the expression on their faces and at once nipped their ambition in the bud. Jean saw, and was doubtful.

They left the byre by way of the tumbledown wall and found themselves in the remains of a hen-run and kitchen garden. Even winter had not suppressed the weeds and they were as high as Jean's waist. Dead grass, leaves and sticks were matted together in a horrid confusion. The hen-run had collapsed completely and lay in rotting planks against the walls.

The Stewarts looked at it in disgust.

"Definitely not the nicest part of the garden." Fiona turned her back on it and climbed over a sagging wire fence into the field. It was the one with the burn running through it, the stone wall surrounding it heaped on the ground and only held up in places by a strand of wire that had once run along the top and acted as a deer fence.

They crossed over to the burn. Once this field must have been ploughed, as a withered stalk or two of barley showed on the rough ground by the burn, but now the turf was short and bitten. The burn itself was one of the nicest kind for a small trout, running deep and still between peaty banks, sometimes falling over a rock into a stout-coloured pool, then a yard or so of shallows.

"Trout for breakfast." Ninian caught Fiona's eye.

"Just imagine this place in the summer," she said.

"We must come here next summer," cried Jean. "Think how lovely. We could sleep out in the hills."

"A bit midgy," Hugh suggested.

"You always think of something," said Fiona.

They followed the burn across the field and over the wall that divided this one from the next. This one was narrow and had reverted much more to its original state of bracken and heather. The wall between the two fields was still fairly intact, but the outer wall was flat in places and it was difficult to see where the grass ended and the hill began. The burn crossed the bottom right-hand corner of this and the top left-hand corner of the next field and then disappeared into the wood.

"I should have loved to have seen this when it was inhabited," said Hugh, as they climbed the wall into the last and largest field. "It's just the right size to be able to work easily and I dare say they had sheep on the hills. Who owned this croft? What were they?"

"Gillies," said Fiona. "Called Mackenzie. They belonged to Lettercarrick, but no one comes here now so it doesn't matter what we do. I expect they were shepherds as well; there's a good deal of feed on Carn Mor."

The wall between the field and the wood had stood up better than most to the long lack of care. Even the wire strand was intact, running from post to post along the wall, high enough to daunt the greediest deer.

"This is just the time of year for them to be low down," said Jamie as they climbed over. "We shall probably see some in the wood."

They dropped down into a soft drift of leaves. Somewhere over on the far side of the trees a cock pheasant was calling.

"A long time since he's had any corn, I expect," said Ninian, even more delighted with the croft at the thought of a pheasant or two in the back garden. There would be grouse too on the heathery lower slopes of the hill, and a lochful of trout. Two wood-pigeons clappered up through the trees as they struggled through, and another two farther on. Beside them the burn chimed over its bed of rocks and gurgled round wads of grass and leaves caught in the low-hung branches of hazel and rowan trees.

"Nuts, too." Sandy spied out a tall tree with several withered-looking clusters at the top. He shook it violently but without effect.

"Rotten, anyway, I expect," said Jamie.

Fiona, who was slightly ahead, stopped as she bent down to crawl under a birch branch.

"Look," she whispered, "deer: we must have frightened them."

In the soft ground by the stream were the slots of a large herd.

"I'm not surprised, we haven't been exactly silent," said Ninian.

"Let's follow them out of the wood," said Sandy. "We might be able to see them on the hill."

It was almost impossible to be silent going through the wood. A stick would crack, a branch swish; a pigeon flap up through the trees. There was no path of any kind that they could follow, only the twisting of the burn.

"Really no point in being silent," said Fiona at last. "We've made much too much noise already."

After that they took no notice of twigs and leaves but hurried on and burst through a belt of hazels into a patch of high brown bracken. The noon sun came streaming down the hill, warm in spite of it being December, and small puffs of cloud drifted over the crown of Carn Mor. They dropped into the bracken and on to rocks, spying out the hill ahead of them, but its long curved side seemed as bare and empty as the fields of the croft.

Suddenly Ninian saw them, down by the loch shore, half-way to Loch Dubh. It was a big herd of hinds, moving slowly now and stopping every so often to pick at a tuft of grass or bracken. They had lost all the sleek smoothness of summer and under their dingy rough hair their bones stood out.

"If we live here," said Jean suddenly, "we shall have them sniffing round the house at night." It was rather an unpleasant thought; bad enough at Carrick where at least it was fairly civilised, but here it would be worse. For a moment Jean had a vision of herself having to jostle past a herd of hungry deer to go out at all, but then dismissed it as rubbish. Anyway, Ninian would be there and she wasn't really afraid of deer.

"We might put out some food for them," said James, who had none of these qualms, but Jean thought this was going a little too far.

"Personally," Sandy got up and brushed leaves and lichen from him, "I think it's lunch-time. What have we done with the food?"

"In the house." Fiona realised she was feeling hungry too. "Let's go back round the wood."

They went right along the top of the trees, parallel with the loch and then turned down towards it. Beyond them along the hill was the gully Fiona longed to explore. She pointed at it.

"We must go there soon," she said.

"D'you think it's a burn?" asked Hugh.

"Maybe."

The hinds were out of sight now beyond the gully. The sun had gone in.

"Come on," said Sandy, and led them charging downhill towards the loch. It was cold if you lingered about, and, besides, he was hungry.

They decided to eat the sandwiches outside, and took them to the smooth clipped grass between the wall and the loch. They sat, sheltering from the west wind, behind a huge rock and ate venison pasties and drank the Thermos of coffee, and wished there was more.

"What'll we do after lunch?" asked Jean, picking up crumbs.

"Let's do the house," said Fiona. "As a matter of fact it must be lateish. What is the time, Ninian?"

"Twoish. Personally," Ninian tilted the Thermos top and drank the last dregs, "I'd like to have a look at the roof.

That strikes me as the hardest job. D'you know anything about tiles and things, Hugh?"

"Well, no, nothing. I mean, one doesn't have much opportunity of learning," said Hugh, "but I dare say we could cope. I've often watched builders, they sort of hang them over the slats."

"Sounds a bit vague," Fiona grinned. "I think chimney-sweeping is the first job. We can't light a fire until then, and if we don't we can't have any hot water for scrubbing." She looked at Sandy, who immediately became enormously interested in the islands half a mile from the shore.

"Right." Ninian uncoiled his six foot four and swung a knapsack over his shoulder. They followed him back to the house, except Sandy and James, who had found some flat stones and were playing ducks and drakes.

Hugh inspected the iron gate on the left as they passed. He lifted it back, kicking tangled grass and leaves out of the way, so that they could go in and out of the garden without having to squeeze through it every time. One hinge was broken, and as it was of the type where a ring stands out of the gate and fits over an upright prong on the gate-post, he felt it was a little beyond him at the moment. The other gate appeared to have been lifted by some super-human force off its prong, but with Ninian's help Hugh got it back.

"A little oil and they'll be as good as new," he said, proudly swinging one back and forth. Fiona looked at the large gap in the wall beside it, but said nothing. After all they could always mend the wall.

"It would be nice to have a seat out here," said Jean, pausing outside the door and pointing along the wall. "Then you could sit here in the summer and look over the loch."

"I'm sure they used to." Fiona could picture the old gillies, the day's work done, sitting in the long summer evenings, puffing their pipes and staring out across the Carna Loch.

"We'll have one, too," she said.

"Now," said Hugh, standing in the kitchen, "how does one clean a chimney?"

"Bunch of bracken tied to a stick?" suggested Ninian, sitting on the table.

"Up or down?"

"Down, of course. How could any one get a stick up this chimney?" Fiona was scornful. The chimney was the usual kitchen-range kind at the bottom, a narrow tube disappearing into a sheet of iron.

"I see what you mean." Hugh did not sound enthusiastic, but Fiona was already hunting in cupboards and dark corners for a stick. Ninian went out to collect an armful of dry bracken from the byre and returned a few moments later with that and also a long and supple hazel he had cut from a clump near the hen-run. They lashed the bracken on with string from the sandwiches — luckily Maggie had tied them with the usual substantial twine all Mr. Swift's parcels were tied with — and made their way up to the attic. Ninian had the brush and Hugh followed with an armful of loose bracken in case the first lot came adrift.

"We should really drop a goose down it," said Fiona. "Or perhaps a duck would do for this chimney."

"Not frightfully helpful." Ninian had reached the attic and stood with his head poking out of the hole.

Sandy and James, seeing this strange sight, came hurrying to join in the excitement.

Ninian looked at the roof and then at his own massive, iron-shod feet.

"I shall go straight through," he said, "as well as slip madly in these."

"Mine are rubber," panted Sandy, arriving in the attic at breakneck speed. Ninian looked at him dubiously.

"D'you think you can crawl along the roof and sweep the chimney when you get there?" he demanded.

"Well, I'll try." Sandy started to worm himself out of the hole while the others watched anxiously in case more slates and laths broke. He crawled up to the ridge and Ninian handed him the brush. Cautiously he edged his way along. When he reached the chimney Fiona was torn between a desire to see what would happen in the kitchen and to watch Sandy's activities on the roof. The kitchen won, and she went downstairs and crouched with her head almost in the range. There was a strange muffled banging and scraping, then a cascade of soot that nearly blinded her, followed by some twigs. The scraping and showering continued for some time until pounding footsteps on the stairs made her turn round.

CAUTIOUSLY HE EDGED HIS WAY ALONG.

"Going to cut another stick." Hugh rushed through the kitchen. "We've come to an end of this one."

During the lull Fiona set her teeth, rolled up her sleeves and put one arm up the chimney. Immediately her fingers came in contact with a matted mass of twigs and hay which made her jump. But she put her arm up again and succeeded in pulling down the remains of a substantial nest.

"Hallo!" she called up the pipe, her voice sounding hollow and muffled.

"Hallo!" came Sandy's distant and surprised answer. "I say," she heard him shout, "I can hear Fiona; there can't be much left."

"It would take more than some soot to stop you hearing Fiona," said Ninian, laughing.

Fiona got up off her knees and went into the attic. The others roared with laughter at her sooty face and arms but, ignoring them, she said to Ninian: "There's an old nest in the chimney. If some of the sticks get left behind on the iron bit above the stove won't there be a fire?"

"I'll come down and look." Ninian sounded as if he had spent most of his life sweeping chimneys. "Now don't fall through the roof, twins," he told them. Jean was perilously near the edge and Ninian had no idea if the laths were rotten or not.

They met Hugh in the kitchen, stripping branches off the hazel stick, and told him to wait a little as they were going to investigate the chimney.

"There must be some way of getting this plate down." Ninian rattled at the sheet of tin. "I wonder how far this pipe goes into the chimney, because the top part seems to be a perfectly ordinary stone thing."

Suddenly and unexpectedly the plate came down with a crash, covering them both with soot and twigs.

"Hells bells!" Ninian rubbed his eyes and made the whole thing much worse. "Supposing we can't get it back?"

"Well, let's clean it up first." Fiona was already peering into the vast cavity left by the removal of the plate. She could see daylight filtering round Sandy's brush and called up to him.

"Stand back," he shouted down, and at that moment the

soot-covered bunch of bracken appeared in the hearth and the last clogged lumps of soot and twigs with it.

"Well, if we can get all this back," said Fiona, surveying the chaos, "it will have been rather successful."

"We ought to save the soot for the garden," said Ninian, dubiously.

"Oh, yes, Ninian, there's a sack in the attic. It couldn't make you much blacker to put it in."

"Thanks very much. What about you?" asked Ninian.

"Feigns!"

"You are the end. What can I do for a shovel?"

In the end a small rusty shovel was found in one of the kitchen cupboards, and Ninian filled nearly half a sack with the soot piled up round the grate. He and Fiona found the secret of the tin plate, and put it back, lodged on the same bricks as before.

"Gosh!" Fiona stepped back and looked at the mess. "This will take hours. And if the fire doesn't burn like a mad thing at the end of it all I shall scream."

Jean appeared in the doorway announcing that Sandy, full of enthusiasm, was going to sweep the other chimneys. He had tied a fresh lot of bracken to his pole and was already standing against the stack when Fiona and Ninian got to the bedroom fireplace.

"Hoy, Sandy!" shouted Ninian.

"Yes, what is it?"

"Don't sweep yet. I want to have a look up."

"All right. There's a tree growing out of the top. I'm going to try and hoick it out."

"Well, don't pull the whole house down."

Ninian crawled into the grate. He could see straight up into the sky. Just as well, he thought, that this house is so old that the chimneys are built on this amazingly simple principle. We could never have coped with curves and twists. He could see Sandy looking down at him and wrestling with the small tree. Presently some chips of stone and moss came tumbling down, followed by a handful of earth. The one in the annexe was clear.

Later they stood outside on the grass and looked at the house, already more civilised by the removal of the tree and several large tufts of grass and moss that Sandy had kicked down.

Fiona and Ninian were black from head to foot and the sweep himself not much better.

"You know," said James, "we've spent the whole day here just messing about and haven't done half the things we meant to."

"We had to look over everything first." Jeannie leant back and looked at the far top of Carn Mor. "It's no good living in a house if you don't like it. And anyway, we swept the chimneys."

No one took any notice of the last part of her sentence. James and Fiona and Sandy turned and looked at Ninian, Hugh took out his pipe and slowly started to fill it. He looked thoughtfully across the Carna Loch, already dusky with evening, and knew what Ninian's answer would be to their unspoken question.

"Are we going to live in it?" asked Sandy at last.

Ninian smiled, his teeth gleaming white in his black face.

"Of course," he said, "you don't think I went to all that trouble for nothing?"

CHAPTER VI

GETTING DOWN TO IT

Sunday, 17th December

A DAMP and subdued party arrived at the croft next morning. It was after ten by the time they got there as they had waited since half-past eight in case the rain would stop. Always it had seemed to be lighter over in the west, but it had continued wet, slight, monotonous, until at last Ninian, sick of sitting in the window-seat with so much to be done at the croft, announced that he was going anyway. The others leapt at the chance, and, buttoned tightly into oilies and mackintoshes and with many instructions from Maggie to keep dry, they had gone once more up to the hut at the end of the track, parked the Ford, and rowed out over the grey water.

"Well, anyway, we shall be indoors when we get there," said Jean philosophically. "And once we get the fire going it'll be lovely."

"There's an awful lot of scrubbing to be done," said Sandy mournfully.

"And window-cleaning and polishing."

"And sandpapering," added James, with a vision of the rusty grate.

"Blacklead," said Fiona suddenly. "We never brought any. I think perhaps with the heat some of the rust will come off the stove, then we can just polish it."

"Well, I hope so." Jamie licked off a raindrop as it trickled down his face.

The boat bumped gently against the stone jetty. Quickly Jean made fast, and, clutching saucepans and brooms, they ran up to the house. Already they were growing accustomed to the hall and stairs and the two rooms, so that it began to feel like home. The walls of the kitchen and hall were panelled in pitch-pine, making it darker than it normally would be; the bedroom was papered with gay pink flowers and buds. Fiona could so vividly imagine what it must have looked like in olden days, its brightly polished brass and tables and panelling, its framed family photographs, its deer-heads and perhaps a stuffed ptarmigan or capercailzie, its tablecloths and antimacassars, and everything clean and fresh-smelling.

"We shall have it like that," she thought, and then wondered. After such imaginings the present dank disorder struck harder than ever, and she felt inclined to sit on the table in despair. However, the twins and Sandy were already hanging up their oilskins on a row of rusty hooks in the hall and volunteering to fetch paper and sticks.

"Let's light a fire in both rooms," Jean said. "That'll get the place properly warm."

"We must remember to bring some lamps," said Ninian, tripping over a broom and nearly falling.

Surprisingly and satisfactorily the fire in the kitchen caught at once and roared and crackled up the chimney. The twins had to go out instantly and stand in the rain to see what the cottage looked like with smoke coming out of the chimney. They reported favourably.

"It looks simply marvellous," said Jamie.

"Yes, really," said Jean. "It looks like a house that's lived in."

Sandy came in with a bucket of water from the burn and they set it on the fire in an enormous kettle to boil for scrubbing.

"And tea," said Hugh, poking his head round the door. He and Ninian were on their way up to the roof to see what could be done about the tiles.

They lit the other fires while the kettle was boiling. Sandy brought several more pails of water and one of coal.

AN ENORMOUS KETTLE BOILING FOR SCRUBBING.

The rest was put in the byre with the peat. Fiona took a broom and swept out all three rooms and the hall and left a mountain of dust and dirt on the back-door step.

"We shall have to burn it or something. I've never seen so much," she said.

Jean was laying out cloths and soap and brushes. Jamie ran from fire to fire, feeding them as they needed it and reporting on the progress on the roof. Fiona, getting warm, took off her coat and rolled up her sleeves.

"It really is beginning," Jean said to herself. "In a day or two we shall be living here, alone in the middle of the hills. I wish Fergus was here. I wish it would stop raining. I hope Ninian can mend the roof, but he's sure to be able to." Looking at her energetic sister, she was vividly reminded of a scene last summer, a very similar scene in a way, in the small dirty cabin of the *Fauna*.

With a long broom Fiona brushed the ceiling, then she and Sandy filled buckets with hot soapy water, took cloths and started to wash the pitch-pine. Under their fascinated eyes the wood became several shades lighter. Jean, inspired, dipped a rag into Fiona's bucket and rubbed at the small windows.

"No use doing the outside until this rain stops," she said.

"It almost looks as if it might," said Jamie, leaning in the doorway.

Above them the ceiling bumped and shook under the heavy feet of Hugh and Ninian. A cheerful sound of hammering started and a voice called down:

"Any one not doing anything?"

"I'm vaguely spare," said Jamie.

"Can you look in the garden and see if you can find the tiles that have come off?" called Hugh.

James disappeared and the hammering continued. "New laths, I expect," said Sandy knowledgeably.

James came back a few minutes later with an armful of slates.

"Most of them are broken," he said, clattering upstairs. By now Jean had finished the kitchen windows and started on the bedroom. Fiona and Sandy, their buckets black, stuck heroically to the back-breaking task of washing the walls. It was such a great improvement that it felt worth the ache of continually reaching up to wash near the ceiling and bending to do near the floor. Meanwhile the fires burned magnificently, and Fiona, rubbing a tentative finger along the stove, found that most of the rust came off.

"What after this?" asked Sandy, sweeping a conglomeration of rusty nails, broken china and string off the high mantelpiece.

"Cupboards, I suppose." Fiona straightened her back and rubbed a dirty hand across her forehead. "Cupboards and table and chairs and things, and the floor last."

"We must have a rag-rug," said Sandy suddenly, looking down at the hearth. "We ought almost to have an aspidistra."

"No." Fiona was definite. "A rag-rug, yes. But an aspidistra, no."

"All right. No aspidistra." Sandy sighed. "But we ought to have one."

The work was going surprisingly well. Everything would have to be scrubbed — cupboards, box-beds, table and floor, but with the smell of clean air and bracken and hills blowing through the house, it already began to lose its shell-like appearance and become a home once more. On the hob a kettle hissed and bubbled, the lid rattling as the water boiled. Fiona emptied her dirty bucket and refilled it with hot clean water, Sandy put down his cloth and, a pail in each hand, went down to the burn. They had found a pool, edged by a worn flat stone, which was obviously the water-place. Also they had discovered above the sink in the scullery a tank which would hold four or five pailfuls of water, drained by a tap into the sink. This was fairly modern and must have been put in shortly before the Mackenzies left.

Fiona was finishing off the cupboards and Sandy had started on the floor when Hugh and Ninian appeared in the doorway.

"We can't do any more," Ninian said, inspecting his thumb which he had just hit with the hammer. "The tiles are all too broken, but if we can scrounge some to-morrow we shall have it finished."

"We need a ladder," said Hugh. "Or else prehensile feet. It's got to be done from outside, and it'll be a bit odd in one corner, but waterproof, I hope."

Jean, hearing voices, came to join them. She stood by the front door, looking out.

"It's clearing," she said. "It's getting quite light in the west. Oh, bliss, it's going to be a lovely day."

"Isn't it nearly lunch-time?" suggested Hugh.

Ninian looked at his watch.

"Gracious, it's nearly two," he said. "Of course we started late, but I hadn't realised the time had gone so quickly."

"Look," said Fiona. "Wait until we finish this room, and then we can have it in here."

"Well, don't be long," said James.

"Out of the way." Sandy slooshed a bucket of water across the floor and sprang at it with brush and soap. Fiona felt pleased with herself. Although Sandy had been very good he had not exactly hurled himself at the scrubbing.

"Well," said Hugh, a quarter of an hour later, swallowing his first mouthful of sardine sandwich, "the thing to do would be to make a list of what furniture it is absolutely essential to bring. We don't want the place cluttered up with things, but there's hardly enough here."

He looked round at the kitchen. Apart from the dullness of the range it was spotless. The floor had been discovered to be worn grey stone, the table had recaptured some of its former whiteness, the window sparkled under the weak light from the sun, struggling through the clouds, on the fire two kettles sang and hissed and a coal fell crackling into the grate. Fiona, thinking as he did, said:

"It isn't bad. With curtains and polished knobs and some china and saucepans it'll look lovely."

Ninian, holding his sandwich in his mouth, rummaged in his pockets and produced a paper and pencil.

"Where shall we start?" he asked.

"Where's every one going to sleep?" asked Jean. This was not so easy.

"There are six of us," began Hugh. "And two, three, five beds."

"Two box-beds, two in the big room, one annexe and one little room," counted James.

"Could one get two into the little room?" suggested Ninian.

"Yes, it's bigger than the annexe," said Fiona.

"Feigns," said James and Sandy instantly.

"Shut up." Ninian ignored them. "The annexe may be uninhabitable."

"Fiona and Jean in the big room, you and I in here, and the boys can fight it out?" suggested Hugh.

"I'd like a closer look at those box-beds," said Ninian.

"They're the same as bunks," said Fiona. "No harder and much straighter than the fo'c'sle ones."

"Don't let's have Sandy and James together, they'll bicker all night," said Ninian.

"Well, would you like to sleep in the little room?" suggested Hugh.

"Look here —" began Sandy, but Fiona interrupted him, saying:

"If I've got to cook the breakfast I think I should be in here."

"But then if we want to sit up late Jean can't go to bed," said Hugh.

"I shall want to sit up too," said Jean.

"If you sleep in here you can light the fire," suggested Fiona.

"Perhaps we shouldn't want to sit up very late," Hugh grinned.

"You could really get three in the big bedroom," Sandy said. "That would be simplest."

In the end that was decided on. Fiona and Jean in the box-beds, Sandy or James in the small room, and the others in the large one, leaving the annexe empty.

"It'd be freezing in there," said Fiona. "There is a fire, but there are three very thin outside walls."

"Are you two really going to use that double-bed?" Jean was intrigued.

"Oh!" Hugh had not thought of that. "Let's go and try it."

He and Ninian got up and disappeared. Loud squeaking and clanking announced that they were indeed trying the springs.

"If it makes all that noise every time they turn over it's not going to be much fun," said Fiona.

The boys reappeared.

"It won't be bad with a mattress," said Hugh.

"The thing to do," Ninian had one of his inspirations, "is for one of us and either James or Sandy to have the big bed and the other the single."

"Toss you." Hugh produced a sixpence.

"Heads!" The coin spun through the air.

"You win!" grinned Hugh. "Oh, well, Jamie, we shared a bed before at Faraway. I think you'd kick less than Sandy."

"All right."

So it was settled. Ninian, meanwhile, had been writing "Two beds" on his list.

"Bedding for six," said Fiona.

"Food for about twelve," said Sandy.

"Usual cutlery and implements," Ninian was scribbling, "and tiles for the roof."

"A mat or two and some curtains," suggested Jean.

"Some chairs and an arm-chair." Ninian looked up at Hugh.

"Steady," he said. "It's all got to come by boat."

"Well, we might as well be comfortable. Let's have two arm-chairs."

"Wicker ones wouldn't weigh much. Let's get some more hooks for things, then we won't need so many chests of drawers," said Jamie.

"A hip-bath!" cried Fiona, inspired.

"For heaven's sake!" Sandy was horrified.

"Very necessary," said Ninian, "if we've got one."

"Lamps," said Jean.

"Paraffin," said Hugh.

"Looking-glass," said Fiona.

"Masses of fuel," said James.

"Strikes me we shall spend the rest of the holidays humping stuff up here," said Ninian, scribbling madly.

"We can all wash in the sink," said Fiona. "That eliminates washstands and things. We've got a kitchen table and dresser."

"We shall think of things as we go along," said Hugh. "I imagine there will be fairly frequent trips to the village and the Lodge."

"Where are we going to get all these things?" asked James. "Surely there's not much at home."

"There's a good deal put away." Fiona wrinkled her forehead. "When we let Carrick House we took a lot of the furniture out and it's in one of the attics."

They finished their lunch, making plans as they ate. It would take several boat-loads with the dinghy piled as high as it could be to ferry the furniture over. James had the bright idea of towing the other boat behind them.

"If there's no wind," he said. "The furniture's not so desperately heavy but bulky."

"We can do several trips and leave some people here to arrange it," said Sandy.

"And the same thing the other end, loading up the car," added Fiona.

After lunch they swept out the attic and the annexe, scrubbed and washed the two rooms, the scullery and larder, the stairs and hall and even the front-door step. The three fires made a tremendous difference and already the house seemed warm and inhabited. Sandy grumbled at his little room, which had no grate.

"You won't be in it much," Fiona told him, "but we'll bring you a little paraffin stove." And she told Ninian to add it to his list.

"Paint, too," said Jeanie, coming out of the bedroom. "White would do, and it would make all the difference inside."

Hugh and Ninian were out on the grass, smoking their pipes, and the others followed them out. It was almost warm and the sun twinkled faintly in the wet heather and drove Jean to finding a cloth and cleaning the outside of the windows. Smoke curled contentedly into the air and drifted away along Carn Mor. Far overhead a buzzard mewed and the burn was a gentle murmur on the right and almost one with the soft noise of waves breaking on the rocks. Warm though it was their sodden hands felt cold and they plunged them deep into their pockets. Fiona had taken one look at her nails and raised her eyebrows in despair. They looked irretrievably black. However, a day spent in scrubbing was not really the best thing for one's hands.

"What are we going to do while we're here?" Sandy's mind, having grasped the first excitement of the croft, had now rushed past it.

"Shoot, explore the hills. We've never been this side before," said Ninian.

"I've never been on Carn Mor at all," said Jean. Ninian tweaked her fair hair.

"There must be miles of uninhabited country north of here," he said. "Perhaps we shall find a lost tribe of Picts."

"Oh, no!" Jean had read Buchan's *No-man's-land*.

Ninian laughed at her, knowing her horror of trolls and similar people.

"I know!" Jamie cried suddenly. "I've got a wonderful, marvellous idea."

"What?"

"Oh, we must, we simply must."

"*What*, Jamie? Do tell us."

"Well, you know that story that father told us, about there being a cave somewhere near here where James Stewart hid after Culloden. Well, let's look for it!"

Nobody spoke. Then Fiona said:

"Yes, there really was a cave somewhere. But no one has ever found it."

"Well, let's."

"Who was it?" asked Hugh.

"James Stewart, our ancestor. It's in a book at home. French ships came into Loch Carrick, I think, to fetch Prince Charlie. But he never came so James Stewart and some others went away in them."

"No Prince Charlie?" asked Sandy sceptically.

"No, this was one of the few places he didn't come to. But the others definitely did."

"Have you any clues about the cave at all? I mean, have

you the remotest idea what we would be looking for?"

"Don't be so difficult, Hugh," said Fiona, who was much taken with Jamie's idea. "We know it must be in a very unfrequented place as no one has ever found it, so perhaps it is quite obvious when one does find it."

"Well, let's look anyway." Ninian glanced at the sky. It would be enough to be just on the hills and they might as well have the added incentive of the cave. He had always had a longing to explore the country north and round Carn Mor, and this would be a perfect chance. He took a deep breath of the air he loved so much and that almost stung his nose, it was so clear and clean.

A star, very faint, beckoned them home.

"Soon," said Jean, happily, "this will be home and we shan't have any farther to go."

CHAPTER VII

SETTLING IN

Monday, 18th December

"WE'LL HAVE to be pretty smart at organising today," said Ninian, spooning sugar on to his porridge. "Some will have to get stores from the village, some take them up to Carna, some row them across and some sort them out. Otherwise we'll never get it done in one day."

"Yes, I see what you mean." Hugh was never at his brightest in the early morning, especially after an evening spent as the previous one had been, in a hectic bout of Racing Demon. There did not seem to be nearly enough people to meet Ninian's requirements. He stirred his coffee thoughtfully.

"We must go in pairs, otherwise it'll be so boring," said Sandy.

"We can't all drive," James pointed out. "At least we can, but Jean and I aren't allowed to."

"Well, as a matter of fact I haven't got a licence," said Sandy, "but that's a minor detail."

Fiona, who had been surprisingly silent, said:

"Hugh and Ninian and I had better separate and each have an infant with us."

"Infant!" snorted Jean, and Sandy, who towered over Fiona by two inches, grinned.

"You ought to be at the cottage, Fiona," said Ninian.

"And either you or Hugh must go to put the tiles on," said James.

"Bother!" It seemed impossibly complicated.

Hugh, who had been chewing slowly, spoke:

"We all go up to the Loch with as much as we can get in the car, perhaps leaving Jean behind."

"Here, I say," said Jean.

"Wait a minute." Hugh smiled at her. "Ninian brings the car back and you and he go and get stores in the village." He knew her preference for being with her eldest brother. "We four row over with the stuff, I put the tiles on and come straight back with Sandy or James. By that time the two shoppers will, I hope, be waiting with the next load and we can either reverse the process if anything more needs to be bought or else all come across." He took a deep breath and a gulp of coffee.

"Well done, Hugh," said Ninian. "That sounds pretty straightforward. Does every one approve?"

Everybody did, except Sandy and James, who as usual could not decide who was to do which.

"I'd rather stay in the cottage," said Sandy.

"Yes, but you're the largest and should be more helpful in the boat," argued James, who wanted to help arrange the house.

"Well, I can row over and probably Ninian will row back." Sandy wanted to stay for the same reason as James.

"For heaven's sake stop arguing. Toss for it or something," said Fiona, who had heard these discussions so many times before that she knew nothing would come of it if they just talked.

A penny was produced, spun, lost amongst the breakfast things and discovered under a plate. Jamie had won and decided to stay with Fiona.

Breakfast finished and beds made, they gathered in the nursery before starting. In the summer the usual place was the grass bank in front of the house, or for more deeply laid plans, the hill above Loch Hernsary. But it was too cold for that, although the sun was shining, and they sprawled round the room. Ninian rocked precariously on the fender, his shoulders against the mantelpiece, Hugh and Sandy were stretched at length in two arm-chairs, Fiona sat on the table swinging her legs, and the twins were in their favourite place each in a corner of the window-seat.

"Loading up the car is the first thing," said Ninian, when they were all there. "Furniture and a few stores, and the precious tiles."

He had been down to the village, earlier, and had scrounged some from the builder, together with a few tips on roofmaking and bricklaying.

"Any furniture we can't take you can pick up on your way back from the shop, you won't have so very much," said Fiona. "We're almost certain to have to do a last trip for all the things we've forgotten."

"Shall we be able to stay the night there?" asked Jean hopefully.

"Shouldn't think so. Might." Ninian was dubious. "Come on, let's get started. It's half-past nine already." He crossed over to the window, unable to bear the sight of Carrick sparkling as the sun melted last night's frost and not be out there too.

It was a perfect day, almost warm out of the wind and a clear cloudless blue sky. Even the wind was not cold and the frost and thin layer of ice was melting quickly. Snow had crept farther down the shoulder of Ben Carrick but there was none by the Lodge, and certainly none on the low ground between the Lodge and the sea. The snow rarely lay on this ground but once or twice Ninian remembered pulling a sledge to the village for food and tearing down the hills on anything from a new toboggan to a meat-tin. He had watched a startlingly lovely dawn this morning from a bend in the track on the way to the village. Slowly the sun had risen behind Ben Carrick, staining its snowy slopes with pink and red and gold. And that had spread, as the sun rose, to the white tops of the Corriedon mountains and the long bulk of Carn Mor. Ninian had stood watching it, his hands in his pockets, his eyes drinking it in, storing it in his memory for other winter dawns when he would not be at Carrick. Ninian, under an unemotional exterior, was passionately and absolutely fond of his home, more fond of it than of anything else in the world. Often, when he was either alone or with strange people, he would find himself back at Carrick, remembering each track and rock, each special dawn and sunset, each lifting of the clouds after rain, the best view of each loch and hill, the white walls and green lawn of Carrick House. It was an inconvenient trick, this switching of the mind so completely to another place. People to whom he had been talking would look at him in surprise till he caught their puzzled eyes and smiled at them and said in his slow voice that he must have been dreaming, which was truer than they knew. He could not bear strangers gushing to him about the beauties of Carrick: he even hated his friends doing it, and squashed them so successfully that most people were not aware of this desperate love for his home. Fiona was the only person who knew and understood, and that was because she felt nearly the same herself. It was a great comfort to him to have her to look at and smile at, knowing that she could almost read his mind.

Fiona, by now, had slid off the table and was half-way downstairs. The others followed and looked with slight alarm at the huge pile of furniture and bedding that was piled in the hall.

"Don't forget the sacks of coal and peat and the logs," said Sandy, whose job it had been to find and fill these.

"We can push odd logs in anywhere," said James. "They can fill up the corners."

"Won't be many corners when we've finished with this lot," said Hugh, walking round it and checking things off.

The two beds were camp-beds and rolled up small. Maggie had actually found a hip-bath in the attic together with two battered wicker arm-chairs, which Sandy pronounced as "super-comfortable with a cushion or two."

Ninian brought the Ford as near as he could to the door

and then put down the hood. He stood inside superintending the packing, while every one else fetched and carried and carefully put things into corners and along the seat.

"What about us?" Sandy asked. "You haven't left us any room."

"Oh, dear! That is a slight bore." Ninian rubbed his hand through his hair. "We were getting on so beautifully, too."

"There's my car," suggested Hugh. "It's too small for stores but it can carry a few people, and perhaps a few odds and ends."

"Good idea. Then you can drive it back this evening." Ninian's face cleared.

"Unless we stay," said Jean, who had heard the last words as she came staggering out of the house under a pile of curtains.

"Well, it can't come to any harm by the hut," said Sandy. "No one ever comes up there."

They had plenty of furniture for the croft as Fiona had gone round the Lodge ruthlessly taking what she wanted. Ninian's vigilant eye had prevented anything good or valuable being whisked off and Maggie had actually been helpful, being used, by now to the family's amazing and unaccountable preference from sleeping and living in what she considered the acme of discomfort. Why forsake the Lodge and the large and excellent meals she set before them for the precarious existence on an island or a boat, or now, in a ruined croft, she could not imagine. Fiona had long ago given up trying to explain and Maggie had grown used to it.

They packed the Ford with all the largest and most unwieldy things — the beds, the chairs, the sacks of coal and peat and, in a large box, the lamps, carefully surrounded by straw, and a big can of paraffin. They were also taking plenty of candles as lamp-glasses had an unaccountable habit of breaking.

The sun shone and a light breeze blew from the south. The morning was warm and clear and alive and the air sparkled. Jamie looked wistfully down to the loch where *Black Swan* lay anchored. They had not taken her out these holidays and it did not seem as if they would have any chance of doing so. It was sad: they were missing so many good things. Not that living up at Carn Mor was not going to be fun — James was one of the keenest to do it — but it meant missing out so much of what made their usual winters, half of it spent on the Loch setting long-lines and lobster-pots and hauling them in with icy fingers; watching winter dawns and sunsets from somewhere on Loch Carrick, the snowy hills tinted every imaginable colour; still, brittle days when the tawny hillsides were reflected, rock for rock, in the calm water; coming home after a long day at sea, cold and happy and hungry, the water darkening and star after star pricking the sky; climbing on the rocks near Foura when the huge icy Atlantic rollers came leaping and crashing ashore, drenching them with spray. Carn Mor was going to be fun but Jamie missed the sea and always would.

Hugh called him and he went to the car and squeezed himself in between Sandy and Jean. There was not much room for three in the back of an M.G., and Hugh drove carefully, following the laden Ford up the track. They were all in a state of tremendous excitement and at one point Hugh had to stop and say he would turn back instantly if they did not keep still. He said it in so fierce a voice and looked so stern that Sandy and the twins were overcome and sat like mice in the back. Hugh winked at Fiona, who was also looking rather startled. Although she and Ninian raged at many things, the twins included, she had never heard Hugh in that mood before and she had not known that he ever was.

They got almost everything into the dinghy at the first

load, leaving behind a sack of coal, a suitcase full of clothes and one of the chairs.

"We'll bring them when you come up with the stores," said Hugh.

Ninian stayed long enough to help push off the immense boatload and then went back to the Ford with Jean. She had the list in her trouser pocket and felt grand and important having been left with Ninian to do the shopping. Ninian, looking at her, thought she looked younger than ever in her tweed trousers and red jersey, her lint-white hair on her shoulders. He turned the car and they drove off, to discover about four hundred yards down the track that they had a puncture.

"I might have guessed it," said Ninian. "I'm more than tempted to take Hugh's car."

"Oh, let's," said Jean.

"Well, I ought not," said Ninian, looking at it.

NINIAN STAYED LONG ENOUGH TO HELP PUSH OFF.

It was almost impossible to move in the boat on the Carna Loch. They had all four oars out but every time they leant back they seemed to bump into something, and the chair, looking rather like a lobster-pot, swayed dangerously in the bows and threatened to fall in completely if any one made any but the most careful movements.

The journey seemed longer than it ever had before. At one time Fiona could have sworn they were not moving at all. Her arms and back ached and her hands were sore, but she would not ask for a rest: none of the others had.

"We must look rather like pioneers or Pilgrim Fathers," said Sandy, between strokes.

"Wish we had a covered wagon," grunted Hugh. He looked at the bilge-water sloshing between his feet and thought it would be the final straw if the boat sank with all their possessions and left them struggling in the ice-cold water of the Carna Loch. He voiced this fear to Fiona, who said hopefully:

"Well, I expect the boat's lower in the water than she has been for years and that some of the side-seams are leaking a bit."

Sandy, on the thwart beside her, craned over his shoulder. He was the only one who could see at all where they were going.

"Starboard a bit," he said, "or we shall ram an island in the near future."

So the long journey went on, Fiona only conscious of movement by the gradual heightening of the hills on her left as they rowed farther away from Carrick.

After about an hour and a half, when even Hugh felt he could not row another stroke and when the water had definitely risen an inch or two, Sandy gave his oar to Fiona and stood up, directing them to the jetty. At last they bumped and a few minutes later were ashore.

"Gosh!" Fiona straightened up slowly. "I shall never be the same again."

"Personally," said Hugh, sitting on a rock, "I absolutely and utterly refuse to dream of rowing the second load across unless Ninian's there too. I wouldn't have believed anything could be so heavy as this boat."

"Don't forget we had coal and tiles in it," Sandy reminded him.

"Oh, this is a heavenly place." Fiona lifted her head and sniffed in a great draught of air. Still the amazing silence reigned — the quietness of the hills, emphasised by the hill noises, the burn, the sheep, the buzzards, the light wind, nothing human or discordant or mechanical.

Their feet slipped and scrunched on the rocks as they carried the stores up to the house.

"The nice part about it," said Jamie, pleasedly, "is that it's all quite clean. We just have to put everything in the right place."

He pushed open the door. Already it was noticeable how different the whole place smelt. Soap, polish and fresh air were predominant, soon, thought Fiona, to be enriched with peat and broth and a roast haunch of venison that was somewhere in one of the boxes.

Hugh and Jamie went straight to the attic with tiles, hammer and nails. Fiona laid and lit the fire and put on a kettle for tea. Sandy distributed furniture as he came to it with, he considered, great taste. Between them they dragged the coal round and dumped it in a corner of the byre. The peat went there too, and the few logs they had shoved in at the last minute.

"We can't have too many of them," said Fiona, dusting her hands on her trousers, "otherwise we shall have to resort to sawing up trees from the wood, and they don't look very big."

"Saw," said Sandy. "Do remember to tell Hugh to tell Ninian to bring one."

"I will," Fiona concentrated, "and a chopper."

They went up to the attic where Hugh and Jamie were

putting finishing touches to the roof.

"Gracious, it looks professional," said Fiona, amazed, but Hugh assured her it was not.

"We really should have taken a whole lot off and worked upwards instead of fitting these ones underneath," he said.

"Well, it looks waterproof anyway, which is the main thing," said Sandy.

"I can hear the kettle," announced Fiona, and on arriving in the kitchen found steam pouring from it and the lid bouncing and dancing like one possessed.

"Tea would be heaven," said Hugh. "Especially as Sandy and I have got that feat of endurance before us."

Fiona poured it out and found some biscuits in a tin. They sat on the edge of the table and in some of the chairs, sipping and talking.

"What chaos this room does look." James, faced with the prospect of straightening it out, felt inclined to volunteer to row back instead of Sandy.

"It is rather formidable," agreed Fiona. "Especially as there's a lot more on the jetty and all the stores from the village."

"Not to speak of the bedding which is still at the Lodge," added Sandy.

"I don't think it'll ever be done," said James gloomily. He walked over to the window and pushed it open. Still the same lovely day outside and the same light wind. "I wonder how *Black Swan* is?" he said.

Fiona looked at him.

"We must go out in her sometime, before we get too ensconced up here. Just once," she said, "to Slaggan and back."

"It gets dark so quickly," said Jamie sadly.

"What's wrong with the dark?" asked Fiona, and Jamie, smiling at her, thought, not for the first time, that his sister did have the most wonderful ideas.

"I suppose it's time we were on our way." Hugh stood

up and lit a cigarette. "Ready, Alexander?"

Sandy took another biscuit and said that he was. They all four walked down to the jetty and Fiona and James helped push out the boat.

"Don't forget the saw and the chopper," called Fiona, as they moved off.

Then she and Jamie turned to what was left of the first load and carried it back to the croft.

Sandy and Hugh did not hurry back over the Loch, but the lightened boat flew along at such a speed that they did not take long. There was no sign of Ninian and the stores so they wandered up to the hut to see if they could find anything amusing amongst the years-old accumulation of fishing tackle, ropes and bits and pieces to do with boats and ponies. As Sandy pushed open the door Hugh suddenly said:

"But where's the M.G.?"

"Someone's stolen it! Perhaps the Starer has come back," suggested Sandy, thinking longingly of the summer they had spent poaching and of the sinister gillie who had lived up in this bothy.

"If Ninian's gone and taken it and smashed it I shall wring his neck," said Hugh, to whom his car was very precious. "At least he might have asked."

Sandy, who had been examining the track for clues, came to a startling conclusion and said:

"The Ford's not here either."

"Curiouser and curiouser," said Hugh. He walked a little way down the track and there before him the whole mystery was unravelled.

"Drat the man," he said, and then called Sandy. "Nothing exciting, I'm afraid. Ninian's had a puncture and left the Ford for us to mend."

"Well, he's jolly well mistaken," said Sandy. "The spare wheel'll be flat too, I bet."

They walked slowly along the track.

"Can't we leave him to change his own beastly wheel?" asked Sandy, but not very hopefully.

"Well, he deserves it, taking my car." Hugh paused. "But it'd be a bit un-Christian if we didn't."

"Well, don't let's hurry," said Sandy.

Ninian and Jean, coming slowly up the track half an hour later, were as surprised as the others had been to see the Ford missing. But when they topped the rise and saw it parked beside the hut Ninian guessed what had happened and felt rather ashamed at having taken Hugh's M.G. without asking. As a sort of sop he had had it filled up with petrol and had put air in the tyres, but all the same he hoped Hugh would not be annoyed. He and Jean had had a pleasant time in the shop buying as much food as they thought it possible for six of them to eat in roughly fourteen days. They had no idea of how long they would stay but Ninian did not believe in going short of anything. He had bought masses of bread as he imagined Fiona would not feel inclined to bake much and also that they would use a good deal as most of their meals were sandwiches. Chocolate, fruit, jam, eggs, bacon, sausages and tinned milk made up the bulk of the stores, with macaroni, butter, kippers and cabbages and a huge sack of potatoes.

"We'll have to come down for things from time to time," Ninian had said to Jean. "And letters and papers and fresh milk and bread."

They had bought two dozen brass hooks, some new dish-cloths, white and green paint, a little mop and a door mat that Ninian had spied high up in the rafters.

"Gosh, we're going to be comfortable," Jean had said, as they loaded up Hugh's car.

"Well, why not?" asked Ninian.

Luckily for them Hugh was a forgiving kind of person and hardly ever minded about anything. He had found it was much less trouble not to fuss about things, at the same time cherishing and appreciating what he had got and longing for some things that he had not.

So apart from a casual:

"Ninian, you are the end. I shall take the key next time." He said no more and they loaded the dinghy for the second time.

Even with the coal and furniture that had been left by the bothy the boat was not nearly so heavy as it had been before. And Ninian could appreciate Sandy's story of their previous herculean efforts. Jean did not take an oar at all but sat in the bows like a Nordic figurehead, perched high above the water and directed them from there.

Already the croft looked different. As they came across the Loch and up to the little jetty Jean's excited voice told them what James and Fiona had been doing.

"There's smoke coming out of both chimneys," she said. "There are curtains at the windows, real curtains, they look lovely. Fiona's scrubbing the step — no, she's just going in. The roof is quite complete, no holes, Hugh, you are clever. Jamie's doing something in the garden, digging or chopping or something. Oh, it does look bliss!"

By this time the dinghy had come alongside and they sprang ashore. A loud shout brought James and Fiona hurrying towards them.

"It really does look super," said Ninian. "I've brought some green paint for the front door, Fiona, and white for inside and for the windows."

"Bags I do the painting." Sandy and James spoke simultaneously.

"Now, don't have another argument," said Fiona. "There'll be plenty to do for both."

Inside, the house looked even more changed than it did outside. The stone floor of the hall was spotless, the pitch-pine panelling gleamed. On the right the door was shut, but on the left was the kitchen, much smaller for its furnishing but warm and homely and unrecognisable. Red curtains hung either side of the windows, and here as in the hall, the panelling had responded to Jamie's vigorous polishing. He and Fiona together had dealt with the range and, having been first scrubbed and then blackleaded, it was now almost a normal grate. Between the bars glowed a coal fire, cinders dropping down to the ash-bucket, and a kettle hissed on the hob. On the mantelpiece Fiona had already arranged two or three blue and white striped jars and a clock. The first wicker-chair was already in place on the right of the grate, a space left opposite for its fellow. The kitchen table and dresser had been re-scrubbed and plates and cups were in the latter, and a brown teapot, casserole and some vegetable dishes. The box-beds were closed, but the door to the scullery was open with a roller towel on the back. A shelf of saucepans above the sink was just visible and two clean cloths hung from a rail. They had even found a mat to put before the fire and a big oil-lamp was hanging from a hook in the ceiling.

They were silent, taking all this in, while James and Fiona leant pleasedly in the doorway.

Jean could hardly speak. She had dreamt that one day it might look something like this but never so soon. And now here it was before her eyes. She took in every detail. Ninian crossed to the fire and stood in front of it, his hands behind him. A glow warmed his back pleasantly and he smiled down on them.

"Very nice," he said. "We shall be jolly comfortable here."

That was the nice part about Ninian, Jean thought. He might be grown up and call you an infant and even tweak your hair and look down at you condescendingly from his great height, but he did like all the things you liked and was never snarky about them.

"You haven't seen the bedrooms yet," said Fiona. "They're not really as nice as this room, and of course we haven't got the bedding yet, but we've made them look as presentable as possible. And we've put the hip-bath in the attic."

She led the way across the hall and into the largest of the two.

Rugs were spread on the clean wooden floor. The bed had been pushed into place. That, three chairs and the chest of drawers made up its entire furniture, but blue curtains hung by the windows, a looking-glass was on the mantelpiece over a blazing fire and Jamie had been out to the wood and picked two branches of evergreen and a spray of red rowan berries and put them in a jar on the chest of drawers.

"With another bed and all our mess this will look quite human," said Hugh. "You've done nothing to the annexe, I take it?"

"Well, it's quite clean but icy cold," said James. "We put the oil-stove in Sandy's room."

"How grand that sounds," said the owner proudly.

"Well, it's a little small, but nice," Fiona told him, "and you can always come into the kitchen to get warm if it's too bad."

They had furnished this with a rug, a chair and the chest of drawers out of the annexe. Blue check curtains flanked the tiny window and they had polished the brass knobs on the rusty bedstead.

"Let's paint it," said James. "And the other. They'll look much better."

"As long as they don't take too long to dry. Think of paint all over the bedclothes," added his twin.

"We'll do it directly after lunch," said Ninian. "By the way, it's two-thirty and I'm ravenous."

None of them had noticed how quickly the time had gone. Fiona rushed into the kitchen to make tea while the others went down to the jetty to fetch in the remainder of their load and the lunch.

"How much more is there to come?" asked Hugh as he and Ninian walked down the rocky path.

"Just the bedding, which is a bit of a load, mattresses and things," said Ninian, with a vision of the hall of the Lodge, crowded with every conceivable mattress, pillow and blanket. "We may have to do two loads."

"We'll never get it done to-day at that rate," said Hugh, picking up the camp-bed and a cardboard box of tins.

"I didn't think we would." Ninian propped the sack of coal on a rock and heaved it on to his back. "It'll be getting dark in an hour or so."

They had a picnic lunch sitting round the kitchen table. Caps and coats on the hooks in the hall, Ninian's stick propped in the corner and a couple of glasses in leather cases on the door took away the temporary atmosphere and made them feel at home.

"No chance of staying here the night." Ninian held his mug of tea between his cold hands and looked at Fiona. "We shall never get the bedding across before dark."

"Does that matter?" she asked.

"I think we'd better concentrate on putting away the stores and doing the painting," said Ninian. "We can come over first thing as we may need more than one journey."

"Oh, dear." Jean had set her heart on staying the night. "We've got all the holidays," Hugh reminded her.

"Yes, but —"

"No, Ninian's right," said Fiona firmly. "It's threeish now, and if we get the painting done at once it might be dry to-morrow morning."

"It's quick-drying," Ninian put in.

"There's not much to do," said James, who had been examining it during the morning. "The door–"

"Might do the back door, too," interrupted Sandy.

"The windows, inside and out, odd bits in the bedrooms and scullery and the beds."

"Well, for heaven's sake don't make too much mess,"

said Fiona, as Sandy and the twins got up. A little was unavoidable, but if James and Sandy started throwing paint-brushes the whole croft would shortly be in a shambles. She, Hugh and Ninian sat drinking a second cup of tea.

"Rifle, bedding and clothes," said Hugh, "then we shall be complete."

"Then we can start looking for the cave," said Fiona, eating crumbs of cake out of a paper bag.

"I wonder if there really is a cave," mused Ninian.

"There must have been one." Fiona tilted her chair. "But it may be such a small insignificant affair that we've passed it often and never bothered with it."

"There are very few caves here, surely," Hugh said. "I don't remember seeing any and Corriedon is full of them."

"There are hardly any." Ninian got out his pipe. "That's why this one must be amazingly well hidden or every one would know about it."

Jamie came in with a tin of paint which he was stirring with a stick.

"I say, Ninian," he said, "if it's fine when we get back, can we go out in *Black Swan*?"

CHAPTER VIII

"NOBODY THERE!"

Monday, 18th December

"QUITE MAD, of course, but do let's." Fiona had nearly won the argument with Ninian over whether they should take *Black Swan* out or not.

They were sitting in the nursery, Hugh in an arm-chair, Ninian in front of the fire, and Fiona on the edge of the table. Jamie's wild plan of taking out their boat in the dark had appealed to her enormously. It would, as Jamie had said, be their last chance before burying themselves up in the hills.

"We can always come down and take her out," Ninian had said.

"Yes, but you know we won't," said Jamie.

And now he and Sandy and Jean were in Maggie's clutches, who was busy with rag and a bottle of turpentine. They had surprisingly little paint anywhere except on their hands, but those were well and truly daubed. Fired with enthusiasm, they had painted all the bedroom furniture, except that which came from the Lodge, and had certainly improved its appearance.

"We shall be sticky for weeks," Ninian had grumbled. "And the house simply reeks."

"It's a nice clean smell," Sandy had said, rubbing his nose and leaving a smear of green. "Anyway it's done now."

Which it was, and no one could but say the rooms looked better.

And now Fiona was trying to persuade Ninian. Hugh looked on with amusement. He was keeping out of this argument. He himself would have been persuaded long ago, but Ninian had more experience of Fiona's scatter-brained ideas, although some, mad though they sounded at the time, certainly turned out well.

Loud screams from downstairs showed that the turpentine was being used with good effect.

"Ouch!" yelled Sandy. "Maggie, you old horror! That's gone right in my cut. A huge graze, oh, you are the end!"

"Stand still then, Master Sandy," said Maggie firmly, and Fiona grinned, she had heard the same thing so many times before.

"Aren't you glad you didn't do the painting?" she asked Hugh.

A few minutes later the twins appeared looking pink and scrubbed, followed shortly by their cousin, nursing with care the "huge graze" into which Maggie had poured the turpentine.

"Have you persuaded him?" asked Jean of Fiona.

She shook her head.

"Nearly. He's being stoogy." Fiona had seldom lost a battle with Ninian, and thought of announcing that they would go without him. She was quite capable of handling the boat, with the help of the twins and Sandy, but somehow it would not be such fun without Ninian's large and comfortable presence.

Jean came and stood in front of him, looking at him with her large blue eyes and small solemn face. There were few things Ninian could resist her.

"Oh, Ninian," she said, "I've got such a blissful idea. We can sail to the Whisky Cave and find Fergus and ask him to come back with us."

After that even Ninian could find no reason why they should not go.

Sandy, as he pulled on extra jerseys and long thick socks, wondered about Fergus. He wondered whether they would find that strange man as they had found him in the summer, sitting in the little room at the back of the big cave, with his stern face and sad eyes and twisted smile. Fergus, silent and lonely, lit too easily to sudden rages, passionately fond of his brother's castle, Taransay, and yet, in spite of all this, their very good friend. They had come upon him mysteriously and he had offered them no explanation. They were all convinced that his hatred for Colin, his brother, was due to more than his love for Taransay and his unhappiness that it was slowly being ruined. But somehow no one could ask Fergus such a thing, except perhaps Fiona, and she, if she did, would never tell his answer. As a matter of fact she never did ask, because she realised that if there was something more and he wanted to tell it he would rather do so himself than be asked about it. Secretly they were all, even Ninian, a little afraid of Fergus Macloud.

To Sandy a life like Fergus's, spent in distilling illicit whisky and other similar things, was the acme of perfection. Fergus knew no law, except his own. His men adored him and feared him and obeyed him; he came and went as he pleased in his ship, the *Wandering Star*. He must be there, he must, Sandy muttered to himself as he tugged on rubber-boots and unhooked an oily from a peg.

"Will you need that?" asked James. "There's not a cloud out."

"It'll be jolly cold," said Sandy. "You seem to forget it's practically mid-winter."

An hour later they were down by the *Black Swan*. Maggie had fed them on big bowlfuls of Scotch broth and slices of bread and cheese and promised them more on their return.

"If ye do return," she said. "Sailin' aboot in the deed o' night on some fey idea o' Miss Fiona's."

"Yes, but Maggie, we've done it hundreds of times before," Fiona had reassured her.

"Nae matter. Ye've all gone clean oot o' your senses. Keep an eye on Miss Jeannie, do, and Master Ninian dinna fergit ye were in ye beid no sa lang syne."

"I'll remember." Ninian had pulled on a huge Iceland jersey and they had slammed the door behind them and gone out into the bright cold night.

It was cold too, there was no denying it. The south wind still held, but it held a touch of frost in it. The stars gleamed winter-bright, larger far than in the summer; north the sky was lit by the Northern Lights. Presently the moon would rise. It was nine o'clock. The Loch water was blown into ripples, shifting the patterns of the stars like scattered coins.

They had forgotten that the dinghies would be up by the boathouse, but it was too late to do anything about that now. Grunting, their fingers numbed, they struggled with one by the dim light from a hurricane-lamp, held by Jean. It was high tide, for which they were grateful, until Sandy said helpfully:

"We shall just about hit the full ebb when we come back. Let's leave it tied up."

"Can't do that," said Ninian. "We may not be down again for several days."

"The rocks'll be wet," added Fiona, "so she'll slip better."

Jamie found rowlocks and oars in the boathouse and joined the others at the water's edge. As he helped push it off he dipped his hand in and found the water warmer than the air. Gosh, he thought.

Ninian rowed out to the dim black shape that was *Black Swan*. She was a fifteen-foot fishing boat, strong and sturdy, with a single brown sail and gaff and a Kelvin engine. They scrambled on board and groped their way about, half-forgetting where everything was. Fiona lit the compass light and put the side-lights into place.

"Just supposing we wanted to, can we start the engine?" she asked.

"I don't know," said Ninian. He and Hugh bent over it

and poured in petrol from a rusty can.

"We shall have to make it go," Jean said. "We can't get into the cave without an engine."

None of them had thought of that. Fergus's cave lay at the end of a long narrow passage in the cliff. You could row or motor down it but not sail.

"We might as well start, anyway," said Fiona, at last. "I mean, having come all this way it'd be a bit silly to go back, and if we can't start the engine we shall have to think of something else."

Ninian agreed and helped haul up the mainsail. The twins went forward to keep a look-out. It was dark but not impossibly so: the bulk of the next headland and the pine trees round the pier were just visible as trees and not part of the hillside. Ripples slapped against *Black Swan*, and Sandy went forward to cast off. Hugh and James were baling, bumping their icy fingers on the bottom boards and swearing with pain. Slowly, silently they moved off into the night. The wind filled the big brown sail and they heeled over slightly, the petrol tin and a spanner clattering as they did so. Ninian was at the tiller and Fiona was content to have him there. She had not sailed since the summer and now it was dark and cold and very different. Ninian had not sailed since then either, but he was the kind of person who never had a moment's qualm about whether he had forgotten anything or not. They sailed on, Fiona, the wind cold on her face and her hair blowing behind her, watching the stars and the movement of the mast against them. It was very calm. The twins and Sandy were talking up in the bows, their voices blown back to the others.

"This is the most fun thing we have done so far," Jamie was saying.

"Specially if we find Fergus," that was Jean.

"Even if we don't find Fergus. It's so super to be sailing again."

"Why don't you go and steer?" asked Sandy.

"Ninian wouldn't let me."

"Fiona wouldn't, you mean." That was Sandy again. Fiona, overhearing, caught Hugh's eye and laughed.

"Would Fiona let him?" he asked.

"Well, she might, when she has steered herself," said Fiona, and called to Jamie that he could when she had.

Jamie leant back, content. His face and ears were tingling with cold but his body was warm under its layers of clothes and the broth warmed him inside. The tops of the hills above Naast and Inverasdale were dark and below them lights from the scattered crofts shone like small yellow stars. A white line of waves showed the Loch's edge and, as they rounded the second point, they saw the water was flecked with white horses. It was colder than ever here, cold and lovely. Jamie would not have changed his place for the warmest and most comfortable room in the world.

Fiona took the tiller and Ninian joined Hugh at the engine. The lantern was so dim that it was almost impossible to see what they were doing. They cleaned the plugs, blew into the carburettor, flooded the carburettor, primed the engine and eventually it started.

Fiona, her cold hand clasping the tiller, was thinking of Fergus. How she had sailed with him over the dark sea from Taransay one night in the summer. It had been warm then and they had been in the *Star*, but there was a certain similarity, perhaps the night, perhaps her mood. Fergus must be there. They must find him in the Whisky Cave and persuade him to come back to Carn Mor with them. He would love it, she was sure, she felt he brooded too much about Colin when he was alone. If he was not there she did not know what to do. They knew of no address; he did not live at Taransay; he would hate them to write anyway; he liked to be left alone. She sighed. Hugh heard her and came and stood beside her.

"I don't remember a more perfect night," he said presently. Fiona looked at him and smiled gratefully.

"Neither do I," she said. "We've never sailed with you in the winter before, have we?"

"No, I can't think why not, it's cold but it's lovely," Hugh said.

They passed where the Loch threw an arm round Isle Carrick towards Beanault. Bright lights were shining from this little town and they heard the engine of a motor boat off the end of the island. Still the lights shone from the scattered crofts on their left: Carrick, Boor, Naast, Inverasdale and Fienn Mor to Cove, the home of the lobster-fishers and the last village before the sea. Past the end of the island and farther north than Beanault a cluster of lights betrayed Mellon Charles, and from then on darkness. There was only one more croft, Slaggan, at the head of the Loch in a small bay of its own, but they would be hardly likely to see it.

Jamie came aft at Fienn Mor and took the tiller, leaving Sandy and Jean in the bows. Jean's pale hair gleamed even in this light and she looked more frail and smaller than ever. Small she might be and frightened at many things, but she was no more frail than Ninian.

Hugh and Fiona sat by the mast talking in low voices. Ninian, his pipe glowing, stood by Jamie, his eyes on the sail, the waves, the sky, searching for clouds that would mean a storm or for white breakers that showed rocks. He shifted his feet that were gradually growing cold and rubbed a strand of hair from his forehead. Another half-hour and they should be there.

Fiona took over when they left the Loch and came out into the open sea. It was much rougher here but no more wind, as they were fairly sheltered by the cliffs. They watched the white waves splashing up on Foura, their special island, and then fixed their eyes on the long dark coastline ahead. Here they put out the side-lights and sailed on, invisible.

"Let's see who'll notice the breakers in Flatfish Bay

first," cried Sandy.

"Shall we see them?" asked Jean, thinking that the night was too black to see anything.

"Of course we shall, silly. Can't you see the waves on the coast?" Sandy was scathing.

"Ye-e-s." Jean did not sound convinced. She peered on into the darkness with the others.

Ahead of them somewhere was Flatfish Bay, that long stretch of white sand, broken into two by a belt of rock, unreachable except by sea. In the far corner stood the Stack, a high pinnacle of cliff harder than the surrounding rock which had gradually been broken off, leaving it alone like a lighthouse in the sea. The ledges all round it were the homes of innumerable sea-birds and in the summer the air was discordant with their clamour and a white cloud hung round the bay, a cloud of fluttering gulls. Behind the Stack was a narrow channel leading up to Fergus's cave, a tricky place to navigate, especially by night. Fergus could do it blindfold, and the Stewarts were hoping they remembered it clearly enough to do it by the dim light of stars.

"It's strange without the noise of gulls," said Fiona. "I wonder what they do in the winter."

"They're still here, I expect," said Hugh. "Only not so noisy. There are no nests now."

"We've never been here in the winter before." Ninian looked up at the sky. "I think the moon's rising at last."

"Is it full yet?" asked Hugh.

"No, a day or two to go. Gosh, what a lovely night."

"Coldish though!" Fiona's chin felt as if it was frozen.

"I seem to have a permanent drip on the end of my nose, but I think it's only an illusion," said Hugh, sniffing.

"I can see the Bay!" came Jamie's clear voice, and they all leant forward peering into the darkness, until they too saw the line of white breakers that were always there whether the sea was rough or calm.

They were tacking now that they had left the Loch, and Ninian, taking over from Fiona, brought *Black Swan* about and headed for the bay. Twelve eyes were fixed on the cliff and the rocks round the Stack, hoping for a glimmer of light that would show that the smugglers were at home. But there was no sign. The cliffs remained black and expressionless, fringed with the white border of waves.

"Doesn't look as if any one's there," said Jamie, at last.

"Well, it's hardly likely really that Fergus'd proclaim his presence to any passing coastguard's boat," said Ninian. "I expect they're all tucked snugly in the harbour. We'll give them the fright of their lives."

Here, under the cliffs, the wind had nearly dropped. *Black Swan* was hardly moving and Hugh bent to start the engine. Sandy and James stood ready to lower the sails, Ninian edged her closer in; they could hear the waves breaking on the Stack and Fiona felt a cold bead of spray on her cheek.

"Let go!" The sails came rattling down and the engine took over.

"Better get into the bows too, Fiona," Ninian said. "It'll be black as ink in the gully."

She scrambled forward and crouched beside Jean. It was, as Ninian said, black as ink.

The big rollers lifted them up and carried them forward between the Stack and the cliff. The waves sounded deafeningly loud, especially when they boomed in the subterranean cave. They seemed to be tearing forward and then to sink, with a sideways swirling motion. Jean did not see how it was possible to avoid wrecking themselves and tried not to shut her eyes. Fiona, a slim blown figure, stood balancing herself against the forestay and calling directions to Ninian above the gurgling of the waves. A fine spray hung all over them, stinging their faces and hands; a loose rope slapped Sandy across the face. Then suddenly they were in the calm of the gully, sheltered by its many curves from any of the sea's violence.

"Whew!" Ninian ran his fingers through his hair. "I've never known it so rough before. Hell of a current runs round that Stack."

"It's beautifully calm in here," said Jean gratefully. But it was still dark and they went slowly, Fiona singing out from time to time that there were rocks port or starboard.

"They must have heard us coming by now," Jamie said, as they entered the little bay. But there was no friendly gleam of a lantern or shout of surprise as they chugged across to the jetty.

"The *Star's* not here." Jamie's voice was full of disappointment.

"There's nobody here at all." That was Jean with a slight quiver.

"Maybe they're inside the cave," said Fiona, but she did not sound very hopeful.

"Yes, they might have left just one person behind as watchman," said James.

They came alongside and made fast to the well-remembered iron rings. It was still and quiet here in the harbour out of the wind. Small waves slapped and rippled on the rocks and the burn gurgled across the stony beach, but otherwise it was silent.

"Better put out all the lights," Fiona whispered, but there was no need to whisper, "otherwise someone might see."

"Let's light the hurricane." Hugh fumbled for matches while Sandy turned down the compass light. Hugh's fingers were so cold that he could hardly hold the match. They felt as if they belonged to someone else. He struck it clumsily and it went out.

"Bother." He groped for another. Sandy and James were picking their way over the rocks towards the cave. Jean kept close by Ninian. In Fiona's pockets her fingers were firmly crossed.

Hugh, with the lantern, led the way, the others close behind him. Above them towered the black rim of the cliff, but there was no time now to look round. Hugh's feet already were echoing on the worn stones of the floor. Left ran the burn, deep and smooth and ahead the cave narrowed.

"If there was any one here they must have heard us by now," said Fiona, and because it was so dark and still and creepy she called:

"Fergus! Duncan! Rody!" in her clear voice and sent the echoes booming and answering from the very depths where the still was.

"Gracious!" Jean had jumped when her sister's voice broke the silence. But there was no answer although they listened intently for several minutes: only the steady drip, drip from the wet walls and the far-away noise of the burn running in from the hill. They went on along the path, bending their heads as the roof grew lower, picking their way over the stepping-stones where the burn crossed from right to left.

"We could leave a message, just in case Fergus comes back," suggested Hugh.

"If any one has any paper," added Sandy, who knew he had none.

"I wish to goodness Fergus was tall, then perhaps he'd enlarge his beastly cave," said Ninian savagely, having bumped his head hard on a snag of rock. "That's the second time I've nearly stove my skull in."

"Lucky you've got a head of bone," said Sandy, well out of reach.

A gust of fresh air met them and they guessed they were in the big inner cave where the still and vats were. Hugh held the lantern high and the dim shapes of the brick buildings loomed out from against the walls. The natural rock roof was lost in shadows as were the far corners. Anything might have been lurking there.

An idea occurred to Jamie.

"You don't think it's been raided since we were here last?" he said.

"Might have been. How frightful." Fiona crossed the uneven floor and inspected the stonework of the still. It appeared to be intact, but the fire in the corner was out and all that remained was a heap of dead, cold ashes.

"That hasn't been alight for ages," said Ninian, dusting his hand.

Hugh carried the lantern over to the heavy wooden door of Fergus's office. The chain and padlock hung across it and a spider had made a web between the corner of the door and the ceiling. From the amount of flies in it, it had been there some time.

Sandy pushed the door but there was no answering shout from inside. The chain rattled and clinked and still the water dripped slowly in the corner by the burn.

"Nobody here." Sandy spoke sadly.

"Well, let's leave a message anyway," said Fiona. "Come on, Hugh, with that lantern. Isn't the table over here somewhere?"

"I'm not surprised they don't live in here in the winter," said James, shivering. "It's as cold as a tomb."

"Wouldn't be bad with the fire going," said Ninian, following Fiona across the burn and into the recess where they had had breakfast one morning at five o'clock. The rough table was still there, and they sat round it while Hugh and Ninian rummaged in their pockets and finally brought to light the blank page from the back of a letter and a fountain pen.

"What shall we say?" Hugh unscrewed the pen and shook a blob of ink from it on to the floor.

"We can't put anything compromising," said Fiona.

"What does that mean?" asked Jean.

"Same as incriminating," and Ninian laughed at her puzzled face and explained.

"Might someone else find it then?" she asked.

"Well, we found the cave," said Fiona.

Eventually they decided on "Croft on Carn Mor," and put the date and all their initials.

"If we push it under the door no one but Fergus can find it," suggested Sandy.

"Yes, but one of the gang might find it if it's outside and take it to him," said Ninian.

"They probably wouldn't know what it meant," said James.

"Let's put it inside, then no one else but Fergus can possibly get it. I think it's safest." Fiona picked up the paper and dried it by the lantern.

"Yes, you're right. It would be frightful if we did anything that got him into trouble," said Ninian. They pushed it as far under the door as it would go. "Now what?" asked Sandy.

"It all seems rather flat." Fiona hunched her shoulders under her coat. "Gosh, it's cold in here."

"Chocolate time, I think." Ninian produced a large slab of Oliver Twist from his pocket.

"Oh, bliss." Jean realised she had been feeling hungry.

"Maggie gave me a flask of coffee," said Hugh. "It's in the boat. She said I wasn't to say, because when she offered them to you, you always refused them!"

"Maggie always tries to pamper us," said Sandy, scornfully.

"Still, some hot coffee would be rather welcome," admitted Fiona, who in days past had always been the one to refuse it.

Sadly they left the cave. Secretly none of them thought Fergus would come back that winter. Whisky-distilling was probably only a summer's job and he would be doing something else extraordinary now. You never knew with Fergus. He never said where he went or what he did but occasionally he would let fall scraps of information about such strange places as Hawaii, Ceylon or Chicago. He must have travelled a good deal but how or why they never discovered, and the *Wandering Star*, although seaworthy, was a bit small to take voyaging round the world.

Back in *Black Swan*, they sat and sipped scalding mouthfuls of coffee. Maggie certainly did her best to look after them and they glowed gratefully towards her as the coffee warmed them.

"It sounds even rougher outside," said Fiona at last, after listening intently.

"Just what I was thinking." In the dim lantern light she could see Ninian looked worried. "It's getting round the Stack that'll be difficult," he said.

"At a pinch we could stay the night," suggested Hugh. "We could make up the fire in the cave and it'd be moderately warm."

"Maggie would have a blue fit," said Sandy. "Surely it can't be too bad, Ninian?"

"You can't tell in here. It's that hellish current I'm afraid of." Ninian lifted his head and listened. "In two seconds it'd sweep you on to the rocks. We don't want to bust up *Black Swan*."

"Well, let's try." Fiona could see no point in hanging about and to her it sounded rather fun. Hugh looked up and saw her eyes bright with excitement and her face, so like Ninian's and yet so different, eager to see if their skill and *Black Swan* could overcome the waves. How strange it was, he thought, that Fiona, a girl, should have not the slightest fear of things like the sea and high cliffs and crossing the hills in the dark. At a time like this, caution, which she hardly possessed, was more valuable than all the fearlessness. Ninian, however, was really in charge. Hugh always felt safe with him.

"We'll go," he said. "Only get ready to fend her off rocks at the end of the gully. The tide's going out, which should help."

They cast off and Ninian started the engine. Hugh and Sandy armed themselves with the two long oars that lay unused in *Black Swan* and Jamie took the boathook.

"It's not going to be bad," said Ninian reassuringly, as they neared the end of the gully. Fiona in the bows could see white-capped waves beating on the Stack and big rollers came sweeping past them, lifting *Black Swan* as easily as a cork and dropping her again.

"Port now!" called Fiona, and they were between the Stack and the cliff. For one moment a wave swept them backwards on to the Stack. Hugh and Sandy pushed frantically at the dark mass that was the rocks, a splinter of oar broke away and then they were off and back in the channel again. A receding wave sucked them out and a moment later they were out at sea and heading east along the coast.

"Gosh!" Hugh wiped his forehead and found it was wet not with spray but sweat. "What a nasty moment." He stowed the oars away and came aft to Ninian.

A WAVE SWEPT THEM BACKWARDS.

"Nearish!" said Ninian. Hugh could see his teeth gleam as he smiled. Fiona came scrambling to join them.

"Once I thought we really were on the rocks," she said. "Rather fun, though. Let's get the sails up."

The dark sea around them and the stars overhead, they moved on into the night.

CHAPTER IX

LOCH DUBH

Tuesday, 19th December

THEY HAD NOT arrived back from Flatfish Bay until two o'clock in the morning. Consequently Maggie had let them sleep and breakfast was not over until ten-thirty. Even so there were deep shadows under Jean's eyes and Hugh decided that a little snooze round about lunch-time would be an excellent idea.

It was one of their favourite kind of days. The south wind, still strong, had veered to the west, a light frost had put an edge on the mud and laid thin cat-ice round the rims of the puddles. Leaves were whirling up from the birch trees and dancing down the track and the smoke from the Lodge chimneys streamed back towards Ben Carrick. Above all, this the sun shone intermittently between puffs of cloud that raced their shadows over the sea and the tawny hills. It was an autumny day, cold but pleasant.

When the Stewarts emerged on to the grass in front of the house, still slightly bleary and disappointed at their failure to find Fergus, one gust of the clear fresh wind blew all that away, and they felt fully awake and aware of the fact that to-day would be their first real day at the croft.

Ninian, regarding the vast roll of mattresses and blankets, said firmly:

"There won't be room for anything but this in the Ford. Why don't you walk on and I'll drive after you?"

That did seem a good idea, although there was a slight argument between Ninian and Hugh as to who should drive.

"You could bring your car up," Ninian said, "only I

don't imagine it would be madly good for it to be left out. It's bound to rain and snow and freeze before long."

"I quite agree," said Hugh. "But that's not the point."

He was finally won round by Fiona, who said she didn't know how any one could be so stoogy as to want to drive in a smelly Ford when there was the chance of a walk up to the Carna Loch on a heavenly morning like this.

"We might see some hinds," she added.

At this Ninian appeared to be on the point of saying he would come instead, but Hugh agreed just in time and walked into the Lodge to hump out the first roll of bedding.

The camp-beds had had their own small mattresses taken up the day before so the only really awkward thing was the mattress for the double bed. This proved completely unmanageable and with a strong will of its own. They struggled and swore at it and eventually got it down on the floor at the back.

Jamie had carefully taken the measurements of the box-beds and they had not been able to find anything small enough to fit them. They had almost given up in despair when Hugh thought of the hay-mattresses they had had in *Fauna* and they had hauled them out of the cupboard where they were stored and refilled them.

"Not so sure the double bed won't be the most comfortable now," grinned Hugh, who had taken care to choose the springiest mattress he could find.

"I'd rather sleep in a box-bed," said Fiona loftily. She unhooked her glass from behind the door, where she had left it until the last moment, and took her stick from the hall.

Ninian came out and watched them start and then climbed into the small place left for him in the front of the Ford. He passed them on the corner on the first hill and disappeared along the track. They paused at the top by the pine-wood and looked back over the low ground to the sea. White horses were blowing across the Loch, and a boat, looking like a water boatman from this distance, crawled from Inverasdale to Beanault. Peat-smoke from the crofts was blown up the hill towards them, and the sound of sheep and cows came drifting with it.

"I wonder how long it'll be until we have to come down again," said Hugh, as they continued up the track.

"We're sure to have forgotten masses." Sandy crunched on the white ice round a puddle.

"There's milk and bread and letters too," added Jean. "And we'll have to reassure Maggie that we're not all dead of starvation," said James.

Up beyond the pine-wood the ground was more or less flat, left irregular small hills and valleys scattered with giant rocks until it met the steep drop above Chuiragarstidh and the Beanault road, right pitted with peat-hags and small lochans until Ben Carrick rose sharply on the borders of Loch Marba.

Half-way along the track Sandy, who had been walking with his eyes ranging the ground on either side, stopped suddenly and pointed. Down to the left at the head of a little glen a small herd of hinds was feeding. The Stewarts and Hugh stood frozen still on the track. They counted five of them, their rough rusty coats blending so well with the dead grass and bracken that they were almost invisible. They were moving down to the next glen, feeding as they went, seeking the low ground and the chance of a little more feed than that they got amongst the bare hillsides.

Fiona had pulled out her glass, and resting it on Jean's shoulder, watched the deer.

"Poor brutes, they look different already from the fat ones you see in the summer," she said, handing it over to Sandy.

"We must be getting on," said Hugh, who was growing cold and yet dared not move nor stamp his feet for fear a torrent of abuse would descend on him. "Ninian'll be livid if he's had to unload all the stuff by himself."

They watched until the last hind had disappeared and then continued on, puffing white steam in front of them on the cold air.

When they reached the end of the track Ninian was sitting out of the wind behind the bothy, smoking and waiting for them to arrive and help him unload the big mattress. The rest he had taken out and piled up on the end of the wooden jetty. From where he sat he could see the whole way down the Carna Loch until it disappeared in a curve of the hills and turned into Loch Dubh, the Black Loch, deep and dark and ringed on three sides by hills. He could see the whole of Carn Mor too, but the house was hidden by the islands. The hills looked more lovely than ever this morning with their tops capped in snow. It lay in thick white drifts down the gullies and seemed to have crept even lower since yesterday. He heard the others for a long time before they reached him, their heavily nailed shoes crunching on the stones and their voices shouting and laughing.

HE COULD SEE THE WHOLE WAY DOWN THE CARNA LOCH.

They helped him struggle with the unwieldy mattress and loaded it aft in the dinghy. Sandy and he put the Ford's hood up and clipped in the battered windows. Sandy, protesting, was made to crawl underneath and poke a heather stem up the tap from the radiator, which somehow seemed to have got jammed. He was successful, and narrowly missed getting a jet of hot, rusty water in his eye.

"Anything else you'd like me to do?" he asked, rubbing earth and heather off his back and head.

"Yes, there's an old sack in the bothy: you might fling it over the radiator," said Ninian, unperturbed. He, himself, was wedging stones under the wheels. Sandy returned with the sack and wrapped it carefully round the car. He inspected Ninian's work with interest.

"Are you expecting a cyclone or something?" he asked.

But Ninian only grinned and told him that although the Ford was old she was worth taking care of. He was fond of the car; it had taken them many miles round Carrick and they had had it almost as long as he could remember. He pocketed the key and they joined the others at the dinghy.

She was looking amazing. Piles of bedding made her appear to be completely top-heavy. The twins were almost buried under mattresses and only the tops of two flaxen heads were visible. Fiona sat in the bows on a bundle of blankets, her legs dangling over either side but nowhere near the water.

"Heavens!" said Sandy. "Where on earth am I meant to go?"

"Well," Hugh had seated himself on one thwart and had the oar out, resting on the water. "Ninian can take the other oar and you can lie along the top of those mattresses and take over if one of us flake out."

"Looks rather comfy." Sandy scrambled carefully into his place and lay in a nest of mattresses looking up at the sky. Ninian followed him on board and pushed off.

The wind was behind them and they fairly blew along. The rowers, of course, were unable to see where they were going and had to depend on shouted directions from Fiona. She, perched high above the bows and swaying as the dinghy slapped against each wave, was having a wonderful time. It was cold but the fitful sun and blue sky made her forget that. The spray pattered against the oilies carefully tucked in by Jean around the bedding. Out in the middle of the Loch it was fairly choppy. Ninian and Hugh were finding the load, although lighter than the first journey to Carn Mor, much too heavy. After a bit Sandy took over from Hugh while he rested and then took over from Ninian. Fiona's shout of "Land Ho!" although they were surrounded by it, was very welcome, and a few minutes later they were in the sheltered water behind the pier.

"What a journey!" Hugh looked at his palms. He had thought them immune to blistering.

"Lucky we haven't got to return, we'd be dead into wind," said Sandy, looking the way they had come and feeling his hair blown back.

It was twelve already. Fiona, staggering up the path, her arms full of blankets, had been hoping there would be time to cook a real lunch on this their first day at Carn Mor. But now there would be only time for something quick: she could see by Ninian's face that he would want to be off on the hill as soon as possible. In her mind she was running over the stores, trying to remember where she had put the sausages. The tinned peaches, she knew, were in a cupboard.

The house smelt cold but clean. Jamie flung open the windows and the air came blowing off the Loch and through it. The curtains fluttered and a door slammed. The clock was still ticking, and when Sandy turned on the tap in the scullery brown peaty water came pouring down from the tank that they had filled the day before.

"Everything works!" cried Jean delightedly.

Fiona was laying the fire.

"Look," she said. "If you all make the beds and generally tidy up I'll cope with the lunch."

"Right, but only you know what most of the things are meant for," said Hugh.

"Well, I can help sort them out," said Fiona, putting sticks and knobs of coal on top of the paper.

"Some things are obvious." Ninian clasped one end of the vast mattress and with Hugh carried it into the bedroom. Large though it was it was smaller than the bed.

"Not enough to matter," said Hugh.

Jamie and Jean pushed the hay-mattresses into place in the box-beds. Privately, Jean still thought they looked rather murky, although they had been scrubbed out. But Jamie assured her there were no spiders inside, and climbed in and examined all the corners to make sure.

The big bed was the first to be made. Four of them did it, flapping the great blankets like sails, and tucking them firmly in round the bottom.

"It looks rather professional," said Sandy at last, smoothing over the big patchwork quilt that covered the whole thing. "Now for the camp-bed."

Fiona was torn from a frying-pan full of sausages and made to sort out blankets.

"All the sheets are all the same from now on," she said.

The camp-beds were easy compared with the box-beds. These, being fairly high, were quite unmanageable, and Hugh and Ninian had to deal with them as having the longest arms.

The sausages were ready first and Fiona tried out the oven at keeping them warm. She was thrilled with the stove: it was her first experiment with anything bigger than the *Fauna's* primus and fires lit on the shores of lochs or at Flatfish Bay.

As they ate they talked.

"What to do after lunch?" asked Sandy, his mouth full.

"Let's begin looking for the cave," suggested James.

"Yes, we might as well; where shall we begin?" said Ninian, longing to start off somewhere.

"Well, let's collect as much as we know about it," said Fiona, "or rather what we don't know about it."

"It's definitely here somewhere." Ninian stretched out a long arm and cut himself a hunk of bread. "We do know for certain that James Stewart hid in a cave near here after Culloden."

"No one's ever found it," put in Fiona. "Therefore it must be somewhere where no one ever goes."

"Or else very well hidden," said Sandy.

"Yes, perhaps. Most of these caves are surprisingly obvious when you find them." Hugh when he was a boy had explored every one around Corriedon, and his family said that his clothes still smelt of that damp musty smell peculiar to caves.

"It must be fairly near, surely," said Jean. "I mean, if he was waiting for a ship in Loch Carrick he wouldn't wait miles away."

"Well, that's not definite," said Ninian. "People in those days thought nothing of walking miles over the hill."

"Well," Hugh summed up, bread and cheese in one hand, beer in the other, "all we do know for certain is that there is a cave. I suppose that's definite?"

"Every one says there is." Jamie stuck firmly to that fact. "All the gillies and crofters talk about it, but they rather laugh at it because no one's seen it for so long."

"Right," said Ninian. "Let's get going."

"No!" said Fiona. "We must wash up and there's dinner to get ready."

"Heavens, you're getting as bad as Maggie," said Sandy impatiently.

"Well, we could leave it." Fiona was no keener than he to do it, but, looking ahead, felt it would be depressing to come back to a dirty muddle of the only plates and cups they had.

"Come on then." Hugh piled up crockery and took it out to the scullery. "If we all do it, it won't take long. Let's have some hot water, Fiona."

It did not take them long, but longer than it did later, when they knew where everything was kept. Fiona, meanwhile, cut up a couple of rabbits and some vegetables and put them in a huge casserole with gravy to stew slowly in the oven. Sandy filled the tank and Jamie the coal buckets. They had discovered in the side of the range a tap leading out of a small hot-water tank. After much twiddling and pushing of wire spikes up the tap it had worked, and now they had a gallon or so of hot water always ready.

Fiona stoked the fire up, filled and put the kettle on one side and surveyed the room.

"It does look nice," she said. "But wait a moment, I haven't seen the bedrooms yet."

Jamie and Sandy escorted her round with pride and she approved of almost everything.

"But don't the rooms look minute?" she said, surprised.

Jean, meanwhile, had been cutting sandwiches for tea, and a few slices of cake. These went into a bag on Sandy's back and then they joined Ninian who was already outside, his glass over his shoulder, watching the small waves break on the gravelly sand of the bay.

There's something, Hugh thought, especially nice about this. Here we are, independent of every one, completely and absolutely free for the next week or so. Whatever happens, whatever we do, this time will be isolated in our lives, cut off and separate from what comes before and after. We shall be able to look back and think of it and be unable to imagine that it really happened. It doesn't seem possible that I'm here again, with the people I like most. The Army seems miles away: I can't really be going back to it and the boring orderliness of its life. His thoughts here were broken into by Ninian and Fiona, arguing loudly about whether there was a bay to be skirted before Loch Dubh was reached.

"Of course there is," Fiona said, shutting the door behind her. "There's a huge bay just over this rise," and she pointed left down Carna. "Then you come to Loch Dubh, right amongst the hills."

"Quite right, except that there's no bay," said Ninian imperturbably.

"Where are we going anyway?" asked Sandy, impatient to be off.

"Well, let's go to Loch Dubh and find out," suggested Jean. "Hardly any one ever goes there as it's so completely cut off and there are pretty cavey-looking cliffs half-way round it."

"Oh, do let's." Sandy had never been there and had always longed to go.

Ninian and Fiona were glaring at each other. They suddenly laughed.

"All right," said Ninian. "Let's go. I haven't been there for years."

"It's a blissfully cavey place," said Jamie.

"Trolls too?" Jean whispered to him.

"No, well there might be. I don't think so," said Jamie comfortingly.

Anyway, thought Jean, I'll stay near Ninian when we get there.

The ground along the edge of the Carna Loch was flat for a few yards inland, tussocky heather and peat-hags, small cliffs down to bays, beaches like the one at the Carn Mor croft, burns that came racing down the hillside, clumps of rowan and hazel and birch, mammoth rocks that had fallen in the ice-age and now gave shelter to Blackfaced sheep, then the hill swept upwards in a long curve and bulged out so that the skyline was invisible. On and up for nearly three thousand feet, the home of deer and eagles, wild cats, buzzards, ravens, ptarmigan and sometimes a fox. The wind blew cleanly up the great shoulder, whistling in the grass and round the rocks, mingling with the noise of the burns.

The Stewarts walked briskly for they had a long way to go. They were all in high spirits, the twins and Sandy chasing each other and jumping on the cat-ice round the peat-hags, the others walking more soberly, their hands in their pockets, their eyes resting contentedly on the long length of Carna and the distinctive shape of their own Ben Carrick beyond.

Ninian was sceptical about the cave. Since childhood he had heard of it but no more than just that there was a cave, no mention of what it was like or where it was situated. Legends, he knew, were apt to spring up and get distorted beyond the truth. Probably if all was known, James Stewart had sheltered in a croft somewhere in these hills and the story of the cave had grown with the years. Every district in the West Highlands had a cave, usually where Prince Charlie had hidden. They were different in that respect. Prince Charles had never visited Carrick nor skulked in the hills around it, although there must have been plenty more Jacobites who had. On a day like this it would be cold in the heather, with no more covering than a plaid, if that. Our ancestors must have been very hardy, thought Ninian, but I suppose even their houses were cold then.

By now they had reached the first rise. They had been keeping an eye on the hill at their left, partly for deer, partly for caves. They had seen neither and, as Sandy said, it was not a very likely place.

"Much too open and bare," agreed James.

"But you could see every one coming," said Hugh.

"I somehow feel it's not there," said Jamie.

"Now we shall see who was right about the bay." Fiona hurried forward. She knew that it was ten to one Ninian was right and yet somehow she remembered that the Loch did not run perfectly straight to Loch Dubh.

They reached the summit and stood looking down the other side. The ground sloped back and then curved out to a point, corresponding to the point on the opposite side, leaving a narrow channel between the two Lochs.

"Well!" said Ninian.

"Well!" said Fiona. "If it's not exactly a bay, it's not exactly straight."

"More straight than a bay."

"Oh, for heaven's sake," said Sandy. "Fiona, you couldn't possibly call it a bay, but there is definitely a curve out to that point."

"Right, let's agree there's a curve," suggested Ninian, as they walked down the slope.

"No caves," said Jamie, disappointedly.

"No, but just look ahead," said Hugh.

It was a magnificent sight.

The sun, slanting westward as the day lengthened, shone through the clouds on to the hills in front of them. Left was Carn Mor which seemed to join Ben Fuar and continued on without losing much of its height. Ahead and to the right the huge peak of Ben Lair towered above the loch and beyond that the great bald head of Slioch. There was a narrow glen between the end of Ben Fuar and Ben Lair, but another smaller hill, Craig an Dubh Loch, rising sharply from the south shore of Loch Dubh, hid this, and thus ringed the water with lowering hills. The lower hills between the two giants were dominated by the vast bulk of Sgurr Ban, white indeed with a cap of snow. Under this overwhelming mass of rock Loch Dubh lay still and black.

"I'm glad we aren't living here," said Hugh at last, and indeed the hills seemed to press in on them and stifle them. Almost they leant across the water, guarding it from sun and wind.

"It's overpowering," said Fiona. "Don't the hills look

huge?"

"Lovely and rocky. Come on." Sandy led the way.

Where the ground stuck out in a point it was flat and tussocky and moderately easy-going, but beyond that the Loch curved east right under the foot of Carn Mor and left only a little flat ground to walk on. There were reeds growing on the far side of the point, and two startled ducks splashed up in a great hurry and went winging down the loch.

"Not used to people," said Fiona.

"We must come here in the spring," said Ninian. "There are sure to be masses of birds then."

The side of Carn Mor looked more hopeful for caves just here, but they agreed that they would look seriously when they came to the far end and where the cliffs were. They passed the point and soon found themselves walking on the side of the hill. Ahead two large burns came racing over the rocks about half a mile apart. One had a long thin waterfall high up on the hill and they watched the narrow ribbon of water falling across a black wet face of rock.

"Might be a cave up there," Jean suggested. "Just the place, under a waterfall."

"We'll look some time but not now," said Ninian. "Let's remember it as a likely place."

One burn was almost a small river for a hundred yards or so. Jean was entranced and they had to stop and explore just in case there was a good pool.

"We must come back," said Jean longingly. "Next year some time."

An hour later they stood at the head of the Loch. Here another burn ran out.

"To Loch Gorm," Ninian said. "The Blue Green Loch. I've never been there. Well, we might," he added to the questioning look on Jeannie's face.

Anything to do with a loch or river or even burn had Jean enthralled at once. Fishing was her passion, and even if it was out of season she could stand by the water and work out the best places to throw a fly or drop a worm. To Jamie the sea, to Fiona the hill, to Ninian Carrick, so fishing was to Jean.

It was dark and cold and sunless. Hugh, looking up, found himself ringed about with hills, their white unfriendly tops lowering down at him. He felt tiny and oppressed, as if he had strayed by mistake into a land in which he was only half-size. He shivered and wished the sun was higher than the shoulder of Ben Lair.

"Come on," said Ninian. "Let's start looking. This is just the place." He took Jean's hand and together they started off up the steep hillside. Hugh worked his way along the burn, looking carefully on either side. Sandy, Fiona and James spread out towards the west. They had arranged a series of curlew calls from any one finding it, and single ones repeated at intervals from whoever had a watch when it was time to go home. Then they would gather at the foot of Hugh's burn.

Fiona, clambering swiftly up and up, soon had a wonderful view across Loch Dubh and part of Carna as well. It was difficult going, being half-precipice, and Ninian, looking up at one moment, saw her far above him standing on a jutting rock where the hill curved round, silhouetted against the sky. She looked down too, and picked out Jean's fair head and they waved, then she disappeared.

Sandy and James stuck to the lower ground, searching diligently but fruitlessly. At one moment Sandy thought he had it, and indeed it was almost a cave, but more of a slight fissure between two rocks. He called James to inspect it but they decided against it.

An hour later Ninian's single curlew calls summoned them to the burn. Hugh, wet and muddy, was there first, the boys came next, shouting disappointedly that they had found nothing. Finally Fiona came leaping down the hill, her black hair streaming, and landed amongst them with a flying leap from a boulder, her nose and cheeks glowing from her run.

"Come on, we must hurry. It'll be dark before we get home," said Ninian, starting off straight away along the east shore of the Loch.

"Not a thing," said Sandy. "We searched and searched."

"It'd be a wonderful place," said Hugh, "but almost too gloomy."

"Of course we didn't search it really thoroughly," said Fiona, who had been longing to go to the top.

"We might, but it'd take hours and the days are so short now."

Ninian hurried them along as the sky was already growing dark.

"We could start at cock-crow," said Fiona, hopping from rock to rock as she crossed the first burn. "Gosh, but it's getting cold."

"And dark," added Jean, taking a little run to keep up with her elder brother's long legs.

"We can't really get lost, we just have to follow the Loch," said James.

"How awful if we passed the croft in the dark." Jean grew quite pale at the thought.

"We should see the boat," said Hugh comfortingly.

"Where shall we go to-morrow?" Sandy's mind was already far ahead.

"What about the far side of Ben Carrick? We've never explored it properly and it's a very good place," suggested Ninian.

"Or the top of Carn Mor," said Fiona.

"Let's do Ben Carrick first, then we'll have finished with that side and can concentrate on this." Hugh looked up at the black curve of the hill and saw an ominous cloud beyond it.

"We must do the cliff above Bearnach some time," added James. "It might easily be there."

"There are so many places," said Jean, who was getting tired.

"What about taking the rifle just in case, if we're going on Ben Carrick?" suggested Sandy longingly.

"Might." Ninian would not promise. "We could do Bearnach on a day that we haven't much time, if it was raining in the morning and cleared after lunch. It's so close," he added.

"Did you bring a map?" asked James. "I'm vague about what happens behind us."

"I'll have a look when we get home," said Ninian, hurrying. He had also seen the cloud.

Home, thought Fiona. The croft is our home. It really is, it feels like one. I like it, I like it better than the Lodge, it's so peaceful. The thought of it beckoned her on.

CHAPTER X

NIGHT AT CARN MOR

Tuesday Night, 19th December

THE FIRE, well banked up by Fiona, was throwing slanted orange shadows across the kitchen as they pushed open the door. The steady singing of the kettle was a warm and comforting sound. They crowded round, shaking off the rain, the forerunner of what Ninian predicted would be a big storm.

Fiona hurried to light the lamp, Hugh took the top off the fire, poked vigorously and added a few coals; the others peeled off damp coats and hung them in the hall.

"Gosh, it's a horrid night," said Jean, re-entering the kitchen. She went to the window and looked out. She could see nothing but the reflection of the firelit room, spattered with drops of rain. It was pitch-black outside and the last half-mile had been stumbled and felt more than walked. They had almost passed the croft in the dark until Hugh, looking at the Loch, had seen the curve of the bay and the pale gleam of sand.

Jamie hurried from room to room shutting the windows and drawing curtains. Sandy, unwillingly, relaid and lit the fire in the bedroom, grumbling chiefly that his room had not got one. Fiona appeased him by promising him the oil-stove.

The kettle boiling, Jean made the tea. They had come back so fast that there had been hardly time to eat and they decided to have some more before dinner.

"We'll have a proper super-dinner later," said Sandy, making toast. He looked critically at his piece and turned it over, scorching his face and hands. Fiona leant over his head, stirring the soup.

"Don't drop things down my neck." Sandy, alarmed, lifted his flushed face.

"Let's roast the leg of lamb." Ninian, who had been prowling round the larder, came back with a pot of bramble jelly.

"Sounds rather ambitious," said Hugh.

"Oh, let's make our first dinner here a grand one." Fiona was full of enthusiasm. "Then when we're feeling more lazy we can have cold meat."

"D'you know how to cook a leg of lamb?" asked Sandy suspiciously.

"Well, I can always try," retorted Fiona.

They sat round the kitchen table, spread with a clean white cloth, and laid with jam and bread and scones, baked by Maggie the day before. A large plum cake stood in the middle. The hanging lamp shone down on their damp untidy heads and eager hands. Their faces growing warmer, glowed red, the room was full of the smell of peat and tea and toast, the fire and lamp filled the corners with dark shadows and a warm orange glow, and on the roof and windows the rain thrashed and pattered, making the croft seem a haven in the midst of a storm.

"Hope the boat'll be all right," said Ninian, through a mouthful.

"Feigns go and see," said every one.

"Typical. Well, I will later." Ninian leant back and looked up at the ceiling. The pattern of the lamp was reflected there and it shook a little as an extra strong gust hit the croft.

He looked round at the others, smiling at their contented faces. They were listening to Fiona, who was, as usual, propounding some mad scheme to climb to the top of all the surrounding hills.

"We might almost stop out all night," she said. "Like they did in the olden days with a plaid. Then we could watch the dawn."

"Not in the winter, please, Fiona," said Hugh, laughing.

After tea, while Fiona was preparing the dinner, Sandy and the twins played Snap on one end of the kitchen table and Hugh and Ninian stretched out in the arm-chairs, on either side of the fire. As Fiona said, there was so little room that it was easier if only one person rushed madly between scullery and kitchen with pots and pans and plates.

"Gosh, though, you do take up a lot of room," she said to Hugh, tripping over his legs for the third time.

"Snap!" shrieked Sandy, scattering cards in all directions, while Ninian, deep in the paper they had brought with them, announced that the weather forecast predicted snow.

"Snow!" Fiona stopped in the act of putting the joint into the oven.

"Snow!" the twins' heads came up, and even Hugh leant forward and knocked out his pipe.

"Oh, think how blissful it will be," Jean's eyes shone. "We should be nearly buried up here."

"Tobogganing down Carn Mor!" Sandy, as usual, was miles ahead.

"The deer'll be right round the house," said Fiona, shutting the oven door.

"How'll we get down to the village?" asked Hugh. "What happens if the Loch freezes?" asked Jamie. This was a new departure.

"Might it?" It sounded better and better to Sandy. "D'you mean we might skate across the Loch?"

"It'd have to be a pretty fierce frost," said Ninian. "But we could always use the Beanault path to get food."

"Well, we must find it first," said Fiona, practically. "But it's miles round."

"Flatter country too, there mightn't be so many drifts," said James. "But seriously, do you think we might get snowed up?"

"It has happened in the old days," Ninian said. "Luckily Maggie knows where we are."

The dinner on, Fiona fetched rugs and coats from the hall and sat on them, leaning against Ninian's chair. On the stove brussels sprouts and potatoes were simmering, the joint was in the oven and the sweet — they had not risen to anything complicated — lay in a glass dish. Tinned pears and peaches and cream.

"Nice and simple," said Fiona.

She leant back, watching through half-closed eyes the smoke from Hugh's pipe curling to the ceiling. Here in the kitchen it was unbelievably warm and comfortable, a fact emphasised by the rain and wind outside. Somehow the weather forecast must have gone wrong because rain and snow did not mix. Every moment the storm seemed to be getting worse. The rain was literally lashing on the roof and streaming down the windows. In the chimneys the wind made a low moaning noise and found a way in under the door, so that Fiona had to go and tuck a rug along it. Every now and then, above the noise, she could hear the roaring of the burn as it gradually filled up. As ever, on these occasions, her thoughts turned to *Black Swan* on her moorings down in the bay. Sometimes after an unusually rough and violent storm they would find bunches of sea-weed blown on board by the gale, and often she would need baling out. Fiona listened half to the noises of the storm, and half to the loud ticking of the clock, to the sizzling of the joint in the oven and the low singing of the kettle, to the twins and Sandy who had abandoned Snap and were discussing the possibilities of tobogganing down Carn Mor, to the rustle as Ninian turned the paper and the creak as he shifted himself in the wicker chair, to the sucking noise as Hugh drew at his pipe, reluctant now to go, and the rasp as he struck another match. After the long cold walk the warmth of the room made her sleepy. She leant back contentedly, clasping her knees, thinking of nothing in particular but of the comfort of the croft.

The dinner was cooked and ready by half-past eight. Ninian sat at one end of the table, the joint steaming in front of him, Fiona sat at the other. With an expert hand Ninian carved great slices of mutton, done, more by good luck than anything else, to just the state of under-doneness they all liked. He managed to find a crisp bit for each and gave the tail to Sandy. Even there was red-currant jelly. Hugh poured the beer, Jamie cut the bread and Jean doled out potatoes and brussels sprouts. They started on their first meal at Carn Mor.

The rain, which had been increasing in volume ever since they came in, now seemed to reach its peak. A vivid flash of lightning flickered through the room, followed by an almost deafening clap of thunder. It came from right overhead and sounded like the hills cracking open. The great roar rolled away to Loch Dubh, where Ben Lair caught it and sent it back to Carn Mor, and it played to and fro between them, gradually becoming fainter only to be caught up by another peal.

They looked at each other with wide eyes. The noise was terrible, far worse than down at the Lodge or even at Carrick House where the hills along Loch Marba echoed at each clap. Here they were so much nearer and they felt thankful that the croft was small and sturdy and not to be shaken by anything less than an earthquake.

"I'm glad we're not up at Loch Dubh now," said Jamie, above the uproar. The others nodded. Luckily none of them minded a thunderstorm. Fiona and Sandy rather revelled in one. Jean was looking at Ninian with big eyes and he leant over and whispered something to her and she smiled.

"Just the weather for trolls," Sandy told her. "You couldn't hear them coming."

"Oh, Sandy, you are horrid." Jean looked at Ninian, who laughed and told her there were no trolls up here. All the same he kicked Sandy under the table.

As they were finishing their fruit the storm died away. They could hear the rumble of the thunder as it faded among the hills. The wind dropped too, and only the steady pouring of rain was left to remind them of the storm.

They cleared and washed up the dishes, and then collected six packs of cards and sat round the table for a session of Racing Demon. They each had a distinctive style of their own. Sandy cheated quite openly, Ninian played slowly and thoroughly with an occasional burst of genius, Hugh was almost always last, Jamie kept silent and watchful. Fiona shrieked and slammed her cards down much to everyone's confusion, and Jean had a habit of retiring into a trance half-way through, mesmerised by the flashing hands and loud shouts and curses. An hour or two of it was about all any of them could stand at their usual pace, but to-night because they were excited and because the air seemed charged with electricity, perhaps a legacy from the storm, they played faster and faster until Hugh was left miles behind and Jean's eyes felt as though they were on sticks.

"Can't cope." Hugh put down his pack.

"Try a little cheating." Fiona leant back and laughed, her face flushed. "Sandy'll give you some tips."

"I don't cheat," protested Sandy. "At least hardly ever."

"We've had about enough anyway." Ninian gathered his cards together. "The rain seems to have stopped, too."

They had been far too busy to pay attention to anything but the game, and now in the pause that followed they could hear nothing but the roar and rumble of the burn as it tore down the hill and over the rocks. Every now and then the wind brought the sound more clearly and they could hear the noise of waves breaking on the shore.

"Almost bedtime," said Ninian, pushing back his chair. "We want to be up early."

"Let's go and look at the night," said Fiona. She went to the door and opened it, the others following.

Outside it was very cold. The storm had passed, trailing in its wake a few clouds that smudged across the stars. Those not obscured were bright and wintery and all around the hills lay black and still against the sky. They walked over the wet grass to the rocks and watched the Loch, still whipped to white horses, breaking angrily in the little bay.

"It's going to freeze," said Ninian, sniffing the air.

"It is freezing." Fiona clasped her elbows and shivered.

"Gosh, it smells good," said Sandy, taking deep breaths.

They turned back to the croft. The window glowed tawny and an oblong square of light fell from the door over the step and on to the grass.

"Bed, I think," said Hugh.

They hurried indoors and shut out the night.

Getting ready for bed was a bit of a scramble. It reminded Hugh of their first night on board *Fauna* in the summer. Now although there was more room the same confusion seemed to reign.

Jean and Fiona undoubtedly had the best of it in the kitchen. It was warm and near the water for washing. Sandy, in spite of his oil-stove, joined the other three by their fire, and the noise coming from their room made Fiona wonder what on earth the mess would be like by morning.

No sooner were she and Jean in their dressing-gowns than Hugh was pounding on the door demanding to clean his teeth.

"Come in," called Fiona. "We thought cocoa would be a good idea."

"Brilliant," said Hugh. "Before the teeth or after?"

"Well, whichever you like." Fiona put a saucepan of milk on the fire and Jean got out the cups.

"Did somebody say cocoa?" Sandy appeared in the doorway, his brown hair on end, wrapped in a Jæger dressing-gown that he had grown out of about two years before. Ninian followed, a candle flickering in his hand, his throat strangely white below his brown face. He came and sat on the end of the table and helped to stir, keeping an eye on Sandy.

"What was all the noise?" asked Jean, watching them. "Sandy pinched my top blanket and I got it back." Ninian picked up another cup.

"Well, you've got six on your bed and I've only got four."

"I haven't got six, I've only got four, or maybe five."

"Have a rug if you're cold, Sandy," offered Fiona, her eye on the milk.

"It's the blanket off my bed at the Lodge," grumbled Sandy. "A lovely red one."

"Well, I've got it now," said Ninian.

"I've got a red one, Sandy, if you like," said Jean, generously.

"I don't really mind," said Sandy, laughing.

The milk rose with a white froth and Fiona mixed the cocoa.

"We haven't really decided about to-morrow yet," said James.

"Let's go to Ben Carrick," suggested Ninian. "We don't know this side of it very well, at least we've never explored it properly."

"All right," said Fiona. "And the rifle."

"If you like to carry it. There's not much chance of all six of us blundering across a hind." Ninian was sceptical.

"Well, let's take it anyway," said Sandy.

"How'll we go?" asked James.

"Row across to Bearnach, I should think," said Fiona, sipping her cocoa. She held the hot cup between her hands and the steam rose into her eyes. "There's a track somewhere round the back of the Little Loch that goes to Lettercarrick. We could branch off up the hill between Ben

Carrick and Mel Vannie, which, by the way, is a likely place."

"What's Mel Vannie?" asked Hugh.

"A small but high hill between Ben Carrick and Ben Lair," said Ninian. "It doesn't belong to us, so no poaching, mind."

"Just supposing we do get a hind," interrupted Sandy, "what on earth are we going to do with it here?"

"We'd never eat the whole thing," added Jean, appalled by the thought of joints and joints of venison and stew after stew.

"Some of us will have to go down to the village soon," said Fiona. "We could take what's left with us. It's always welcome."

"There's not much room in the larder for a hind," said Hugh. "In fact I can see us rueing the day we shoot one."

"If we do," added Sandy.

A shower of cinders rattled into the grate and the coals subsided with a crunch. In the silence that followed the clock sounded extra loud and Ninian looked at it. Ten to eleven.

"If the cocoa wasn't so hot it's time we were in bed." He blew at his and took a scalding mouthful.

"Has every one got a candle and matches?" asked Fiona.

"Yes, at least we've one between us," said Hugh. He yawned, suddenly sleepy. Fiona, on the contrary, having half-dozed before dinner, was now feeling wide awake.

"I simply must see Jean in her box-bed," said Ninian. "Come on, Jeannie, I'll lift you in."

"I can get in quite well myself, with a chair," said Jean "Oh, Ninian, stop, you're spilling my cocoa."

Regardless of her protests he picked her up and carried her over to the cupboard-like aperture in which she was to spend the night. She felt ridiculously light. Inside, the bed looked most inviting, the red blanket turned down, the white pillow-case and sheets clean and uncrumpled.

"Mind your head." Ninian thrust her in, still clutching her cocoa. She sat cross-legged like a goblin, her head just below the top of the bed.

"You won't be able to sit up, Fiona," said Hugh.

"If I'm unconscious in the morning you'll know I've knocked myself out trying to." Fiona inspected her bunk with interest. "I shall be able to lean on an elbow if I want to read," she added. "Or drink my early morning tea."

There was silence.

"Let whoever's up first make the tea?" suggested Ninian. "Well, whoever starts banging about on the range will pretty soon wake us," retorted Fiona. "Still, it'll be pleasant lying in bed and watching someone else lighting the fire."

"Maybe," said Hugh. "Come on, Jean, get right in and tell us if it's comfortable."

Jean took off her blue dressing-gown and wormed her way into the bed.

"It's lovely," she said. "Much nicer than you'd think. Beautifully warm, too."

"My beastly cold cell," grumbled Sandy.

"It'll be boiling. You've had the oil-stove in there for hours," said Fiona.

They put their cups in the sink and Hugh picked up a candle in a red enamel stick and lit it at the stove. He yawned and opened the door. Across the little hall the door of his room was open and flickering shadows from the peat fire lay on the floor and walls.

"Good night," said every one, and they went out, leaving Fiona alone. For some time she heard their voices, gradually growing more spasmodic.

She lit her own candle and turned down the lamp. Jean, curled up in bed with the blankets up to her chin, called drowsily:

"Come on, Fiona, it's so blissful."

"Must open the window," said Fiona, thinking vaguely that perhaps it was not the most healthy thing in the world to sleep in a room full of smoke and fire and the faint smell of cooking. She drew the curtains back from the window opposite the beds and decided to open the one facing the Loch. She left the candle on the table and pulled back the curtains. Outside was the moon. She opened the window and knelt on a chair, leaning out. It was very cold and she wrapped a rug round her. The air stung her throat and tingled on her face; she had never felt so wide-awake.

The moon shone full on the Loch, still shaken by the wind and breaking the silver into a thousand pieces. The clear shape of Ben Carrick was sharp against the stars, almost, the moon was so bright, she could see the shadows of the cliffs and corries. Mel Vannie, Ben Lair and Slioch were each outlined, snow-capped and immovable and somehow comforting by their solidness. Left bulged the shoulder of Carn Mor, right was the flat country and the tree-humped islands, dark on the silver water. The moon was as bright and as silver as a sixpence, an old sixpence, rubbed flat in one corner, not yet full, and the vast continents and hills on her face seemed close to-night. About the chimneys of the croft and back in the wood all that was left of the storm lurked in the shape of a frosty breeze, cold and sharp. The grass was still wet with rain, from the feel of the air it would be frost in the morning. Far away and faint in the hills by Loch Dubh a stag roared and was answered by one yet fainter. If the cold weather held they would be all round the house, roaring and fighting. It was an eerie sound, here in the quiet night, and Fiona's thoughts went ranging further and further as she knelt, wrapped in the rug, looking out on to the silver water. Quietness and emptiness and peace seemed to press upon the world, leaving her the only person in it. She found she was able to think more clearly about all the things that troubled and puzzled her ordinarily: she

THE MOON SHONE FULL ON THE LOCH.

realised briefly and half-unconsciously, how much too much self and material things mattered to her, that somewhere, somehow, there was an answer and a meaning to so many things that seemed pointless, that the quietness and beauty of this night was more important than almost anything else. Her eyes on the stars, she found herself on the brink of some great truth that had eluded her and every one else in the world, the meaning and the purpose of life. She felt detached and one with the stars.

The rattle of ashes falling in the grate startled her.

"Bother," said Fiona, her train of thought completely lost.

She felt cold and alone and small. She turned back to the room. The candle on the table had burnt sideways, heaping a mountain of wax down one side and lighting the dark room with a bright yet gentle glow. She unwrapped herself from the rug and hurried over to the bed, putting the candlestick on a chair beside it. Suddenly she felt sleepy.

She could hear Jean's soft and steady breathing and saw the hump she made under the bedclothes and a gleam of her fair hair. Hurriedly she climbed between the cold clean sheets and lay curled up, not daring to stretch her toes in to the icy unexplored corners of the bed. We must have a warming-pan, she thought. She turned on her side, watching the candle flicker, deciding not to read though the book lay close to her hand. She leant and blew out the light and smelt the bitter smell of a snuffed candle. Suddenly the room was dark and full of the sound of the clock ticking, then gradually the moon lit the windows and fell in silver squares on to the floor.

Fiona uncurled a fraction and snuggled her nose into the pillow. Again a stag roared and again it was answered, faint and far away, in the cold hills round Loch Dubh.

CHAPTER XI

JEAN'S CAVE

Wednesday, 20th December

THE SUN was over the top of Ben Carrick by the time the golden eagle from Carn Mor steadied his great wings and swooped on each current of air from the hill down over the Carna Loch. His bright telescopic eye raked rock and peat-hag, tuft of heather and stunted tree, alert for the twitch of a whisker, the flick of a tail, the washing of a face. Something new and unknown caught his eye and he soared north-east, across acres of tawny heather and sparkling threads of burns to the little bay opposite Bearnach. Something new and unknown was happening. From out of what he had come to consider as a heap of rocks and a useful hiding-place for rabbits and shrews, was coming a curl of blue smoke. A fair-haired boy in a green jersey was running down to the burn with a bucket and whistling as he went. The eagle swooped lower, the air rushing through the great pinions, his strong feet curled, his hooked head and bright eyes turning suspiciously. The boy, splashing cold water on his face, looked up as he heard the rush of wings, and the eagle, disgusted, turned and soared back, up the shoulder of Carn Mor and over the other side.

Fiona had awakened late that morning after her vigil the night before. The room was grey with the dawn of nearly half-past eight when a stifled whisper and the clatter of a bucket interrupted her dream and jerked her into reality. Jamie was over by the fireplace, his fair head tousled. The room looked grey and forlorn and depressing, the chairs crumpled and scattered with rugs, the grate full of ashes and cinders, muddy footmarks on the floor.

THE GOLDEN EAGLE FROM CARN MOR.

"Hallo!" Jean said, from the next bunk as she saw her sister move.

"I'll bring some more coal in," and Jamie took out the bucket while Fiona lay back drowsily.

The room grew lighter but it was very cold. Through the open door to the backyard came the vigorous sound of coal being shovelled, and a robin singing. Fiona drew the blankets up to her chin. She felt lazy and hoped Jamie would light the fire.

"I'm going to get up," announced Jean, and sprang firmly out of bed. "Come on."

"It's cold." Fiona was still only half-awake.

"The others'll be in soon." Jean dressed like lightning. That statement had the effect of rousing Fiona. Hugh and Ninian, and certainly Sandy, would be sure to throw a cold sponge or something equally nauseating at her. She followed Jean's example and then sent Jamie down to the burn for water.

By the time he returned, his face cold and pink from the icy splashing it had had, Fiona was raking out the fire and Jean tidying up the room.

"It's going to be a simply super-day," said Jamie, drying his face on the roller towel behind the door. "It froze last night and now the sun's shining. Do let's hurry, there's snow half-way down Ben Carrick."

"The hinds'll be lower," was all Fiona said to that as she set a match to the paper. The room was filled with the smell of newly lit sticks. Fiona hovered anxiously above them until they caught, then went to wash her face. Cold though the burn water might be it certainly woke one up. As she was slooshing madly in the sink, Hugh appeared with a razor in one hand and a sponge in the other, demanding hot water for shaving.

"Give us a chance," said Fiona. "You can't expect miracles."

"Don't tell me you've only just got up?" demanded Hugh. "Isn't breakfast ready yet?"

Fiona's only reply was to splash him with cold water.

"I'll put on a kettle for you, some time," she added.

Jean and Jamie had opened the front door by now. The cold air came rushing through the cottage, fluttering the curtains and blowing the *Bulletin* on to the floor.

Porridge had been slowly cooking on the stove all night. Fiona looked in and stirred briskly. Kippers or eggs and bacon to follow? Kippers perhaps. They might go bad.

The twins had vanished from sight when Fiona looked round for someone to lay the table and make the toast. They were down by the Loch, breaking the thin ice and throwing stones far out to see whose would splash best.

"Come on with that kettle," said Hugh, leaning in the doorway and grinning at Fiona as she rushed backwards and forwards with frying-pans, bread-knives, milk and plates.

"Make the toast while you're waiting," she said.

"Where's Ninian, by the way?"

"The last I saw of him was the top of his head and a muffled voice saying it was much too cold." Hugh knelt in front of the fire and looked at it dubiously. "I say, this thing hasn't been lit nearly long enough, it won't even warm the toast."

"Well, you'll have to have bread then," said Fiona, frying the kippers over his head.

The cold fresh air had gone to the twins' heads like wine. Fiona had a glimpse of them rushing madly past the windows on their way to the wood. She hoped they would bring back some sticks. The smell of kippers and toast invaded the kitchen, the sunlight fell in a square through the open window, the shaft of light full of dusty specks. Fiona, pausing on her way to the larder for the butter, pulled-to the doors of the box-beds. She decided they looked too untidy.

A shriek from Sandy's room proclaimed that he had got out of bed, and five minutes later his sleepy face came round the door.

"You'll have to wash in cold water," Fiona said before he could open his mouth. "The twins are somewhere up by the wood. If you're going, you might tell them to bring back some sticks."

"Right," said Sandy, vanishing.

For a little while there was peace in the kitchen. The fire crackled as it caught fresh lumps of coal, the kippers hissed and spluttered on the stove, Fiona whistled softly as she laid the table, and outside the robin still sang. Far away came the shouts of the twins and Sandy. Fiona went to the window and looked out. Gone was the magic of silver and black that had entranced her last night. Now the Loch was blue and gold, the hills tawny under the sun and capped with white, the grass outside still crusted with frost, but the same stillness and peace reigned, until it was broken by Hugh burning his fingers on the toasting-fork.

She left the window and went across the hall to the boys' room. She opened the door and looked in. A long hump and a curl of black hair was all that showed of Ninian. And yet he must be awake. Sandy and the twins had made enough noise to rouse the dead. She went over to the bed and pulled back a corner of blanket. A bright blue eye regarded her.

"Come on, Ninian," she said, using her first name for him. "Or would you like breakfast in bed?"

"Is it nearly ready?" he asked, turning over and stretching his arms above his head.

"Just about. Hugh'll use all the shaving-water if you don't hurry." Fiona looked round at the room. "Good heavens, what have you been doing? I didn't know you possessed so many clothes."

Ninian propped himself on an elbow.

"Yes," he said, "it does look a bit odd. Must be young James."

"Rubbish." Fiona picked up a shirt and sock clearly marked with Ninian's name. "Don't leave it in too much chaos, because we must keep a vague semblance of tidiness."

"Can't think why," said Ninian, sitting up. "No one here to mind."

"Well, if you don't mind I don't." Fiona went over to the door. "But you'll have to sweep it and dust and make the beds."

"Shan't bother. Might occasionally smooth my bed."

"You are the limit." Fiona scowled at him. "You know you hate living in a mess and always shriek for someone to come and tidy it up and find your things. No Maggie, so that means me. Why are men so helpless?"

She vanished, unanswered, as a shout from Hugh warned her that the milk was boiling.

By the time breakfast was on the table everyone was hungry, especially the twins and Sandy, having arrived back from the wood, dragging a small tree behind them.

"We must get organised before going out," said Fiona, ladling out porridge. "Let's get plenty of coal and sticks and water in, otherwise it'll be misery if we get back in the dark."

"D'you think the fire'll be out?" asked Hugh, his face still flushed from the toast-making.

"Sure to be. If we leave some sticks near it it'll light quickly. I've seen Maggie do it," said Fiona.

"Wouldn't she be surprised to know how comfortable we are?" Sandy took a large mouthful and was speechless for nearly a minute.

"How did everyone sleep?" asked Hugh, looking at Jamie and laughing.

"Why? Were you very uncomfortable?" asked Fiona.

"No, we only came across each other about once. But the bed's pretty iron-like," said Hugh.

"Mine was lovely," said Jean. "A bit hard but lovely."

"Mine's lumpy," said Sandy, through the porridge. "I shall get curvature of the spine or something?"

"You fuss too much," said Fiona. "Just wait until you haven't made it for several mornings." Her mind was still on the subject, conscious perhaps of the fact that she and Jean would have to tidy their things away whatever happened.

"Do you remember how beautifully neat Fergus's ship was?" said Jean, who was reminded by her box-bed of the bunk she had used in the *Wandering Star*. "Although there were only men on board it was as tidy as anything."

"I expect Fergus is pretty strict,' said James, remembering his stern face.

"I wonder if he ever went back to the cave and found our note," said Sandy. "I don't suppose so."

Breakfast was finished and washed up, beds were aired and made, rooms were swept and dusted, grates were cleaned and polished, wood and coal chopped and carried, the tank filled, the lamps cleaned, the shoes brushed, the stock-pot added to, even the doorstep was scrubbed, sandwiches were cut and tied up, knapsacks filled with them and fruit and beer, the rifle slipped into its case and a clip of ammunition into Fiona's pocket.

"We can't be really ready?" said Sandy.

"I feel quite exhausted already." Hugh got out his pipe and filled it.

"Well, the house looks a dream of tidiness," said Fiona, with housewifely pride. "We've worked jolly hard, too."

"And someone's got to row across to Bearnach Bay," added Jamie. "Feigns."

Everyone else said feigns a fraction of a second later, not that they really minded rowing across to Bearnach.

They picked up the knapsacks. Fiona took the rifle and her glass, Ninian and Hugh their sticks and a coil of rope. The twins and Sandy decided you could look for caves better unhampered but for torches.

"Oh, it is a heavenly day," said Fiona, as she stood still on the grass outside the cottage.

It was cold and clear and sunny. The wind was north-west, strong enough to send the white patches of cloud chasing across the sky and making wavelets break sharply on the sand of the bay. Across on the islands the trees were dipping and tossing, their branches bare and black.

"Come on!" cried Sandy, and they ran down to the boat.

It was hard work pulling across the Loch with the wind dead on the starboard quarter. Spray flew into the boat at extra large waves, and Hugh, looking over his shoulder after they had been going for what seemed hours, found that they were only half-way across.

"Glad we're not bringing the stuff across to-day," said Jamie, dodging a bead of spray.

"The wind'll be behind us from the bothy," grunted Ninian.

Hugh kept his eyes on the cottage, which did slowly, although he doubted it, grow farther away. It looked small and grey and solid above its apron of green grass, it was friendly with its newly painted door and the curtains showing at the windows and a faint wisp of blue smoke blown south-east by the wind. From this angle Carn Mor seemed to rise straight up behind it in an almost sheer precipice, for the few fields were hidden by their stone walls. Right, the small wood was a dark patch on the tawny hillside and high up a burn was falling in a silver thread across a sheer face of rock. Hugh, pulling steadily, looked higher up to where the snow met the wintery hill and beyond that belt, shadowed and seamed by gullies, was the bright sky and the clouds and a black shape that was the eagle.

"We're nearly there." Never had Jamie's voice been more welcome. Hugh, looking over his shoulder, saw the curve of the bay and the peak of rock on the left. They grounded a few minutes later and pulled the dinghy up on the sand alongside the one there already. This was well up the beach by the boat-house and turned bottom up, not used during the winter months.

They followed a rough track beside the burn, that ran out over the sand. At the top of the first rise they could see Lochan Bearnach below them and the pine-wooded island where they had camped two summers ago. It was difficult to believe it ever could have been warm enough to sleep out in the heather in a blanket, now it was too cold even to stand about for long. Left, a burn connected Bearnach with the Little Loch and their track wound away round the edge of that and branched at the far side, the right fork going between the loch and Ben Carrick and round to Carrick House, the left ending up at Lettercarrick half-way down Loch Marba, winding between Ben Carrick and Mel Vannie. This was the track they were going to follow, exploring the south east slope of Carrick and coming back over the hill.

It was good going on the track, made mostly of rock but with the mud frozen hard. Fiona was the first to call a halt, at the far end of the Little Loch. She pulled out her glass and spied out the ground that sloped down to the left from the top of Ben Carrick. Sandy, with no telescope, was the first to spot half a dozen hinds feeding just below the snow-line on the hill facing them.

"The wind's right, too," said Ninian, taking Fiona's glass regardless of her protestations. Having seen the deer he was as keen to get one as she was. "If we don't make too much noise, we can look for the cave and work our way up from beneath them. Not the ideal way, but still."

Fiona snatched back her glass and trained it on the distant brown specks.

"We'll have to be careful," she said.

Jean, who had not seen them, whispered as much to Ninian, who immediately confused her even more by saying:

"Well, you see that flat rock?" when to her all the rocks looked equally flat.

By the time she had seen them Fiona had spied out the ground below the hinds and discovered all available cover. "Who'll shoot?" asked Jamie.

"Let's argue on the way," suggested Hugh, who was growing cold.

They continued along the track, keeping a wary eye on the hinds who were not moving much but staying in a small corrie out of the wind.

"Really," said Fiona at last, "it ought to be Sandy. He saw them."

"Really?" Sandy dared not sound too hopeful.

"I think so," said Ninian.

"Well, in that case you can carry the rifle," and Fiona handed it over. Sandy took it joyfully. He had not dared hope he might be allowed to use it.

They still had a mile to cover across rough boggy ground before they came to the foot of Ben Carrick. Lochans lay on either hand amongst peat-hags and burns and mounds of rock, and several snipe got up and zig-zagged away, making Ninian wish he had brought a gun.

"We must remember that, whoever goes down to the Lodge," he said. "There may easily be a rabbit or two in the wood."

Jamie was the first one to see a big bunch of hinds feeding on the lower slopes of Mel Vannie.

"Oh, look," he said, and stopped. "Masses of them."

Ninian counted fifteen while they stood there.

"Shall we?" asked Sandy.

Ninian shook his head.

"It's poaching," he said, "and they'll get our wind in a minute."

They were very near. Fiona could see them moving about and several lying down, even one scratching.

"I suppose we'd better go on," she said, but they walked with their eyes on the hill.

Suddenly one hind got their wind. They were too far away to hear the short bark of alarm but the rest of the heads came up. The ones that had been lying down were on their feet, all the big bat-like ears were pricked, every head turned towards them. The Stewarts stopped to watch. For a minute or two they stared at one another, then the hinds turned and went cantering off round the side of the hill to the slopes of Ben Lair.

"Oh, well," said Fiona, and led them on.

The track ran along beside a biggish burn, dotted with pools that made Jean's mouth water, and she resolved to come and try them in the summer. Smaller burns came down the hills on either side and ahead the pass narrowed and opened out again above Loch Marba.

"This is as good a place as any for a cave," said Hugh. "Let's start looking."

He and Jamie crossed the burn and went a little way up the lower slopes of Mel Vannie. The others spread out on Ben Carrick, slipping on the steep rocks.

"Not too far up yet," warned Fiona. "And don't make a noise."

They moved slowly on towards Loch Marba, keeping an eye on the track below so as not to wander too far. At one moment Sandy, coming to a slit in a cliff, nearly gave a shout. But it only went in a yard or so and was much too open and obvious to be called a cave. The others were equally unsuccessful.

They met in a sheltered hollow above Loch Marba and got out the lunch.

"Not a sign," said Jamie gloomily. "We've looked so thoroughly, too."

"It's an awfully difficult thing to find, a cave," Hugh said hopefully. "And we've covered very little ground really."

"We may easily have walked over it." Jean bit despondently into a sandwich.

"If it's here we'll find it," said Ninian. "After all someone found it in the first place, somehow."

Fiona leant back in the heather and watched the dark shadows of clouds moving over the water. Loch Marba lay below them, stretching left and right, slender and blue. Across on the opposite shore were the dark pine-woods along the Asheenach road and the grey hotel and scattered white crofts and green fields. Plumes of smoke were smudged above each house and a car roared along the road. On the Loch below them were the islands, dark and wooded, and Fiona could see the pine trees on the largest of them that grew round the grave of the Norwegian princess. It was pleasant sitting here in the sun with nothing in particular to do and the whole day stretching ahead. Vaguely, as she chewed, she hoped the hinds had not moved.

"Where'll we go to-morrow?" Jamie's voice broke in on

her thoughts.

"Somebody'll have to go to the village," she said. "We need more milk and eggs and bread."

"Wish we'd got a cow," murmured Sandy. "Then we could have pints of milk and masses of butter."

"Someone would have to milk it," pointed out Hugh.

"We'd be back by then," said James.

"Six o'clock in the morning? No thank you." Ninian took another sandwich.

"It seems a pity to waste the fields," said Jean.

"The walls need rebuilding," said Hugh. "Which reminds me, we ought to do some gardening."

"It'll be too hard soon." Ninian banged his heel on the ground. "Well, it's heathery here but it'd be hard on the grass."

Lunch finished, they stuffed the paper back in the knapsacks and brushed off the crumbs.

"Let's climb a bit higher and work our way back towards the hinds," suggested Ninian. "The wind's still right and we can go carefully."

"Let Sandy and I go first," said Fiona. "It's no use us all trailing along, and there's much more chance with just two of us on ahead."

"Right. We'll give you quarter of an hour." Ninian leant back again. The other two leapt up, and shouldering the rifle, were out of sight in a few minutes.

It was two o'clock before the others got to their feet and turned their faces to the hill. Ninian and Jean climbed nearest to the summit, Jamie and Hugh spread out below. They walked slowly with the sun before them, half-dazzling them. It was tempting to call out to each other, but, remembering Sandy and Fiona, they were silent. The hill was very steep and it was almost impossible to stop slithering down. Ninian was soon out of sight somewhere around the summit and Jean found herself alone. Hugh and James were beneath her but she could neither see nor hear them. The cold air came buffeting into her face and the heather stalks caught at her feet. At one moment she found herself on a nearly sheer rock and a sudden gust of wind caught her and made her slip, bumping her down into the heather. Below, the hill fell away, rock-strewn. Jean's heart beat faster as she got up and crawled onwards. She looked up but there was no sign of Ninian and she stumbled on, feeling small and alone. There was no sign of a cave either, she looked conscientiously, she wished one of the others were with her. A hundred yards farther on she came over a rise to find the ground fall away into a deep narrow gully down which a burn was hurrying. There were several cavey-looking rocks and Jean, sliding downwards, saw a black hole on the hill in front of her. A cave! Her heart stood still with fright. She hated caves, especially on her own. She decided she would look at the entrance but not go in. To her horror she realised she could not shout her discovery to the others, she might not see them again until after Sandy had shot the hind, or not, as the case might be. She scrambled down and stood for a moment looking for a way over the burn. She knelt by a pool and took a long drink: ice-cold it was and made her gasp. Must be near the snow-line, she thought; Ninian would be in it. She looked for a stick among the rocks but there were none so high up. Well, a stone would be better than nothing. She picked a knobbly one and crossed the burn. It was steep going up the other side and she had to use a hand as well as her feet, so almost before she realised it the cave-mouth was in front of her. She stood up, breathing hard, and swallowed. Oh, how she hated caves. This one was tall and black and thin and a small path was worn to it between the rocks. Trolls. Their little feet would wear just such a path and here she was, alone, unable to call for help unless she brought the united fury and scorn of Sandy, Fiona, and probably Ninian, down on her head. She felt sick with fright and cold and numb. Should she pretend she had never seen it and go back and climb up the hill again farther down? Yet it might be *the* cave. Equally it might have a troll in it. She looked round desperately. There was no one in sight. Clutching the rock in her arms she advanced. The nearer she got the blacker seemed the entrance. Everything was silent but her pounding heart and the eerie whistle of the wind. Except something moved in the cave. She could hear it. Half-hypnotised she took a step closer. Something was breathing, something stamped. With a rush and a grunt two sheep came bounding out. Jean dropped the rock and gave a stifled shriek. The fat silly things. Still there would hardly be a troll in it as well. She picked up her weapon and went on again. Gradually she could see that the cave, dark though it appeared to be at first, was really quite shallow. When she was near to it she could see right in, the walls all round and the back. It was much too bare and open to be the hiding-place of any one, except, she had to admit, a sheep. Boldly she walked in and looked round. It was quite

JEAN DROPPED THE ROCK AND GAVE A STIFLED SHRIEK.

empty, the floor trampled by the sheep but otherwise no sign of habitation, no fire-blackened rocks, no scratchings on the walls. She threw her stone back into the burn and went on and up. Five minutes later a rifle shot and then another echoed over the hill.

Sandy and Fiona had made their way up to where the first fingers of snow crept down from the summit and had then gone on round the hill. They found, as Jean did later, the going more than difficult. In some places Ben Carrick seemed to drop in a precipice to the glen below. After half an hour slipping and stumbling, their ankles aching with the strain of walking sideways, they stopped.

"Must be soon," said Fiona.

"Not nearly yet, we've another half-mile to go at least."

"Can't be, Sandy. Don't forget the hill is smaller at the top than it is down below."

"Not much. We ought to be able to see the Carna Loch before we see the hinds."

"I think we're nearly on them."

"I don't. Come on."

"For heaven's sake don't rush like a mad thing."

"You're tired."

"Don't be absolutely idiotic."

"Well, come on."

Well, if you want to frighten them all. But let's load anyway." She took the clip from her pocket and Sandy put it in. On second thoughts he took the rifle out of its case, which he gave to Fiona. It was not often that she was wrong about anything to do with stalking, but he was convinced that he was right. The rifle under his arm, they hurried on.

So it was not altogether to Fiona's surprise that they came across the hinds as they topped a rise. Two of the beasts were lying down, the rest feeding and moving towards the Stewarts. One animal, ahead and downhill from the others, was almost in a line with Sandy. The farthest was only a hundred yards away. A bark of alarm and the two lying down sprang up: already some were off down the hillside. There was only one thing to be done and Sandy did it.

"Go on. Fire!" Fiona's voice was sharp with excitement.

As she said it the rifle was up to Sandy's shoulder. He fired at a hind just going over the skyline below him. The beast broke into a limping run.

"Quick! You've wounded her!" Fiona was off, down the hill like a flash with Sandy behind her. Below them the hind was limping away amongst the rocks.

Sandy knelt and steadied the rifle. The hind disappeared from view behind some rocks and Fiona and Sandy waited in agony. She reappeared, nearly three hundred yards away, and Sandy fired again. Again the hind disappeared

"You've got her," said Fiona comfortingly. "She'll be amongst those rocks. Come on, let's get down."

They were on what appeared to be a small precipice. How the deer had come down it at such a speed was a mystery. Sandy, looking up, or down rather, saw the other five on the flat ground and cantering through the burn.

"I don't like to say, 'I told you so,'" said Fiona, "but —"

"Sorry," and Sandy was sorry. "I could have sworn I was right, too."

They came across the hind lying dead amongst the rocks. The first shot had broken her near hind-leg, the second had gone through her heart.

"Not too bad, considering." Fiona got hold of a fore-leg and hauled her into the open. "Bother, I've forgotten my knife."

From away up the hill came a shout from Ninian and Fiona answered it.

"Gosh, it's getting cold," she said. "What d'you bet the fire's out."

CHAPTER XII

"IT CAN'T BE!"

Wednesday Night, 20th December

"AND SO," said Ninian, tugging on the rope as they pulled the hind down to Bearnach, "James Stewart came home from Culloden over the hills, and when he got home he found the redcoats waiting for him. Luckily he saw them first, so he went to the cave he had found as a boy and stayed there for ages. Then eventually a French ship came into the Loch to pick up Prince Charlie, but got tired of waiting and went back to France, and James Stewart went with it. Years later he came back, with his wife and children, but he died on board ship."

"He just managed to get a glimpse of Scotland before he died," interrupted Fiona. "Which was lucky, because he'd been longing to for years, all the time he was in France."

"He was going to show his son, Ewen, the cave," continued Ninian. "But of course he never did. So that's why nobody knows about it."

"Two hundred years," said Hugh thoughtfully. "Any amount of brambles may have grown over it or there might have been a landslide."

"Ewen looked everywhere," said Jamie, "but he never found it."

"Well, it's not on the east side of Ben Carrick anyway." Sandy sent a stone spinning down the hill. "But of course there are masses of other places."

"Was he alone?" asked Hugh.

"No, there were four of the clan with him," said Fiona. "Davy's great-great-great-grandfather was one."

"People kept coming and going," said Ninian. "I see

what you mean, Hugh, it must have been a pretty substantial cave."

It was half-past three and they were half-way down the shoulder of Ben Carrick and about two miles from the nearest end of Bearnach. Soon it would be dark and Ninian was hurrying them. He wanted to find the track along by the burn before it was too dark to see. He and Hugh were pulling and Fiona and Sandy acting as brakes when the hill became too steep. The twins carried knapsacks, the rifle and sticks. It was going to be a hellish long pull to Bearnach and it was getting colder every minute, his hand was nearly frozen on to the rope and the others must be as bad. They hardly ever wore gloves as they always lost them. Ninian changed hands on the rope and thrust the cold one into his pocket. He caught Fiona's eyes and she nodded.

"Me too," she said.

Jean's teeth were gritted together to stop them chattering. The sticks caught and tangled in her legs: she had plunged one foot into an icy burn and it now felt as though it was freezing solid. The grey and wintery gleam of Bearnach looked miles away and she almost despaired of ever reaching it. Ninian was taking such long strides that she had from time to time to run. This was most tiring on such a steep slope as the one they were on. Anyway one ray of comfort was that she had been the only person to have found anything approaching a cave. Ninian had looked at her with raised eyebrows and an incredulous grin on his face when she told them she had been right inside and that she was sure it was not the place.

"Really, I did go in, Ninian," she had said earnestly. "Really."

"No trolls?" Sandy had asked.

"Of course not." She could be emphatic now, but she was glad he had not been watching when she first saw the cave's mouth. She hurried on, running a few steps to catch up as the others almost disappeared below her.

The sky was still practically cloudless but now the sun was sinking and the wind, which had been cold all day, had nothing to counteract it. It was a poor sunset, the sky smudged red for a few moments behind the western tip of Carn Mor, then turning an uninspired grey with the dark shadow of the night creeping up behind them.

"Oh, please — please let the fire be in," said Fiona to herself. She could not bear the thought of the dead cold range and the dank icy feel of the cottage. Oh, but she was cold, her jersey and coat might as well be made of paper for all the good they did. She had been led astray by the sunny look of the morning and was only wearing one jersey over her shirt. Never again.

"It must be freezing already," said Sandy, trying to blow smoke-rings with his breath in the cold air.

"I should think it is. I suppose we didn't bring a Thermos amongst all this junk?" asked James, as the knapsack holding the beer bottles slipped off his shoulder for the tenth time.

"I'm afraid not." Fiona regarded her hand and thought it looked the same, although it did not feel as if it belonged to her.

The hill was growing less steep and across the burn ahead rose the slopes of Mel Vannie.

"Keep your eyes skinned for the track, we must be almost on it," said Ninian.

"That's it — no, it's not, it's a peat-hag," said Jamie, ice crackling under his feet.

"Let's stop a minute and get our bearings," suggested Hugh, whose arms were aching.

The hind slid to a standstill. Fiona dropped her rope and put her hands in her pockets. Sandy, Ninian and James went on ahead towards the burn. Jean leant against a rock until it felt as though she was leaning against a block of ice. Hugh lit a cigarette and the orange flame of the match showed how dark it had suddenly become. They stamped their feet and blew on their frozen fingers. Behind them, up the glen, a stag roared, answered by another from Mel Vannie, picked up again by one somewhere near the Corrie, so that the dusk seemed full of them.

"Are they fierce?" Hugh asked as the noise died away.

"Not often, sometimes. I don't think they'd attack all of us together," said Fiona.

"Well, that's something," said Hugh.

A shout from Jamie announced he had found the track.

"Well, stay on it," called Ninian, "in case we lose it again."

He and Sandy came hurrying up and they picked up the ropes once more.

It was nearly dark: Jamie was only just visible.

"We must go carefully," Ninian said. "We don't want to keep losing it."

"We ought to have brought a pony," said James, after two hundred yards or so.

"This won't take us long." Fiona hunched her shoulders under her coat.

It had been dark an hour by the time they reached Bearnach. The moon was a glow in the sky behind Ben Lair.

"Wish it'd hurry up and rise," grumbled Jamie, tripping over a rock.

"Does anybody except me think the wind's dropping?" asked Ninian, who had been turning his head this way and that until Fiona almost asked him if he had got a stiff neck.

"No, definitely not," said Hugh, who had turned his collar up half an hour before but was feeling no warmer.

"Pity. It didn't feel quite so fierce." Ninian stopped for a moment and listened to the waves breaking on the shore of Little Loch Bearnach. The path was rocky here and it was hard work pulling the limp body of the hind. Again a stag roared, much closer this time and Jean jumped, and again he was answered from the Corrie. They went on bellowing for several minutes.

"They sound like lions," said Jamie. "Listen to that one, he's in front of us somewhere."

The night was discordant with the noise, blown backwards and forwards by the wind. The grass and a clump of hazels on the shore of the Loch whistled as it blew through them, the waves splashed and broke on the rocks, again the stag in front of them roared.

"He's unpleasantly near the boat," said Ninian. "Come on."

They hurried on round the Loch and down beside the burn to the bay. On their right they could hear the stag roaring but they did not see him, much to Jean's relief. The hills seemed to be full of them.

"Funny," said Sandy. "We never see so many during the day."

They decided it would be drier to embark the hind before pushing the dinghy down to the water. Here the torches came in useful, and Jean held one while the others heaved and tugged the beast on board. It seemed to take up an astonishing amount of room and weighed, Hugh vowed, more than the heaviest lot of stores.

"That's because the wind's more or less against us," said Ninian, pushing off with an oar. He and Hugh rowed; Sandy, protesting, was sent up in the bows to keep a look-out.

"I shall freeze," he said.

"Well, someone must look out," pointed out Ninian.

"We can't see a thing here, it's absolutely pitch."

"Well, I can't see anything either."

"Look at the top of Carn Mor or something," suggested Fiona, crouched on the bottom-boards, out of the wind.

"Carn Mor's a huge place," objected Sandy.

"See if you can see the islands somewhere on the port

bow," said Jamie. "The wind'll blow us to Loch Dubh if anywhere."

"Gosh, it's strong." Hugh's oar went in deep as they hit a wave outside the bay. Spray flew up and pattered icily on Jean's face. The boat rocked violently and to Ninian and Hugh, rowing, it felt like a gale.

"Better aim for the shore much higher up," said Fiona. "The wind's blowing us down the Loch all the time."

"You're telling me," grunted Ninian.

At one time they were out in the middle of the water, no land in sight but the tops of the hills around them. Doggedly they rowed on, the dinghy tossing madly, the wind buffeting them and half-blinding them by blowing their hair across their faces.

"I can see something," cried Sandy at last.

"What sort of thing?" panted Ninian, not daring to rest his oar.

"Well, the shore, but I don't know which part."

"Let's get closer," suggested Hugh, looking over his shoulder. "We're drifting all the time."

They pulled a bit farther in.

The shore looked dark and rocky and uninviting.

"It's sure to be too much to the right," said Fiona, who had emerged from the bottom of the boat. "Let's go up the Loch a bit."

"Dead into wind," grunted Hugh, his oar almost missing the water as an extra high wave lifted them up.

They struggled along for about a quarter of an hour, recognising nothing, until at last Jamie gave a shout:

"There's a point just ahead! It must be the bay!"

It was. A few minutes later they were in its sheltered water and Sandy was leaning forward to leap ashore.

"Thank goodness," said Fiona. "I'd begun to think we never would make it."

"I'm so hungry," said Jean.

"Who's going to cope with the hind?" asked Sandy,

suddenly struck by that unpleasant thought as he helped unload her.

"Let's not worry about that, let's get indoors," said Fiona, her numbed fingers refusing to obey.

"We can't bring it in with us," Sandy objected.

"Oh, don't be so idiotic, we'll put it in the byre and light a lantern." Fiona could hardly think of anything but whether the fire would be alight.

They hurried up the path, over, or rather through, the burn and up to the cottage. Ninian and James dragged the hind round to the byre; the others followed Fiona inside.

It felt cold and unfriendly. The fire was out. Fiona could have wept.

"First, let's get a lamp lit," said Hugh, cheerfully. He groped his way into the scullery and found the lamp. Lit and hanging from its hook it made the room look a different place.

"I'll rake out the fire," he said, looking at Fiona's cold white face. They crowded round him, thawing their hands on the still-warm stove. Presently Jamie felt thawed enough to take paper and sticks and struggle with the one in their room.

"The soup's still warm anyway," said Ninian, testing it with a finger.

"Let's wash some hind off," said Jean. "Or shall we keep the kettle for tea?"

"Might as well use it, I'm so dirty and it'll be warm at least," said Fiona.

When she returned to the kitchen the sticks were crackling and the flames roaring up the chimney. Sandy had pulled the curtains and turned up the lamp. The clock on the mantelpiece said seven.

"Who'd have thought it?" said Hugh, brushing coal dust off his hands. "Ninian, I hate to suggest it, but wouldn't it be a good thing to cope with the hind now and get it over?"

"Yes, we'd better." Ninian went over to the door. "Get something good and hot organised, Fiona."

"I certainly will," said Fiona, stirring the soup. "Thank you for the fire, Hugh, it was preying on my mind."

"I know it was," said Hugh, smiling.

She consulted with Jean and they decided that the broth they had in the saucepan, plus barley and potatoes, would be sufficient if it was followed by bread and cheese.

"Quickest, too," said Fiona. "Let's only scrub the potatoes."

"And have coffee, instead of tea," said Sandy, on his way out to the byre.

"Right. But it'll take a bit longer," said Fiona. "In fact everything'll take hours unless this fire hurries up a bit."

Luckily the hind took hours to deal with too, and the boys and supper more or less coincided.

"It certainly smells good, whatever it is," said Ninian, coming into the scullery cold and hungry. "Any hot water, Fiona? I simply reek."

Hugh and Sandy joined him at the sink and they scrubbed off all traces of the hind. Jean and Fiona ladled huge helpings of broth into the bowls and Jamie cut hunks of bread. The kitchen was full of the smell and steam and warmth.

"Beer, I think," said Ninian, drying his hands. "Beer, or perhaps a small whisky first, Hugh?"

"I couldn't agree with you more," said Hugh. He went to the cupboard and looked along the shelves.

"None of 'Fergus's Special' left?" he asked.

"No, we finished the last a few days ago. We'll try and get some more one day." Ninian poured out three fingers for himself and Hugh, and a tot for Fiona.

"You're much too young," he told Sandy, but gave him one all the same.

Outside, the wind was dropping and no longer whistled round the chimneys of the cottage and found a way in under doors and windows. Jamie had a look at their fire and threw on another log or two.

"We must do some sawing," he said. "There's lots of wood up at the back."

"Do hurry up. I'm so hungry." Jean could hardly bear to watch the others dallying over their whisky while the plates of broth on the table steamed and grew colder.

"Yes, come on." Hugh drained his glass and sat down. He dipped his spoon into the bowl of broth and promptly burnt his tongue.

"Not so much hurry after all," said Sandy, laughing.

They sat round, sipping.

"What'll we do to-morrow?" Jamie put the usual question.

"There's a bit more of Ben Carrick," said Ninian. "The cliffs above Bearnach."

"I want to climb Carn Mor," that was Fiona, "and see what's the other side."

"There's Ben Fuar, by Loch Gorm," said Jamie, "and Ben Lair."

"Really, someone should go for stores." Ninian looked critically at the butter-dish. "There are one or two things we've forgotten, too."

"We need bread and milk and matches," said Fiona.

Sandy kicked James under the table and mouthed something at him. Light gradually dawned and Jamie's face broke into a grin.

"What's up?" asked Fiona, suspiciously.

"Just something I thought of," said James.

Jean, a spoonful of broth half-way to her mouth, stopped, her mouth open.

"Shsh!" she said. "Listen!"

They were silent, hearing nothing but the wind and the burn racing over the rocks.

"Can't hear a thing," said Fiona. "What was it?"

"There's a stag roaring," said Jamie helpfully.

"No, silly. Do shush for a minute."

Again they were silent, the clock ticking loudly and the fire crackling.

Then they heard it too, and looked at one another. Someone was coming over the rough track that led to Beanault. They could hear feet clattering over the rocks by the burn and then growing silent as they reached the grass, scraping occasionally on rocks.

They looked at one another. No one ever used this long and difficult track to Lettercarrick, perhaps the glow from their windows had aroused the curiosity of a shepherd. But not as late as this, and on such a night. Whoever it was was quite close now. Ninian half-rose and sat down again with a look at Fiona. From outside came the sound of whistling. The kitchen door was open and they sat with their eyes on the hall. A foot rasped on the doorstep, the whistling was clear and tuneful and vaguely familiar.

"It can't be!" said Jean.

"It is!" said Fiona.

The door swung open and the cold air rushed in, making the lamp flicker and the curtains move.

It was.

It was Fergus.

CHAPTER XIII

"SOMETIMES IT'S THERE AND SOMETIMES IT ISN'T"

Wednesday Night, 20th December

HE STOOD in the doorway, his hands in his pockets, his cap pulled over one eye, the same half-smile on his lips that they remembered so well. They stared at him, unable to believe that this slim broad-shouldered figure in the blue fisherman's jersey and old stained trousers would not vanish before their eyes.

"Can I come in?" asked Fergus. "Or shall I go away again? Don't you remember me?"

That broke the spell. They leapt up and crowded round him.

"I thought you were a troll," said Jean.

"Did you get our note?" asked Sandy.

"You must be frozen: come and have some broth." Fiona suddenly felt shy. You could never tell whether Fergus was pleased or not.

Ninian poured him some whisky and Hugh laid another place. Fergus took off his cap and threw it into a corner with a sack he had been carrying. As usual his brown hair needed cutting, as usual his thin, dark face was more brown than his forehead, as usual when he was not smiling the stern lines came round his mouth and his eyes scowled. He stood by the fire, warming his hands and looking at them all.

"You've none of you changed," he said. "Are you all well?"

"Of course we are." Jean was hardly ever afraid of Fergus now. She looked at him with fascinated eyes. "How did you get here?" she asked.

"Before you tell us, come and have some supper,"

HE STOOD BY THE FIRE.

suggested Ninian. "Are you going to stay?"

"May I?" Fergus looked at Fiona.

"Yes, of course, we wanted you to," she said. "This is fun: I can't wait to hear how you got here and everything."

They sat down once more, Fergus with the remains of the broth in front of him. Between spoonfuls, he told them.

"I came over from Taransay in the *Star* yesterday," he said, "and went to the cave and found your note. I had some things to do and I came on up here as soon as I could."

"What have you done with the *Star*?" asked Jamie.

"She's at Beanault. She needed some new ropes. Duncan's seeing to that." Fergus took a piece of bread. "I came up the track from there."

"I can't believe you're here," said Fiona. "How long can you stay?"

"How long *can* I stay?"

"We shall be here for ten days at least," said Ninian. "As long as it's not too uncomfortable."

"It doesn't seem uncomfortable." Fergus looked round.

"By the way," said Hugh, who had not been able to get a word in edgeways, "where's he going to sleep?"

"Oh, heavens!" Fiona looked at Ninian, who raised his eyebrows.

"There is a spare bed," said Sandy.

"I'm not too particular," said Fergus, laughing.

"With a fire the annexe would be all right," said Fiona. "It's quite clean."

"Or another bed in Sandy's room?" suggested Hugh.

"Bit of a squash." Sandy was a little awed at the thought of sharing a room with Fergus.

"Never mind." Fergus took a huge spoonful of broth. "This is good. What a wonderful place. Tell me about it."

They told him how they had found the cottage deserted and cleaned it and brought up the furniture. Fergus did not say much but listened and laughed at their descriptions.

"How's Rory?" asked Jean, remembering his huge young brother.

"He's fine."

"Why didn't you bring him too?" asked Sandy.

"Well, I didn't know I was coming," said Fergus.

"Is he at Taransay?" asked James.

"Yes." Fergus's face grew hard and they knew better than to ask him any more.

Jean took away the plates. They cut huge slices of bread and cheese and chewed slowly.

"Where have you been since the summer," asked Ninian.

"Brittany," said Fergus, laughing at their surprised faces. "I have, really."

"Was it nice?" asked Jamie.

"Some of it. Have any of you realised it's nearly Christmas?" Fergus reached out an arm and dragged his sack out of the corner. "I've brought some things."

He dived in and produced a large turkey and two live lobsters.

"Who's cook — Fiona? Can you deal with that? It should be a good bird." He reached in again and brought out a couple of bottles.

"Fergus's Special?" asked Hugh, and he nodded.

"Not much else but clothes," he said, rummaging, "and some things that'll keep. This, for instance," and he handed a large box of crystallised fruit to Fiona.

"Keep that away from young Sandy," he said. "We'll have it for our Christmas dinner."

Supper finished, they put the things in the scullery and decided to wash up later.

A fish-kettle went on the fire and the lobsters into it for twenty minutes or so.

"Let's look at the annexe," said Fiona. "We'll light a fire

in there to warm it."

Fergus, when shown it, approved. Luckily they had brought spare bedding and another camp-bed.

"We'll put it up later," said Ninian, and led the way back to the kitchen.

With the seven of them in it the room looked rather small. Fergus and Hugh, as guests, were given the armchairs. The others sat round and on the table, or, like Fiona, on the floor. The fire was made up and a kettle set on it, for a later brew of tea. The lamp was trimmed and the three pipes lighted. From time to time the windows of the cottage rattled and the wind sighed in the chimney. Sparks and cinders pattered into the grate, and Fiona, cross-legged before the fire, poked pieces of twig between the bars and watched them flare. For the moment she was content to leave the talking to the others and just listen, throwing a word in from time to time.

Fergus, his pipe well alight, leant back and stretched out his legs. After his long cold walk the warmth and food were making him sleepy.

How pleasant and cheerful it was here, how warm and friendly, how simple and straightforward life seemed after Taransay.

"Tell me what you've been doing, as well as moving house," he said lazily.

"Well," began Jamie, "we've been doing a rather special thing but you may not want to do it too."

"I might," said Fergus, trying not to smile.

"Do you know the story of James Stewart of Carrick?" said Jamie. "The one who went to Culloden and came back here?"

Fergus nodded.

"He was here for ages, hiding in a cave, until he went to France. But nobody knows where the cave is. We know it must be somewhere, so we're searching for it."

"Sounds rather fun." Fergus drew at his pipe. "Where

have you looked?"

"We went up to Loch Dubh yesterday," Sandy said. "We looked pretty thoroughly at the foot of the hills but not far up."

"We went on the east side of Ben Carrick to-day," said Ninian, "and it's certainly not there. We've still got the steep bit above Bearnach to do."

"And Carn Mor," added Fiona, watching the red coals in the heart of the fire.

"Oh, there are thousands of places," said Ninian, "but it's as good an excuse as any for exploring all the hills round about."

"I suppose you haven't heard any stories we haven't about the cave?" suggested Jean.

"No," said Fergus slowly. "No. But I have heard of something. You say that people have looked before and never found it?"

"Yes," said Ninian. "My father and Sandy's used to search and search when they were young, and I suppose everyone else has who lived here."

"And yet it's not a legend but a real fact?" asked Hugh.

"Oh, it's true all right," said Ninian. "But I can't help feeling that a landslide or something has covered the entrance."

"Brambles or a lot of heather would do that," added Hugh.

"Could it be under a waterfall?" suggested Sandy.

"Well, we haven't seen any likely ones," said James. "But what do you know, Fergus?"

"Have you ever heard of the Sithean, the Fairy Hill?" asked Fergus, in his deep voice.

Hugh looked up to see if he was laughing at them but he was perfectly solemn. They shook their heads.

"Funny," said Fergus. "Perhaps the people are less superstitious here than they are at Taransay. But this is more than a superstition. The man who told me about it was a very unromantic sort of person."

"But what is it?" cried Jean, unable to bear the suspense. "Wait and I'll tell you." Fergus was not to be hurried.

"This man told me that the Sithean really existed. He said he had seen it himself but that very few others had."

"What do you mean?" interrupted Sandy.

"Listen, Sandy," said Fiona, annoyed.

"This Fairy Hill comes and goes. Sometimes it's there and sometimes it isn't. He couldn't explain it," said Fergus. "I can't either."

He saw Hugh's puzzled face and smiled.

"But he was speaking the truth," he said. "I'll swear that, and he wasn't drunk either. Somewhere, there's an explanation of course, but he said the fairies did it. Now wouldn't you be thinking that that is where James Stewart must have hidden?"

"Whenever any one looked for it, it wasn't there," said Fiona, entranced at the idea. "Of course it's the answer. But how can we find it?"

"If we walk over every inch of ground we can't miss it," said Ninian.

Fergus looked at him.

"I wonder," he said. "It's easy to say 'walk over every inch of ground,' but in hills like these it's almost impossible."

"It might be some trick of light," suggested Hugh, who found it hard to believe a hill could vanish and reappear. "When the sun shines in a certain way, it throws a shadow. Something like that."

"I dare say you're right," said Fergus, who was Gaelic enough to believe some sort of a charm might be cast over even a hill.

"Did the man say what sort of fairies?" Jean asked, struck by a horrid thought.

"If you say trolls, Jean won't dare go outside again,"

laughed Sandy.

"No, just fairies," Fergus said. "Nice ones, I should think, if they guarded James Stewart for so long."

"Who was the man?" asked Hugh.

"He is a shepherd," said Fergus slowly. "He's very old, he may be dead. I knew him when I was a boy. He lives up here."

"Here?" Fiona sat up.

"Yes, the other side of the hill in Glen Darrach. He saw the hill from Carn Mor."

Then there really was excitement. The room buzzed with questions and suggestions. Fiona could hardly wait to start exploring.

"How do you mean 'sometimes it's there and sometimes it isn't'?" asked Sandy, frowning.

"That's what he said," Fergus leant forward. "He said he saw it and then when he looked again it was gone, and when he went up to it, it wasn't there, and that that happened again."

"We must go to-morrow," said Fiona.

"What about the stores?" asked Ninian.

"Bother the stores!"

"Someone ought to go. There's the post too."

"Bother the post!"

"Hugh and I might be recalled. We can't cut ourselves off entirely," said Ninian.

"I should have thought it better if you did," said Fiona. "Do you want to go back?"

"I wish we didn't have to," said Hugh. "Ninian's right, really, but it's most unlikely that we should be."

"Shall we go, James?" asked Sandy.

"You can take the car if you like," offered Ninian, as a bait. "As long as you leave her by Rody's cottage."

"Can we?" Sandy's face lit up.

"Bags drive back," said Jamie, who would really rather look for the Sithean.

"Well, be careful for heaven's sake," said Ninian. "It's the only car we've got."

Fiona, finding the floor grow hard, pulled another rug under her and leant back against Hugh's knees. She was feeling warm and lazy, much too lazy to get up and make Fergus's bed or to do the washing up. She had a kind of feeling that another bucket of water was needed from the burn and that there were no sticks for the morning. Leaning back, she watched the blue smoke curling up to the ceiling among the shadows thrown by the lamp. We shall be asphyxiated to-night, she thought. It seemed strange to see Fergus sitting in a chair in front of a fire. He belonged to the cabin of the *Wandering Star*, to the cave behind the Stack, to the huge empty rooms of Taransay. The fireside of a croft was as unreal to him as he to it, and yet he seemed and looked happy. Perhaps it was what he wanted, and yet, looking at him, she could not imagine that strange restless person ever settling down anywhere, especially in a croft. He would be wanting to go after a very few weeks. What would happen to him? Where would he stay? What was his island, Hanga, wasn't it? What was that like? Fergus, looking down, smiled at her.

"What are you thinking?" he asked.

"How strange it was to see you sitting by a fire. It doesn't seem right somehow." Fiona spoke without thinking.

"Doesn't it?" Again Fergus's face became stern and distant. "Perhaps you're right."

There was silence. He stared into the fire, his eyes focused on something miles away, his thoughts at the same distance. Oh, Taransay, with your thick walls, your winding passages, with your great rooms and strange corners, with your strength and quiet and sense of absence from the everyday world, with your foundations washed by the waters of the Minch and your roofs and turrets caressed by the winds of the Hebrides, with the sun warm on the old stones and the sleet lashing on the narrow windows, with the tree-trunks burning in the great fireplace and the deerhounds lying watchful, their noses on their paws, with the faces of the Maclouds that went to my making and of others that died and were killed or disappeared, home of my fathers and of my heart, am I never to sit at peace before your fireside and watch the red caverns in the peat and the soft grey ashes? Never that warmth and comfort. Only the cold sea and the keen wind and the wet heather, a cave, a ship or this, this brief happiness to torment me.

"Ninian," said Fiona in a low voice, unable to bear the look on Fergus's face any longer. "Ninian, what are we going to do with the hind? We can't keep it all."

"We must deal with it in the morning," said Ninian, grateful to Fiona for having broken the silence. "How much do we want?"

"Let's keep plenty," said Sandy, anxiously.

Fiona smiled and counted on her fingers.

"Seven of us," she said. "We've got some cold mutton left, and Fergus's turkey and lobsters. Sandy and James can collect the beef. I should think a haunch and chops and a shoulder for soup and stews."

"Sounds good," said James. "Please will you make us a list? We're certain to forget everything."

Hugh pulled a paper and pencil out of his pocket and handed them to Fiona.

"Beef," she said, writing.

"Post," said Ninian.

"Butter, eggs, milk, bread." Fiona scribbled madly. "Matches."

"Paper," suggested Hugh. "The *Bulletin*."

"Chocolate." No need to guess who that was.

"Cabbage or cauliflower or brussels sprouts," wrote Fiona.

"Well, which?" asked Sandy.

"Might as well get them all. Call in at the Lodge and

reassure Maggie on the way down, and she'll have them ready on the way back," said Fiona, and wrote "Reassure Maggie."

"Ask for my other shoes," said Jean. "I've only got one pair."

"More beer," said Hugh. "We're running out, Ninian, and we've got an extra body now."

"Saw for the wood," said James.

"Everyone got enough blankets?" asked Fiona. "And pillows and things? Oh, dishcloths; ask Maggie, Sandy, for two glasscloths."

"Anything else?" asked Ninian, yawning. "I'm getting sleepy."

He looked at the clock. It was eleven.

"Time we were in bed. Oh, help, there's the washing up." Hugh looked round in disgust.

Fiona sat up slowly, stretching.

"I'll make some tea," she said. "You can use the water for washing up and I'll make Fergus's bed." She got up, feeling suddenly tired.

The tea revived them all. The boys disappeared into the scullery, Jean and Fiona, followed by Fergus with his sack, went into the annexe. It could hardly be called warm, but the chill was off the air and the fire looked nice if nothing else. Jean drew the curtains while Fiona thoughtfully hung the sheets in front of the flames for a minute. She looked up at the ceiling, made of laths and tiles.

"It looks most unsafe," she said. "I hope you don't get one on your face in the night."

"I should think a spider's about all that'll come down," said Fergus. He helped her tuck in the blankets.

"The walls look frightfully damp." Jean ran a finger along the plaster. "Don't get a chill."

"I don't suppose the cave's much drier," said Fergus.

Back in the kitchen they found the boys just finishing a

wet and noisy washing-up session. Water seemed to be everywhere and a broken plate lay under the sink.

"What a mess," said Fiona. "I don't suppose there's any china left."

"Only one plate gone," said Sandy, aggrievedly. "Nothing else."

They finished their tea and tidied up the room.

"Jamie, dear," said Fiona, "we must have some more sticks for the morning."

"Well, can I have a lantern?" said Jamie, obligingly.

"We need some water too." Jean peered into the tank.

"I'll go," said Fiona. "I'd like to."

She took her coat from a peg in the hall and the bucket from by the sink. Jamie went with her as far as the byre, then she was alone.

It was cold and dark, with the same wind racing up the Loch and the sky full of bright stars. The wind blew through her hair and into her eyes, making them sting, and the bucket handle was icy to her bare hands. Great purple-black clouds moved over the moon, already up above Carn Mor and silvering the Loch. The birch-wood rustled and sighed up by the fields and a stag was roaring somewhere in the hills. It was too dark to see properly, and Fiona groped her way to the burn more by sound than anything.

She found the flat rock and the pool, and knelt, dipping the bucket into the icy liquid. Foam glistened white round the rocks and the stars flickered on the broken water. Despite her cold hands she stood for a minute listening to the night, to the quietness of the great hills. Then she turned back to the cottage, small and square, its glowing windows a safeguard against all perils of the night. She walked back over the grass, trying not to hurry as she remembered how, when a child and out at night, she had been convinced that something was following her. She must not and could not look round, but once inside and

DIPPING THE BUCKET INTO THE ICY LIQUID.

the door shut she would be safe. Even now she could feel a qualm of fear as she saw the distance between herself and the croft.

Someone was out on the grass down by the Loch, she could see the shadowy figure and the glow of tobacco. Hearing the bucket handle squeak, he came towards her, a tall, quiet figure, his face lit by his pipe.

"Hullo, Hugh," she said, and they walked back together to the house.

CHAPTER XIV

HUGH'S CAVE

Thursday, 21st December

FERGUS woke as usual, swiftly and completely, not lying awake half-drowsy and trying to recapture the fast-fading dream but with unblinking eyes and mind alert. The room was cold so he pulled up the blankets and lay watching the dusty rafters and clotted spider's webs dangling from the corners. The plastered walls were patched with damp and long cracks ran across them. The half-open window rattled as the wind shook it, and Fergus could see, from his bed and without sitting up, the foothills of Ben Carrick and the sky, already glowing with the dawn. It should be a fine day, sunny and windy and a clear view from the hill. He resolutely shut his mind away from all that troubled him and lay there thinking of the present, of the few days ahead and of the fun of them. So unlike anything else he did, he might be a different person, and it was nice to feel that the Stewarts knew only that different person and were apart, but from the briefest meeting with his brother Colin, from the rest of his life.

He lay still, listening to the first early morning noises of the croft — a robin singing piercingly from one of the bent apple trees in the garden, the sound of a door being shut quietly and of someone creaking as they turned over in bed in the next room. Then came the muffled rattle of the grate being cleaned, and somebody flashed past the window: it looked like one of the twins.

Fergus decided to get up.

He dressed quickly because of the cold. The old blue trousers and jersey he had worn yesterday were put on again — he had brought nothing else. There was no sound coming from the room next door so Fergus pushed up the window and jumped out.

It was, as he had thought, a lovely morning. White horses still raced down the loch but the sun took the keenness out of the west wind and shone, gold and pink, upon the snow-covered hills. The grass sparkled with frost, not yet thawing, and on either hand the hills were clear and sharp-lined, the rocks and burns and corries, the tawny grass and green heather and brown peat standing out clearly as though seen through a magnifying glass. Fergus took a deep breath and then walked slowly along by the wall to the left. The ground became rougher as the short clipped grass was superseded by heather and bracken. After about two hundred yards the stone wall turned to the left, and the small wood started fifty yards or so up the hill.

Fergus, hearing the noise of sticks breaking, walked slowly up to see who it was. He pushed his way through the thin trees, a confusion of birch and rowan, hazel and pine and a few small oaks, and carpeted with mossy grass and sphagnum, until he heard someone whistling: rather a blowy whistle that left out the high notes. Coming round a large rock he saw Jean, her fair hair bright against her red jersey, picking up sticks. He leant, watching her. She was trying to whistle his song, "Oh, who will go with Fergus now?" and getting it wrong. After the third attempt Fergus whistled it himself, and then laughed at her amazed face.

Jean, looking up as the clear notes dropped into the morning air, could not at first see Fergus. She knew it was him, because she would know his whistle anywhere, and then she heard him laughing.

"Where are you?" She turned then and saw him leaning against the rock, his face half-hidden by the shadow of the trees.

"Oh, Jeannie, why do you look so anxious?" he asked, as she stared at him, her eyes large above her armful of sticks.

"I was surprised," she said. "You are up early."

"Well, it's a lovely morning." He came towards her. "Let me help. Any kind of sticks?"

"Yes, any'll do. I've got almost enough."

They pushed their way through the trees, several rabbits scuttling away in front of them. Fergus reached up and pulled down dead branches.

"Fiona will be pleased," said Jean. "These'll last days."

As they approached the cottage it was plain that the boys were awake and getting up. Loud sounds of splashing came from the scullery where Sandy and Hugh were washing in the icy burn water, with Fiona beside them trying to fill a saucepan under the tap.

"Oh, Sandy, stop splashing, I'm simply drenched." She wiped her face.

"Well, go away, I'm washing! Ouch!" cried Sandy, blinded with soap.

"Serve you right, get out of the way." Hugh pushed him aside, and groped his way to the roller-towel. Ninian appeared with a toothbrush, having been cleaning his teeth at the burn, his hands blue with cold. Jamie was putting on his socks in the kitchen, where they had been drying all night.

"My shoes are as stiff as stiff," he grumbled, forcing his feet into them.

"We might get some dubbin. Don't forget," said Fiona, stirring scrambled eggs in a large pan.

Breakfast took longer than usual as they had to discuss the best way up Carn Mor and the most likely places to search. James could hardly bear not to be going with them but was consoled by a whispered conversation with Sandy. Fiona could see they were up to something, but what she could not think.

"Let's go down to the point," Ninian said, "and climb from there. Then we can work our way back and come down above the croft."

"What about the rest of the hill the other side of the croft?" asked Hugh.

"We can do that to-morrow. I think the Loch Dubh end is most likely, myself. What about you, Fergus?"

"I don't know." Fergus leant back, his eyes on the slope of Ben Carrick that showed through the kitchen window. "I hardly remember what's over the other side."

"Ben Derg Mor, the Big Red Hill, is the next one," said Fiona. "But I've never been there. And beyond that a loch and beyond that my hill, Sgurr Fiona, the White Peak, higher than all of them."

"Can we go there?" asked Jamie.

"It's too far," said Ninian reluctantly. "James Stewart would never have been hidden there."

"We might go one day, perhaps," said Jean.

"We might," agreed Ninian.

"This end's the highest end of the hill, too," added Sandy, still thinking about Carn Mor. "Pity we're going to the village, because I should have liked to have climbed it, but there's masses more."

"We might find the cave," pointed out Jean.

"Bet you don't."

"Well, we might."

"If we haven't found it after to-morrow's search let's go and see the old shepherd," suggested Fergus.

"Oh, do let's. How do we get there?" Fiona thought he sounded intriguing.

"He may not still be alive," Fergus said. "But anyway, there's a track up from this end of Loch Dubh, between Carn Mor and Ben Fuar. It's pretty steep, but a lovely place. Of course we might find the cave on the way."

"Come on, let's get started, there's masses to do." Fiona stood up. "I'll cut sandwiches if someone'll wash up, and Ninian, what about the hind?"

"Hugh and I'll deal with it."

Ninian led the way towards the byre. "Better take the meat to the shop, Sandy."

"What about our lunch?" asked James.

"Have it at the Lodge," suggested Fiona. "Maggie'll love to see you and she always has masses to eat."

"Perhaps she'll give us a cake. We've finished the other one," said Sandy.

An hour later they were ready to start.

The others helped Sandy and James carry the venison down to the boat.

"Have you got the list?" asked Fiona.

"Yes." Jamie fluttered it in the wind.

"For heaven's sake don't do anything idiotic." Ninian banged the ground with his stick, impatient to be off.

"No, we'll be as good as gold," said Sandy, with a suspiciously innocent face.

"Come on." Fergus had already started. The others followed him along the shore, glancing back to watch Sandy and James slowly pulling the heavy boat down the Loch.

They walked fast until they came to the point separating Carna and Loch Dubh. Although the sun was bright the latter looked as black and gloomy as ever, somehow it seemed as if the sun never got past those high hills to warm the dark water, which, compared to Carna, was calm and still.

"It looks just the place for a cave," said Fiona, as they stood on the point looking east.

"We've walked all along there so we know there's no Fairy Hill, unless it literally does disappear," said Hugh.

They looked long at the hillsides, trying to see if a shadow would fall and reveal another smaller hill, but there was nothing. No shadows fell on those steep dark hills; they remained black and inscrutable above the silent Loch.

"Well, there's nothing there," said Ninian at last, turning away. "Is it worth looking on the way up, Fergus?"

"I don't know." Fergus glanced at Fiona. "Myself, I think we should search for the hill and when we find it, then we can find the cave."

"I agree," said Fiona. "Of course, if we see a large inviting-looking opening in the hillside we won't ignore it. What about you, Hugh?"

Hugh, who was as doubtful about the existence of the hill as he was about finding the cave, agreed with her.

"Come on, then," said Ninian, and started towards the hill.

Typical, thought Hugh, after the first few minutes, that he should have chosen the steepest part. The ground seemed to rise unendingly perpendicular before him and it was impossible to see enough of the hill on either side to make it worth looking for caves. They climbed on for about twenty minutes, then Ninian stopped and looked round.

It certainly was a glorious view, even though they were much less than half-way up. They could see the black dot of the boat as it crawled along amongst the islands. Away down to their right was the croft, invisible behind the little wood. The wind felt strong enough to blow them off the face of the hill.

"It is steep," said Jean, her heart pounding. Looking down it did not seem as if they had come far, but it felt like miles. Above, the hill sloped up, its summit out of sight.

"We shall come to the snow soon," said Fiona, struck by the thought. "I hope it's not too deep."

They were directly above the point now, the hill curving round Loch Dubh to the east. About two hundred yards to their right a burn was falling down a steep gully left, the ground fell away sharply, almost a cliff, and then sloped on and up.

"Let's spread out a bit," suggested Ninian, pausing by a tall rock. He leant against it, looking down the way they had come.

HE LEANT AGAINST IT.

"I can see the sea!" cried Jean, delightedly.

"There's Skye," said Ninian, recognising the tall peaks beneath which Sandy lived.

"Doesn't the sea look lovely?" Fiona's voice was wistful. There still were white horses out in the Loch, but the water glinted under the sun and the rocks on the headlands were white with spray.

"I can see Lewis," said Fergus, in his deep voice, and Fiona glanced at him. The far-away look she knew so well was back in his eyes, his face stern and inscrutable.

"Can you see Taransay?" asked Jean, staring in the same direction.

"I can always see Taransay," said Fergus.

They spread out along the hill, Ninian going to the edge of the gully on the right with Jean next to him, then Fergus with Hugh beyond him and Fiona on the edge of the precipice. They climbed slowly, like beaters keeping in line, watching each other out of the corners of their eyes. It always seemed as though the next person had a more likely clump of heather or fall of rocks to explore and it was tempting to poach on his beat. Also it was hard not to look round and scan the ground between the track and Ben Carrick, between Ben Carrick and Mel Vannie, between Mel Vannie and Ben Lair, and on round across Glen Tulacha and the shoulder of Ben Fuar to where the burn from Lochan Feith roared down to Loch Dubh beside the pony-track to Darrach. It was such a lovely view, the bright slips of blue water that were lochans; the dark chocolate of peat and the emerald and rose and rust of sphagnum moss; the great grey elephantine rocks coated with yellow crottal and lichen; the golden-tawny grass of the flat country, and bogs patched with pine-green heather and seamed with burns; the hills themselves shouldering their way up, no two the same yet all cut and crossed with gullies, rock-strewn, white-capped, with, through the snow, black rocks sticking up, down by their foot bare winter woods and rusty bracken clustered round burns and in small sheltered pockets.

On Fiona's left was the precipice. Ahead she could see that it curved into a shallow corrie and then out again, sloping gradually once more. Across on the other rim of this corrie half a dozen hinds were feeding, out of the wind. Fiona, looking to her right, saw Hugh standing on the top of a rock and whistled to him. He came scrambling across the steep face and they watched the beasts together, about six hundred yards from where they were standing.

"Wish we'd brought the rifle," whispered Fiona.

"Well, we've already got one hind to deal with," Hugh reminded her. They watched for several minutes, until a gust eddied round the corrie and the hinds got wind of them. Each head with the widespread ears came up, the beasts stood watching for a moment or so, and then turned and trotted off over the hill.

"Pity," said Fiona, and they climbed on up towards the snow.

As she climbed past the head of the corrie she looked down into it. A burn ran down the centre in a well-worn, rocky bed, a cavey-looking place but no sign of one among the rocks. The place must be somewhere near a burn; James Stewart could not have lived long without water and would not have wanted to walk far for it. Yet this corrie was too shallow and open, more of a curve in the face of the hill. She stood still a moment, brushing the hair off her forehead and taking a deep breath of cold air. Ahead the hill climbed steeply, almost too steeply, and yet it would mean a big detour to go round by another way; left the ground dropped; right was Hugh. She took her hands out of her pockets and pulled herself up by the rocks.

After fifty yards or so the ground flattened out into a small cup scooped out of the hillside. On either side the hill continued, jutting out past this enclosure like two arms and sloping steeply up above. The floor was carpeted with grass, short and green, unlike the long dead stalks on the hill all round.

Fiona stopped, entranced. Here it was warm and still and sheltered from the wind, so steep was the ground below that it seemed as if she was standing on a chip out of a precipice. Was the place too good to be shared or should she call them all? No, not all. She climbed up the left-hand slope and saw Hugh struggling along a little farther down.

"Hugh!" she called. "Come here."

"Found it?" asked Hugh, rather breathless.

"No, but something equally nice."

In a few moments he had scrambled up and over the rim of the little cup. He sat down on the short grass to regain his breath, feeling, as Fiona had felt, that he was poised between sky and earth. Looking over the edge, the steep hill rolled on and down, smoothly, till it ended in the orange-gold bog-grass on the point. Carna lay to the right, blue under the sun, and left was the curved, overhung Loch Dubh, ahead the hills, the flat country and the sea.

"What a wonderful place," said Hugh at last.

"Isn't it peaceful and quiet?" said Fiona. "What a lovely place in the summer, to spend all day here, in the sun with a book."

"Eagles must feel like this in their eyries." Hugh leant back and looked up into the spinning blue.

"That's a good name for it, The Eyrie," said Fiona. "I suppose we must go on, though."

"I'd like to stay." Hugh smiled.

"Well, so would I, in a way. But I want to see what's over the top."

"I know the feeling."

"I shall come here often," said Fiona, as they climbed on. "You'll never have time," Hugh teased her.

"One day I shall."

He shook his head, disbelieving. Fiona would always

want to see what was over the top.

They had been climbing through the snow for about half an hour when they heard Ninian's voice calling that he was at the summit. They gave an answering shout and another shriller one came from Jean, a little higher up than they were.

The snow was not deep here although occasionally they plunged into a drift up to their knees. Their boots scrunched on it and left an uneven trail of footprints. Here and there a lone forlorn grass stuck through it and behind rocks the ground was bare.

"I don't believe this hill has got a top," panted Hugh.

"What an awful thought. D'you mean we shall suddenly find we're half-way down the other side?" Fiona, as usual. was going at a tremendous pace and hardly breathless.

"It wouldn't be sudden for me," said Hugh. "I should know it at once."

Another, nearer shout came from Ninian, and a few moments later they saw him and the others standing by some rocks. Suddenly before them, they could see the hills of the next range, Ben Derg Beg and Mor and the hills beyond.

"We're here!" cried Fiona, hurrying on.

Below them Carn Mor dropped down to an expanse of hillocks and lochs and burns until it rose again at Ben Derg. Carn Mor was not the kind of hill with a definite top but was more like a down with a long rounded back, wide and almost flat in places.

The others came to meet them, cold with waiting.

"We found a nice place," said Fiona, in explanation. "Not a cave but a sort of scoop, lovely and warm too."

"Inconsiderate brutes," said Ninian, shivering. Certainly it was cold here on the summit.

"Where now?" asked Hugh.

"Let's get out of the wind," suggested Fergus. "I'm frozen."

THEY COULD SEE THE HILLS OF THE NEXT RANGE.

With a last look round at Carna and the sea they turned and hurried down the hill.

"No sign of a Fairy Hill," said Jean, disappointedly. She had been half-expecting to see it directly she was over the top, and now there was nothing but a large shallow glen, dotted with lochs and hillocks, rising up again to Ben Derg.

"Where are we?" asked Fiona. "I've never been here before."

Ninian looked round him, finding his bearings. "That's Lochan Cnapach, the Loch of the Hillock," he said, pointing down to their right. It was a small round blue patch of water at the top of the glen. "And that's Lochan na Bearta," he added, pointing left. "Ben Derg's the one ahead, then Sgurr Fiona, then Loch Bruaich."

"Let's go down to the Lochan and along the glen to the next one," suggested Fergus, who, like Jean, had been half-expecting to see the Fairy Hill once they were over the skyline of Carn Mor.

Fiona explained her theory that the cave must be by a burn, and they agreed.

"Don't forget the Fairy Hill depends on light and shade for its elusiveness," said Ninian. "It might be anywhere quite unexpected," and he turned and looked left along the hill to Ben Fuar.

Fergus had already started down towards the Loch and the others followed. It was so long since he had been here, a boy, that he had half-forgotten what it looked like. Yet it was as he remembered, the rough glen and the two lochans.

They were silent on the way down. All of them were disappointed. The shepherd's story had sounded so much as though it had been true and that the hill would be there below them. Certainly, there were hillocks in the middle of the glen, but they could see the whole way to the foot of Ben Derg and there was nothing remotely like a Fairy Hill amongst them.

"Look, ptarmigan," said Jean suddenly, and they stopped, looking where she pointed. In their winter plumage they were almost indistinguishable from the snow. So seldom did they see human beings that they had no fear of them, leaving small tracks in the snow, and ran about quite close. Hugh had noticed these tracks up on the summit but had paid no attention to them. Now, as he looked more closely, he could see the footprints of a wild cat and the long, loping track of a rabbit.

Lochan Cnapach was a nice small loch, almost round with a burn that ran down to Lochan Feith. They sat on its shores on a huge fallen pine-trunk and ate their on sandwiches. The pine was a giant, a relic from the time when the West Coast had been wooded and covered with these trees.

"It must have been lovely," said Fiona, biting into a hard-boiled egg. "Think of all these hills covered with huge pine trees."

"And not planted in rows or anything, just at random," said Hugh, thinking of the neat lines of pine and larch where a hill belonged to the Forestry Commission.

"D'you suppose that in a thousand years or so the rain will have washed all the earth away and leave only the bare rock?" asked Fiona, who had read that somewhere, and been haunted by the thought of her beloved hills barren and grey.

"Who knows?" said Fergus, looking at a long bare rock below the snow-cap on Carn Mor. "It's a sad thought, but in a thousand years so much will be changed, and people too, perhaps, that no one will like or want the things we do now."

"It may be less than a thousand years," said Hugh, thinking of the people.

"It may, indeed," said Fergus, but he was thinking of the hills.

"I don't think people will change." Jean looked around her at the stern beauty and the clear line of Ben Derg against the sky. "I think they'll always want hills. They're in the Psalms."

"Perhaps there won't be time," said Ninian. "Life will get faster and faster until no one knows what they're looking for."

"We'll always know." Jean was unconvinced. "And our children and their children."

"I think you're right, Jean," said Hugh, surprised at Jean's insistence. "I hope you are."

"Your children's children may not want to live here," suggested Fiona. "They may be bored stiff."

"Or have to work," put in Ninian with a smile.

"You can still work and yet live here," said Fergus quietly.

He had been silent, listening to them, knowing the truth in his heart as he had found it.

"Yes, but if you lived somewhere else and only lived here in your heart." Ninian leant forward. "Your children couldn't be expected to. They wouldn't know anything about this kind of place."

"My children?" Fergus's mouth twisted in his sideways grin as if he found the thought amusing. "My children are about as improbable as —"

"As the Fairy Hill?" suggested Ninian.

But Fiona, reading more than amusement in Fergus's face, pointed upwards at an eagle floating out from Carn Mor and so changed the subject.

They buried the eggshells and sandwich-papers in peat around the Small Loch of the Hillocks and walked on north-west under the steep shoulder of the hill. They were some way up, even here on the moderately flat ground, about seventeen thousand feet above sea-level, and Carn Mor rose sharply beside them.

"Just the place for a cave," said Fiona, looking up.

"If your theory about a burn is right this isn't a good place," said Ninian, looking about him.

"There are plenty of little burns," said Jean, jumping one, "and the Loch."

"These'd dry up." To Ninian's long legs that size of burn was negligible. "And the Loch's probably a bit brackish."

They walked on in some depression. It was proving, as Fergus had said, much more difficult than it sounded. The hill just was not there. The only shadows on the slopes of Ben Derg were those thrown by corries, there was no question of anything being in between where they stood and the next hill, the tawny grass and grey rocks were unbroken. The only consolation was the sight of masses of deer. There really were masses. Fiona had brought her glass and for some time they watched a herd of about twenty hinds feeding across the glen.

"I wonder what the others are doing?" said Jean, as

they walked on.

"Probably just driven into the ditch," said Ninian, who regretted his offer of the Ford.

"Sandy's really quite good," Fiona reassured him.

"So's Jamie, but they're so mad when they get together," said Ninian.

"Perhaps they'll have some tea ready for us," suggested Hugh. "That is, if they get back first."

"Oh, they'll do that all right," said Ninian.

It was half-past two by the time they reached Lochan na Bearta. This lay below them as the glen sloped down steeply, and left Carn Mor curved back as the mouth of the glen widened. Still there was no sign of the Fairy Hill, nor even of a cave. Fiona had begun to feel that perhaps it was easier to look for the cave, there was a definite story about that. And yet Fergus's shepherd had seen the Hill.

"Shall we go down?" asked Jean, looking at the Loch with a speculative eye.

"We ought to be getting back," said Ninian. "We've a long way to go and it'll be dark before we're home."

So they turned reluctantly from the lochan and set their faces to the hill once more.

"We won't have to go so high this time," said Fergus, looking along the ridge.

They were spread out along the face of the hill, finding the slope a good deal less steep than before, when a shout from Hugh made them turn and then hurry towards him.

"What is it?" called Fiona.

"A cave of sorts." Hugh's voice sounded less enthusiastic than it had at first.

They crowded round him, looking at the dark triangular hole in the hillside.

"I've forgotten the torch," confessed Jean.

"You're a helpful person to take looking for caves, I must say," said Fiona. "Has any one got a match?"

Three boxes were produced. No one seemed over keen

to be the first to crawl into that small black hole. A rock overhung the entrance and large boulders were scattered all round. It was impossible to see into it at all, but it seemed almost too small for what they were looking for.

"No Fairy Hill," said Fiona.

"Wait." Fergus smiled. "We may all disappear with it."

"Who's going in first?" asked Ninian, rattling his match-box. "Come on, Hugh, you found it."

"Well, all right." Hugh got down on his hands and knees. "You might come in after me if I don't reappear in about ten minutes."

"Right," said Fiona, laughing.

They watched him crawl into the entrance and strike a first match. To them the light seemed microscopic, to Hugh it was not much better. There was nothing directly in front of him so he crawled on, feeling above his head in case he could stand, but the rock pressed down as low as ever. He looked behind him, but the daylight half-blinded him and he turned back again. There was a horrid musty cavey smell, but it seemed dry so far and not inhabited by dead sheep or anything else unpleasant. He struck another match and was surprised to find himself face to face with the wall. He reached out a hand and could touch rock on three sides and his head. Half a crawl to the left and he could touch the wall there too. He started to back out.

"What's the matter?" came Fiona's voice.

"Much too small." His own was muffled. "Go in and see. I can touch the walls all round."

"No scratchings or carving?"

"As a matter of fact I didn't look, but as I could hardly move my arm it's not likely to be the place." Hugh rubbed earth from his coat. "Go in and have a look."

"Does it smell?"

"Not much."

Fiona disappeared with the matches and returned a few minutes later saying there was not so much as a chip out of the walls.

"No more successful than mine," said Jean.

"Well, we've all seen it, which is more than we did with yours," said Hugh, grinning.

"Oh, Hugh!" Jean's eyes became, as he knew they would, larger than ever. "Oh, Hugh, really it was there!"

"I know it was, idiot," said Hugh.

CHAPTER XV

SANDY AND JAMES GO SHOPPING

Thursday Night, 21st December

A COLD BLUE evening had set in by the time they came over the top of the hill. It was freezing hard and they hurried, their nailed shoes scraping on the rocks. Carn Mor had sheltered them, but now as they came down the other side the icy wind struck them, making them plunge their hands even deeper into their pockets.

"Can't see a light from the croft," said Ninian, as they slid and scrambled downhill. It lay directly beneath them and they could see the dark patch of roof.

"Perhaps we're too far away," suggested Fiona.

"They may not be back yet," added Hugh, straining his eyes in an attempt to see the boat.

"They must be back." Ninian looked down the Loch. Apart from the wooded islands its iron-grey surface was unbroken.

"They may be there," said Fergus. "Perhaps they haven't lit the lamps yet."

This strange wintery blueness was like a cloud of smoke. Ahead of them Ben Carrick was almost black and they could see no farther than that.

"It is dark for four," said Fiona.

They plunged on down the hill, at moments their legs almost running away with them. They scrambled over the broken wall round the highest of the fields.

"Sandy! James!" called Ninian.

There was no reply. The small window turned a dead eye towards them, no smoke curled out of the chimneys into the cold air, the back door remained shut.

The next wall was in good repair and had to be climbed

over, then there was the burn to cross, their feet slipping on the wet stones and crackling the ice.

No lantern glow came from the byre, no sound of sticks being chopped nor wood sawn, no shout of laughter that was never long absent when Sandy and James were together.

Fiona and Ninian looked at one another.

"They're probably hiding." Fergus's deep voice was reassuring.

Jean opened the door and they followed her into the house. It was dark and cold, a faint glow coming from the last embers of the fire and the dusk showing more blue than ever through the small windows.

"Perhaps they're having tea at the Lodge: Sandy would think of that," said Fiona, suddenly inspired.

"That sounds an excellent idea," said Hugh. "What about some for ourselves? I'm cold."

Ninian went to the door.

"I'm going to see if the boat's back," he said, and disappeared.

Fiona made up the fire, Hugh trimmed and lit the lamp, Jean brought out cups and saucers, and Fergus leant against the table and watched. It amused and intrigued him to see them, he felt so out of place himself. He could manage well enough in the *Wandering Star*, where the only range was a primus and cups and pots hung ready to hand, where the cabin was not meant for comfort or beauty but only for convenience, for the easy storing of food and charts, for the least space of beds, for the handy outstretching of an arm to reach whatever was needed. Neither could the cave pretend to be a home, yet this cottage, after so few days' inhabitance, was that already, with the kettle simmering and socks drying above the fire, a table-cloth not quite as pristine as it had been, spread over one end of the kitchen table, the clock's slow ticking, the polished lamp, the rag-rug (Sandy's speciality), the plates and dishes and gleaming pots of jam on the dresser and the snug curtains drawn against the night. So Fergus, with his half-smile, leant and watched them, vaguely surprised that Hugh, too, should know his way about and not feel awkward.

Ninian came back from the landing-stage as the kettle began to boil.

"Not a sign of them," he said, warming his hands across Jean's head as she knelt to make the toast. "I gave them a shout that must have been heard over at the bothy, too."

"No car-lights?" asked Hugh.

Ninian shook his head.

"They are a bore." Fiona returned from the larder. "There's hardly any butter and this is the end of the bread."

"Let's have dripping," suggested Hugh.

"And cake," said Ninian, looking at the large one Fiona had put on the table. "We certainly shan't starve."

"When do we embark on the venison?" asked Hugh, as they drew their chairs in round the table.

"Gracious, I hadn't really thought." Fiona cut a piece of toast. "It has to hang for about a week."

"Don't let it go bad," said Ninian.

"Not in this weather," said Jean.

They ate tea slowly, half an ear cocked for the noise of oars or footsteps coming up from the boat, but there was no sound. Ninian had reported the wind dropping and the air colder than ever.

"What's happened to your snow?" asked Hugh. "That was days ago."

"Something went wrong, I expect." Ninian piled high some toast with bramble jelly. "There isn't a cloud in the sky now."

They talked spasmodically between mouthfuls of the best place to set snares for rabbits; of the most likely hide to get a duck if they came flighting in to Loch Dubh; of the most promising snipe-bog on the ground at the Beanault end of Carna.

"Are there any duck?" asked Hugh.

"I saw some the other day," said Ninian.

"What about geese?" Fergus looked up from his toast and dripping.

"There are usually some by Tournary and up at the Goose Loch," said Fiona. "No reason why they shouldn't come up here."

"We've never looked," said Jean.

"We've got stacks to eat at the moment, even for us," Hugh said. "But what about a plum pudding?"

"Trust Maggie," said Fiona. "She put one in and even wrote down what to do to it!"

As Jean leant across to get her cup filled, Ninian grasped her arm.

"Keep still," he said. "My dear child, your neck is black. You must be scrubbed."

"Ninian, I'll scrub it myself."

"We'll all scrub it," said Hugh.

"If Jean's is black I dread to think what Sandy and Jamie's will be like," said Fiona. "Oh!" She was struck by a sudden thought. "I know. The hip-bath!"

"That's a thought. But how?" asked Ninian.

"Kettles and kettles of water, and all the saucepans." Fiona looked at the range. "We'll get it simply red hot and put the bath in front of the fire. Rather nice."

"How many of us can have it?" asked Hugh, feeling that he would rather like one himself.

"Well, there are two kettles and two saucepans and the fish-kettle, as well as the tank by the side," began Fiona. "A bucket, too, could be warming. I think, if we get the water really hot, we could do three baths."

"Two in each and one over?" suggested Fergus, grinning.

"Rather fun, but we must fill the cold tank," said Fiona.

"We'll start directly after tea."

"What about supper?" asked Jean.

"Let's have a cold one," said Fiona.

They were washing up the tea and the fire was roaring under an accumulation of pots and pans when a strange noise came floating up the loch.

"What on earth?" Fiona and Ninian looked at each other.

It came again and then a shout of laughter and a splash.

The tea things were left strewn round the sink. They rushed to the front door and opened it. The sound of oars was plain and the boy's voices giggling over something.

"There's the boat," cried Jean, pointing.

A dark blur took shape on the water and the creak of rowlocks sounded even nearer.

"Sandy!" shouted Ninian.

A shriek of laughter answered him, followed by a low unhappy moo.

"Oh!" cried Fiona, suddenly realising everything. "They've got a cow! I can't bear it!"

She collapsed on the step in a fit of giggles.

"What?" Then Ninian, hearing another moo and a shriek from Sandy, understood as well and leant helplessly against the door-post. Even Fergus threw back his head and laughed till the tears stood in his eyes.

"They are the end." Ninian, recovering, straightened up. "What on earth are we going to do with it?"

"They'll have to look after it." Fiona, feeling cold, got her coat from the hall.

A shout from Sandy came across the loch:

"Hoy! Ninian! Come and help. Bring the lantern." In a few minutes they were all rushing down towards the jetty, the hurricane-lamp swinging madly.

Sandy and James had brought the boat alongside and were now sitting there, too exhausted with laughing and rowing the heavy load to do anything else. The cow, a small black one from the Lodge, stood lowing miserably, tied in with ropes and piled all round with sacks of peat and coal and stores and masses of hay.

"Poor wretched animal." Fiona stroked its head. "How on earth did you get it in?"

"I don't quite know, but gosh! she was heavy." Sandy rested his aching arms on his knees. "It's taken us hours."

"You are mad," said Ninian. "Who's going to look after it?"

"Well, we all can. We've thought it out," said James.

"She can live in the field and we can milk her in the morning and evening."

"Thanks very much. And what unearthly hour are we meant to spring out of bed at?" Ninian glowered at them. "You two'll have to be responsible for it. And come back early in the afternoons to milk it."

"Well, we will be back by four, most evenings," said Sandy. "At least one of us can be."

"We don't get back till six sometimes," pointed out Hugh.

The cow, meanwhile, who was hating her sojourn in the boat, lowed again.

"Poor thing," said Jean. "Let's get it out anyway."

"Did you bring the stores and the post?" asked Fiona, as Sandy got to his feet.

"Yes, three letters for you." Sandy stretched his arms. "Gosh, I'm aching."

"Serve you right." Ninian bent to untie the ropes.

"No message for me?" asked Fergus, heaving out a sack.

"No, were you expecting one?" asked James.

"Yes, I told them to leave it at the Lodge, but I don't want to get it," said Fergus.

The cow, who could smell dry land, began to get restive. The boys had tied a halter to her and Hugh took this while Ninian undid the last knots. His fingers, numb with cold, fumbled at them, and the cow struggled and mooed, which did not help.

The others hauled out packages and sacks.

"We're going to have a bath to-night," Jean told Jamie. "Who is?" asked Jamie suspiciously.

"You are, and Sandy and me," said Jean. "Ninian said my neck was dirty."

"It probably is," said her twin.

"I don't want a bath." Sandy tied the painter more securely to a ring-bolt.

"I dare say, but you must reek of cow," said Fiona firmly. The cow, feeling the last rope grow slack, gave a sudden bound and spring that nearly pulled Hugh off his feet, and stood heaving on the jetty.

"Well, that's something," said Jean. "Where are we going to put it?"

"Her," said James.

"Well, 'her,' then. Where are we going to put 'her'?"

"None of the walls are good enough, she'll get out," said Hugh.

"Tether her, if you've got a rope." Fergus, suddenly bored, strolled off along the jetty. Fiona looked anxiously after him. You never knew with Fergus: he might disappear and not come back.

"We'll put her in the bit of garden near the henhouse." Sandy had been discussing this with James the whole way back. "She can't hurt anything there."

The cow bounded along ahead of Hugh. Sandy and James, still liable to collapse giggling, followed behind, their arms full of stores. Jean ran in front with the lantern.

"We'll leave the coal," said Ninian to Fiona. "It won't hurt for to-night," and they hurried after the others.

"Is there anything for 'her' to eat in here?" asked Jean, when they stood among the ruins of the henhouse.

"Plenty of grass," said James. "Poor cow, but she'll be happy now. We'll make her a nice field to-morrow and clean her a corner of the byre."

"You'd better say good night to 'her' and come in," said Fiona, who was getting cold. "There are buckets of water to be fetched for the baths."

"Feigns!" said James and Sandy.

"Oh, no, you don't. Especially as they're mostly for you," said Ninian.

They left the cow wandering round her temporary home and lowing occasionally.

"She'll settle down," said Sandy. "We'll go out last thing and see she's all right."

Back in the cottage the kettles were singing and the fire needed stoking. There was no sign of Fergus.

"He can't have gone," said Jean to Fiona.

"He might have," said Fiona.

"Did we say anything he might have got livid about?" James was worried.

"We were talking about cows," said Ninian.

"Well, perhaps he's got a thing about cows," suggested Sandy.

"He's not that sort of person. He's not silly, only queer," said Jean. "He wouldn't mind about cows. It's Taransay and Colin and things like that."

"Perhaps he was reminded of something," said Fiona thoughtfully.

"Perhaps he was bored," said Hugh, and she looked at him.

Several pans on the fire were almost boiling. Fiona moved them to one side and pushed on others. Sandy and James, ravenous, so they said, were given huge slices of bread and jam and sent to the burn with buckets to fill the tank. Supper would be soup and cold meat and a winter salad, cheese afterwards if any one was still hungry.

Heavy feet tramped in the loft overhead and a moment later Hugh appeared with the hip-bath in his arms. He and Fiona pushed aside the arm-chairs and cleared a space in front of the fire.

"What about a bath-mat?" asked Hugh.

"Well, do you think the rag-rug will do?" Fiona ruffled her hair. "We haven't got any towels left."

"It's going to be rather pleasant," said Hugh, looking at the bath and the firelight flickering on its curved back. "Who's first?"

"Jeannie, I think. Me next."

"Yes, then the boys, and Ninian and I last. But what about Fergus?"

"If he comes back we'll ask him. He may be cleaner than us."

"Perhaps he's swimming in the Loch," suggested Hugh, improbably.

"I hope not, he'd get frost-bite." Fiona poured the first kettle in and the steam rose in clouds. Sandy and James came sloshing and shivering into the scullery.

"How's the cow?" asked Hugh.

"Very well, thank you," said Jamie politely. "We went to see her."

The fire in the boys' room was being carefully tended by Ninian. He now appeared, his hair flecked with grey ash from blowing the flames, and seized the arm-chairs. "We may as well be comfortable," he said.

Jean followed him and was grabbed by Fiona.

"Come on," she said. "You're first."

"Then who?" asked Jean.

"Me, probably."

The boys left them, shutting out the draughts, and Jean undressed while Fiona poured alternate hot and cold water into the bath until she approved of the temperature. The kitchen was filled with steam and it was wonderfully warm. A towel and Jean's pyjamas hung warming over a chair-back, soap and flannel lay in a saucer: the bath smelt faintly of hot paint.

Jean, her hair pinned on top of her head so that her

neck could be thoroughly scrubbed, put one toe in and shrieked.

"It's simply boiling!" she said.

"Nonsense." Fiona, in an apron and with her sleeves rolled up, looked like a fierce nanny. She poured in a negligible amount of cold water and stirred.

"Come on, silly, it's quite cool."

"Ouch!" Jean sat down. "I shall be boiled. Honestly, it's agony, Fiona!"

"It'll be cold by the time I get in." Grudgingly Fiona poured in another pint or two of water from the bucket. Jean leant back, still half-cooked but enjoying the warmth and comfort of the fire flickering on her through the bars. Fiona soaped the flannel vigorously and advanced on Jean's neck. It was satisfyingly black, but the shrieks its cleansing produced brought Jamie to the door to demand whether his twin was being killed.

FIONA ADVANCED ON JEAN'S NECK.

"I might as well come in after you," said Fiona, when Jean stood enveloped in the warm bath towel, and she allowed her sister the pleasure of scrubbing her neck in return. Certainly it was pleasant to sit like this in a bath in front of the fire, lazily trickling water over yourself with a sponge, while Jean powdered herself liberally with your talcum powder till the room was full of the smell of it and the steam, and the floor splashed with water and wet footsteps.

"Hurry up!" It was Ninian's voice. "We all want ours before supper."

"Bother you." Fiona squeezed an extra large spongeful over herself and got up. Surprisingly enough the water looked quite clean and she called this information through the door.

"Sandy can have it," said Ninian. "What's it like when you're in?"

"Lovely," said Jean, pink and sweet-smelling in her blue dressing-gown.

Fiona tidied up the mess as well as she could and put more pans on the fire. She emptied the hot kettle into the bath and stirred. Poor Sandy, but it was not really dirty.

"How are we going to empty it?" asked Jean suddenly.

"Gracious! Bale it out, I suppose, unless Ninian and Hugh can lift it." Fiona had not thought of that. She called them in and explained.

"We'll tip it away outside," said Hugh, tentatively lifting a corner.

"Will it go through the door?" asked Sandy.

They measured and it would, just.

James was left with his cousin to see that he was properly clean and the others went to sit by the fire in the boys' room. Ninian and Jean stretched in the arm-chairs, Fiona and Hugh curled up on the bed.

"You mustn't get cold after your bath," said Hugh, and Fiona said she was beautifully warm.

"Somebody had better light Fergus's fire," she said. "Not me, because I'm clean."

"Sort of horrid thing you would think of," said Ninian, from the depths of his chair. "Just as I'm comfortable and have finished blowing this one."

"It'll be awfully cold in the annexe if you don't." Jean was worried. "Poor Fergus, he'll be cold too when he comes in."

"Why he wants to go hareing off into the icy night beats me," grumb!ed Ninian, heaving himself out of his chair.

With the brilliant idea of removing a shovelful of red-hot coals from the kitchen, the fire was lit in a few moments and Ninian was back before Sandy was out of the bath.

The mess he and Jamie had made had to be seen to be believed.

"You might have been hippopotami," said Fiona, inspecting it. "Anyway you can wipe it up, there's a dishcloth in the scullery."

However, that mess was nothing compared to the one Hugh and Ninian made carrying out the bath. It slopped all over the floor and they had to end by pouring it into buckets and emptying them. Also the bath leaked and a pool of water was found underneath which trickled away over the uneven stones.

"Never mind," said Fiona, picking her way between puddles. "It'll help clean it, it needs scrubbing."

Fergus, meanwhile, alone in the night, was standing on a rock by the water's edge. It was bitterly cold but he did not feel it, nor did he hear the sound of the waves lapping at his feet nor the wind sighing in the grass on Carn Mor. He gazed at the water with unseeing eyes, not noticing the broken reflections of the stars nor the stars themselves, frosty and bright. He was conscious only of the deep and overpowering sense of loneliness and depression that had flooded over him, underlined by the madness of the

Stewarts, making him feel an outcast. He was thinking, as ever, of Taransay, of his brother, Black Colin, who would even now be sitting in the tall chair before the fire, whisky at his elbow, his weak mouth drooping, his narrow eyes on the flames, his dark head resting on the worn leather chair-back, Ruadh and Bradhan, his deerhounds, at his feet. The room would be dark and full of shadows, Murdoch would not yet have brought the lamps, and it would be lit only by the flames, kindly lit, for the flames would not show the tattered coverings, the unpolished wood, the signs of decay and disuse that the daylight showed. But in spite of the torn rugs, the cracked windows, the stained, discoloured walls, the smoke-blackened mantel, it would still be Taransay, the only place he cared about, the only place in which he could not live. Colin could live there, Colin who hated it, Rory could live there, who did not care, but he, Fergus, who loved it with all his heart, could not live there unless he lost the pride that made up half his soul. Half-conscious of the sound of the water lapping on the rocks and the soft hush of the wind he felt himself back at Taransay on any winter night, standing on one of the grassy slopes at the foot of the great rock while the Minch, calm for once, sparkled before him under the stars. He lifted his head, expecting to see the bright fingers of the Northern Lights, and was startled when there was only the dark shape of Ben Carrick across the water. Ben Carrick . . . Carrick . . . he was not at Taransay after all, this was not the Minch but the Carna Loch, behind him was Carn Mor, not Taransay, that was as far and as inaccessible as the stars. He shivered, returning to reality, and found himself cold and hungry. Slowly he turned and walked back to the croft, longing for the warmth and friendliness and happiness of the Stewarts.

And it was as he had hoped. He opened the front door and a cloud of steam and light and laughter and the smell of soap and powder came out to meet him. They were mopping up the last of the mess.

"There's lots of hot water left, Fergus," said Fiona, thinking how tired he looked. "D'you want a bath?"

"Can I?"

"If you're not long," said Ninian.

"You can borrow my powder if you like," offered Fiona.

"And my sponge," added Jean.

He looked at them and smiled and the hardness left his eyes. They had comforted him with their friendship; they took him so much for granted.

"I don't know what I'd do without you," he said.

CHAPTER XVI

JAMIE'S CAVE

Friday, 22nd December

TO FIONA and Ninian's astonishment Sandy and James were not only up in time to milk the cow but they got up quietly. No slamming of doors and shouting, no clanking of pails and shrieks of laughter. Fiona, who dimly heard them go, turned over and went to sleep again. Ninian, also awake, lay half-drowsing until he found himself annoyingly wide-awake. He lay on his back looking at the grey light filtering in through the window, wondering what the time was, too lazy to look at his own watch.

Outside, the morning looked horrid: drab, grey and cold. Perhaps it was very early. More likely it was cloudy. They could not expect the weather to continue as it had, frosty and sunny. Snow had been predicted again in the paper the boys had brought from the village. Snow! That was a thought. Ninian raised himself on one elbow but the grass and rocks outside were as cold and grey as ever. His watch said eight o'clock. There was no noise coming from the kitchen, perhaps Fiona was still asleep. Well, I might as well, thought Ninian, and leapt out of bed to dress.

When he softly opened the kitchen door steady breathing was coming from the two box-beds. Fiona's back was towards him and the top of her head was the only thing visible. Jean was lying on her back, one arm flung out. Ninian went over to the range and began to rake it out.

The fire was blazing and Fiona, in a dressing-gown, was spooning tea into the pot, when the back door burst open and Sandy and James came in. Sandy was carrying the bucket, which he thrust in front of Fiona, saying proudly:

"Look! Isn't it lovely? Now we can have simply lashings of milk."

Fiona obligingly looked. The bucket was half-full of milk, creamy and frothy, with small pieces of hay and hair floating in it.

"Wonderful," said Ninian, peering over her shoulder. "How is the wretched cow?"

"Much happier now it's light and she can see where she is," said Jamie. "We must mend the walls after breakfast."

There was no muslin to strain the milk through, so Ninian provided a clean hanky and Sandy managed to fill two jugs without pouring too much on the floor. Everyone had two helpings of cereal for breakfast and Jean and Jamie had mugs of milk.

"If we have any over we can make cheese or something," said Fiona.

"Sounds rather vague, do you know how?" asked Hugh.

"I can make crowdie, you know, sour-milk cheese," said Fiona.

"Like cream cheese only not creamy," explained James. "Rather good."

After breakfast everyone went out to help mend the stone walls. The morning had not improved since Ninian first woke. The sky was grey and cloudy and it was very cold. Out of the wind it was just bearable, but on the unsheltered face of the hill it was icy.

They had decided that the big field nearest to Loch Dubh and below the wood had the best walls. In fact the one near the trees hardly needed repairing at all. But down by the loch the stones lay in heaps and they concentrated on this bit.

"The coldest thing we could have thought of doing," grumbled Fiona, as her frozen fingers slipped.

"We needn't make it high," said Fergus, who was working next to her. "Look, the big one underneath and wedge that little one above it."

"I've never built a wall before," admitted Fiona. "Have you?"

"Yes, as a matter of fact, but it wasn't a very good one. However, it served its purpose."

"Where was it?" asked Jean.

"On Hanga; it was more to keep rabbits and sheep out than a cow in." Fergus wedged a large stone into place. "It keeps the sheep out but rabbits seem to crawl in everywhere."

"Which reminds me, we ought to do some digging," said Fiona.

"And some sawing," added Hugh, who had filled the wood-box that morning. "We're almost out of logs."

"Bother," said Ninian.

"Hell!" said Sandy, as his newly-rebuilt wall came rattling down.

"We haven't even collected any wood to be sawn," continued Fiona. "Hadn't some of us better do it now?"

"Yes." Ninian straightened up. He looked round the field. There was not such an awful lot more to be done. "You can saw all right, can't you, Jeannie?" he said. "You and Jamie go and do it."

Jean, who was not strong enough to lift the largest stones and who was also nearly frozen, stood up gladly.

"All right," Jamie said. "But don't put the cow in here without telling me, will you?"

They promised that they would not, and the twins climbed over the wall and disappeared into the wood.

"You know, this wall is rather a nuisance," said Ninian. "We shan't get started much before lunch, and then someone will have to come back early to milk the dreaded cow."

"James or I will," said Sandy. "We could do some more sawing then."

"True." Fiona stood up and looked out across the grey Loch. "What an odious day; I think it's going to rain or something."

"Hope not." Fergus rubbed moss off his hands. "Seven of us would be rather a tight fit in the house all day!"

Half an hour later, Fiona, sucking a squashed finger, said: "Couldn't we tether the cow; most people do?"

"What, all this work for nothing?" Hugh looked round the field. "Come on, we've only got a couple more holes to fill in."

"Yes, but they're vast." Fiona inspected her finger, off which she had scraped a good deal of skin.

A sound of vigorous sawing came from the back of the croft.

"There was that tree Jamie brought in the other morning, too," said Ninian.

"I thought we'd burnt it," said Fiona.

"You haven't. I tripped over it last night." Fergus grinned.

"We can get some wood from the island if there's not enough here." Hugh looked across to where they had gathered wood secretly one night last summer and nearly been discovered. The stark trees were clustered round the pines like beggars round a rich man, yet they would be clad in finer leaves than he in a few months. Again the great eagle from Carn Mor came sweeping overhead on his huge wings. He never seemed to move them but got carried along on currents of air. He circled round several times, obviously unable to make out what they were doing, then turned and floated off. Six duck flew down the Loch, low above the water. Ninian watched them till they disappeared towards Aird Dubh. He guessed they were going down to feed on one of the lochans and would return at dusk. It would be fun to hide and watch them, perhaps with a gun, when they came flighting in. There were no end to the possibilities of this place.

The wall finished, Sandy went to fetch the twins and the cow. The others walked more slowly back to the croft, rubbing their sore hands.

With a ceremony the cow was driven into the field. They watched with pride as she wandered a few steps and then began to feed.

"She'll be all right," said Fergus. "Come on, let's get started."

Half an hour later they were following the track that Fergus had come up along. So seldom was it used that it was difficult to decide which was it and which were rough rocks from the hillside.

"How on earth did you find your way in the dark, Fergus?" asked Jean admiringly.

"Cat's eyes," said Fergus, and smiled at Fiona. "I can see in the dark."

Jean looked at him with interest, but his eyes were the dark blue she had thought they were, not green or tawny as he made them sound.

"I say," said Sandy, "this is our last chance. If we don't find the Fairy Hill this afternoon we go and see the shepherd to-morrow. Isn't that right?"

"Yes," said Ninian. "We may be on entirely the wrong track. But he definitely said Carn Mor, didn't he?"

"Yes." Fergus looked up at the steep-rising hill beside them. "Yes, he said Carn Mor, but I don't remember if he said he was on Carn Mor or it was."

"You couldn't have a hill on a hill," objected Fiona. "No?" Fergus raised his eyebrows.

"Well, could you?"

"You could have a Sithean anywhere," said Fergus.

Ahead of them the faint outline of the track wound on, at times disappearing completely as it dipped down to cross a burn, then showing itself again as it climbed a rise. Presently it forked, the left hand path going round the head of the Loch, the right-hand following a wide dip between Carn Mor and Carn Beg.

They climbed a few feet, then stopped and turned.

Below them to the right the largest of the islands lay in a shallow bay. Two burns ran out here, big ones, and on the right-hand arm of the bay was Loch Beg, the Small Loch, scarcely bigger than the island on Carna. Over the other side was the bothy, its reed-thatched roof almost indistinguishable from the surrounding grass, and a scattering of lochans on either hand. Farther away, a blue slip on the horizon, was the sea. On to the right the track reappeared at the head of Carna and wound down to Beanault. The land looked cold and bare and uninviting. Fergus turned again to the hill.

Yesterday, and on all of their previous climbs, Ninian had led. To-day it was Fergus, who climbed as if he knew the hill from long ago. Before it had seemed wrong for Fergus not to be leading, yet now it seemed strange to see Ninian walking behind with Jean. "Where I am my word is law." Fergus had said that long ago, and Hugh wondered if it applied here as much as it did amongst his men. Hugh could not see Fiona leaving it all to him either. Generally, she was far ahead of the others, climbing some improbable rock or precipitous gully.

Gradually the track grew steeper as it wound on between the two peaks. They would soon be on a level with the top of Carn Beg, but Carn Mor still towered above them, and ahead the track curled up and disappeared over the shoulder.

In spite of the cold they were getting warm at last. Their feet were still numb but their cheeks glowed.

"Keep a look-out for caves," Sandy reminded them, and they scanned the slopes on either side.

"What happens at the top?" Fiona took two long strides and caught up with Fergus.

"There's a river and a loch and lots of hills, but maybe not enough," he said, smiling. "And perhaps the sea."

"Fergus, you are maddening! Which hills and how do you know?"

"The things I know," he said slowly, "would fill a book, several books, but they don't matter."

"Shsh!" Jamie stopped and pointed. A solitary stag was picking his way along beside the burn below them. He was shaking his head and roaring. They stopped to watch. Another answering roar came from farther down the burn and a smaller, light-coloured stag came slowly towards the first one. He, too, lowered his head and shook it. The hills echoed to their roaring.

"Late for them to be fighting," whispered Ninian.

"Shsh!" Fiona hushed him.

They leant against the rocks, watching.

The stags, their heads down, ran at each other and the horns clicked. They shook their heads impatiently and came at each other again and then again. The small beast was getting the worst of it. After a few runs and clinches he limped off down the burn. The big stag followed and roared after him. He stood watching until his victim disappeared, then lifted his head and roared again, looking round for the next opponent.

"Bad-tempered brutes." Fiona went on up the track.

"Perhaps better to have all your bad temper over in a few months," suggested Hugh, with a grin.

"D'you mean my bad temper or bad temper generally?" asked Fiona, suspiciously.

"Generally, of course," said Hugh, laughing, and she threw a handful of heather at him.

They reached the top of the pass at half-past two and sat in the shelter of a rock to have their lunch. As Fergus had said, there was a river and loch and hills before them and beyond all that the sea. The river lay directly below them, running from Loch an Eilean down to Loch Vaddai, and from there into the sea at Gruinard Bay. The long stretch of sand there was a dull gold, white waves breaking on it and on the rocky shores of Gruinard Island. West were the Hebrides, a distant iron-grey range of hills upon the horizon, north was Loch Bruaich and Summer Isles and all the hills up to Suilven, east the hills they knew, Ben Derg Beg, Ben Derg Mor, Sgurr Fiona, Dundonell and Sgurr Ban.

"The shepherd lives down there," Fergus pointed vaguely over the top of Ben Derg Mor, "but we get to him another way."

"No Fairy Hill," said Jean, sadly.

"Wait a bit, we haven't looked properly," said Fergus.

"Besides, the sun's not shining," added Hugh.

Sandy looked at the sky.

"It looks as if it might," he said.

"You'll have to be going back," Ninian told him. "There's your precious cow to milk."

"I'll go," Jamie offered.

"You'll have to go to-morrow," pointed out Fiona.

"Bother. Let's toss up, Sandy."

Hugh produced a sixpence and Sandy won. He chose to go back now.

"Because I think to-morrow'll be more fun," he said.

"I'll do it one day," said Jean. "As long as she's not difficult to catch."

"Well, I haven't tried yet," admitted Sandy. "But Maggie always caught her quite easily."

"She knows her corner of the byre anyway," said James. "You should be able to drive her in."

"I'll wait a little longer." Sandy took an apple. "Just in case the sun comes out. What are you planning to do?" and he looked at Ninian.

"Well, I don't know. Fergus, you know this country, what's the form?"

"Let's go down to the Loch," said Fiona. "It looks such a nice one."

"Right. Then we could spread out like we did yesterday," said Fergus, "and come up over the top."

For an instant the sun gleamed palely. Half-hearted

shadows were thrown on the shoulders of the surrounding hills but nothing betrayed the Sithean.

"Oh, well," Sandy got up, "I'll be going."

"You might do some sawing," said Ninian.

"Yes, I might," agreed Sandy.

"And make up the fires," added Fiona.

"Right. Any cooking?" He started up the hill.

"Peel some potatoes and put on the soup," said Fiona. "It's in the blue pan."

"Good-bye!" called Jean.

"Bye," and Sandy hurried away over the hill.

"You'll live to curse the day you brought the cow up," Ninian told Jamie.

"Well, it does give us fresh milk," Jamie defended his precious cow. "But I dare say you're right."

It did not take them long to reach Loch an Eilean, a long, slim slip of water about the size of Chuiragarstidh. It bulged on its northern side, and in the bulge lay the island, dark and tree-covered.

"Strange how all these islands have trees," said Hugh.

"The only relics of the days when all the hills had trees, I suppose," said Ninian.

The track crossed the burn that was almost a river, at a ford about a mile from the northern end of the Loch. This, according to Fiona, was silly. There must be hundreds of ways across a rocky place like this particular river without going a whole mile away. Accordingly they spread out and Hugh found a way over via a small island and a precariously wobbling rock. No one fell in and they continued round the Loch, scaring duck and snipe out of the reeds. There were masses of deer, too, feeding there. They seemed surprised to see people here in this remote place and moved off slowly, looking back to make sure that they were there after all. At the south-east end the Loch was almost as dark and overshadowed as Loch Dubh. Carn Mor and Craig Vaddai encircled it closely, leaving only just

SCARING DUCK AND SNIPE OUT OF THE REEDS.

enough room to walk round.

The sky was growing grey with dusk, and the sun, after its pale flash of light, retired behind the clouds again.

"We might as well start back," said Ninian, looking up at the almost perpendicular slope above them. "It's going to take us some time."

"Shall we meet anywhere or go straight down the other side?" asked Hugh.

"Let's go down, we might miss each other if it gets dark," said Fiona.

"Right!" Ninian looked up again. The hill seemed startlingly steep. "I'll go along to the end, that's the longest bit really."

He went off along the Loch, followed by Fiona and Hugh. Jean, Jamie and Fergus covered the ground that was left.

No one could have hurried on this hill. At times it was so sheer that a long detour had to be taken. It'll be dark before we get to the top, thought Fiona, as she found another precipice. What a nasty place to get stuck at night. It was necessary to concentrate so hard on climbing that it was almost impossible to look for caves. Once or twice she turned round in case the Fairy Hill had thrown off its cloak of disguise, but there was never anything but the grey shield of Loch an Eilean and the brown slopes of Craig Vaddai and Ben Derg beyond.

Jean, climbing steadily, was concentrating too hard on keeping up to think of anything else. Much though she hated to admit it, these steep cliffs above this dark Loch looked ideal places for a troll to lurk. Long slits ran down the face of the rock, too narrow to be caves, but just right for Anything Else. Resolutely she turned her mind from that subject and felt the comforting bulge of the torch in her pocket. She had not forgotten it this time. Occasionally she, too, stopped, but it was not to look back but to steady the beating of her heart. Most of the time she was alone. Sometimes she glimpsed Jamie's fair head on her right and waved to him. There was no sign of Fergus. He was probably nearly at the top, climbing with that peculiar swift stride of his. Cat-like cat's eyes. He could see in the dark. So, she supposed, could They. She swallowed. Dusk was already dimming the hills. She had never been perfectly sure of Fergus.

Neither left nor right, however hard he might look, could Jamie see anything that could be called a cave. Conscientiously he investigated every slit and cranny in the rocks but they all ended within a few yards. Somehow this looked such a promising place, quiet, deserted, seamed with burns and yet not inaccessible. Because of his thoroughness he was going more slowly than the others, except Jean. He lost all sight and sound of Hugh at the beginning though he kept his ears strained for a shout that would show someone had been lucky. Jean, he saw occasionally, scrambling along, and away up on the left he caught a glimpse of Fergus. Otherwise the hill was quiet and deserted.

Pulling himself up over the rim of a steep face of rock, James found himself on a rough plateau. It was about one hundred yards long and fifty wide, bare smooth rock, with tufts of dead grass and heather growing from the long cracks that zigzagged over it and several trickles of burns staining it brown where they ran, not strong enough to have worn any but the most shallow groove in its hard face. Icicles hung down amongst the grass that somehow clung beside them and a few small stunted bushes sucked a meagre living from the crevices. Jamie stood still for a few minutes, regaining his breath after his recent strenuous climb, and looking round him. His eye lit on a dark crack in the face of the rock, deeper and wider than all previous ones, almost, in fact, a cave. He walked over to it, his heart beating with excitement. It was indeed a cave, a sort of cave, long and black and narrow, continuing out into the plateau of rock so that it formed a deep abyss. It looked, to Jamie, a likely place. A narrow ledge ran along it inside on the right, then vanished into the gloom. He felt for his torch and pulled it from his pocket. He pressed the button and it threw a pale gold circle into the dusk. Not much good, thought Jamie, but better than nothing. No horror of trolls lurked in his mind, he was only thinking of James Stewart, his namesake, and what he must have thought when he lived here, if this was his cave.

At the moment when Jean scrambled up on to the left-hand edge of the plateau Jamie advanced towards the cave. Jean saw him, his pale head bright against the dark slit in the rock.

Then, to her horror, he vanished.

She stood, transfixed. A moment before he had been there. Now he had disappeared completely. Trolls. That was it. They had snatched him into their fastness before her eyes. She felt sick with horror, unable to move or call, unable to go forward or back or to do anything but stand rooted to the spot waiting for the little dark hairy men to creep out into the dusk and spirit her away.

This couldn't go on. She could not leave her twin to his fate without an effort made to save him. She took a step forward.

"Jamie," she called, her voice hoarse with fright. "Jamie!"

"Jean!" The relief of it. "Jean, where are you?" "Here!" She hurried over. "What's happened?"

"Careful." Jamie's voice seemed to be coming out of the ground under her feet. "Don't slip. I'm down here." Below her in the crevasse she could see the gleam of his head. She knelt down, peering in.

"Don't fall for heaven's sake," called Jamie.

"But what happened?" asked Jean.

"The rock's all wet there." She could feel it was with her hands. "I slipped down here, but I can't get out."

"What? Are you all right?"

"Yes, it's soft earth but the walls are quite smooth."

"How far down are you?"

"I don't know, it looks miles." Certainly his voice seemed to come from the depths of the earth.

"What shall I do?" asked Jean.

"If you took off your coat and let it down I might clutch it," suggested Jamie.

Jean stripped off her tweed coat, shivering in the wind. She knelt down, but the sleeve did not reach, so she lay on her face. Still Jamie's hand groped for it in vain.

"Oh, dear!" Jeannie's voice shook with concern. "What shall I do?"

"Try shouting."

"Fergus, Fergus! Hugh, Hugh!" screamed Jean. "Fergus!" But there was no answer.

"They must be up farther, let's both try," said James, and they shrieked together, but only the echoes answered. "You'll have to go for help," said Jamie at last.

"I'll take hours." Jean looked round at the darkening sky. "How'll I find you?"

"I could flash my torch and shout if I hear you," suggested James. "But do be quick."

"Shall I leave you my coat?" Jean felt rather like the Good Samaritan and it was icy cold on the plateau.

"Yes. No, you'll be colder, I expect. Hurry, quick, before it gets dark," said Jamie.

"I'll shout on the way." Jean pulled on her coat again. "Good-bye, twin, I'll be back soon."

"Good-bye." Jamie sounded forlorn down in the crevasse. He had tried to go back into the cave, but although his crack ran right into the cliff the walls remained as smooth as glass.

"Anyway it can't be the right one," he thought.

Jean, her face to the hill, was climbing as fast as she could. It seemed to grow steeper if anything and her heart pounded like a hammer. Every now and then she looked up, but the hillside was bare. No sign of Hugh or Fergus. She called repeatedly, but there was no answer.

By the time she reached the top she felt quite exhausted. The wind came racing up to meet her, cold and frosty. It was almost dark but she could just see the grey gleam of the Carna Loch below her and the black mass of country beyond. Ben Carrick was there with its familiar shape and left was the peak of Ben Lair. I must take bearings, thought Jean, looking wildly round. It was too dark to see much, and anyway by the time she came back it would be night. Back. The thought of facing that hill again was too much. Already her legs were aching with her frantic climb up. A tear trickled down her cheek but she brushed it away. Gone were all, or almost all, thoughts of trolls. Poor Jamie, cold and lonely in the crevasse, must be her first consideration. A bearing, a landmark, a star. A star, that was it. Low over Ben Carrick was a pale point of light, and in front of her was a huge loaf-shaped rock. Ben

Carrick and that in line and the star over the top, Jamie would be beneath her.

She looked down. The hill sloped away gradually to the shore and it looked simply miles. She could not see the croft nor any pin-prick of light. Oh, but it was cold and lonely. Her feet, deep in the snow, felt numb. The snow, they could follow her footprints, that would be something else in case a cloud obscured the star. The sky had been cloudy all day, too.

"Ninian! Fergus! Hugh!" she shouted, but the words were whipped back over her shoulder. A stag roared in answer from higher up on the hill. Oh, no. Not stags, too, please. A sick feeling of fear crept into Jean's stomach. With tears starting in her eyes she stumbled off down the hill.

The snow was far behind and she had been slithering for what seemed hours on the hard frosty ground. Again and again she called, but the night was empty but for her and the stags and the cold mountain wind. Her legs ached with hurrying and where she had bumped into rocks, her face and hands and feet were frozen. Still the Loch lay beneath her, that long grey shield that did not seem to get any nearer. Still there was no gleam of light from the croft: perhaps she was miles out of the way. Perhaps she was lost. Another tear followed the first down her cheek and she bit her lip.

Then, from below her, came a laugh. There was no other laugh like it in the world. She would know it anywhere.

"Fiona!" she screamed. "Oh, Fiona!"

She started to run, stumbling over the long grass and heather, calling her sister's name. She tripped and fell and lay with her heart pounding. Then in the silence that followed she heard Ninian call her name.

"Ninian!" she shouted.

"Jeannie!" Never had his voice sounded so deep and

comforting. "Jeannie, I'm coming."

She got up and went on down the hill. The others were all beneath her, hurrying up towards her. Ninian reached her first and held her in his arms.

"It's all right, Jeannie, we're all here. Where's Jamie?" She clung to him for a moment and then held his hand as the others crowded round.

"It is Jamie," she said, and told them.

"I'm sorry, Ninian." That was Fergus. He had forgotten that Jean might not be able to keep up with him and had not bothered to look round for her. "I am sorry."

"That's all right. We must get going." Ninian ruffled his hair. "Fiona, there's rope in the croft, can you go and get it and the lantern? I'll go back with Jean, slowly."

"Right." Fiona turned and was off down the hill like a flash. "I'll meet you at the top. Straight up, Jeannie?"

"Yes."

Fergus followed her, and their feet went pounding off down the hill.

"I should have looked back, too." Hugh was as sorry as Fergus.

"It's all right, Hugh," said Jean.

Holding his hand and Ninian's she turned to the hill once more and tried not to look at its long steep face.

Before they were at the top they could hear Fiona and Fergus panting up behind them. They waited for them and continued together.

To Jamie, huddled in his narrow prison, the night seemed endless after Jean left. He heard her feet scrambling away up the rocks and a farewell shout. Then he was left alone.

Again and again he explored the smooth rock walls, searching with his fingers for a chink or crack that would serve as the hold for a finger or toe. But the place might have been polished, it was so smooth. He could just squeeze up to the end, which was right in the cave, and thought it worth switching on his torch for a moment or two just in case there was anything to discover. The yellow beam lit damp black walls which soared away out of sight into the roof. Trickles of brown water rolled down them, and moss and ferns grew there high up out of his reach. This crevasse continued right to the back of the cave, gradually getting so narrow that no human could have squeezed through. Definitely, then, this was not it, although it would have proved an excellent hiding-place for a fugitive. No one would have thought of looking in here, but then, of course, once in you could not get out. Jamie abandoned that idea and paced up and down the mud floor in an effort to keep warm.

Overhead the sky grew darker and the narrow slit in the rocks became as cold as a tomb. The one question in Jamie's mind was would the others ever be able to find him in the dark. He did not look forward to the thought of spending a whole night in this place. Hard though Jean would try, Jamie was not sure she would be able to find her way back. Not an easy task for anyone.

He watched a star gleam and flutter above him in the narrow strip of sky. A dark cloud passed over it, and then, as he stared, it reappeared once more. He felt like the prisoner in "The Ballad of Reading Gaol," and tried to remember that stone walls do not a prison make, but it was desperately dark and cold and lonely.

Above him the wind made an eerie, whistling noise in the back of the cave and the trickles of water fell with a persistent drip-drip-drip. There were stags roaring down by the Loch and a rabbit screamed suddenly. Jamie held his breath and listened. His pounding heart was the only noise; not even the friendly tick of a watch.

The mud floor felt damp to sit on after a bit so he tried jumping up and down to warm himself, but gave up as he banged his elbows on the rock walls.

There was nothing to do but to wait, and the silence waited with him, while a hush like a deep breath passed over the hill every now and then and he was left alone with the thudding of his own heart.

"A loaf-shaped rock," repeated Ninian. "What sort of loaf, Jean?"

"Well, just a loaf," Jean gestured. "You know."

"Round? Square?" suggested Hugh.

"Oh, round, two rounds."

"Cottage!" panted Fiona, out of breath for once.

It was Fergus who saw it, and Jean's footprints at the same time.

In a moment they were behind it, looking at Ben Carrick, but the star had vanished.

"We'll follow your steps," said Hugh, and they hurried down the hill.

"Mind, it's steep," said Jean.

Sandy had come back with Fiona and Fergus and went in front with the lantern.

"Jamie! Jamie!" they called.

At last his faint voice came up to them.

"Thank God!" Fergus's voice was so low that only Fiona heard. "Well, it is really my fault," he said, seeing her look at him.

"Silly," she said. "You couldn't help it."

It was no use trying to hurry on these steep rocks. Hugh slipped once on a loose stone and started a small avalanche. After that they went slowly.

At last Jamie's voice grew louder. Ten minutes later they slithered down on to the plateau and uncoiled the rope. Ninian let it down and they held on behind him ready to haul.

Then Jamie, cold and bruised but otherwise all right, stood amongst them.

"Gosh!" he said, laughing.

"Have some of this," offered Fergus, handing him a thin silver flask.

" 'Fergus's Special'?" asked James, and Fergus nodded. He took a gulp and choked at the fiery spirit.

"I think we all need it." Fergus handed it round and finished it himself.

"I'm so hungry," said Jamie, as they climbed once more up the steep side of Carn Mor. "How's the cow, Sandy?"

"Flourishing," said his cousin. "And there's some wonderful soup waiting."

On the summit the moon struggled weakly through the clouds and faintly lit the ground ahead. Ninian swung Jeannie into his arms and they went on down the hill.

CHAPTER XVII

THE SHEPHERD OF GLEN DARRACH

Saturday, 23rd Decemebr

THE BOYS were up early next morning having a tremendous log-sawing session while Fiona and Jean did some serious bedmaking. Even Fergus's did not pass Fiona's critical eye. It was a cloudy morning, frosty still, but with the sun sparkling on the grass from time to time. Mattresses were turned and sheets and blankets hung on the stone wall to air. Fiona and Jean appeared at the window shaking dusters and brooms. The croft hummed and clattered with activity, and the sharp air rang with the sound of an axe from the wood where Ninian and Fergus were doing some felling, and with the rasp of the saw from behind the croft where Hugh, James and Sandy were adding to the log-pile.

Fiona was not sure what was wrong with the cottage, but it certainly did not sparkle and shine like most of the ones she had visited. So the red-brick kitchen floor was scrubbed and the grate polished, and all coats and socks and jersies left lying about were ruthlessly hung on pegs or stuffed into drawers, regardless of their ownership.

They had finished breakfast by half-past eight and were planning to start early for Darrach. Jamie was none the worse for his imprisonment and had been up at dawn with Sandy to milk the cow. Certainly, thought Fiona, Vimming the sink, it was pleasant to have so much fresh milk. If they left early they should have reached the shepherd's croft before Jamie had to start back. Fiona supposed she ought to volunteer to come back early and she would one day, but not to-day, with the sun and the clouds and the cold air and all the unknown hills at the head of Loch Dubh to be explored.

She took the bucket and went down to the burn. At the rate they were going there would be time to do some washing before they started. The boys had thrust several wet, peaty socks at her, too dirty to be just dried, and there were shirts and underclothes too. To-day was a fine day for drying; she would get Ninian to rig up a line in the sun.

The frost was white on the grass on the way down to the burn and sheets of ice lay across the stillest pools. They crackled as she dipped in the bucket, gasping with cold as a ripple washed over her hand. She stood still for a moment or two, looking east up the Loch, rubbing her hand on her trousers and content with what she saw. The blue and white water rippled by a light wind, stretching on until the tall hills threw the shadows that gave Loch Dubh its name; the rough brown curve of Carn Mor on her left, rising steeply to the sky; the far white-topped peaks that edged Loch Marba, Ben Carrick, Mel Vannie, Ben Lair and Slioch; the russet, tawny country across the Loch, the colour of a hind's coat; the apron of emerald-green turf before the croft and the patchwork of fields behind encroaching on the slopes of Carn Mor; the croft itself, low and grey, the slate roof starred with lichen, smoke rising steadily from one chimney and the windows flung open and gleaming in the sun; the bare-branched wood behind it with the few ever-green pines lifting their heads above their neighbours. And then the noises, the rush of the burn and the tinkle as ice broke and was sucked into the stream; the steady knocking of the axe and the crack as a branch broke; the saw grating and shouts of laughter from the boys and Jean calling to them; and all the noises of the hill, the whisper of the grasses, the chirp, the rustle, the patter, the brush of wings. She picked up her bucket and hurried back to the house.

Fergus and Ninian in the wood were creating havoc among the dead branches. They had pulled all they had sawn into a small clearing and it was a formidable pile.

"This'll do." Fergus rested on the axe. "It'll be dark by the time these get sawn up."

"Oh, they can wait." Ninian unhooked his coat from a tree and swung it over his shoulder. He and Fergus laid hold of a couple of large branches and dragged them back across the field.

"Heavens!" Sandy stopped sawing. "What are we preparing for? The Ice Age?"

"Well, you needn't do this now," Ninian told him. "But it's as well to have plenty near at hand. There's masses more in the wood; I'll show you."

Fergus went on into the house while the others followed Ninian. It felt cold and clean inside and he looked approvingly at Fiona, who had finished the housework and was cutting sandwiches at the kitchen table. He came and leant against it, eating pieces of cold mutton in his fingers and watching while she spread and cut the bread.

"You wouldn't like to do the lamps, I suppose?" she asked him.

"No," said Fergus truthfully, "I should hate it. Where are they?"

"There." Fiona gestured with the knife at the one swinging above his head. "And two in the scullery, and all the bits are on the shelf."

"Row or walk?" asked Hugh, half an hour later. The branches were stacked by the byre and the lamps filled and trimmed and cleaned.

"Shorter to walk, really," said Ninian. "We don't want to go right to the end of the Loch."

"Come on, then." Fergus was bored with hanging about. He set off along the track, east this time, and into the hills.

They did not stop for anything, not even to look for deer, until they reached the fork in the track. One went over the point, across the shallow bar between the two lochs, then branched into three separate paths. Beside them it climbed abruptly up Carn Mor along the track of a burn, the steepest and most sheer part of the hill on its left, Ben Fuar on its right. They paused here, looking round. Even to-day, with the patches of clear sky and the sun flashing, Loch Dubh did not look cheerful, but lay as dark and still as ever amidst its circle of hills.

Fiona's glass was produced and the country scanned for deer. Jamie saw a big bunch under the snow-line on Mel Vannie, and Ninian saw some more on low ground at the head of the Loch. Two buzzards flew round them, high up, uttering shrill mews, and again the duck started up and spattered across the water from the reeds by the point.

Hugh leant back against a rock and followed the faint track up the hill. Only in places was it visible, growing alarmingly steep before it vanished over the head of the pass. The Burn of the Waterfall beside it was well named, and cascades of water fell across the steep face of rock. Very beautiful it looked, with the sun shining and the spray lit to an iridescent halo, but to Hugh the rocks looked absolutely sheer.

"Oh, well." Ninian clicked in Fiona's glass and handed it back to her. "I suppose we might as well go on."

"It's pretty steep in places," Fergus warned them. "Don't go slipping into any more crevasses."

At first the track sloped gradually but presently they found themselves in single file climbing from rock to rock.

"How on earth ponies come up and down here I can't imagine," said Sandy.

"Especially with deer on their backs," added Jean.

Beside them the burn roared and splashed over the rocks.

"We're just coming to the best waterfall," Fergus told them. "It should be pretty good to-day."

It was a lovely one, a white ribbon of water across a black rockface.

A WHITE RIBBON OF WATER.

"Don't forget the cave," said Fiona. "That's the most likely waterfall we've seen."

She left the track and scrambled over the rocks until she was right beside the burn. She could feel the cold spray on her face, and long icicles hung down where the water had frozen. But there was no cave and no slightest track or path that could have led to it. She joined the others who were waiting for her, Fergus with his mouth twisted in his sideways smile.

"You knew there wasn't a cave," said Fiona, indignantly, and he laughed outright. "You are a maddening person."

"When were you here before?" asked Jean.

"Years ago, when I was a boy." Fergus was uncommunicative on the subject and Jean knew better than to ask him any more questions. That was so strange about Fergus, he said the most intriguing things and would never explain them.

The roar of the burn faded as it curved away from them

and for a few yards the track flattened out. Looking back they seemed to have climbed a long way, Jamie thought. Loch Dubh lay curved below them, and west the sun was glittering on the sea.

"It's not a bad day," Ninian said. "Does anyone see any shadows that the Fairy Hill might throw?"

They stopped again to look round.

"It gets better farther on," said Fergus. "You can see up to where we were yesterday," and he hurried them on.

They startled three hinds as they came over the hill, who were feeding in a grassy hollow. So hard was the ground that their feet made no impression on it.

"I shouldn't like to be a hind in this weather," said Jean.

"They've got nice thick coats," said Sandy.

"All the same, I shouldn't like it."

Over the top of the next ridge was Lochan Feith, the Boggy Loch. It was really two lochs, like Bearnach, joined by a wide stream and half-covered with reeds. A flight of duck rose from it as they approached and went north over the hill.

"What about lunch?" suggested Hugh, who was carrying the knapsack and getting tired of it.

"It's early," said Fiona.

"Half-past twelve isn't really early." Hugh stopped by a convenient flat rock.

"And we had breakfast hours ago," added James.

"It's a nice place anyway," said Ninian.

They leant back against the rocks in the sun and munched their sandwiches. This was a new place to the Stewarts and their eyes were exploring every fold of the hills. In front of them across the Loch rose Ben Fuar, its big loch up higher than they were and out of sight. Left the track sloped gently on across the brown sunny hill, behind was Carn Mor and the long hollow between it and Ben Derg, with Lochan Cnapach over their shoulders in a fold of the hill. They were nearly at the top of the pass and the track had flattened out a good deal and looked even less used than it did farther down.

Fergus, leaning back against a rock, looked up at the clouds. The buzzards were still there and he watched them lazily, enjoying the brief warmth of the winter sun and the quietness of the hills. So many days had he spent like these, years ago, at Taransay. He knew the hills there like the palm of his hand, yet he had not climbed them for four years — was it? — or five. Yet he could still remember them and the way the shadows fell across them and the folds of the corries and blue slips of water. There was one so like this. His mouth hardened as he thought of it; he had cause to remember it.

Watching him, Fiona wondered for the hundredth time what was the mystery about him. Why would he not tell them? Why did his eyes scowl and his face grow hard when he was thinking? What had Colin done to him? She wished she dared ask, but the knowledge that Fergus would either go off and not return or fly into one of his rages prevented her.

Jean, sitting cross-legged like a goblin on a high rock above the water, thoughtfully considered the Loch in front of her. No use for fishing, the weeds spread almost entirely over it, reeds, rushes and water-lilies, yet there were probably big trout in it if they could get up here. They would have a job coming up the waterfall, impossible really. She dismissed it as a place not to be visited in future with a rod and decided that it was ideal for a kelpie. The reeds would make perfect cover for him to lurk in, he could spring out on you as you came, unsuspecting, down the track, spring out with splashings and snortings and fiery eyes. She was a little vague about how a kelpie really looked. Maggie had plenty of stories about them, but she had never actually seen one. No one seemed to see them nowadays, perhaps that was just as well, only they might still be lurking under the surface, ready to spring if you were not watchful.

"We ought to be going on." Ninian sat up and looked at Fergus. "How much farther is it?"

"Couple of miles or more." Fergus came back with a start.

Fiona prodded Hugh with her foot and he opened his eyes.

"I wasn't asleep," he said. "I heard him say two more miles."

"I shall have to whizz back," said Jamie. "Let's get going."

When they reached the summit of the ridge in front of them the ground sloped on and down in a series of rough steps.

"It'll take hours climbing back up here," said James. "I suppose I have got time to come the whole way?"

"Oh, yes." Fiona looked back as they started downhill. "It won't take you long."

A mile farther on they met another burn and followed it down to the glen where it joined what might almost have been called a river. There were plenty of deer about on these long slopes and Fiona could hardly bear hurrying past them. Fergus led them relentlessly on, over rough bridges and stepping-stones, past a cairn and a little wood, past what Sandy swore was a cave. The hills swept back on either hand from a wide glen, and far below and in front of them was a glimpse of green fields.

"Darrach's down there," said Fergus, pointing.

Ben Derg was on their left, a large snow-covered mass, and beyond that a long loch — Darrach, in its clump of oak trees, stood at the Loch's eastern end, green fields about it and the big burn running past.

"What a lovely place," said Hugh. "You could live here in the hills, have a whole village if you liked, and no one would ever know you were here."

"I expect there was a village once," said Fergus. "There

are the ruins of several crofts down there, It'd be fun to start a tribe, wouldn't it?"

"Yes, all the nice people," said Fiona. "We'd grow our own food; plenty of fish and deer in these hills: we need never leave."

"Let's do it one day," said Hugh, looking down the glen. "I'll build my house under that big rock with the heather on top. The burn'll run right past my door."

"I'll have mine up the hill in that little hollow," Ninian pointed. "Then I can look down on you all and keep you in order."

"Where would you live, Fergus?" asked Jean. Fergus smiled.

"I'd come and stay with you all in turn," he said.

How lovely, thought Fiona, to live in this wide green glen in the very heart of the hills. She could imagine the white crofts scattered along the banks of the burn, smoke rising in the still air, cows lowing from the hills, hens cackling, and dogs and sheep and people all adding to the sounds, which would not seem strange in this place that was waiting for them. There would be walls built on the green sides of the hill and crops growing there and hill ponies, too, belonging to them all. Now there was just one croft, the old shepherd's. How lonely it must be, as if haunted by the ghosts of the future.

As they rounded the corner of the oak wood they came upon the croft, whitewashed and thatched newly with yellow straw. It faced the Loch and had no garden nor wall in front of it but only the long grassy hill. The wood looked dark and cold and a path wound into it and was lost to sight. They avoided that and kept outside in the light. As they approached, a collie ran out, barking. A few seconds later an old woman appeared, drying her hands on her apron.

"Mairi Macloud?" called Fergus in Gaelic.

She answered him after a moment as if she could not

believe her eyes.

"Is it Fergus?"

"Yes. Are you well? And himself?"

Hugh, not understanding a word, stood watching. Fiona translated in an undertone.

"He's telling her who we are. Now he's asking for her father; that must be the shepherd."

The woman nodded her head.

"Himself's inside, but go carefully, he's very old," she said.

"How old?" asked Jean.

"A hundred and two." The woman smiled at her amazed face. "There are not many live to that age. He's blind, you know, but wonderful considering."

She led them round the house and in at the front door. It was like a stable door in two halves, the top half open and a hen sitting on it.

"Shoo!" cried the woman, and it flew off cackling.

The cottage was built with two rooms only, a small one on the right, and on the left the kitchen living-room into which she led them. A wide, open fire burnt at one end with a big kettle hissing beside it, the floor was trampled earth, the ceiling showed rafters and the inside of the thatch. It was dark after the sun outside as the small windows gave hardly any light. Jean caught hold of Ninian's hand and he squeezed it reassuringly. Then, as their eyes became accustomed to the gloom, they saw the shepherd.

He was sitting in a chair by the fire, a plaid tucked round his knees although the room was warm. He was the oldest man they had ever seen, not creepy, but old, old as the hills. A snowy white beard curled from his chin half-way down to his waist, his brown face was gnarled and lined like an old tree, his white hair was long and fluffy like sheep's wool round his head and his twisted hands were folded over a hazel stick. He turned his sightless blue eyes towards them.

"Fergus." His voice creaked like a tree. "Fergus, what brings you so far?"

"He knows him," whispered Jamie, in amazement.

"The Sithean." Fergus went up to the chair and put his hand between the shepherd's.

"It's a long time," said the old man. "A long, long time. Many's the time I've remembered you, Fergus, and thought of you, but little I thought you'd come to me. Why didn't you come before?" He seemed to sense what Fergus was thinking, for without waiting for him to reply he went on:

"Ah! the proud heart and the anger. I told you, Fergus, to beware."

"Yes, Alec, you told me." They had never heard Fergus's voice like this before; he sounded like a different person.

HE TURNED HIS SIGHTLESS BLUE EYES TOWARDS THEM.

"I told you, yes, I told you," the old voice quavered. "Ah, well, what's done is done, and they that have gone have gone and will not return."

"Yes, Alec, I know." Fergus sighed. "But the Sithean. You saw it, didn't you?"

"Ah, the Sithean." Alec stopped, and was silent for so long that the others thought he was asleep. He still held Fergus's hand, and Fergus himself waited patiently without moving. They heard the old man muttering to himself.

"The Sithean," he said. "Yes, I saw it, twice. It was there and then it was gone. Yes, I saw it."

""Where did you see it?" asked Fergus.

"It was there, where there had only been the hill," continued the old man. "And when I looked again it was gone and it was cold. Yes, I saw it."

"But where, Alec?" Fergus's voice was gentle. "Where were you?"

"I was on Carn Mor, after the sheep," said Alec. "High up and the sun on my back. And I saw it, but only once more."

"Whereabouts on Carn Mor?" Fergus repeated his question, but the old man did not seem to hear. He stared hard into Fergus's face as though he could see him.

"There is great happiness in this room," he said at last, "but not for you, my son."

"I know," whispered Fergus.

"Great happiness," the old voice went on, "but happiness is not everything, don't forget that. Happiness and unhappiness, what are they? They come and go. Like the Sithean, they are there and they are gone. You understand?"

"I understand." Fergus's voice was so low they could hardly hear him.

"It is always so for some of us." Alec stopped and stared into the fire. Presently his daughter came up.

"You must go now," she said kindly. "He is like this.

He is so old. He can't tell you any more. I think he is asleep."

Gently Fergus laid the gnarled hand on the plaid and they went out into the sunlight. After the quiet still room it seemed like another world of light and noise.

"Thank you," said Fergus to the woman. "He is wonderful for one so old."

"I am sorry." Alec's daughter looked worried. "He would tell you if he could."

"That's all right: he told us a lot."

"Will you stay for some tea?"

"No, we've a long way home — back to Carn Mor."

"Ah, Carn Mor. Yon was a fine croft, once."

They left her standing outside the house and went back round the oak wood. Fergus looked distant and preoccupied. They waited for him to speak, bursting with curiosity.

"I'm sorry," he said at last. "I hadn't realised he would be so old."

"He's an amazing man for a hundred and two," said Ninian.

"I didn't understand," said Jean. "What did he mean about unhappiness?"

Fergus smiled at her.

"What should you know about unhappiness?" he asked. "He was talking nonsense. He's fey, I think."

"Has he got the second sight?" asked Sandy.

"I don't know."

"Well, anyway, he said one thing that made sense," said Ninian. "He said the sun was shining when he saw it and that when it was gone it was cold. That proves Hugh's theory of the shadow of one hill against another."

"That's right," said Fiona. "And he was on Carn Mor."

"Of course I didn't understand a word," said Hugh. "Did he say anything else?"

"Lot's about happiness or unhappiness," said Jean.

"And people who were gone."

"Nothing that made sense," added Fergus. He stopped where the burn forked. "This is the parting of the ways, young James, if we're going round the hill."

"It's three o'clock," said Ninian. "You'll have to hurry."

"See you for supper then." Jamie looked for a moment up the burn where they were going and then hurried off the way they had come.

"Poor Jamie," said Fiona. "I thought he'd regret the cow."

Ahead of them the glen ran on, laced by the burn. It was a long glen with steep hills on either side, Ben Fuar on the right and the almost precipitous side of Sgurr Ban on the left.

They went on in silence, thinking of the strange scene in the cottage and of the old man's words. Fergus seemed completely lost and strode ahead, deep in his own thoughts. At last he gave a sigh and smiled.

"A hundred and two," he said. "And ending his life in that glen."

"It's a nice place to end it," said Fiona.

"I know. I envy him," said Fergus. "But I'd hate to be a hundred and two."

"Oh, well." Unaccountably Sandy felt depressed although he had understood as little of the conversation as Jean. "I suppose we might as well keep an eye open for the cave. It may not be on the Fairy Hill after all."

"No, it may not. What about those cliffs?" Ninian nodded at the black rocks of Sgurr Ban. "They should be white," he added, thinking of its name.

"Well, the top's white," said Hugh.

"It'll take us all night if we start climbing them," said Fergus.

"Well, we needn't climb, just look," said Fiona.

They kept on the right of the burn, under the shoulder of Ben Fuar. It was growing cold and they hurried until the hill got too steep.

"Who was Alec?" asked Sandy at last, putting the question they had all longed to ask.

Fergus came back from some far-off land with a start.

"Alec," he said. "He was my grandfather's shepherd. He went to Taransay after he married and I've known him all my life. He's always been strange like that, able to tell things about people, but I suppose he's getting so old now that he wanders a bit."

"What's been done and who's gone?" asked Ninian, while Hugh listened, intrigued, determined to ask Fiona what really had happened when he could get her alone.

"It's a long story," said Fergus, his eyes on the great shoulder of Ben Lair.

"We've a long way to go," suggested Ninian, and Fiona held her breath.

"No," said Fergus, "no way is long enough," and he gave a hard laugh and his mouth took on the bitter sneering look that it had had before. He looked at Ninian, his eyes gleaming, his face dark with anger. "No way is long enough." They had heard his voice like that before, at Taransay. "And most ways are too long." So soft his voice they hardly heard him. "So you see, Ninian, I can't tell you," he added unpleasantly.

"Sorry, Fergus." Not even the most black and evil rage could worry Ninian, and Fiona looked at him enviously. "But all the same, it was a nice glen, Darrach."

"Alec wasn't really very much help," said Jean sadly. "What shall we do to-morrow?"

"We've done Carn Mor pretty thoroughly." Sandy wrinkled his forehead.

"I know." Fiona, as usual, was struck with an idea. "We've never been up Glen Tulacha, just ahead of us. Let's go up there and explore Loch Fada."

It was as good an idea as any.

"Yes, all right," agreed Ninian. "We'll be right under

Ben Lair, too, and it's very steep and rocky."

"Loch Fada, the Long Loch. I've always wanted to see it." Jean had heard of the salmon that had been caught there.

"There it is." Fiona pointed at it below them as they came to the top of the glen. It lay about a mile away to the left. A smaller loch, Loch Gorm, was on their right, and they passed close to it as they rounded the foot of Ben Fuar.

There were a few sandwiches left and they divided them for tea. It was too cold by now to sit about, so they ate while they walked.

"Somehow I don't think we'll ever find it," said Jean, gloomily.

"Oh, we must," said Fiona.

"If we don't, I shan't believe the legend," said Hugh.

"Do you believe in the Fairy Hill now?" Fergus asked him, in a more normal voice.

"Yes, you couldn't help believing that man," Hugh said. "Although I couldn't understand him, he had a very truthful face."

They were climbing up a rough hill now and at the top they stopped and looked down. Loch Dubh lay below them, curving away to the left, dark and cold and gloomy. They went round to the right and Carna seemed a long way ahead and the hills about them looked never-ending. Fiona sighed. The hunt for the cave that had started so well seemed to be ending in failure. They had searched as thoroughly as one could search all the possible hills. There remained only the unlikely Glen Tulacha behind them and the improbable Loch Fada. The Fairy Hill seemed to be as elusive as the cave, and yet old Alec had seen it; it must be there. She pondered over his words, wondering if they meant what she thought they meant, and if they did, how they fitted in with what she thought. Glancing at Fergus she saw that his face looked much happier than it had before, and yet the prophecy had not been a nice one. Evidently there was much that she did not understand. She sighed, finding it difficult to accept, but there was nothing she could do about it.

A shout from Sandy made her look up. They had come to the top of a rise and there, in front of her, lay the Carna Loch, dim with the dusk, and far away a friendly wink of light under the slopes of Carn Mor.

CHAPTER XVIII

SANDY'S CAVE

Sunday, 24th December

A SHRIEK from Jamie brought them all out of bed at dawn the next day.

"Snow!"

Despite the cold they were at the windows gazing out into the grey early morning. The boys came into the kitchen, wrapped in blankets, and joined Fiona and Jean as they peered through the small panes.

"It really is snow," said Sandy. "Quite thick, too."

It had come down heavily during the night, and, settling on the hard frozen ground, none of it had thawed. The hills were white, right down to the shores of the loch; the grass in front of the croft was a smooth unbroken blanket; across the water where it had fallen on the rough tussocky ground tufts of grass stuck through like small black wig-wams. The pine trees on the island had white hats; each frozen branch was topped with a thick crust.

"Snow!" shrieked the twins and Sandy, tearing round the kitchen like maniacs, their mantle-like blankets flapping. "Snow! Bliss! Rapture! Calloo! Callay!"

"Shut up!" cried Fiona, laughing and half-deafened, while Fergus poked a tousled head round the door to ask if they had all gone raving mad.

"Snow!" screamed Jamie and Jean, seizing him by the hands and dragging him into the room. "Real wonderful snow."

"I know, I know." Fergus was laughing, too.

"We must get out the meat-dish. Oh, why haven't we got the toboggan?" mourned Sandy, opening the window to feel if the snow on the ledge was indeed real.

"Shut it!" Ninian slammed it down, nearly squashing his cousin's hand. "We shall freeze to death."

"I must say it does look rather lovely," said Fiona, yawning. "And it's going to be fine, too."

She looked out of the window at the sun rising behind Ben Carrick and tingeing the whole countryside with pink and gold. The Loch was black this morning between its white banks, and over on the other side some specks moved. Hinds! Poor things, down low to find some food. There would not be much here, and she guessed they would be amongst the trees before long, just behind the house.

Snow does make some people temporarily mad, and it seemed to do so with the twins and Sandy. Their first burst of wild spirits had not died down and they were tearing from room to room, up the stairs and into the loft and down again, shrieking madly, their flying blankets knocking over chairs and sticks and sweeping a cup off the table.

"For heaven's sake," said Fiona, as they tore past.

"We're sprites, we're spectres, we belong to the snow," they chanted, whirling through the room. "Snow, snow, glorious snow! Wonderful, beautiful, glorious snow!"

This went on until eventually Sandy tripped over his blanket on his way down the stairs and fell, bringing the others with him. They lay in a heap in the hall, exhausted, giggling, heads and legs and arms protruding from the mass of blankets.

"Talk about raving lunatics," said Hugh, stepping over them on his way to dress. He was so thoroughly awake by now that it was pointless going back to bed.

Before he had pulled on his jersey, Jamie burst into the room like a tornado, flung on his clothes and shot out again, calling something over his shoulder about the cow and hay.

Hugh shrugged his shoulders and finished dressing.

Jamie opened the front door. Luckily it swung inwards, because three inches of snow lay on the doorstep, as smooth and crisp as icing sugar. It seemed a pity to step on it: however they had to get out. Jamie scrunched down towards the Loch, leaving a trail of footprints. He was not the first. Although the snow looked untouched from the windows, a rabbit had hopped across it, leaving its strange three legged print; birds had criss-crossed over it too, and along the east of the wall were the tracks of deer, quite close to the house. The air this morning felt cleaner and finer than ever. Jamie took deep breaths and felt them tingle in his throat. Left and right, as he looked along Carn Mor, it was white, rocks breaking the even blanket, but still white, right up to Loch Dubh and beyond.

A snowball caught him on the shoulder and he whirled round in time to see Sandy's brown head bob behind the wall. In a minute the air was thick with flung snow and shrieks until Sandy called Pax and they went to milk the cow.

"Lucky we brought plenty of hay," said Jamie, as he leant against the byre door. "But oughtn't she to have cow-cake or something?"

Sandy, his head against her black flank, grunted. Jamie took this for yes and went on:

"Well, we haven't got any. What shall we do? We must go and get some."

"How?" asked Sandy.

"I don't know. I say," a thought dawned upon James, "if it gets any worse we'll be snowed up!"

"Gracious!" This had not occurred to Sandy. "D'you suppose we've got enough food?"

"Masses. There's all the hind." Jamie nodded to the joints still hanging in the byre. "Then, of course, we've plenty of milk. Lucky we've got the cow."

"Not if we haven't enough to give her to eat," pointed out Sandy.

"Well, the hinds live somehow," said James. "Bracken. They probably eat that and leaves and things."

"She won't give very good milk on a diet of dead leaves." Sandy paused in the milking.

"Hay's only dead grass," said Jamie.

"Don't be silly."

"Well, we'll ask Ninian." Sandy had great faith in his cousin.

"He's livid about the cow anyway," said Jamie, sadly, stroking the rough black hair.

"Not really," said Sandy. "As long as he doesn't have to do anything about her."

By the time they returned to the house with the pail of warm milk Fiona had broken the first of twelve eggs into the frying-pan. The boys and Fergus had two, she and Jean could not manage more than one.

An air of excitement buzzed through the cottage. People kept wandering into the kitchen in varying stages of undress and asking questions and wandering out again. Socks and shoes seemed to have vanished during the night, vital things like knives and coffee-pots had been spirited away, only to reappear in an unlikely place. Hugh returned from the burn, the bucket chinking, reporting that there was ice right across and that he had had to break it. Jean, looking out of a window, saw hinds just beyond the western wall of the croft. Ninian, putting on his shoes in the kitchen, broke a lace and swore loudly. All the time outside the sun crept higher and higher, sparkling and gleaming on trees and rocks and grass, on the roof of the house and the top of Carn Mor, on the still water of the Loch and the racing, ice-blue burn.

All through breakfast people kept leaping up to look out of the window to see that it was really still there, in case a hind was snuffling outside; to throw crumbs to a fat, cold robin who came and perched on the sill. Jean broke up a whole dish of crusts and pieces of toast and scattered them outside, and more birds than they had thought lived in this deserted place came fluttering round.

"We mustn't forget them," said Jean. "We must put out food every day for them while the snow lasts."

The sun gleamed on her fair hair as she stood outside scattering the crumbs. The robins, made bold by hunger, came right up to her feet.

"They're quite tame," she said, entranced.

Somehow, this morning, it was impossible to get anything done, decided Fiona. As soon as you said you really must start washing up someone called you to look at the icicles hanging from the eaves or the patch of snow melting round the chimney. Sandy and James were fussing about the cow, and the byre had to be inspected to see that it was comfortable and warm enough. Fergus's only remaining clean socks had a hole in them, and the others and literally hundreds of pairs of the boys' simply had to be washed. Jean called from the back of the cottage that the wood-pile had simply vanished, was there a spade so that she could dig for the logs? When a snowball, thrown by Hugh, thudded on the kitchen window, she gave up and rushed out to join them.

A furious fight was going on. Fergus and the twins against Sandy, Ninian and Hugh. She stood watching for a moment or two until a wild shot from Sandy hit her on the leg, then she joined in on the other side, and their combined efforts drove the three boys into a corner of the wall. Rallying with a tremendous cry, Ninian rushed out and chased her along the Loch shore until she tripped over a tussock and lay laughing while he pelted her with snow.

They walked back together, watching the end of the battle by the house. Sandy and Hugh were definitely getting the worst of it, although white patches on Fergus's blue jersey showed that several hits had been scored. As Ninian and Fiona came up they stopped and tried to brush the snow off.

Fergus, strolling down towards the Loch, decided that it was one of the most lovely mornings he had ever seen. It had that peculiar stillness that some snowy mornings have, as though the whole world had been crystallised and turned to ice. Each sound was magnified and voices came clearly on the still air. He felt in the highest spirits, his black mood of yesterday vanished, it would be impossible to be anything but as mad as Sandy this morning when the air went straight to your head like wine.

The twins and their cousin had escaped from Fiona's clutches for the washing up and were out along by the wall building a snow-man. Jean's red jersey and Jamie's green one were bright splashes of colour against the white. They paused in their building every now and then to throw handfuls of snow at each other. Fergus went slowly up to join them.

Fiona, looking out of the window a few minutes later, laughed.

"What is it?" Hugh, who was helping with the washing up, peered over her shoulder. "Fergus seems in a better mood this morning," he said.

"Yes, thank goodness." Fiona went back to the sink.

"You like him, don't you?" Hugh asked.

"Well, don't you?"

"Y-e-e-s. Yes, I do. Almost always," said Hugh.

Ninian, coming in with an armful of logs, stopped in the scullery.

"I say," he said, "we'd better row down to Loch Dubh; it won't be very good going on this rough ground."

"Glen Tulacha'll be awful," Fiona rubbed at an obstinate plate, "if it lives up to its name."

"Why, what does it mean?" asked Hugh.

"Tussocky, hillocky," explained Ninian. "But actually they're bigger hillocks than the ones along by the Loch and won't be so difficult to walk on."

He dumped his logs and went down to the boat to see if

BUILDING A SNOW-MAN.

it was full of snow.

An hour later they were all on the jetty, bags of food and beer and a couple of Thermoses of hot coffee with them, and long sticks to prod the drifts, and Fiona's glass and some oilies to spread on the thwarts where they were wet.

Fergus and Ninian took the oars and pulled out into the Loch. It was still glassy calm and blue now that the sun was up. They rowed slowly; seven people in the dinghy was no light weight, besides, they had the whole day ahead of them.

The shores of the Carna Loch seemed alive with deer, scraping amongst the rocks for grass and leaves.

"There must be masses down by the Lodge," said Jamie. "I do wonder if it's thick there as well."

"Sure to be." Ninian looked forward over his shoulder. "It must have snowed like mad last night to be so deep this morning. Of course the ground is hard."

"And it's still freezing in spite of the sun," added Hugh.

Fergus, keeping time with Ninian's long stroke, rowed slowly, his eyes on the white side of Carn Mor, his thoughts at Taransay. How lovely it must look there now — the turrets and towers and steep roofs white-capped, rising out of the dark mass of the castle, and, on the rock on which it was built, each grassy ledge carpeted with white like all the uneven stones in the castle walls. He remembered seeing it like that on just such a morning as this. The Minch had glittered with gold under the sun, the distant hills of the mainland had been as white as clouds, and Taransay itself had jutted out into the calm water, its dark walls glistening as the snow melted, each window gleaming, each sloping roof soft-white. And above it in the still air the smoke from the countless chimneys drifting in a haze, and the great red flag hanging motionless from its standard. That had been many years ago, but it would look the same now if it had snowed there last night, save that one chimney only would smoke and most of the windows would be broken and the flag-staff would be bare, for the flag had been burnt one wild winter night on the top of the hill. Fergus jerked his mind back from such memories, and caught Jean's eye as she sat in the stern and smiled at her. She had been watching his face cloud and grow black as he stared into the distance, and smiled back at him.

Sandy and James were still in wild spirits and rocked the boat alarmingly in their efforts to see how far they could stare into the golden-brown water. Ninian had to use his sternest voice to prevent them from upsetting it altogether; but although they stopped they were far from quelled and giggled and poked each other until Fiona, sitting between them in the bows, was nearly driven mad.

To her great relief, on looking over her shoulder, she could see the Narrows just ahead.

"Steady, Ninian," she called, "we're just up to the Narrows."

Ninian, knowing the place of old, stopped rowing and glanced over his shoulder. It was more of a shallows than a narrows really, and as they grated against a rock he told Fergus to stop rowing. The boat bumped on for a moment or two and then came to rest on the bottom. Fiona stood up, stretching her cramped legs, and jumped out on to the nearest rock.

"We'll have to get out and drag her over," she told Hugh. "It's a kind of causeway."

They gladly followed her ashore, stiff and cold after their hour's confinement in the boat. It was easy to see the bottom here and possible to walk across without getting your feet wet. They laid hold of the heavy boat and heaved and tugged her over, their cold fingers slipping on the wood. Then she was across and afloat in the calm black water of Loch Dubh.

"It almost feels as if one has to whisper," said Jean in a hushed voice as the boat lay still on the water.

Certainly they had never known Loch Dubh so quiet as it was to-day. They waited there for a moment or two, looking round them, almost in awe. The mighty hills, so close and overpowering, soared up on either hand, majestic, wonderful, their shoulders carved in marble, great noble sweeping lines rising sheer from the water's edge, utterly silent and still. They seemed empty, devoid of any living thing, and no one dared speak and let his voice be the one to break that clear, brittle air. They stared and stared. The Loch curved right out of sight into the arms of the hills; they felt uneasy at the thought of rounding that corner although they knew that before them would be the narrow opening of the glen up to Loch Gorm. Even Sandy and James were quelled. They, too, sat silent, staring round them at the familiar and yet different hills.

Fiona broke the silence.

"We needn't row right in," she said, and her voice seemed to echo down the Loch. "The head of Glen Tulacha is just here," and she pointed right to where a small hill — Craig an Loch Dubh — lay just beneath Ben Lair.

"Yes, you're right," said Ninian, glad that she had broken the spell. "Row in behind that little island, Fergus. I think we can land there."

They turned the boat and pulled in towards the shore, coming nearer and nearer to the sheer side of Ben Lair. Behind a rock, that could hardly be called an island, a small shelving beach lay and they ground the dinghy here and pulled her up.

"Hardly likely that anything will happen to her here," said Sandy, as he watched Ninian making her fast to a rock.

"You never know." Ninian tugged at his clove-hitch. He liked to be on the safe side with a boat.

Fiona led them up the beach and into the snow. It was no use trying to hurry as tufts and tussocks tripped one at every step. They climbed the side of the Craig, leaving patches of bare frozen grass as they kicked and scrunched four inches or so of snow underfoot.

At the top of the hill they stopped and looked down, picking out the best route up Glen Tulacha, which lay below them under Ben Lair and driving south-east into the hills. This end of Ben Lair was so precipitous that no snow could settle there, so that it was as black and grim as ever. A burn, falling from rock to rock, sounded far louder than usual as it poured down the cliff with a clear ringing sound. There was a good-sized burn running down Glen Tulacha, too, half-frozen over in places, but the water, instead of peaty-brown, was as clear as ice from the snow. It ran from Loch Fada, but was fed by numerous small channels off the surrounding hills. There were bare, twisted birch and rowan trees growing along its banks, their branches black against the snow, and hinds were down beside it, trying to find grass here where the ground was flat.

"Come on," cried Sandy at last. "If there's going to be a cave it'll be in those cliffs," and he started off down the hill. The others followed, but they had really given up all hope of finding it. They had searched all the possible ground that James Stewart had owned and known. This was off his forest and therefore unlikely that he would have explored it thoroughly enough to have known of the existence of the cave. Carn Mor no longer belonged to them, but it had in the old days, and Ben Fuar had marched with his land and therefore been a possibility. Anyway this was a lovely place, and there was no harm in keeping an eye open for the cave.

Sandy ran ahead of them, kicking up drifts of snow, and they followed him, capturing something of his high spirits, until they were all flying downhill, almost out of control.

They slowed down by the burn and walked up it, looking for a place to cross. Sandy had insisted on their going as near to the cliffs as possible.

"There'll probably be an avalanche if you make so much

noise," said Fiona unwisely.

"Oh, will there? What fun! I've never seen one," cried Sandy. "Ahoy!" he shouted at the top of his voice.

"Ahoy! Hoy!" came back from the cliffs of Ben Lair.

"What a wonderful echo, a double one," said Fiona. "Jamie!" she cried.

"Jamie!" called the echo.

"Fergus!"

"Fergus!" It repeated both syllables.

"Come back!" called Jean.

"Come back!" This was fascinating. They stood in the snow, shouting at Ben Lair until they were hoarse. Ninian gave a tremendous bellow. "Ahoy!"

"Ahoy! Ahoy! Hoy! Hoy! Hoy!" It died away in the hills.

"I'm cold!" screamed Jean at last.

"I'm cold!" answered the hill.

"Good-bye! Good-bye!" yelled Sandy.

" 'Bye! Good-bye!"

They went on.

"It's the best we've ever found." Fiona cleared her throat.

"Talk about 'reverberate hills'," said Hugh.

"No avalanche," said Sandy, sadly, and Ninian threw a handful of snow at him.

That was fatal, of course, and they scattered like a flock of birds, each behind a rock, and pelted one another until Ninian, looking at his watch, called to them to stop.

"It's nearly one," he said.

"Your watch must be mad; it can't be." Fiona tried to imagine how the morning could have gone so fast.

"Well, we were hours messing about outside the croft," said Fergus, "and it took some time to row down here."

"I suppose so." She was not convinced. It still seemed early morning.

They crossed the burn where it ran shallow over some rocks and continued up the other side.

"I say," said Jamie suddenly, "I've thought of something rather frightful."

"What?" asked Ninian suspiciously.

"I think I can guess," said Fiona, eyeing him. "The cow."

"Yes, one of us'll have to go back to milk her." "And feed her," added Sandy.

"We'll all have to go," said Fergus pointedly. "There's only one boat."

"Yes," said Jamie in a small voice. He looked sideways at his brother, who, as he so rightly guessed, was scowling.

"You are the absolute end, James," he said. "Why you had to bring that wretched animal up here I can't imagine, but now to inflict it on all of us by making us go back early is the limit."

"I'm sorry, Ninian." Jamie was sorry. Ninian did not appreciate the cow, her friendliness towards him, and the homey feeling it gave him to see her in the field.

Ninian, from glowering at the ground, suddenly looked up. The clean white faces of the hills were smiling in the sun and they smelt good and it was warm and pleasant. He glanced at Jamie. He was, after all, very like Jean. He grinned and scooped a handful of snow off a rock.

"Never mind, Shamus," he said, "we'll have plenty of time to see the Loch and get back. We don't want to be out in the dark to-day." His arm went back, and instead of throwing the snowball at his brother he sent it spinning through the air, so that it broke in a splosh of white on the black cliff face.

"Lunch soon, I think," said Hugh, relieved.

"Let's wait till we get to the Loch," said Jean, and they hurried on.

Hugh, who had been frowning to himself and counting on his fingers, suddenly shouted.

"What on earth?" Fiona looked round.

"Has everybody realised something?" he asked. "No,

what sort of thing?" said Sandy.

"We're all quite completely raving mad," said Hugh, grinning. "It's Christmas Eve."

"Christmas Eve? It can't be!" Ninian started reckoning the days. "But it is!"

This was too much, and it set the twins and Sandy off again.

"Christmas Eve!" they screamed. "Christmas, Christmas Eve!"

"Oh, not again, please," said Fiona. "I can't bear it." They went tearing off over the snow and came back again, panting.

"We must hang up our Stockings!" cried Jean.

"Have you brought your squeeze-box?" asked Jamie, and Fergus nodded. "Carols! We can sing carols."

"Oh, bliss!" Jean's eyes shone.

"We are rather mad, though," said Ninian. "Fancy not remembering."

"We haven't got any holly," said Fiona practically.

"Pine branches with rowan berries tied on," suggested Fergus, much amused. "What about mistletoe?"

They thought hard, but could not imagine anything that would do instead.

"Anyway," said Jean at last, "it's not as if we really need mistletoe," which made them all laugh.

They were about half-way along the glen by now, a long, narrow, hillocky place, drifts of snow lying on the weather side of the hills, the ground almost bare on the lee.

"The wind must have fairly shrieked up here last night," said Ninian, looking at the smooth side of a drift. "Hope it doesn't get up again."

"Yes, it'd be a nasty place to get caught in," agreed Hugh. "I can imagine this glen seeming the longest in the world if you were in a hurry."

There was a great monotony about the place, almost two miles of it — narrow, humpy, steep-sided.

"Well, we're nearly there." Sandy looked on to the ridge ahead. "Loch Fada must be over that."

The cave, the Sithean were forgotten. Even Jamie only gave the hillsides the most cursory glance. Previous Christmases were discussed; large, noisy ones at the Lodge; dim, half-forgotten ones at the House; and the Hogmanays that followed; dancing in the village hall, and long ago, in Carrick House; ceilidhs, weddings, children's parties, and the weeks of gaiety from Christmas to Hogmanay.

"We must go to church to-morrow," announced Fiona suddenly. "Mustn't we, Ninian?"

"Yes, we should. It'll be rather unpopular if we don't." Sandy looked mutinous, but Fergus said, looking at the sky:

"I doubt if you'll get there if we have any more snow."

"We'll have to try," said Ninian.

"I haven't got a skirt," said Jean.

"You'll have to change at the Lodge," said Fiona.

"As a matter of fact we'll all have to change," said Jamie. "At least, none of us are exactly dressed for church."

He looked round at them. Ninian in his oldest kilt and a coat patched with leather, Sandy and Hugh in ancient stained and torn tweeds, and Fiona not much better, Jean and himself in three jersies apiece, and huge bright ones on the top, Fergus looking like a disreputable fisherman.

"You can count me out," he said, laughing. "I've got nothing but this, this side of the Minch, and I haven't been to church for years."

"That's no excuse," said Fiona firmly. "Ninian can lend you something."

Ninian, who was at least six inches taller than Fergus, grinned.

"We're not there yet," said Fergus, who was not making any promises.

Still, the day was clear and cloudless, the snow thawing slightly in places and sliding off rocks and down the cliffs.

"Wish we'd got the sledge," said Sandy.

"Fat lot of good the sledge would be up here," said Ninian. "The ground's far too rough. You want something like the track or the road by Invercarrick."

At last they reached the head of Glen Tulacha and looked down towards Loch Fada, Ben Lair and Slioch on the right, Ben Tarsuinn on the left and open flat country beyond. It was nearly as dark as Loch Dubh at this end, but farther down the hills stood back, leaving it unprotected. It was an uninspiring Loch, they thought, with none of the character of the ones at Carrick. Even Jean was disappointed.

"I suppose it might be here," said Jamie dubiously.

"What? Oh, the cave. Yes, it might." Fiona was feeling cold and not at all inclined to slither about on the hill looking for a non-existent cave.

"Let's have lunch," said Hugh again.

The place looked bleak and bare until Fergus spied a little wood half a mile away at the foot of a corrie on Ben Lair. They found a sheltered place here in the snow, and the warm coffee revived them.

Sandy, seeing a pine tree, insisted on being boosted up by Hugh to pick branches, although Fiona swore there were some just behind the croft.

"Well, these are extra nice," said Sandy. "Come on, James, we'll find some rowan berries."

They crackled off through the trees and up the corrie. There must have been a glacier here once or else a landslide, for the ground was littered with enormous boulders of every shape and size. The trees grew up the side of the hill, and Sandy, climbing over a vast rock in his effort to get to a rowan tree, looked down and found himself staring into the mouth of what appeared to be a vast cave.

His piercing shriek brought everyone hurrying and scrambling towards him.

"What is it?" called Fiona, with a vision of a broken leg

and dragging Sandy home on a hurdle of branches.

"A cave!" shouted Sandy, dancing on the rock with excitement.

"Where?" they all yelled.

"Here!" Sandy slipped on the snow and fell practically into the entrance. They came panting up and stood round him.

It did indeed seem a likely place. Hidden by the rocks, sheltered by the wood, a burn only a few yards away.

"It must be it," said Jamie. He produced a slightly bent candle from his pocket and Ninian gave him a match. They watched with eager faces as Sandy advanced, the candle in one hand. All except Fergus, who was grinning broadly. Fiona looked at him and wondered why. He had believed in the cave as much as they had; surely he couldn't know?

Sandy ducked his head and went in. He straightened himself gingerly and stood up, looking round. Certainly it was a better cave than Hugh's or Jamie's but it was not good enough. It was far too small. No smoke had ever blackened these walls; it did not look as though any foot had disturbed the drifts of leaves on the floor for thousands of years.

They crowded in behind him.

"Is it it?" asked Jean.

Ninian shook his head. There was not room for them all inside; the cave was no wider than its opening and only a little deeper.

"Too small, surely," said Fergus, coming back into the sunlight. "But a lovely place."

"We must remember this in case we ever get caught uphere at night," said Sandy. "It must be warm with all these leaves inside."

Sadly they went back to where they had left the lunch things, picking up the branches Jamie had strewn on the ground in his excitement.

"We must go home. Come on." Ninian looked at his watch, and they followed their footprints back out of the wood.

Grey clouds were piling behind them, and the wind had sprung up, north-east and cold. Fergus and Ninian glanced at one another and strode quickly back along the glen.

The kitchen fire was open and stacked up as high as it would go with peat and logs. The windows and doors, securely shut, rattled under the rising wind. The lamp hung above them from its iron hook, throwing the now familiar pattern of shadows on the ceiling. The curtains were drawn tight and chairs and rugs pulled close to the flames. The kettle was singing and the smell of peat and pine-wood and tobacco filled the room. On the table was a pile of green branches and red berries, tied on with black cotton from Fiona's work basket and looking almost like real holly. She and Jean were curled up on rugs, pulling stockings from a huge pile in front of them and darning slowly. The boys sat and sprawled on the chairs and table; their glasses of beer and a whisky were on the floor somewhere, in imminent danger of being kicked over. The back door opened and slammed, and a rush of cold air rustled the curtains and swung the lamp. Sandy and James came in, stamping snow off their feet and rubbing their hands.

"Gosh, it's cold out," said Sandy, stepping over Jean to get near the fire.

"Snowing yet?" asked Ninian.

"No, patchy clouds. The moon's coming up."

"It's freezing, I think," said James.

"How's the cow; all tucked up?" asked Hugh.

"Yes, it's lovely and warm in the byre. We've given her plenty of bracken and hay and she seems quite happy," said Jamie.

"Umm! I'd rather be in here." Fergus held the glass between his hands and looked into it, the whisky full of light from the fire. "There couldn't be a nicer Christmas Eve."

"Glad I'm not out, anyway," said Ninian, as an extra hard gust rattled the windows.

"Wretched deer," said Fiona. "They're probably in the byre with the cow if they've got any sense." She rolled up a pair of stockings, Hugh's, and threw them at him.

"I can't darn another thing," she said. "Fergus, where's your squeeze-box?"

Fergus reached down beside his chair and picked up the box. He finished his whisky and nodded as Ninian held up the bottle. He waited until his glass was refilled and then plunged into a tune, his own.

"Oh, who will go with Fergus now?"

From that he changed to a carol, and they nearly lifted the roof off with "Hark the Herald Angels Sing." All the other well-known ones followed, and Jamie sang solo for "The Holly and the Ivy." Fergus played till his fingers ached. They kept thinking of others, some that he did not know, but picked up as they sang.

Hugh got up to throw a log on the fire and they stopped, and finished their glasses.

"I know." Fiona leapt up and rushed to the window. Outside the moon shone fitfully on the snow while banks of cloud moved up from the east. There was a lull in the wind for the moment, and everything looked startlingly lovely "I know, oh, do let's!" Fiona turned round to them, her eyes shining. "We can act 'Good King Wenceslaus'; it's absolutely perfect for it."

"Much too cold." Ninian shivered, but the twins and Sandy sprang up and came to peer over her shoulder.

"Oh, do let's," said Jean.

"It needn't take long." Jamie stared into the night, set before him like a stage.

"We can wrap ourselves in rugs and blankets," Fiona went on. "I'll make a crown."

"Who'll be who?" asked Hugh, resigned.

"Jean had better be the page." Fergus smiled.

"And Ninian the King," said Jamie. "You'll have to be playing, Fergus."

"We'll be the chorus." Fiona cut zigzags in the top half of a paper bag. "Who'll be the peasant?"

"Bags," said Sandy and James, so they had to toss and Sandy won.

"Come on and get dressed." Jean pulled Ninian out of his chair.

A quarter of an hour later they opened the front door and went out. It certainly was a perfect night for the carol, a shade too cold and cloudy, but there was the snow and the moon.

The hills were white and silver and black; the Loch was black and silver. The wind, keen and frosty, stung their faces and made them shiver.

"Fergus will get cold hands," said Jean, draped in a blanket.

Ninian strode on to the grass, magnificent in a rug, draped like a cloak, a sword (Hugh's stick) and Fiona's crown. Sandy, almost invisible under towels and rugs that were meant to look like rags, capered wildly.

"Where shall I go?" he asked.

"Down by the burn," said Fiona. "We'll stand outside the far side of the door and Ninian can come 'looking out.' Is that all right?"

"Fine." Sandy rushed off, the chorus arranged themselves, Ninian followed Jean into the house, thoughtfully shutting the door behind him.

Fergus, Jamie, Fiona and Hugh stood in the wings of their impromptu theatre, the stage itself being the sloping ground in front of the croft, the orchestra the cold water of the Carna Loch. The sky was full; moon, cloud and stars patterned there and moving in a way that, if you stared, it was difficult to tell which did move, the planets or the clouds. The set was Carn Mor and the cottage, lit by one glowing window, and the tumbled wall. The snow sparkled white as, for a moment, the moon shone out.

Fergus struck a chord. The door was flung open and Ninian in cloak and crown, a King indeed, stood silhouetted against the dim-lit hall, his little page behind him.

"Good King Wenceslaus looked out
On the feast of Stephen,
When the snow lay round about
Deep and crisp and even."

The voices of the chorus rose high into the cold air on clouds of white breath.

"Brightly shone the moon that night
Though the frost was cruel,
When a poor man came in sight
Gathering winter fuel."

Moon and frost were there, and Sandy, a bent old man in fluttering rags, seeking firewood by the burn.

"Hither page and stand by me
If thou know'st it telling
Yonder peasant who is he
Where and what his dwelling?"

That was Ninian's deep voice, as he pointed with outstretched arm at the bent figure.

"Sire, he lives a good league hence
Underneath the mountain,

Right against the forest's fence
By St. Agnes fountain."

The page sounded as if already he felt cold and faint, but his voice steadied as he gestured at the tall hill and the little wood behind the croft. By now, Ninian was out in the snow, a long black shadow thrown before him. The chorus stood silent. The first flakes of snow began to fall.

"Bring me flesh and bring me wine,
Bring me pine-logs hither,
Thou and I will see him dine
When we bear them thither."

The props, arranged by James, lay just inside the door, and it only took Jean a moment to reappear with a haunch of venison, a bottle of whisky and a huge log. She struggled out into the snow, her hair silver under the moon. The chorus took up the song.

"Page and Monarch forth they went,
Forth they went together,
Through the rude wind's wild lament
And the bitter weather."

Fergus moved out of the shadow and the others followed. If they had but known it they fitted in well with the legendary scene, looking, in their cloaks, like wandering minstrels.

"Sire, the night grows darker now
And the wind blows stronger,
Fails my heart I know not how,
I can go no longer."

Loaded down with meat and wine and logs, it was no

wonder the page felt tired. Fiona whispered as much to Hugh, who grinned and answered that the King should have carried it himself. The present King was having too good a time with his cloak, swinging it back across his shoulder in a dashing manner, to be concerned with anything else.

"Mark my footsteps, good my page,
Tread thou in them boldly,
Thou wilt find the winter's rage
Freeze thy blood less coldly."

The tall King and the little page must have looked very much the same long ago, thought Fergus, with the moon lighting their way and the tall white hill above them.

"In his master's steps he trod
Where the snow lay dinted,
Heat was in the very sod
Which the saint had printed."

The page was having a job to stretch from step to step behind his master. The wine slipped and fell, and Fergus missed a note, but went on again as it was picked up intact.

"Therefore Christian men be sure,
Wealth or rank possessing ;
Ye who now do bless the poor
Shall yourselves find blessing."

Even the peasant joined in the last verse, tearing pieces off the joint and wolfing them in a realistically famished way. Then they came tearing back over the snow, Jean stumbling in the folds of her rug, while the chorus applauded.

"Oh, it was lovely!" cried Fiona. "I wish we could do

some more."

But Fergus, blowing on his cold fingers, was firm and led the way indoors.

"Can't we do 'While Shepherds Watched'?" asked Sandy.

"No, not so good. Why, do you fancy yourself as an angel?" asked Ninian, as he shut the door.

An hour later Fergus, Fiona, Hugh and Ninian filled stockings for the twins and Sandy, who were already in bed, and then some for each other.

"All go to bed," cried Fergus, "and I'll come and hang them up. You might pretend to be asleep."

"All right," said Ninian, laughing. "We won't look."

"I'll pin yours on, Fergus," said Fiona. "But you mustn't look either."

"No, I won't," he promised.

One by one the lights dimmed and were blown out and the croft curled up, as it were, for the night under its blanket of snow.

CHAPTER XIX

SNOWED UP

Monday, 25th December

"HAPPY CHRISTMAS!" Fiona's dark head came round the door of the boys' room. On seeing several drowsy eyes open she came in with a tray of tea. At this unusual sight the boys sat up, and Sandy and Jean followed Fiona in.

Sandy had been up early and gave James a favourable report on the cow. Jean went and banged on Fergus's door until a sleepy voice called:

"What is it?"

"Come and have some tea," said Jean. "And bring your stocking."

"What sort of a day is it?" Ninian sat up and pulled on his dressing-gown. It certainly was cold and Sandy shut the window with a bang.

"Masses more snow," he said. "Huge drifts. Really an awful lot."

"Wonder if we can get down the track," said Jamie.

"We'll have to try." Ninian took a sip of tea.

The door of the annexe opened and Fergus appeared, dark and unshaven in an old dressing-gown. He sat on the end of the big bed and pulled a blanket over him, and Fiona gave him some tea.

"Tremendous luxury," he said.

"It's a treat for Christmas morning," explained Jean. "I'm going to open my stocking."

"Oh, you might unpin mine." Jamie pulled the bedclothes up to his chin.

"One at a time," said Hugh.

"All right, but just give it to me, Fergus," said Jamie.

Jean, meanwhile, had pulled out a carrot from the top,

which was the nearest they could get to a cracker. A skein of mending-wool, an egg, a bar of chocolate, some biscuits.

"I'm afraid there wasn't much scope," said Fiona.

"These are lovely," said Jean, pulling out a small, carefully wrapped parcel. She stared at it, turning it over. "Who from?" she asked.

"Me." Fergus smiled. "Go on, open it."

She untied the string. Inside was a simply-carved wooden statue of a man. He wore a cloak and hood and his hands were folded in front of him as if in prayer. Although his face was roughly cut, it expressed great calm and peace and happiness. His back was uncarved, the plain wood charred as if by a fire.

"He's a little saint," explained Fergus. "His church was burnt down, that's why he looks black at the back. He's especially good at keeping away horrid things, so I thought of you and the trolls. He might help."

"Oh, Fergus, thank you so much." Jean was amazed that he should have thought of such a thing. She had always thought he laughed at her, and now, although he was smiling, it was a nice kind of smile.

"He's called St. Yves," Fergus went on. "There was another, but he

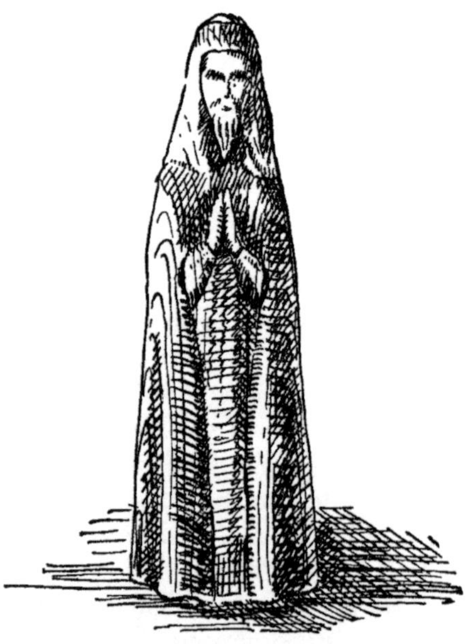

"HE'S CALLED ST. YVES."

was, too, burnt. Of course he's frightfully old."

After the unexpectedness of Jean's presents the others could hardly wait to see what they had got.

"Hurry up, Jean," said Sandy. "I want to open mine." Jean dived into the stocking's toe and brought out an orange.

"That's all," she said.

Sandy and James's stockings were the same; carrots, turnip-tops (for the cow, Fiona told them), chocolate and biscuits, an orange and a clip of bullets; and from Fergus, Breton fisherman's berets. These were instantly tried on, and they looked so funny that every one was weak with laughter by the time Fiona opened her things. She had packed it herself, and thought she knew what was in it, and was tremendously surprised when she pulled out some writing-paper, from Ninian, a new silk handkerchief from Hugh, and Fergus's parcel, which contained the most lovely hand-made lace and embroidered ribbon.

Hugh's and Ninian's were identical, too, as far as the chocolate, oranges, biscuits and an egg each. Hugh had a pipe from Ninian, and Ninian a tin of tobacco from Hugh. Fergus gave them each a bottle of smuggled French brandy.

"What a wonderful Christmas!" said Fiona. "More fun, because everything's so unexpected."

"Open your stocking, Fergus," said Jean, running her fingers down the carved folds of St Yves' cloak.

"There won't be anything like the things he's given us," said Jamie sadly.

He had the same things as the others, but his special presents were a pair of socks that Fiona had originally been knitting for Ninian but had hurriedly finished for Fergus, a new knife Sandy had bought for himself but not used, and a tin of tobacco, from Ninian this time.

"Just what I wanted, all of them," said Fergus, snapping shut the knife. He unrolled the stockings and looked at them, wondering if they would fit.

"They will," Fiona said. "They're the same size as the ones I was darning!"

Ninian looked at his watch and sat up.

"I hate to disturb everyone," he said, "but it's halfpast eight and we must get going. Church is at eleven, and we've got to change at the Lodge, and goodness knows how long it'll take us to get down the track."

"I'll rush and get the breakfast then," said Fiona, who was already dressed.

A quarter of an hour later they were sitting round the table, plates of scrambled eggs and bacon in front of them.

Ninian, who had been looking out of the window while he dressed, was more dubious than ever about them reaching the Lodge. Snow had fallen so heavily during the night that all their footsteps from the day before had been covered and new humped drifts lay where the wind had blown them during the night. Across on the other side of the Loch several rocks he remembered seeing yesterday were hidden, and the hills all round looked smoother and more blanketed than ever. Down at the Lodge Maggie would be getting in a fuss if she did not hear from them. Perhaps at the other end of the Loch it would not be so bad.

Sandy, who had gone down to the burn with the bucket, came back, reporting that there were drifts over his knees and that yesterday's snow was a mere nothing.

"The sooner we get started then, the better," said Ninian, gulping down coffee.

Washing up and bedmaking were hurried through. The stove was well banked up and a big supply of wood and coal and water brought in. They put on their warmest clothes and thickest boots. Fergus pulled on his thigh-boots. Jamie opened the front door, and about a foot of snow that had drifted on to the doorstep fell into the hall.

"We'd better take a spade," said Hugh. "Where is it? In

the byre?"

"Yes, the far end." Sandy swept the step clean.

Hugh returned with the spade, reporting that there were deer-tracks all round the house, especially by the rubbish dump, and also big claw-marks which might be an eagle. Everyone had to go and see, and it was decided that it was an eagle. Sandy discovered the pad-marks of a wild cat.

"Rather unsafe to go out at night," said Fiona, "with all these ravening animals about."

There was a great flock of birds around the dish of food Jean had put out.

"Hundreds of them must die most winters," said Hugh as they went back to the house. "I wonder what they do when we're not here?"

Once out of the drifts the going was not so bad, although seven or eight inches deep in most places. The boat was white, thick slices of snow lying along the thwarts and half-filling her.

"Nice easy way of bailing," said Sandy, throwing handfuls of snow overboard. She did not take long to empty and they pushed her down alongside the jetty.

Ninian and Hugh took the oars, and slowly they moved off over the still water.

It was calm and windless. Sky and loch were the same dull grey; all the surrounding countryside was the thick, smooth white of newly fallen snow, rocks and trees breaking the monotony with patches and strips of black. The oars splashed sharply as they pulled north; hinds, down by the Loch shore, flung up their heads and stood staring, but did not move off.

Fiona, looking back over her shoulder, found her eyes aching with the immense whiteness. The croft itself, with the snow driven up against the walls and on the low roof, was nothing but a grey smudge, though the chimney showed black as the snow melted. Smoke rose high into the still air, misty against the white slope of Carn Mor. Right, the wood was hardly visible, so coated were the trees, but beyond that, the gully running from top to bottom of the hill had one side almost uncovered where it had been sheltered from the wind. It lay, a dark furrow of rocks sticking through a layer of snow.

They rowed quickly up the Carna Loch and arrived warm and breathless at the pier below the bothy. High, unbroken banks of snow rose to meet them.

"We'll never be able to use the Ford," said James.

"Where is it?" cried Sandy, as they came to the top of the rise up from the shore.

A great drift had blown against the side of the bothy, leaving only its high steep roof and chimney protruding.

"I can see a wing and a bit of the roof," said Hugh, as they floundered towards it.

"Poor thing," said Fiona. "Will it be all right, Ninian?"

"I hope so, but there's nothing much we can do about it now." Ninian struggled up out of an extra deep drift.

Fergus, in his thigh-boots, had the best of it. Jean was up to her waist at one time. The drift in places was like great rollers frozen in the act of breaking so that they curled under and hung there. It seemed a pity to break such loveliness but there was no other way up to the car. At last they reached it, and stood laughing. They scraped a little snow off and Sandy attacked it with the shovel.

"It's useless," said Ninian. "It'll probably snow again to-night."

"I hope it doesn't tear the hood." Hugh looked up at the weight of snow on the roof. "As far as I remember it's not too strong."

"I suppose it was mad to leave it here." Ninian ruffled his hair. "Oh, well, we couldn't really do anything else."

"And now what?" asked Fiona, stamping her cold feet.

Ninian looked dubiously at what he imagined was the track.

"We might as well try," he said. "If it gets too deep we can turn back."

The first part of the road was flat and straight, rough, hillocky country and lochans on either side, then curving downhill to the right. They managed the first mile fairly well, although it was tiring work struggling over the snow. At the ridge they stopped and looked down the curving glen ahead. There was no sign of the track except for what might have been a slight depression across the smooth white hill. Where it bent out of sight round a knoll, a huge drift lay across it and there was one just ahead.

Fiona, Hugh and Ninian looked at one another and Ninian slowly shook his head.

"Not worth it," he said. "The snow'll be up to our waists some of the way."

"What do we do now?" asked Hugh.

"Are we snowed up?" asked Jamie eagerly.

"Yes, more or less," said Ninian. "Look, the thing is we ought to get a message down to Maggie, otherwise she'll be sending up search-parties. As a matter of fact she's probably snowed up, too, but she's got the telephone. Anyway, we want some more things, don't we, Fiona? Bread or something?"

"Bread, cabbages, coal is always welcome." Fiona racked her brains.

"Christmas letters," suggested James, "and more hay."

"My message," said Fergus.

"A book or two if we're going to get really snowed up," suggested Hugh.

"Well, you see, there are lots of things. I'll go," Ninian said. "Who'll come with me?"

"Bags." Sandy and James and Jean were instantaneous.

"I will." Fiona and Hugh were not far behind.

Fergus grinned, rocking to and fro, his hands in his pockets, his cap over one eye.

"I'll go," he said.

"Not Jeannie," said Ninian. "What about the dinner, Fiona? We don't want that to be a bish; it's got to be something special. Sandy, you've got long legs. Only it'll be hard work."

"Fun," said Sandy, grinning.

"Sure you don't want more than one?" asked Hugh.

"Yes, there's a bit of organisation to do this end." Ninian looked up at the sky and a patch of blue appearing over Ben Carrick. "You'd better take the boat back and then some of you come for us. We'll try not to be too late, but it'll be darkish, I'm afraid."

"How shall we know you're not stuck in a drift?" asked Fiona, with visions of them freezing to death.

"Wish we had a St. Bernard," said Sandy. "You could send him out after us with a keg of brandy tied round his neck."

"Oh, Sandy, do stop." Fiona could not help laughing. "No, honestly, Ninian?"

"Well, we'll promise to be very careful. We've got the spade. We may not make it; if it's too bad we'll come back."

"And just wait?" asked Hugh.

"Either that or come and shriek at you from the other side, if we can get as far," said Ninian. "Come on, Sandy, we don't want to hang about. If we're not back by seven don't wait."

"Good luck," said Fergus.

"Don't get stuck," said Jean.

They watched the two start off down the hill, plunging about and tripping over hidden tussocks as they strayed off the track.

"Oh, well." Fiona turned and they followed her. "What are we going to do?"

"Wish we could see the *Star*," said Jamie longingly. He looked at Fergus.

"If we can't get down this track, we'd be hardly likely to

get down the other, which is more than faint, anyway," pointed out Fergus.

"Yes, I suppose so." Jamie sounded so disconsolate that Fiona said:

"There's the turkey to pluck and the pud. to boil. What else does one have for Christmas?"

"Mince pies?" suggested Hugh.

"Oh, yes, let's try and make some. We've got some raisins and things," said Jean.

"Brandy butter," added Fergus. "I hope you've got a cookery book."

Considerably cheered, they retraced their footsteps, while overhead the sky grew lighter, and even the sun came out and set the trees dripping and small avalanches of snow sliding off the branches.

It took Sandy and Ninian nearly three hours to reach the Lodge. From time to time, where the wind had come whistling down the glen, huge drifts of snow had banked up across the track, especially where it was cut into the hill-side, steep above and falling away to the burn below. They were thankful for their spade as they dug through these drifts.

"It won't be so bad coming back," said Sandy. "We can follow our trail."

"We shall have the sledge loaded up," Ninian reminded him.

"Wish we had it now," said Sandy. "We'd fairly whizz down here and over the top of the drifts."

"We'd get bogged," said Ninian, hacking with the spade at the soft snow.

"It certainly is lovely." Sandy looked round him as they emerged the other side. "I feel like an Arctic explorer."

Ahead of them over the sloping ground the snow stretched on and on, unbroken save by the tallest rocks, which were themselves white-capped. The tufts and tussocks and peat-bags that had been visible the day before were hidden; nothing broke the whiteness; no foot had trodden this track before save deer and rabbits and birds. Ben Carrick looked in fact like a sugar mountain, sparkling as the sun came through the clouds. The Corrie was a blue shadow on the snow, the cliffs above Bearnach still black and uncovered as though someone had sliced them down with a knife. The burn at the bottom of the glen on their left was a dark trickle between white banks, boulders and fronds of bracken humping up beneath the blanket. The other side the flats stretched on until they dropped in the ridge above Chuiragarstidh.

"We shall soon see the sea," said Sandy.

"A couple more corners," said Ninian. "Oh, look at those hinds."

There were five or six of them below the track, trying to feed where they had scraped a little snow away. They moved off, but listlessly, as if they knew the Stewarts had no rifle.

"Poor brutes," said Ninian. "I hope Davy puts out some hay."

When eventually they saw the sea above the far white tops of the fir-wood, the sun was up, and Loch Carrick gleamed with gold between its snowy banks. Right out by Cove and Slaggan the snow was not so thick and dark tufts and marks showed through. But inland above Carrick village it looked heavy.

"I bet Maggie is snowed up," said Ninian.

It seemed to Sandy that the track must have stretched in the night, it was so much longer than he remembered. Or perhaps Ninian was right, only not right enough, and they had passed the Lodge completely buried. It seemed as though they had been trudging and digging and scrambling for hours and hours. He was just going to suggest that they might have passed the Lodge when Ninian gave a shout and pointed. There were the tops of the trees above the house and a wisp of smoke smudging across the snow.

"Hooray!" cried Sandy, and tried to run, but ended by rolling over in a drift.

They struggled across the last half-mile or so, dug through a tremendous drift just above the house, and came plodding round the corner just as Maggie came up out of the byre.

She gave a scream of astonishment and waited on the edge of the swept path for them to come up to her.

"Happy Christmas, Maggie!" called Ninian. "Are you snowed up?"

"Aye, just aboot," said Maggie, beaming at the sight of them. "Duncan was up frae the village this morning wi' the post. He says it's verra thick. He was worrit aboot ye up by the Loch."

"Oh, we're fine," said Sandy. "As snug as . . . as . . . dormice. But we've come for the sledge and some stores."

"And some lunch," added Ninian, following Maggie into the house. "But we want to be off as soon as possible. I don't want to get stuck here in the dark."

"Ye're not going back?" cried Maggie, horrified.

"We can't leave them," said Sandy. "We've come miles and miles through the blizzard, panting and struggling, half-frozen, only spurred on by the thought of the others dying by inches in the snow."

"Stop it, Sandy. He's talking nonsense, Maggie," said Ninian, reassuring her. "They all sent their love and Happy Christmasses."

"Have ye found your cave?" asked Maggie, going into the kitchen.

"No, not yet," said Sandy.

She made them some lunch, and they sat eating it and reading letters and looking at cards.

"We'll take them all up with us," said Ninian, scrutinising an envelope addressed to Fiona. "Now I wonder who this is from?"

"Steam it open and see," suggested Sandy.

"Idiot," said Ninian, putting it down. He thought he recognised a brother officer's writing.

They found the sledge in the byre, cobwebby and rusty but serviceable after a little sand-papering. They loaded it up with bread and vegetables, cow-cake, coal and hay, an armful of books, some extra jersies, the cards and letters, and a few of the smaller parcels.

"There was a message for a Fergus Macloud. Are you knowing him?" asked Maggie, as they filled a lantern in the scullery.

"Oh, yes, most important." Ninian put down the can. "Is it a letter?"

"No, it was the telephone." Maggie produced a sheet of paper from the kitchen mantelpiece. "It says, 'Tell Fergus that Rory Macloud says "high tide waits for no man." ' "

" 'High tide waits for no man,' " repeated Ninian. "That sounds like Fergus's marching orders."

"He'll have a job," said Sandy, looking at the white hill through the window.

"Where was Rory speaking from?" asked Ninian, but Maggie did not know. "Oh, well, we must be off."

With many injunctions that they were not to lose themselves or get wet ringing in their ears, they set off up the track. The sledge weighed a ton until they got used to its weight, then it weighed about a ton and a half. Ninian tried pulling alone, while Sandy pushed from behind, crying:

"Mush on there! Mush on!" until Ninian was too weak with giggling to move another step.

They rested, looking back. They seemed to have gone only a few yards.

"Oh, dear," said Sandy. "Shall we ditch the coal?"

"No, stop playing the fool and come on." Ninian picked up the ropes and Sandy came round to help him,

"MUSH ON, THERE! MUSH ON!"

muttering "Mush" under his breath.

"We ought to have snow-shoes," he said after a bit, "and a team of huskies."

"Well, we haven't got either," grunted Ninian, glancing up at the sky. He struggled on even faster, knowing it would be dark before they reached the end of the track.

After lunch the twins took Fergus to the island to explore and pick up any dead sticks that might be protruding out of the snow. Fiona and Hugh were left to tidy up the confusion in the kitchen.

Turkey's feathers seemed to be everywhere, although they had done their best to keep them in the scullery. Some slightly burnt-looking mince pies rested on a plate. Hugh and Fiona decided to share one just to see, and found they tasted much better than they looked.

Every now and then they glanced out of the window and across the Loch in case the figures of Sandy and Ninian should appear.

They swept and dusted and polished, they rearranged the "holly," and pulled the table out into the middle of the room so that everyone could sit round it in comfort. They made up the other two fires, brewed pints of coffee, inspected the trussed turkey and wondered if it looked all right, made sage and onion stuffing, peeled potatoes and prepared brussels sprouts, and eventually turned out a concoction that was meant to be brandy butter and that at least tasted of brandy. Fergus, before he went out, insisted that it should be cold, so they put it in a pudding-basin and buried it in the snow.

"Mustn't forget where it is," said Fiona, and Hugh marked it with a stick.

The twins and Fergus returned at about half-past three, the dinghy loaded with wet branches. They were all more or less soaked to the skin from falling into drifts.

"Impossible to move on the island." Jamie kicked off a sodden boot.

"I wonder where Sandy and Ninian are now," said Jean, warming her cold hands. "I say, this does look nice."

"Well, don't mess it up," said Fiona. "It's got to stay like this until dinner-time."

"When are you going for the others?" asked Hugh.

"Let's have some tea quickly and then go." Fiona looked at Fergus, who was going with her. He nodded.

While they sat round the table munching toast and dripping, Fiona gave instructions for the cooking of the dinner.

"The pudding's on," she said. "Just keep an eye on it to see the water doesn't boil away. You'd better put the turkey in at about five, as the oven's not madly hot. There's a clean tablecloth in the cupboard, and you can cope with all the rest."

"Yes, I think so." Hugh grinned. "What about the spuds?"

"Well, they're round the turkey and should roast, one hopes," said Fiona. "Also the sausages."

She looked once more across the water, but the white shore opposite was empty. She got up.

"We ought to be going, Fergus," she said. "And please, for goodness' sake, twins, don't make a mess."

"No, we'll be as good as gold," Jamie assured her. "We'll make it look beautiful."

Fiona and Fergus put on boots and coats and oilies and huge gloves, preparing for an icy wait for the boys. The hurricane-lamp was filled and ready and Fergus had the matches. He looked out at the greying sky, it was dusk very early this evening.

"Come on," he said, and opened the door.

Fiona followed him out into the cold.

They walked quickly down to the boat and got in, each taking an oar. Fergus pushed her off and they settled down to row, glancing over their shoulders across the Loch.

Gradually the sky grew grey as the sun sank. Once its warmth was gone it stopped thawing and froze. The short twilight was soon over and then it was night, dark and still but for the creak and splash of the oars and the ripple of water under the bows.

They hit the opposite shore too far down and rowed slowly up, but there was no shout to welcome them, nor gleam of light. It had been a long pull up the Loch; their arms were aching slightly, but they were warm.

"I wonder how long we took," said Fiona as they pulled along under the bank.

"About three-quarters of an hour or an hour," said Fergus over his shoulder. "We didn't exactly hang about."

"No, we didn't." Fiona rubbed one hot sore hand on her cold oily. "Here, steady, we'll overshoot the bay."

It was shallow here: she knew it of old, with an island to the north.

"Keep in the middle," she told Fergus. "It's rocky."

They grated once, and then were paddling in the calm water by the jetty. The boat bumped alongside, and Fiona, shipping her oar, grasped at the unseen wooden uprights of the pier. She scrambled ashore, clumsy in her long oily, and tied up. Then she and Fergus stood listening. It was silent and still. No sound of voices, nothing but the lapping of the waves below them.

"Oh, well." Fiona picked up the lantern. "They're not here yet. I suppose they will come?"

"Yes, I should think so." Fergus stamped his feet. "Can we get into the bothy? We shall freeze to death here."

"We can try." Fiona led the way up the hill, following carefully the footprints they had made before. "They'll see the lantern from the bothy, too," she added.

They skirted round the big drift where the Ford was buried and groped their way to the front. Stars were coming out all over the sky, giving a faint frosty light. The snow had piled up across the bottom of the door but it was not too deep. They kicked and scraped and eventually got it clear. Then the hasp stuck and they had to battle with that for several minutes. The orange glow of the lantern fell on their intent faces, Fiona's white, cold, fringed by wisps of blown black hair; Fergus's thin and dark, with its hard mouth and cleft chin and the tip of his nose below his cap brim. Then the door swung open and they went in.

It was not much warmer in the bothy, but at least they were out of the small cold wind that had got up as the sun went down. They wandered round, inspecting heaps of rope and straw, old oars and broken rods, an ancient bridle, some trestles, tins, cups, a table and other odd bits of junk. Then they hung the lantern in the doorway so that it shone down the track, and sat down to wait.

The minutes passed slowly as they sat, growing colder and colder, in the hard chairs. Fergus lit his pipe, which made a warm glow and a comfortable smell; Fiona tried thawing her hands at the lantern, but it was quite useless, so she stamped up and down and finally went back to her chair. They talked spasmodically, Fergus seemed on the verge of one of his black moods.

"You knew Alec well, didn't you?" asked Fiona.

"Yes, he was shepherd with us for years and years."

"Why did he leave?"

Fergus glanced at her; in the dark he could see nothing but the pale oval of her face.

"He didn't like it any more," he said at last, and added softly, "neither did I."

"It must have been when his father died and Colin became Master," thought Fiona, and dared not ask more.

Suddenly a faint shout reached their ears and they sprang up, rushing to the door. There, far away in the snow, bobbed a small glow of light.

"It's them!" cried Fiona, and gave an answering yell. "Thank goodness they've got through."

She seized Fergus's arm and capered madly in the snow.

"Come on," he said, laughing, "we ought to go and help."

They met the returning expedition on the flat ground by the first lochan. They were nearly exhausted after pulling the heavy sledge for about four miles, and most of them up-hill.

"Well done," said Fiona, seizing a rope. "You must be nearly dead."

"We are," said Ninian. "The worst bit was thinking we should be too late and you would have left."

"If you'd been much later you would have found two frozen images in the bothy," said Fergus.

With four at the ropes the sledge fairly flew over the ground, and by seven o'clock the boat was loaded up and pushed off. Sandy and Ninian sat back in the stern and Fiona and Fergus took the oars.

"We'll help in a minute or two." Ninian stretched his arms, trying to imagine they did not ache nor his hands feel so sore from the rough ropes.

"You certainly brought enough stores," puffed Fiona. "I don't think the boat's moving."

"It is just," said Sandy, watching the stars over Carn Mor. They gleamed down and the air seemed to crackle with frost.

"Oh, yes, there was a message for you, Fergus," said Ninian, "from Rory. 'High tide waits for no man'."

"Thank you," said Fergus, and sighed.

"Does that mean you've got to go?" asked Fiona, behind him.

"Yes, some time."

"Not to-night?"

"No, not to-night."

They rowed on, their oars creaking rhythmically, Sandy, who was humming, started to sing and the others picked it up, going through all the songs they knew. The twins and Hugh, listening from the croft, heard their voices from away down the Loch.

"They're all there!" cried Jean. "I can hear Ninian!"

"Just in time," said Hugh. "The dinner's almost ready."

The voices grew nearer and louder. Then Fiona called to them, and they shouted back and hurried down to the jetty.

A few minutes later the boat bumped and they were staggering back to the croft with the stores.

"How's the dinner?" asked Ninian, who had been ravenous for hours.

"Simply wonderful. Wait until you see it," said Jean, from behind a sack of hay.

"Thank you for bringing the cow-cake," said Jamie, who had been presented with a sackful by Ninian. "She'll love it."

"How is she?" asked Sandy.

"Oh, fine. This can be her Christmas dinner."

They dumped everything in the hall and took off their boots and coats before Hugh would let them open the kitchen door. The most delicious smell came wafting out from under it, making them realise their hunger. Then James flung it open.

Fiona and Fergus had seen the beginning but even they were impressed. Sandy and Ninian gasped with astonishment.

The curtains were drawn and the room was snug and warm, full of lamplight and firelight and the smell of roast turkey. The table was spread with a clean cloth white and decorated with sprigs of "holly." St. Yves stood in the middle, a wreath round his feet, and on either side a candle, and beyond two pudding-bowls of apples, oranges and bananas. Seven places were laid with plates and cutlery and glasses, and an eggcup each for a wineglass. Bottles of brandy and whisky stood at either end, and beer in between. Saucerfuls of Fergus's crystalised fruit were arranged at intervals, with others filled with raisins and nuts and the two dishes of mince-pies. The lamp and candles gleamed on the fruit and silver and glasses, the brandy shone like a topaz, the whisky in its green bottle, like a tourmaline. The pine-needles spread dark fingers over the cloth and round the feet of St. Yves, the fire-red berries were points of light on the sombre colour. They had arranged "holly" round the lamp and it added thin fretted shadows to the ceiling, in addition to the usual ones.

A gust of wind rattled the windows and broke the spell. Hugh hurried to get the turkey from the oven, Jean arranged dishes of vegetables, Jamie brought the gravy, Fiona turned the lamp down so that it only shone on the table, a circle of light in the dark room.

They sat down, their eyes shining, Fiona at one end of the table, Ninian at the other. He stood up to carve, his dark head in the shadows, watching their faces, Jean, Sandy, Hugh, Fiona, Fergus and James, aware in his tired mind of a great and indescribable content.

CHAPTER XX

FIONA'S CAVE

Tuesday, 26th December

THE CROFT lay still and sleeping until late the next morning. A tousled Sandy had staggered out in the grey dawn to milk the cow, but had gone back to bed again. The others lay like logs until nine o'clock. They had not been to bed until after one the night before: they had sat up talking and planning and reminiscing and telling silly stories, laughing till they were weak. Even Fergus had thrown away all trace of his fierceness, and was more gay than Sandy and more human than they had ever known him. The glass beside his plate had seldom been empty, but it had no effect other than making his eyes gleam and his laugh come more freely. Fiona refused to let any one wash up, so, after dumping everything in the scullery, they had sat round the fire on rugs and chairs drinking huge cups of coffee and licking the stickiness of the crystalised fruit from their fingers. The night had gone on and on until everyone was too warm and sleepy to move, and it seemed as though it would go on until the dawn. Clouds of smoke eddied round the ceiling, the fire snapped as Hugh threw on another log, and so it went on until Ninian, seeing Jean's eyes grow large with sleep and a suppressed yawn quiver across her face, uncoiled himself and stood up. Then a niche had to be found at the foot of Jean's bed for St. Yves, and Fergus had to be made to promise he would still be there in the morning.

And now — Fiona turned over and woke up. Light was streaming into the room from a clear fine morning. The room itself looked appallingly untidy and depressing. She shut her eyes again, trying to recapture the dream from which she had awakened, but it was gone, and the horrid reality of the morning was there in its place. She yawned, stretching, and lay on her back looking at the dark boards of pine that lined her bed and the curtains moving by the window. She could see the Loch in front of the house dancing with gold ripples, and the white shores on the other side and Ben Carrick beyond with its dark cliffs and snow-covered peak. Out of the other window was the tumbled garden of the croft and the long smooth shoulder of Carn Mor. A robin, perching on a bent branch of the apple tree, sang piercingly, each note as clear and cold as the morning. Fiona had never felt less like getting up.

At nine o'clock everyone had put in an appearance but Fergus, and were wandering round the kitchen with sleepy faces and tousled heads, feeling thoroughly grumpy and morning-afterish. Everything seemed to go wrong, too — a plate was broken, the fire would not light, the kettle refused to boil and the milk boiled over, Fiona cut her finger and Jamie burnt the toast. The table, that had looked so gay the night before, was now a depressing conglomeration of candle-ends, empty bottles and limp sprigs of holly.

And then Fergus appeared, dressed. He looked in at the front window and stood laughing at them, his eyes shining, his hair damp and curly where he had slooshed it while washing his face at the burn.

"Gracious!" said Fiona. "What have you been doing?"

"I've been up hours." Fergus leant into the room. "Hurry up, it's the most glorious morning. The snow's quite hard and the sun's shining. We could climb Carn Mor!"

"Well, let's," said Ninian, catching some of his enthusiasm.

"Why not?" Hugh rubbed his bristly chin. "I'd love to see what it looks like from the top when everything's covered in snow."

"Could we do it?" asked Fiona. "Oh, do let's."

"We could try." Fergus left the window and came in, his boots covered with snow, and drops of water sparkling on the front of his jersey. It was a garment that fascinated Jean, and knitted with minute stitches in a soft strong wool with a pattern that seemed to involve everything a knitter could think of, tiny cables, diamonds, diagonals, vees, purl and plain and rib. As bad to knit as a Fair Isle one, Jean thought.

"No, but honestly," said Ninian, "what's the snow like, Fergus? Would we get stuck?"

"I expect so, it must be very deep. But there's a gully where the burn comes down that is practically bare on one side."

"Let's try anyway," said Sandy. "I feel like climbing miles this morning."

There was so much to be done in the cottage that they were not ready to start until about eleven o'clock. Everything seemed to be dirty and dusty. They had had to do a certain amount of washing up before breakfast because they had no clean plates or knives and forks left. But there were pans and dishes and glasses, the floor to be wiped clean from the marks of snowy feet, sticks to be chopped and the tank to be filled. But it was, as Fergus had said, a lovely morning. Patches of white cloud floated across the sun from time to time, but they were not large enough to last long, and the whole white countryside gleamed and sparkled for most of the time.

There were more tracks of deer round the croft. Sandy said he had seen them on his way out in the dawn, and also something large with a bushy tail, a fox perhaps. They searched for tracks, and found not only fox but wild cat and the claw-marks of the eagle. All the rubbish they had put in the stone incinerator had been pulled out and everything edible eaten.

"We ought to put food out for them." Fiona could not

bear the thought of the cold, hungry animals outside.

"We haven't got enough," said Sandy. "The cow will want all the hay and stuff and we eat the rest."

"It's awful," said Jean. "Think of them starving. Perhaps we could get hay from Davy."

"We can't even get to Davy," pointed out James.

"Well, the shepherd at Darrach, then."

"He does feed them," said Fergus. "If I know him of old the glen will be full of hay. His daughter does it for him now."

"It must be lovely up there to-day." Fiona cut bread and butter to eat with the cold turkey for lunch. She could imagine it well, the wide sunny glen and the long white slopes. The croft by the oak wood, each black branch ridged with snow, sending a column of blue smoke into the morning, the burn racing between ice-covered rocks, and the buzzards, high up, circling and mewing, sailing on currents of air, their strong wings outspread.

They packed up the lunch and set off.

It was more difficult going than they had thought. The ground here by the edge of the Loch was rough at the best of times, and now, with the covering of snow to hide peat-hags and ridges, it was impossible to help stumbling and falling. They managed to reach the foot of the gully, and there they stopped, looking up at the steep white face of the hill. Carn Mor was nearly three thousand feet high just here; they had to crane their heads back and then could only see half-way up. On and on it seemed to stretch, up and up. One side of the gully was choked by a deep drift but the other was comparatively clear.

"Well," said Fergus at last, "we may as well try."

He and both Ninian and Fiona guessed it was impossible. To Hugh it looked raving mad even to attempt it, but Sandy and the twins were convinced that it could be done, especially with Fergus, Fiona and Ninian anywhere about.

They scrambled up a few feet. James was the first to slip up to his waist in a drift. They hauled him out, but almost at once someone else was in another, and so it went on.

"Hopeless," said Ninian eventually, leaning against a rock. Their legs were aching already from the effort of plunging in and out of drifts. Looking up, the hill seemed steeper and whiter than ever.

"Yes, I'm afraid it is." Even Fergus had to give in.

"Oh, hell! Are you sure?" Fiona scowled up at Carn Mor. "Surely we can?"

"It'll get much deeper," Hugh reminded her.

"Oh, bother! We've only come so short a way."

"Fiona, you must see we can't go on plunging about in this." Ninian kicked at a drift and the snow flew in all directions.

"We could," said Fiona obstinately.

"Don't be mad."

"Well, what do you suggest doing? Going back and sitting all day in the croft?" Fiona had set her heart on climbing Carn Mor and was now in a rage.

"I thought you liked the croft," said Sandy maddeningly.

"Well, so I do, but not to waste a day like this in. Oh, well, I suppose if you want to," and she started off down the hill again, scattering snow before her.

Hugh and Ninian grinned at each other, and followed her more slowly. The twins remained silent, having learnt by long experience that it was better not to speak when Fiona was in one of her rages.

They overtook her at the bottom of the gully leaning against a rock and staring at Loch Dubh.

"I say," she said, when they came up, "let's row right into Loch Dubh. We haven't yet, and it should look blissful to-day. Unless you've thought of anything better."

No one had thought at all.

"Sounds fun," said Hugh. "It must look lovely from the

middle of the Loch, especially on a day like this."

"And it won't take too long, either," added Jamie.

"Come on then, let's hurry." Ninian strode off. "It's late already."

"Sure you hadn't thought of anything else, Fergus?" asked Fiona, who usually approved of his plans.

"No, nothing." Fergus stared absently at the grey walls of the croft ahead. Fiona was relieved: he had not said anything more about going, perhaps he had forgotten it.

The dinghy was empty of snow, as they had used it the day before, but the oars and rowlocks were icy and the water had frozen round her so that it crackled as they pushed her off.

Fergus, Ninian, Sandy and Hugh each took an oar, Jamie perched in the bows. Fiona and Jean stretched themselves out in the stern in great comfort. They fairly flew up the Loch. The water glinted like diamonds as it dropped from the oars and splashed up on to Jamie's face as they hit a wave. They kept near in to the shore, and in places the Loch was frozen far out. They rammed through it, the ice clinking like glass.

"We might be in the Arctic," said Jean. "Only I suppose there'd be polar bears."

"And penguins," Hugh reminded her.

Fiona, leaning back, stared up into the sky, revelling in the faint warmth of the sun. A cloud passed across it, making her shiver, and she turned to see if there were more coming, but there were only a few. She looked at Loch Dubh thinking that perhaps after all to-day was not going to be so gloomy as it had at one moment seemed. It was cold but fine and the hills looked so lovely. A sudden strange creaking noise made her turn and look up. At first she could see nothing, then Jean cried:

"Look, swans!" and pointed.

Five of them were up there, flying south, their long necks outstretched, their great wings moving steadily. The boys stopped rowing to look and the boat danced up and down, the waves slapping against her, the only sound now that the rowing had ceased. The swans flew on, straight for their destination, not straggling or turning aside but flying unerringly to where they wanted to go.

"I wish they'd stop here," said James. "They do sometimes."

"There's something lovely about swans flying," said Fiona as the boys started rowing again. "So quick and smooth and graceful."

Half an hour later they had grounded once more on the Narrows. This time the ice crackled and smashed as they dragged the boat across, although in places it bore their weight.

"Skating!" said Sandy suddenly. "Why haven't we got our skates?"

"Well, where should we skate? Heave now!" Ninian pulled and the boat slithered and scrunched.

"Some of the lochans must be frozen. Perhaps we could find one to slide on," said James. "Do you know of any near here, Ninian?"

"Loch Fuar Beg on the side of Ben Fuar." Ninian frowned, trying to remember. "Loch Beg, up at the other end of Carna. Bearnach might be frozen."

"Shall we go and try?" asked Sandy longingly.

"Having hauled this blessed boat over the Narrows we're jolly well going to row down Loch Dubh," Ninian told him. "You should have thought of it sooner."

"We could try Bearnach on the way back if there's time," suggested Fiona.

"It may have thawed by to-morrow," said Sandy.

"Well, let's go to-night," suggested Jean, inspired.

"I don't think there's a moon," said Hugh. "Sorry, but there it is."

"Well, we've days and days anyway," said Jamie. "And it doesn't feel like thawing."

They paddled slowly on over the dark water of Loch Dubh.

"Funny how it still looks black although the sun's shining and the hills are white," said Fiona.

"It feels almost as gloomy as ever, but not quite," agreed Fergus, looking round.

The hills, white now, but as tall and overhanging as ever, shouldered up on either side, Carn Mor, smooth and curved, immense twin-peaked Ben Fuar with Ben Derg over to the left and vast Sgurr Ban, truly white, to the right, and Ben Lair to carry on the chain, and behind Ben Lair, Slioch, and to the right Mel Vannie, and beyond that Ben Carrick. They were a wonderful sight in the snow, better than any one had expected, so vast and still, almost as if they watched and waited or guarded something or else slept until the thaw. They were remote and inaccessible now, no one could cross them or climb them, no rifle-shot break their great stillness nor shout wake their echoes. The Stewarts felt like pygmies beneath them, hardly daring to speak.

"Let's land at the end by the burn," Sandy broke the silence, "and have lunch and then go back via Bearnach."

"Well, we'll land at the end anyway." Ninian did not believe Bearnach would be frozen.

They rowed on, slowly, rounding the last corner so that the opening into the Carna Loch was out of sight and they were alone in Loch Duhh. Their oars sounded loud in the silence. Clouds drifted across the sun and away again. None of them wanted to land; the place felt bewitched. Ninian, who was stroke, rowed slower and slower. Then he stopped, resting on his oar and listened.

"What was that?" he said.

"What was what?" Fiona's voice was hushed.

"I don't know, I thought I heard something."

"A stag perhaps." Sandy was the most prosaic of them all.

"No, it was a kind of feeling." Ninian shook his head, unable to describe what it was he had heard. Jean edged closer to Fiona. She, too, had that sense of apprehension, of watching and waiting, of expectancy. They were completely shut in by the hills now, encircled on all sides. A breath of wind blew off the tall, white slopes and sighed across the Loch. Fergus felt a prickle of fear run through his body. He looked up and caught Fiona's eye, and saw for the first time a glimmer of fear in it.

"We shouldn't have come," she whispered, her voice hardly distinguishable above the lapping of waves against the boat, the only sound they could hear.

He shook his head, half in agreement, half in wonder. There was more in this Loch than he had thought, and yet, perhaps, brought up on stories of kelpies and trolls and Sitheans, of a host of fairies good and bad, told to him in awed Gaelic by his nurse, perhaps he was more susceptible than the others. Yet they had been brought up in much the same way, but not to the same extent nor surrounded by legend in Taransay.

Again came that breath of wind like a sigh, and a cloud passed over the sun. Fergus, faced by nothing but hills, looked over his shoulder to the head of the Loch, but no comfort there. The hills sloped back, white and steep, cut with corries and burns, studded with black rocks. Then the sun came out again and Fergus drew in his breath.

"Look!" he said softly.

They turned and looked. There, a hundred yards up from the foot of Ben Fuar, was a hill, a small steep, pointed hill, almost a hillock, its smooth sides rising five hundred feet or so up to a neat rounded top, its pyramid-shaped shadow, blue-grey on the snow-covered slopes behind it. At the identical point where a burn running down the big hill disappeared behind the small one, so another burn appeared, making the two look one. Where a gully gashed across Ben Fuar so a gully gashed across the hillock.

Without the shadow it was invisible.

"The Sithean!"[1] Jamie's voice was a whisper. "Alec said when the sun shone he found it."

So they, too, had found it. Loch Dubh had given up its secret. They had seen the Sithean. As it happened, Ben Fuar curved back in a great hollow and encircled it on three sides, so gently curved and sloping were those arms that they were hardly noticeable. But, while the shadow was falling, the hill was plain, a small ordinary hillock but different somehow.

"Shall we go there?" Jean hardly dared ask.

"Yes, of course." Fergus dipped in his oar and broke the silence. "Come on, we must find the cave."

It seemed a matter of course that they would find the cave. Even Hugh was taking it for granted. Now that they were talking and the oars splashing there was hardly any fear left on the Loch, and yet, Jean especially, was feeling that she didn't want to land. After all it was a Fairy Hill, and if so, where were the Fairies? Wouldn't they resent their hill being invaded? She looked up and found Fergus watching her.

"St. Yves," he said softly, and she felt comforted.

Another cloud blotted out the sun and instantaneously the Sithean vanished. Some trick of the land, of course, thought Hugh, glancing over his shoulder, but it certainly was invisible. And yet there it was a moment later, and the sun dazzling his eyes.

"I can't believe it," Sandy was saying. "After all our searching. We've walked past it twice."

"We didn't know about it then," said Ninian, thinking back.

"Yes, we did. The time we went to Glen Darrach; that's the third time," said Hugh.

"It was dusk then and very cloudy the time before."

---

[1] The Fairy Hill is marked on the map by a ★

Jamie spoke over his shoulder; he was not taking his eyes off the Sithean.

Fergus was grinning.

"I believe you knew about it all the time," said Fiona indignantly.

"I told you it was there," he said, laughing.

"Did you know?" asked Jean, but he only laughed and said:

"Of course not."

The boat grated on the rocks and Jamie leapt ashore. They followed him on to the snow and made her fast.

"Awful if she got adrift," said Sandy. "We'd take years walking back in this and it's too cold to swim out and fetch her."

"What a horrid thought, don't." Fiona shivered, suddenly cold, and looked back at tall Ben Lair and the dark Loch beneath.

Having been so elusive, it now seemed as though the Sithean had decided to remain visible, and it lay before them, its smooth sides sharp against Ben Fuar. They walked towards it slowly. There was no hurry now, and yet, supposing the cave was not there? Supposing all their plans had been based on a wild idea of Fergus's? Supposing there was no groove or hollow in the white blanket of snow before them? They could see nothing yet, but the gully looked promising and there was no knowing what lay the other side.

Slowly they walked on across the hundred yards or so of rough ground before they reached its foot. The snow was deep and smooth here. Nothing had touched its surface, no slot of deer nor print of bird. It was blown into small ridges, curling over like a wave above each hollow, piled high beside rocks where it had drifted, shining under the sun like salt. It was very dry and their feet kicked it up into showers. Jean bent and pressed her outspread hand on to its smooth surface and felt it melt beneath the warmth of her palm.

"I must do that," cried Sandy, and going one better, buried his face in it, and then leant back laughing, a white mask in the ground before him, his cheeks and nose tingling.

"It's lovely," he said. "You must try." So they all knelt, like Buddhists, and buried their faces in the snow, leaving a row of masks before the Fairy Hill.

At last they stood beneath it, looking up at its sloping sides.

"It doesn't feel so frightening now," said Jean, and indeed the sense of silence and waiting was gone.

Ninian shifted the bag of lunch on to his other shoulder.

"We must eat soon," he said, tiring of carrying it.

"We can't yet," said Fiona. "What shall we do first?"

She turned to Fergus, who somehow seemed to be the

THE SITHEAN HAD DECIDED TO REMAIN VISIBLE.

one to ask.

"Unless the entrance is blocked it can't be here," he said. "And if that's the case we'll have to come back in the spring. But I should think, try the gully, or round the other side."

"Let's go round the other side first," suggested Ninian. "We don't want to struggle up to the gully for nothing."

"It may have drifts in it, too," added Hugh.

They were close to Ben Fuar now, and presently were in the narrow glen that ran up and round the back of the Sithean. It was difficult to walk in the snow and look up at the same time, and they found it easiest to walk a few paces and then stop and scan every inch they could see of the hill on their left. Hugh gave Ben Fuar a glance now and then, up on his right. You never knew. Soon they were in the tell-tale shadow that had given the hill away. It was cold here, out of the sun, and a small breeze seemed to be creeping round the Sithean as well. The sheer steep slope of Ben Fuar on their right was overpowering; they were so close under it that it was impossible to see far up, but giant boulders and short cliffs stood out from the snow.

"There doesn't seem to be a thing," said Sandy, dismally.

"Patience," said Fergus. "We haven't been all round yet."

"It's rather creepy, this walking and wondering what's round the corner," said James. "I wonder what sort of Fairies they were?"

"Perhaps Green Laddies," suggested Fiona.

"Black Laddies up here," said Sandy, giggling.

"Don't be disrespectful to them, they might send an avalanche," warned Hugh.

"The last place we explored like this was your harbour, Fergus," said Fiona. "And that was a successful expedition, so perhaps this will he too."

"Oh, it must!" said Jean.

By now they were out in the sun again, back to where their own footsteps branched off.

"Well, that's a blank." Ninian ruffled his hair. "Now what."

"The gully?" asked Hugh.

"Yes, the gully," said Fergus. "It's our last chance."

They retraced their steps for about a hundred yards until they reached the foot of the gully, which ran out so that it faced north-west. They stood for a moment or two working out the best way up. Luckily, through facing this way, it was moderately free from drifts. It was a deep narrow gully that might have once been the bed of a burn. A few snow-laden trees hung from its banks and a clump of withered bracken was just visible at the foot.

"Well, come on," said Fergus, and led the way up.

They had to go slowly, partly because it was steep and partly because it was snowy. They spread out to search better, Ninian keeping an eye on Jean, who was liable to disappear from sight if she slipped into a deep drift. They hauled themselves up by tree-trunks and rocks, calling to each other:

"Have you found it?"

"No, have you?"

"No!"

It was Fiona who found it.

A particularly inaccessible ledge, fringed by trees, was just above her head and it seemed essential that she should reach it. Grasping the stem of a rowan she hauled herself up, scraping skin off her hands and knees. She found herself on a small flat shelf about ten feet by twenty, and there, in a crack in the rocks between bent trees, was the cave. There was no mistaking it — a dry cave, with an entrance just low enough to make you bend your head beneath a smoke-blackened rock. A queer sick feeling of excitement seized her, for a moment she could do nothing but stare, half-hearing the others on the rocks beneath.

IN A CRACK IN THE ROCKS BETWEEN BENT TREES WAS THE CAVE.

She turned, and a view straight down Loch Dubh and the Carna Loch almost took her breath away. Ben Lair and Carn Mor framed the picture, and beyond the long miles of Carna and the flat country lay the track. No one could approach from Carrick, Beanault, Lettercarrick or Darrach without being seen and there was no track over Ben Fuar. There could not be a more perfect place.

At last she heard her voice calling:

"I've found it! I've found it! Come quickly!"

Screams of excitement followed, and a few minutes later they were beside her on the platform, gazing with her at the dark entrance.

Suddenly she felt she did not want to go in. It was James Stewart's cave, carefully guarded for all these years, where he had spent so long and lived on such high hopes, only to leave it to die of a broken heart far away in France. She turned to Ninian, who would understand. He smiled at her and nodded. She walked away to the edge of the plateau and looked down the Loch, where James Stewart must have looked so many times.

"Don't let's go in," said Ninian.

"Not go in?" said. Sandy, horrified. "Whyever not?"

"It doesn't belong to us; it belongs to James Stewart." Ninian spoke slowly, trying to explain what was in his mind and Fiona's. "It's his cave, you see, and —"

"Oh, nonsense, we must go in," interrupted Sandy. "He wouldn't mind. Besides, he's been dead for hundreds of years."

"Yes, I know, that's why. Go in if you like."

Fergus looked at him, his mouth twisted in a smile, and said:

"I would like someone to feel like that about me, one day."

Jean looked from Fiona to Ninian and then to the cave. She passionately wanted to go in, and Sandy and James were on the threshold, their torches alight, and Hugh just behind them.

"May I?" she asked Ninian.

"Of course, if you want to." He smiled at her, and she followed them in.

To Fiona, looking down the Loch, it seemed as though they were in there hours. Her heart was beating painfully, she felt full of some strange emotion that she could not name. Fergus and Ninian were behind her, talking, then the others came out.

"There's nothing much in there," Jamie said. "His initials carved on the wall and lots of black from smoke. Nothing horrid."

"Lots of leaves, perhaps just blown in, but maybe his bed," said Hugh, "and chips of wood, from carving."

"And this knife," said Sandy. "Look!"

He held out a sgeand-dhu, black-hafted and small, with a dull blade.

"No!" cried Fiona. "No! Put it back, it doesn't belong to us!" She swung herself over the cliff and went tearing back down the gully. Somehow she hadn't expected to feel like this and it annoyed her. She had wanted as much as any of them to find the cave, and now that it was found it was horrid, like the breaking open of a tomb, the tomb of James Stewart's hopes, and the hopes of every one that had followed Prince Charles.

They came upon her sitting on the end of the boat and swinging her legs.

She grinned at them.

"Sorry," she said. "I was mad. I'm glad we found it, really."

"Well, let's have lunch anyway," said Sandy, "I'm ravening."

"We put it back," Hugh whispered to her as she bent forward to seize a piece of turkey.

"It's all right, Hugh," she said.

They rowed home in the dusk, and while Jamie went to milk the cow, the others sat round the kitchen table discussing the day.

"I wish you'd been inside, Fiona," said Sandy. "Especially after finding it. It wasn't a bit creepy."

"I was rather mad," Fiona smiled, "but I had a creepy feeling."

The others nodded. They had had that kind of feeling too, at different times. Jamie clattered into the scullery and came through into the kitchen rubbing his hands.

"Gosh, it's cold," he said. "Freezing like mad and dark already. But where's Fergus?"

They looked round, thinking he was with them.

"Fergus!" But there was no answer. They looked at one another.

"He's not out at the back," said James.

They leapt up and rushed to the front door, throwing it open. The cold night and the stars came in to meet them, the dark water lapping and the burn roaring over the stones.

"Fergus! Fergus!" they called, and the hills caught up their cry and echoed his name, and a lone stag answered them from the other side of the Loch.

But Fergus had gone.

THE END